The PENDRAGON™ fiction line presents the best of modern Arthurian literature, from reprints of long-unavailable classics of the early twentieth century to new works by today's most exciting and inventive fantasists. The titles in the series are selected for their value to both the casual reader and the devoted scholar of the rich, varied story cycle known as the Matter of Britain.

PENDRAGON™ Fiction

PENDRAGON

W. BARNARD FARADAY

Introduction by Raymond H. Thompson

Please address questions and comments concerning this book, as well as requests for notices of new publications, by mail to Green Knight Publishing, 900 Murmansk Street, Suite 5, Oakland, CA 94607.

Green Knight Publishing
Publisher: Peter Corless
Executive Editor: James Lowder
Consulting Editor: Raymond H. Thompson

Visit our web page at: http://www.greenknight.com

FIRST PAPERBACK EDITION

10 9 8 7 6 5 4 3 2 1

Green Knight publication GK6213, April 2002.

ISBN 1-928999-29-8

Printed in the United States

INTRODUCTION

W hat we know of the life of Wilfred Barnard Faraday, the author of *Pendragon*, amounts to little more than tantalizing fragments. We might infer from his name that he was related to Sir Michael Faraday, the eminent nineteenth-century scientist who married Sarah Barnard, but since Sir Michael had no children, any relationship would have been through his brothers. After studying law, Faraday was called to the bar in 1900, and in 1925 he was appointed the recorder of Barnstaple and Bidford in Devon. He joined the Fifth Battalion of the York and Lancaster Regiment, which served with great distinction on the bloodiest battle-fields of World War I, but from 1917-19 he was Secretary of the Royal Aeronautical Society, for which he edited *A Glossary of Aeronautical Terms* (1919). We do not know whether Faraday saw action, but since seventy-two out of every one hundred men in his regiment were wounded or killed, it is highly likely that he was invalided out of the army after being wounded. He would hardly have been appointed Secretary of the Royal Aeronautical Society, preferred among three hundred and fifty applicants, had he not possessed an impressive record.

Perhaps the most convincing piece of evidence that Faraday saw military action, however, is Artorius' account of the Battle of Mount Badon at the climax of *Pendragon*:

> ". . . there was a wailing of men, and people falling piecemeal to the earth, and many shouts of anger and bitter woe, and colour before everybody's eyes as it were black or red, and dazzling rainbows and stains of blood, and pain, and noise, and clash of arms. . . .

> There was anger and damage and blindness, whereby
> men lost their eyes, their most treasured possession,
> so that they were doomed never to see the sweet
> colours of the flowers, or the sun, or the laughter in
> their children's eyes."

The emphasis upon the dazzling colors, especially
red and black, upon blindness and bodies falling piecemeal, seems more appropriate to a battlefield in the
twentieth century than to one in the sixth. Moreover,
when Artorius shifts from a general description of the
battle to his own part in it, fighting on despite his
wounds, the passage has the distinctive and intense
flavor not just of a powerful imagination, but of the
author's personal experience:

> "As I rose the whole of everything that I could see was
> bright scarlet, and my face was wet, and I had a most
> dreadful pain in my side. . . . Now I had a pain in my
> head that seemed to belong not to me, but to a great
> cave in which I was walking, and that arched over my
> head; and I wondered that the cave, being so great
> and so many miles away, should allow any pain so
> great as that to live."

Whether or not such passages reflect his own battlefield experience, *Pendragon* was, in Faraday's opinion,
the best book he ever wrote, and while its literary mer-
its are uneven, it deserves to be recognized as a groundbreaking work in the field of modern Arthurian fiction.

Published in 1930, it is, in the first place, one of the
earliest novels in the twentieth century to make use of
a Dark Age setting for the story of Arthur. The com-
posers of medieval chronicle and romance placed figures from the past, including not only Arthur but also
Charlemagne and Alexander the Great, in a setting that
was of interest to their aristocratic and wealthy patrons.
As a result the stories unfold in a feudal world of elegant
courts and lofty castles, bold mounted knights and
fiercely contested tournaments, fair ladies and devoted
lovers. The story of King Arthur and his Knights of the

Round Table thus was shaped by the High Middle Ages, during which its popularity spread throughout Europe, and most writers in succeeding centuries followed this tradition.

In choosing to draw not upon these medieval models, but upon Dark Age material such as Gildas' sixth-century *De Excidio Britannia* (*The Ruin of Britain*) and early Welsh writings on the one hand, and on the other upon the research of historians and archeologists in his own day, Faraday was striking out into little-traveled territory. While some details, like the use of chariots with scythe-blades upon the axles, no longer seem plausible, we would do well to remember not only that "historical fashions" keep changing, but that "for the purpose of a tale less scientific methods are permissible," as the author himself points out in his Introduction. That so many have followed his path since is a tribute to the far-sightedness of his approach.

Secondly, this is the first novel told from the point of view of Arthur himself. Not only does this keep Arthur—or Artorius, as Faraday calls him—firmly at the center of the story, rather than push him into the background as happens so often, but also it allows us to share his understanding of the situation in which he finds himself. The result is a sympathetic portrait of an heroic leader, determined to save his people from the threat of invasion despite the heavy odds.

Thirdly, Guinevere—or Gwendaello, as Faraday calls her—is presented as a proud and self-reliant figure, fierce in defense of what she values, yet clear sighted enough to recognize the need for cooperation against a common foe. Unlike traditional portraits of Guinevere, both before and since, Faraday's heroine would scorn to manipulate events through other people, to use moral blackmail and indirect influence to achieve her aims, to rely upon a champion to save her from ravishment. Although Arthur does escort her to safety when he finds her fleeing from the Saxons, he soon discovers that she is not the helpless and swooning maid he first assumes her to be.

Throughout *Pendragon*, Gwendaello's actions and accomplishments are impressive. When threatened with rape and enslavement by her Saxon captor, she stabs him with his own knife, picks her way through the enemy camp amidst the mutilated bodies of her fellow Britons, swims across the river, then travels, alone and hungry, through wild and desolate countryside to warn her compatriots of an imminent Saxon assault. At the Council of Princes, she cunningly outmaneuvers the British rulers who seek to divide up her kingdom of Dynevawr in southwest Wales, then takes the initiative in planning their mutual defense against invasion. At the Battle of the Islands she personally leads her warriors against the Irish—stripping naked and blackening her body as is their custom; paddling first a coracle, then a raft, in water rough enough to capsize many of the frail craft and drown their occupants; scrambling over slippery rocks and wielding a sword against superior numbers of foemen. She then immediately rallies her followers—and unlike Maelgwyn, who sets sail for Ireland to capture slaves—leads them by forced marches all the way to Mount Badon, where they arrive just in time to save Arthur in his battle against the Saxon hordes: "and in front of all the others was a chariot driving with wild horses, with manes and tails blowing about, and in it a figure with red hair streaming in the wind, holding a spear and shrieking aloud in fury."

This fury arises, in no small part, out of her love for Artorius. Yet here again Gwendaello departs from traditional portraits of Arthur's passive queen, for it is she, not he, who takes the initiative in developing their relationship. While Artorius' feelings toward her change rapidly from scorn to respect, and then ripen into love, he remains curiously shy and diffident for so valiant a soldier—even if we excuse him for being preoccupied with his duty to save Britain from the invaders. It is Gwendaello who eventually asks him for the gift of the blue cloak that he bought for her in the first place, a gift she wears proudly at the Council of Princes; and it is she who first openly proclaims her feelings, for when

Artorius tells her she has saved Britain by bringing her warriors to Mount Badon, she replies, "Truly . . . And also something that I value even more. For I have come, and mine with me, forty miles this day that I may keep it." She then wipes the blood from Artorius' face and kisses him.

In the figure of Gwendaello, Faraday has created one of the most spirited and resourceful women in all of Arthurian literature, the match of any hero, and this long before such figures became fashionable in the pages of fantasy literature.

Two other distinctive aspects of *Pendragon* deserve recognition here. The first is the generally positive treatment of the British rulers. Novels that make use of Gildas as a source almost always share his condemnation of their selfish ambition and wicked deeds. Certainly this was the case in Edward Frankland's *Arthur, The Bear of Britain*, a novel reprinted earlier in the Pendragon Fiction series. Yet Faraday shows these rulers rising above their political rivalries and helping one another because of their shared concern for the general good of the British people. Even Maelgwyn's notorious lechery is transformed into an amiable fondness for women. He would prefer to be rid of them, but, Artorius reveals, should Maelgwyn, "so much as hint that there were too many of them, their tears and upbraidings destroyed his peace of mind."

Much of the sting is taken out of Gildas' railings by showing that they are an art form in which he takes considerable pride. His listeners, and even the objects of his rebuke—like Maelgwyn himself—admire his verbal skill and wit. They are part of the often grim humor that is another distinctive element of the novel. Directed at friend and foe alike in the form of insults and sardonic comments, it adds a refreshing liveliness to the narrative, as when Artorius explains why he was slow to read some tedious verses dedicated to him: "so valuable being the material that I thought it disrespectful to hurry over it." Such irony not only makes more enjoyable the many digressions in which the author introduces background information on the era, but also makes more acceptable the characters' attitudes toward enemies like the Irish and Saxons. Moreover, although these attitudes may strike the modern reader as cruel and prejudiced—if not actually racist—they recreate accurately the heroic mood of Dark Age tales like *Culhwch and Olwen*. There, too, the warriors show no mercy to their enemies whom they taunt verbally and slay savagely. They even insult their friends in the form of the *englyn*. Faraday's Britons can at least argue that they are not the aggressors in the wars that threaten their very survival, even if they respond with as much ferocity as their foes.

—Raymond H. Thompson
February 2002

Born in 1941, Raymond H. Thompson lived in many different parts of the world before emigrating to Canada. He currently resides in Nova Scotia, having recently retired as a professor of English. His fascination with Arthurian legend dates from student days. He has written *The Return from Avalon: A Study of the Arthurian Legend in Modern Fiction* and serves as an associate editor of *The New Arthurian Encyclopedia* and a consulting editor for Green Knight Publishing. Most recently, he prepared *Taliesin's Successors: Interviews with Authors of Modern Arthurian Literature*, which can be found on-line at <www.lib.rochester.edu/camelot/intrvws/contents.htm>.

TO
MILLIE

Author's Introduction

The story of Arthur is the great territorial epic of the British Isles. Round it as centre has gathered a vast accumulation of folklore, tradition, myth, and poetry. For the Welsh, Arthur is their own national hero, but his fame extends far beyond; he has become almost a divinity among the descendants of those who were his bitterest enemies. On this story have been grafted wild tales handed down from prehistoric ages, immemorial customs and myths of agricultural ritual, the mystic vision of the Grail, the origins of Christianity in Britain, the wars which surrounded the fall of the Roman Empire, the legends of North Germany, the bitter struggle of Moor and Carolingian in France, the terrors of the barbarian inroads throughout Europe, and the chivalric ideals of the later Middle Ages. In the mountains of Wales, of Cumberland and the Yorkshire dales, there still lingers, or did a generation ago, the belief in his return as Deliverer; in the Pennine hills of the old Strathclyde, it is said, lies the cave where King Arthur stands with his knights and horses, waiting to restore at the proper time, happiness and prosperity to Britain. As I used to hear said forty years ago, by unlettered shepherds and wayside labourers, 'When Arthur comes again the poor man shall come into ease and happiness.' Malory made him the hero of a princely romance, Tennyson translated him into an allegory, the incredulous historians of a past age denied his very existence. Yet he did in fact live and perform great deeds, and he was never, in name, a king.

Those who desire to study what data there are in historical fashions must look for them in some book such as Mr. Edward Foord's *Last Age of Roman Britain*, but for the purpose of a tale less scientific methods are

permissible, and in the following pages the true story of
the life of Arthur, as far as I can gather it from many
scattered sources, is told. He is a part of history. His
descent can be traced, the record of his victories followed. He was, it is fairly safe to assume, a mercenary
of the later Roman Empire, of royal British descent, of
the most ancient living house of Europe: a man of simple life, with his own just grievances, loyal, somewhat
cynical, with a strong sense of duty and a powerful military genius. He saved Celtic Romanized Britain for a
space, and it was his work which, in a world falling into
ruin, preserved for Britain its great name. Roman
Britain did not fall at a touch as did Italy and Gaul. The
smallest and most remote province of the Roman
Empire in the West, abandoned by its natural protec-
tors, held out with epic heroism against a storm of hor-
ror for the lives of five men, a hundred and fifty years,
and even at the end was never entirely defeated.

This was the work of Arthur. He is the Artorius of my
story. The moral may be drawn, that patriotism is more
than a superstition, and that the good that men do lives
after them. Artorius was born in A.D. 460. His great victory was in 503, at Mount Badon, the Badbury Rings of
Dorsetshire. He died in 540, full of years and honours.
He found Britain distressed, in the grip of nameless bar-
baric fiends; he cleared the land of evil and died in the
full glory of success. For forty years after his death the
land was free and prosperous. The battle of Deorham
Down (Camlan), A.D. 582, marks the end of Roman
Britain; though it was not, as legend says it was, Arthur
himself who fell there, but rather the dream of his heart
and the work of his life.

His estates, or those of his wife, were overwhelmed
by the sea a decade later, A.D. 593. This inundation of
the Creuddyn may explain the part played by water in
all stories of the Passing of Arthur: the Lady of the Lake,
the sinking of Excalibur, and the voyage of the three
Queens in the barge, veiling in mystery the disappear-
ance of the grave of the national hero. If we want to find
it, the most likely place is the sandbank of the Sarn

Gwynfelyn, about fifteen miles due west of Aberystwith. It is here that the boatmen still claim to see, at certain states of the tide, the remains of a city under the waves. But the Welsh poet writes:

> Whose grave is this?
> One sleeps under the oak,
> Another where the surf beats upon the shore;
> One on the crest of the hill,
> Another in the lowly dale.
> One grave is long and narrow,
> Another is covered with dead grass and leaves.
> It was not known who lay in one grave;
> In another it was Cynddlan slept,
> He of the ruddy sword and the white steeds.
> Among the graves on hill and dale
> And on the seashore
> There was no grave of Arthur:
> It would be folly to expect him to have a grave.

The story of Artorius is the record of a man who did as much as a man can do, and reaped the reward of his work. He stood for eternal things, for freedom and order, for love of home and love of the land; and the memory of the people is not unthankful. Their legends called him truly the King who cannot die but will come again: for he served what is immortal.

—W. B. F.

This tale was told to me, Beli ap Rhun, by my grandfather Artorius, my mother's father, the year before he died, which was in the year of our Lord five hundred and forty. It was during his narration well impressed upon my memory, and was written out by me, who am King of Gwynnedd and overlord of Powys and Dynevawr and of the principalities of Morgannwg, Dyfed, and Morfan, in the scriptorium of the Monastery of Bangor ys Coed, in the year five hundred and seventy-eight. Many tales have been told of the times of which I write, but this, the full story which I now communicate in writing for the first time, is the true story of those former ages. It is freed from all magic and illusion, which so many have introduced, and which are contrary to the true records of my forbears.

My mother was Yseult, daughter of Artorius, Duke of the Britons, by his wife Gwendaello of the Creuddyn, in her own right Pendragon of the Island of the Mighty. My father was Rhun, son of Maelgwyn Gwynnedd and of his wife Regan, daughter of Meirion of Pennal. So I know the things of which I write. It is in me that the principalities and Kingdoms of Cambria are united under one head for the first time.

Principal Characters in the Order of Their Appearance

ARTORIUS	*A Roman General*
AURELIAN	*King of Locris*
GWENDAELLO	*Princess of Dynevawr*
MERDDIN	*A Bard*
GILDAS	*Abbot of Bangor*
CADIFOR	*A Farmer*
ESSYEULT	*His Wife*
ANEURIN	*A Bard*
MAELGWYN	*King of Gwynnedd*
CADELL	*King of Powys*
REGAN	*A Girl of Pennal*

The action of the story begins in Britain in A.D. 502.

REX EST QUI METUIT NIHIL: REX EST QUI CUPIT NIHIL

CHAPTER 1
SAVERNAKE FOREST

DEEP IN THE WOODS WHERE BEECH AND OAK
CAST SHADOWS ON THE GRASS,
A TALE BEGINS OF ANCIENT FOLK:
HEAR NOW WHAT CAME TO PASS.

My horse showed signs of overwork, and as I had a long journey before me and no certainty of obtaining a second mount, it was necessary to rest the beast. A horse is but a means to convey a soldier, for the man is ever more important than his steed; but I had a fondness for the creature such as one might have for a favourite slave. He was faithful and affectionate in his way, and in one quality surpassed many men, having never yet deserted me in a close corner.

We had travelled now for over thirty miles, having been upon the road since leaving Cirencester at dawn, and as I was obliged to travel in full equipment and alone, he had no light load to carry. I have at no time believed in the modern pattern of fish-scale body armour, but have always adhered to good and solid plate. The foreign mercenaries, who have for so long corrupted the old Roman armies, introduced this barbarian fashion, but I prefer the defences of my ancestors. It was not in fish-scales that Æneas fought at Troy. Still, the gear is heavy, with helmet and greaves, with shield, javelins and sword to boot, and after thirty miles I was as weary as my horse.

The forest through which I rode was a pleasant place, and had I been engaged upon a less pressing business, I should have found some delight in loitering. The grass upon the rides had been kept short by the wild animals of the woods, either rabbits or the goats

which had wandered from the farms in the disturbed
times, and had bred wild in thousands. The beech trees
too, after their kind, were wide apart, and gave no trouble from undergrowth, while the late sun shone golden
through the summer foliage. Still, it was hot beneath
those wide-spread boughs and their thick canopy of
leaves, and I was sweating as badly as my horse with
heat and weariness.

When, therefore, I came upon a little brook which
widened into a pool by an overhanging bank, I determined to rest, at least for some hours, until the moon
rose, when I could continue my journey at a gentle pace
until dawn. I dismounted and rubbed my horse down
with a handful or two of dry grass, and, after easing him
of all the burden of his harness, tethered him. He was,
in truth, not sorry to be so relieved. For myself I had a
bathe in the pool to clean off the dust and sweat, and
then, resuming my armour, sat down to wait until I
could again continue my journey.

Its urgency had been impressed upon me by
Aurelian during our long conference in Bath, where I
had met him two nights before. I was sorry to leave that
pleasant city, where for so many years I had dwelt with
no small honour and success; for though Aurelian was
rightful King of all Britain, and I but the General of his
armies, we had been friends since my boyhood, and had
trust one in the other. Now, seated by this pool in the
lonely wood, with no companion but my horse, I meditated a while upon what I had left behind; for though,
indeed, a soldier must go upon his service, I have not
yet met the man of war who did not prefer campaigning
among the comforts of the city and the graces of the
ladies rather than among the more uncouth pleasures
of war and destruction. I have some skill in war, and
have so far succeeded in ending to my satisfaction those
contests in which I have engaged; yet I am well aware
that my fortune might at any time take me upon the losing side, a result best prevented by living at peace for as
long as possible. I am no fire-eater, and have never yet
met a soldier who was, and who was at the same time

any good at his trade. Still, needs must, and my motto has always been to fight as well as I can, when I must, and no oftener. By following this rule, I suppose, I have attained the age of forty without mischance.

Bath, with its hot springs, is indeed a pleasant place. There are the streets and squares where the ladies, fair to see, attired in white and purple, or green and blue, and here and there a scarlet cloak, with their flowing hair and smiling faces, walk in the mornings; the markets where they chaffer for such things as women buy, the constant gossip and small festivities, as when one seeks an iced drink at some pavilion, with cakes, or the Arabian or Egyptian holly dissolved in boiling water. Or again, in more stately style, there are the gardens of the villas, even that of Aurelian himself, the ordered entertainments, the banquets and the stage plays. Then there are the heated chambers in winter time, the soft beds, and waiting slaves with everything ready to hand. I am of an age to enjoy all this, and am not indifferent to the relief that the hot springs, and the skilled attendants there, may bring to those twinges in legs and shoulders which are the fruits of earlier campaigning.

I mind me of two girls in particular. One was the daughter of a prince who, angered at the conduct of affairs in Demetia, had crossed the forest of the Gwent with his family, and lived in retirement in Aurelian's capital. She was a pleasant companion of the mischievous Silurian type, black-haired and sparkling-eyed. The other was from Teyngrace, a Damnonian, golden-haired and with eyes as violet as the skies in her pleasant home at evening, but, though calmer in spirit than the other, in no way less gifted with the arts of her sex. However, all this was now behind me.

At the baths Aurelian met me, and, saying that he desired to speak to me in secret, invited me to his villa. The people stepped upon one side to allow our passage, for Aurelian, though King, walks about his capital unattended, beloved by all, and needing no protection. He smiled and exchanged words with those whom we met from time to time, and appeared to be cheerful and at ease, but when we were closeted together his glance grew grave and his speech serious.

"Artorius," he said, "there is gloomy news, both from east and north, and your time of ease is over."

"That is indeed gloomy news," I agreed. "For at my age I seek a measure of repose. Has some outlying tribe of Britons refused tribute? Tell them that they are in common cause with us Romans, and their safety, as well as ours, depends upon the adequate maintenance of the State."

"No," he answered. "I have no complaints against my feudatories, but some old stories from Demetia; but provided that I receive nothing beyond disloyalty, I fear the Silures little."

"They are treacherous," I suggested, "and would join with an enemy of Roman Britain, even to their own destruction."

"True," he agreed, "but short of actual treason, I fear them not at all. I do not like Guitolin, but I do not fear him."

"What then is your necessity?"

"I have received messages from the north. The pagans are making great landings, and the Kingdoms of Reged at the Wall, and of Strathclyde, are in some danger. It is for Reged that I fear. Coel is old, and the Picts have joined with the pagan Angles in a common attack."

"The Picts indeed," I retorted in some scorn, "the savages who conceal their villainous faces with bushy hair, while they expose their scraggy knees to the winds of heaven. I will go north myself, and drive these marauders back to their glens and hovels."

"It is indeed for you that Coel has asked. He requires a military leader. The thing is serious, Artorius."

"With what force, Aurelian?"

"Nay, with no force at all. I have not a cohort to spare. I must watch both Guitolin and the East."

"I guessed as much, Aurelian. You would not send me on such a mission alone, could you be spared here."

"It is true," he said. "It is a danger to the State, but say nothing. We must have no alarm among the people, and if the rebellious raids of these Picts are quelled, we shall hold our own. Strike the adder while he is raising his head, and not afterwards."

In truth our problems of administration and defence were no light ones. Rome, our bulwark and shield, was gone. The mother city was in the hands of the barbarians, and Italy was a chaos of conflicting tribes. The divine Emperor, our rightful Lord, was far away in distant Constantinople, and powerless to aid us; though in this, it is true, there was a certain advantage, as he had ceased to collect any taxes. Britain, a minor province of the Empire was left to her own resources, and for a hundred years we had borne the full assault of the wild tribes from Caledonia, and from the Saxon and Danish shores, who sought to overwhelm us.

Nor were these the only problems. The population of the old Roman Provinces of Britain needed careful handling. Aurelian himself was not of the true royal house, as all knew well. He was but the scion of a Proconsular family, of Imperial descent, and long settled in Britain. That he was mainly British in blood and speech goes without saying, for though his ancestors on the agnate side were Roman, they had, for as long as could be reckoned, taken wives of British stock; for which they cannot be blamed, as the women of this nation are pleasing and faithful. Still he was not, by the reckoning of these Celts, of the true descent; many aspirants could follow their ancestry back to the gods of the island from the primeval eras, and they were haughty about it too.

The trouble was worst in Cambria, though our rule in Cornubia and Damnonia was not without its anxieties. The people of Strathclyde and Reged in the north, being in greater danger than they of Cambria, were more reasonable in their dealings with us. On the east there was sore danger. The abominable Saxons, or people of similar or no character in the beastliness of their manners, the cruelty of their minds, and the dishonesty of their purpose, were well established. Kent, Hampshire and Vectis were in their hands, and ever they received fresh additions to their strength from overseas, and sought to extend their boundaries. We therefore in the west, in our great and beautiful cities of Bath, Gloucester, Cirencester and Isca were alone. We had, it is true, the legions, which we maintained in their discipline and courage, and still armed in the Roman style. We were attempting to rebuild and re-arm Gloucester, our fortress against the Cambrians. We ruled from the Trent to the Channel for the safety of the people, and we were, as far as I am able to judge, the only government in the island able to see beyond the immediate calls of temporary ambition, and the profits of theft and rapine. So Aurelian reigned; for his father, realizing that Rome, as far as we were concerned, was dead, had cast off the shadowy dignity of Proconsul, and called himself henceforth the King of Britain. This was Ambrosius, a great man and a patriot, and Aurelian was a greater man still. He was my friend, cool, cautious, and wise beyond the ordinary run of rulers. I loved him well.

That Ambrosius was right in assuming the crown there is no doubt. He claimed to be a Briton ruling in the name of the people, and not of the alien power of Rome, as myriads, after five hundred years, still considered her. These Celts have a respect for royalty, and when they knew that the produce of their fields, taken by Aurelian's tax-gatherers, was for their own defence, they were more complaisant than they had been to the foreign levies, for the maintenance of the dignity and luxury of the Imperial power, in which they had little share.

There were still the barriers of pride and foolish ambition, and the murmur went round, "Who is this Aurelian? and who was his father Ambrosius? Servants or slaves of the Romans were their humble breed, yet I am of the sacred blood of Britain, for a thousand generations have my stock ruled the land, a greater and nobler man am I than this Aurelian, the descendant of slaves." We might smile at these pretensions, but they were founded on fact, as I, a Briton by ancient descent, well knew.

But I had been well educated as a Roman citizen, and had served since boyhood in the Emperor's armies, from Dacia to beyond the wall of Antoninus. I had learned that it is not always the haughtiest general, but the most skilled, who achieves the victory. Ancient descent is an excellent thing, and my own family can be traced back to the time when there were dragons flying about the sea of Ireland, and elephants in the woods of Britain, or so the story goes; but I am a practical man, and would rather have a snug villa or a prosperous farmstead, than a castle rightfully mine, but in process of being burnt by the barbarians.

That the ancient royalty has survived is not surprising. Rome did not disturb the native kings and princes in their small royalties, provided they maintained the Pax Romana. She ruled through and by them as her Reguli. Hence, even after Rome had gone, the land was full of kings, and the rule of the country on the ordered lines continued without interruption.

Yet to say that Rome departed from Britain is a misunderstanding. It would be more true to say that Britain departed from Rome. The legions in Britain under the command of Rome were British and not Roman. For the Romans always called their legions by numbers, the 10th, the 21st, or the 5th as the case might be, but it was long since we had seen any of these famous armies. Our own legions we had, for two hundred years or more, called by our own names such as the "Fur-caps," the "Grumblers," the "Defenders," the "Breeches-men," and the "Never-say-die." Though they were good troops and well armed, there was more than enough work for them to do, and so the friendship of the feudatory kings was necessary. We had a legion in each of our cities, as at Cirencester, Bath and Isca; one was engaged at Gloucester in rebuilding the defences, and another watched the mouth of the Thames; but apart from these, scattered parties in smaller fortifications were all our force. In all we had five, or sometimes six, legions of six thousand men each, to defend a kingdom of wide extent in very evil times.

This is a military matter and should be correctly recorded. No Roman legion left Britain, for there was none there. Rome deserted us because it was useless any longer to collect taxes. These were indeed paid but, in process of transmission to the Fisc of the Emperor, were almost invariably stolen on the way by either the subordinate officials in Gaul, or by pirates or barbarians. The Emperor became discontented, as may be imagined, saying that there was no profit in Britain. He therefore neglected to send the pay for the legions; at this the legions too were discontented, and we had to pay them ourselves, in addition to the Emperor's taxes. At last we neither sent money to Rome nor took any from her. All we did was to send reports of our operations, and all the Emperor did was, from time to time, to express his gracious approval of these same reports.

By Aurelian's desire then, I was now well away from my home and all the comforts of the baths and luxuries of the city, bound on my long journey to the realms of Coel the Old in the far north by the Roman Wall, there to lead his troops into small affrays and expeditions of chastisement against those blue-skinned, unshaven sons of the devil, the Picts. Well, I hoped that the work might be soon over.

Yet there were signs which gave cause for misgivings, even so near to Bath and Cirencester. Within thirty miles from one of Aurelian's cities I had met two sights which indicated trouble to come. There was that body I had seen, not six miles back, a poor man dead from loss of blood with his right hand lopped off. He might be only some woodcutter hurt by accident whose mate had gone for help. Having no time to waste, I had lost none in examining the matter; but coupled with another sight only two miles back, a cottage burnt to the ground, its little garden and fields destroyed, the home of some small cotter of the woods, it might point to outrage. Like Aurelian I did not trust Guitolin, whose marauding bands might have crossed the Gwent in secret night marches and raided our lands. That he was trafficking with the Saxon I well knew, and Aurelian knew it too, little as he said. The woods were deep and wide, and little watched, for we of the western cities guarded our own rich fields and prosperous tenantry, with small regard for the wastes and marshes of the interminable forests of the Midlands; nor had we forces to spare. Away to Severn-side these forests stretched, wild and valueless, and in parts impassable through undrained rivers. But whatever danger lay hereabouts was as yet secret and treacherous.

Suspicious therefore, as an old soldier in a lonely country, I re-armed my horse, which the beast did not relish, and waited, as the sun set slowly and the dark came, until the moon rose and I could press on through the night. Before me there was no town of any force until I reached Uriconium, a hundred miles away. I was upon my guard, for these raiders, even though they spoke our own British tongue, were not such pleasant companions in the night as some inhabitants of Bath I could name. They would sally forth from a recess in the woods, with their knives and arrows, with blackened skins that could not be seen in the dark, having, like the naked savages that they were, left all their clothes at home, and would cut the throat of any chance traveller for his few valuables. Had I caught any one of these gentry in flight it would have meant for him a flogging and a stay in Gloucester for at least as long as his compatriot Mabon enjoyed, who was, I should guess, deservedly enough, in gaol for three thousand years according to the old story of the Ousel of Cilgwri.

The last relic of the daylight faded, and I sat silently in the dark for perhaps an hour, when there came a sound. It was but a whisper in the branches of the alders which fringed the little pool, but to the ear attuned to the silence, and familiar with the noises made by the wild creatures, it was distinctive enough to draw the attention. I rose, as silently as I might, and stepped gently to my horse. It was no wild goat that I heard moving, for no goat would approach so near a man and horse even in the dark. I gazed hard in the direction of the sound, but there was no repetition. It might be one of those black-faced villains from Demetia, some stray rascal of a blackguard tribe, detached to follow me silently through the dark, waiting his chance to leap upon me unawares, and, having slain me, rifle my horse and arms. There was not more than one, I could swear, and he should receive a welcome. I could wait in patience, as I waited for two days at Verulam for the Jutes to attack. So stilling my horse by rubbing his neck, I waited to slay this sooty-faced scoundrel from beyond the Gwent.

But gaze as I might, I could see nothing. What with the shade of the trees, and the hour of the night, the darkness was intense, a blackness as of Erebus, in which no living thing could see, except one of those cats to which these Cambrians are so greatly attached. At last a faint ray of light permeated the gloom. It was the moon, which having risen high enough to illumine this dark jungle from above trees, shone at length upon the patch of alders by which I watched. I was aching to be away. Much depended upon my haste, but even more upon my life. To the aid of Coel I had been pledged by Aurelian, and I was determined, for this, if for no other reason, to be slain in no break of undergrowth by a midnight thief. That I had some personal objection to being pierced in the back by a Silurian arrow goes without saying, and if I hurried into the light of the moon my assailant would have my horse and armour for loot and I should be powerless to dispute his possession. Cursing to myself, therefore, I waited. Diana was always my friend, and she shone upon where I suspected my enemy to be, rather than upon me, her humble client.

I saw the moonbeam upon the alder leaves. It glimmered with a reflected light. Yet it was no alder leaf that shone so fair, but a white face, and in it two cavernous black spots of eyes that caught the light. I moved forward. No charcoal-smeared thief from Britain beyond the Gwent was this. It was a young maid, terrified and bewildered at the sight of an armed man standing sword in hand to await her.

CHAPTER II

THE SEVERN GATES

THE ISLAND WHERE THE LADY DIED,
WHERE TREASON WAS BEGOT;
HERE IS A TALE OF OLD THAMES-SIDE,
THE ISLAND OF SHALOTT.

At this I laughed to myself. I have been fooled but
rarely, yet fooled I had been this time. Fortunate for
me, indeed, if all my surprises be so pleasant. I stepped
across the sward, and, with a sudden grasp, seized the
girl as she hid in the bushes, and held her fast. She
gave a faint scream, so faint, so terrified, that it was little more than the chirp of a night-bird held by some
young owlet who has taken its first fledgling, or of a
mouse in the claws of a tiny beast of prey.

"Silence," I whispered as I drew her forward. Without
ado I placed her upon my saddle, across or anyway, seeing that she had fainted, and led my horse from that
suspicious copse. Down the ride we went for half an
hour or more, the girl gradually recovering from her
faintness, stirring a little, and moaning feebly, until we
had arrived at a clearing; and there, in the full light of
the risen moon, I halted my horse, and holding firmly to
her arm, slid her to the ground.

I did not know who or what she was, but thinking
that she might be some bait set to befool a wandering
Roman soldier, or that she might know more than I of
the happenings in those parts, I was determined that
she should not escape until I had put her to some exam-
ination. Yet she was not without her sting, for, even as
I held her, with a quick movement she drew a knife from
some hidden place in her dress, and struck viciously at
me. The blow rebounded harmlessly from my breast of

plate; had I been wearing one of those cursed fish-scale hauberks it would have found a cranny, as its curved blade was made for just such work. I knew its make and shape, a shape that it shall be my life's work to expel from Britain if it lie in my power. It was the weapon of murderers and thieves, of robbers and outragers of women, a "seaxe." How they get these knives I know not, in that accursed plague-spot overseas from which these pests come. I have heard that they are made from bits of ore dredged up from some muddy pool in the Northland; in that case they have the same origin as the stinging flies that come from sour water.

It was not the blow, but the knife, which made me tighten my grip upon her hand the harder, and speak in harsher words than I had thought to use to so fair a creature when I took her. She was one of that foul scum then, was she? And fair-haired too, which confirmed my suspicions. But what was a woman of that accursed race doing so far from the southern shore? Was this some further secret raid by the wielders of the seaxe, to vex the realm of my Lord Aurelian?

She was a spy, and if I let her go free now she would betray me to her masters, for these Saxons hold their women in serfdom, as do all barbarians. I would rather she died than I for three good reasons; for I owed my life to three, to Aurelian whose insigne I bore within my shield, to myself in no small degree, and now, it seemed, to Coel the Old of Reged. Two kings and a general were worth more than this Saxon bitch. I raised my sword, but she dropped her knife and spoke.

"Strike then, foul Saxon. Within these last two days have I seen more than a few noble ladies of my race suffer worse than death at the hands of greasy animals such as you."

"I am no Saxon," I said, surprised.

"Then, Sir, I claim your protection against the Saxons, and I command you to guide me to safety. You shall be well rewarded."

To her request, made in my own tongue, no man need have made demur, but the stately insolence of her demeanour now was more difficult to understand than her possession of that accursed knife.

"Who are you to command?" I asked curtly.

"Soldier, for such I perceive you to be, I am one who is not unaccustomed to command. I am the Princess Gwendaello of Cornwall. Here is my proof, if you are wise enough to know it."

She pulled out from her bosom by a string a small piece of black polished stone, carved into the shape of a raven, as big as a man's thumb, bored through the middle with a hole, and of ancient make. I knew it well, for at least two of these badges lay in the treasury of Aurelian, taken doubtless as dowries with some bride of his forefathers. None of the other British houses wore such things, and they were held sacred by the Cornish. To Aurelian they were toys and nothing more.

"I know the badge," I said. "You are truly of the House of Cornwall."

"Of the race of Corineus," she said proudly, "whose domains once extended to the ground on which we stand and far to the north beyond. That very town to the south, which before a year or more is out, will be closing its gates against these foul Saxon invaders, is named for our great founder."

"So I have heard," I answered, for her sudden pride and boastfulness were becoming a little tiresome, particularly in our situation. "But why is such a noble lady wandering alone in the woods at night with a knife, attacking innocent strangers?"

Relief had weakened her. Her pride, I now suspected, was but a pose; she began to tremble, and her mouth opened weakly.

"Well then," I said, "we will defer our explanations until we get to Uriconium, though we have a long way to go as yet. It is several days' journey, with two upon one horse."

"My news," she replied, "will not wait until we get to Uriconium. Take me back to Cirencester."

"I cannot," I replied. "I have lost time as it is. I speed on duty to the State. Behold."

I turned towards her the inside of my shield, and there, painted in bold colouring of blue and red, upon a square label, lay the insignia of my rank, those of the Duke of the Britons, showing the badge of my authority, the scroll of my commission, and the fourteen named forts upon their island. It was a lordly badge indeed for one who now journeyed unattended, bestowed upon me by no less a person than the most sacred Emperor Flavius Anastasius himself. It was, I confess, all he ever gave me, beyond instructing the clerks to record in the Notitia that I was his trusty and well-beloved servant.

"Uriconium will then be well enough," she said sulkily, "though I should have thought that I, a princess of the ancient house, was more fitted to command than a lackey of upstart Rome."

Truly I never met a maid more quick to take offence. There was no humility about the creature at all. She seemed to believe that her privileges were endless. It was evident that she was of the House of Cornwall. They had always made a favour of assisting Aurelian, even when he was acting according to their own requests. They never paid the tribute for their marchlands at all, and it was only by intercepting their own tax-gatherers that the officers of Aurelian were able to collect what was due.

Aurelian himself made no particular protest against their refusal to acknowledge him as their overlord. "Provided," he used to say, "that we obtain what sums are due to us, these civilities would appear to be of minor importance."

"That you are of the House of Cornwall I do not doubt at all," was what I said in reply to the lady, "but Cornwall is of the dominion of my Lord Aurelian, and is ruled by Constantine. Your house now dwells on smaller thrones, a cadet branch in Strathclyde, and your main line driven into wild Demetia. You are from Brecknock, I guess?"

In any case the maid was interesting. If she had come from Strathclyde, what had happened in that far north to which I was bound, and what did a princess in

peril, so far from her home? If on the other hand she
were of Demetia, her story would still be of import. I
considered that she might be some cousin of that rascal
Guitolin.

"Yes," she replied, "I am from Brecknock, or beyond."

"Then what do you in this country, and who came
with you?"

"I, and those who accompanied me, have the right to
travel unquestioned where we will in the realm of
Britain, or anywhere else in the Island of the Mighty, by
ancient right of conquest," she said proudly. "I came
with no less than Guitolin my uncle, Pendragon and
King of all Britain."

"There is no Pendragon," I answered. "The rule of
this land depends now on the strong hand. That old
claim of Pendragon is the cause of most of our woes. To
Aurelian alone belongs the overlordship, and on him,
and those who serve him, hangs the fate of all of us
against the barbarians."

At this she looked contemptuous, and I said no
more. This girl had escaped from the Saxons; therefore,
there were Saxons somewhere near. Guitolin himself
was plainly not far away, with, probably, some hundreds of his fly-by-night and thieving kerns. It was
indeed time to be gone.

"To Hades with the Pendragon," was all I said. "We
must get away. You may ride pillion, if you have no
other knife upon you."

She was but a light weight, and my horse made no
account of the added burden, beyond a disapproving
shake of his head; and so we jogged on, for the next two
or three hours, at an easy pace, taking a path through
the woods which I remembered from a former expedition, until, many miles to the north, we came at last to
the Severn-side. At this point the river flows fast,
between steep and high cliffs, forming the gate to as fair
a valley as any in Britain: a rich country when Rome
ruled the world, but now waste and depopulated. I said
no more to the girl, whom I began to dislike most
heartily. I would take her to Uriconium, as I had

promised, but once there I longed to be rid of her, as did my horse. Still, I must get her story.

Accordingly, when I had made my camp by the waterside under cover of the trees, which here grew down to the river's edge, and after I had scrubbed down my horse and we had fed plainly on what bread and meat I had in my saddlebags, I ordered her to tell me her story; at first she demurred.

"My tale is for myself alone. That I was on business of the Pendragon, and with him, you know. The rest is no tale for you, a mere servant of the usurper Aurelian."

"What concern then was it of mine to carry you for these many miles into safety? Many men would have declined your acquaintance altogether, after that play of yours with the knife."

"I should have killed you indeed had you been, as I thought, a Saxon."

"A poor excuse, to insult a man first and try to murder him afterwards. You are too fierce altogether, you Pendragons. But tell your tale, or I shall leave you here alone. Do you know where you are?"

"I am in my family's dominions."

"The main population of your family's dominions would appear to be Saxons and murderers, if my own experience of these regions goes for anything. But, if you are content, so am I. I shall then leave you, with trust as to your ultimate safety, upon the rich and peopled estates of your kingly ancestors."

"But you promised to see me to Uriconium."

"I will escort you to Uriconium on one condition, that you tell me truthfully what was your affair with your Pendragon King of thieving tribesmen, and where you have been, and what it was you sought, so far from your capital city of wattle-and-daub huts."

"I shall tell you no more."

"Then find your own way, either to Uriconium or to Brecknock, or to your friend the Pendragon himself."

"Alas, but the Pendragon is taken."

At this I sat up with attention indeed. There was more in the air than had reached me. Guitolin had been taken, and the girl, his niece, and a princess of Britain, was a fugitive. Who had taken him, and what had the fool been doing. That there were Saxons in the business was clear from the knife and the few hints that the girl had made. I professed indifference however.

"Then the realm will be more peaceful. His followers are all hanged, I hope."

Many may think that I was hard upon this girl. She had doubtless seen some horrors of the sort that are usual in any matter concerning Saxons, but she had recovered so completely, and shown so little gratitude, and so much arrogance, that my patience was at an end; for, though I liked her appearance well enough, she was but a trifle in the scale of my affairs. The land had been despoiled by the constant raids of the barbarians and the fighting between all parties for a hundred years back, and though Aurelian and his father Ambrosius had done much to restore peace and a moderate prosperity, and to rebuild the ordered fabric of society under the centralized rule of their house, much remained to be done; many towns and villages had been laid waste and never rebuilt, while vast areas of once fertile lands lay depopulated and derelict. The wild forest through which we rode had once been cornland. Here and there were clearings which in the old time were happy and wealthy homesteads. Now the young trees, self-sown, were already of timber size.

So I hated this girl as I hated and despised her house. She belonged to a race of the same blood as ourselves, who were yet not content to be on the side of the fair land in which they dwelt, aiding the strong hand in the interests of all, but were for ever jealous and scheming. The higher we raised our power, the fiercer became the desire of these cursed Pendragons to possess the inheritance of their fathers; a throne which, before they were driven from it, was not worth the having. There was but one of the breed for whom I had any respect, and that was Maelgwyn of Gwynnedd; he, at all events, was a man and a soldier, though a notorious evil-liver. The last was his private concern, but the fact that he had slain the Irish and despoiled the Scots was to his credit, and a matter of public importance.

Maelgwyn, moreover, held sound opinions on many subjects. Though himself of the House of Cornwall, he asserted with oaths that the claim of the Pendragonship by his kin was nothing to him, and that, whoever was Head-King by legitimate claim, it would never be himself, inasmuch as he had never heard that his great grandfather Cunedda was ever married at all. Moreover he had small sympathy with any of the religions of the time. "The Christians," he said, "stated that it was right to spare their enemies, a dogma upon which the Christians with whom he was best acquainted, namely the Irish pirates, never seemed to act, and therefore the Christians did not practise their own preaching; more-over it was folly to spare your enemies." Personally I agree with him; it appears that the doctrine of sparing enemies was first advanced by those who were acquainted with neither Picts nor Saxons.

The Druids Maelgwyn rather favoured, holding that their gospel of kill or be killed was sound common sense and true religion. He encouraged them, so far at least as to leave them in peace, unless they offended him. On these occasions he hanged them with much respect and many compliments. As for Jupiter and the ancient Gods of Rome, they were all dead, except Venus, to whom he himself was devoted.

I had known Maelgwyn since we met at Carlisle in the war with the Dal Righs, and he explained his religion to me after many mugs of wine. I found him to be a good soldier, and a trustworthy ally, for though, like all his countrymen, he preferred to fight in the dark and by way of surprise, he happened at this time to be slaying those whom I particularly wanted to be put out of the way. A good friend, if he happened to be on one's own side, and until he actually joined the other, as he would if he saw profit in the change. Yet if Maelgwyn changed his views it was well for others to take them into consideration. He was a man who always prospered, and like myself had no liking for the Saxons,

who he said had no business in Britain at all. He was
well advanced in his cups when saying this, but he was
nevertheless quite sincere. Britain, he held, was a country for gentlemen who were entitled to kill and rob each
other as they liked; let then the best man win, "who," he
added with a hiccough, "is myself." But the Saxons,
according to him, were never gentlemen at all. Their
breath smelled of beer, and they spilt fat on their
clothes. If ever they came into Gwynnedd he would
make candles of them, and being greasy they would
burn well. A savage man in truth, and one whom on the
present mission I wished to avoid. Let him remain in
Gwynnedd, out of the present quarrel, for the foes
against whom we were engaged had little in the way of
loot, and Maelgwyn would claim a price for his sword
which neither Aurelian nor I had any wish to pay.

I must certainly know from this girl what had happened, if Guitolin had been out of his own territories
and had met with Saxons. These swine had never troubled him; to reach his lands at all they must cross the
country of Aurelian, which they had never done yet. We
lay like a bulwark, a sure and certain wall, between him
and these savages. How to get the news out of the girl
was the problem, so I determined to try such guile as I
had, and before we lay down to rest, I began to talk with
her again.

"You doubtless wonder why I am alone upon the
road, maiden?"

"I have no concern with your business, Sir. I pre-
sume you act under your master's orders."

"And yet a friend of Guitolin's might well take some
interest in my errand."

She remained silent, and, indeed, turned her back
upon me.

"The truth is," I continued, "that we are tired of that
nest of whelps in Demetia. Only a year ago, Gloucester
was sacked by your friends, and burned by ignorant
kerns from your barren hills, looting our ancient city as
if it were one of your own pigsties, by surprise in the
night."

She spoke at last. "You know well why Gloucester was punished. The city had refused tribute to its overlord."

"So the tribute was taken by thieves, housebreakers and murderers, for such are the people of Demetia. Poor as are their barren hills, stinking like their own goats, black-faced as their poor half-starved sheep. Why, in order to get an excuse for violence you set up a fraudulent claim. We who have both culture and sense are not prepared to submit to further outrages. Ere a month is over, the throne of Guitolin will have vanished. I am journeying to complete the military arrangement by which the Princes of Gwynnedd and Powys will join with Aurelian in stamping out this nest of vipers." I said all this, which was not in any way true, in order to frighten her.

"Fool," she cried, "ere the year is up the Saxon will be at your gates." Then she was silent.

But she had said enough. I saw what was in the wind. Guitolin had travelled east, and was, or had been, trafficking with the barbarians. His mad ambition and pride in his shadowy claim to the Pendragonship had tempted him into a shameful alliance with the pigs from the muddy sloughs of the Northland overseas. It seemed, moreover, from what the girl had said, that the plan had miscarried in some way. She had said that Guitolin was taken. If so, by whom? I rose from my seat on a fallen tree, and stood over her where she sat.

"So you are a Princess no longer, or in a month at most you will not be. You will be a concubine, or a kitchen-maid, in one of our nobles' houses, if any want such a tainted vixen. The manner of your future tuition can begin at once. Tell me everything, or I shall flog you." I gripped her harshly by the arm.

She groped wildly with her hands, but was powerless in my hold. Her eyes closed and she seemed to faint, relying, as I suspected, on woman's weapon of pretence, by which they weep and deceive, and then afterwards laugh at those in whom they have inspired pity. She roused herself, for I could see the effort, and falling upon her knees, prayed for me to spare her.

"Then tell me all," I said, "for I know a part of the tale. Who has taken Guitolin?"

She began to weep. "Alas, alas," she cried, "it is the Saxons, and thus is my ancient race and noble and faithful country threatened on all sides. I can bear no more."

"Your story, fool."

"It is like this. A year ago, Guitolin made alliance with the Saxon King, or Duke, for he is nothing more. The terms were that he and his hordes, who are sorely oppressed in their own lands, were to have settlement here. It was the Consul Aetius, by defeating Attila many years ago, who caused the pother. The Saxon tribes were driven from the south of their country by bands of defeated Huns and now, overcrowded and poor, seek fresh homes. For these poor refugees, in his charity, Guitolin offered accommodation."

"And what advantage was this charitable monarch to get out of this for himself?"

"He has no lands which could accommodate them. We are but a poor and mountainous country in Demetia, but in the lands of the Thames valley, even to the White Horse upon the hill, there is room for many thousands. There the Saxons could have settled and prospered, and become the warlike and wealthy subjects of the Pendragon."

"And in time, doubtless, when they were numerous enough, they would help him to recover the entire realm of his ancestors."

"That was in the treaty," she said; "it was a noble scheme."

"It was indeed. Were any beside Guitolin in this plan?"

"Some minor chieftains from Builth and Morgannwg, no more."

"I follow. So you blackfaced sheep from the west, protected from the barbarians in your wretched fold by the sword of Aurelian, have been trafficking with his enemies behind his back. Is that the tale?"

"That is the tale," she said stubbornly.

"And now it has miscarried?"

"In grief and disaster. We went with our guard, a small force of kerns and some few knights, Guitolin, and some of his ladies, to lend trust to the gathering. With us were the Princes of Builth and of Morgannwg and some royal squires, those they call the golden-haired, from Cydweli, Ysgarn and Isnafyr. In all there were some twenty noble gentlemen and their ladies, with servants to give them dignity, proceeding under safe-conduct from the Saxon Duke. The meeting was to be secret, and in an unknown place."

"And was the meeting held?"

"Alas, it was; upon an island in the river, a place of ill-omen. You know it from the ancient tale; it was the island where the Lady died."

"I know the story, and the isle. Well?"

"The feast began. A pavilion had been prepared by these Saxons for the ladies, and there we were seated with such coarse entertainment as these poor savages, as we thought them, could afford, with mead to drink, and roasted pigs, and cakes with honey. The Saxon women ate greedily, and we, my friends and I, were laughing to see their hog-like manners. Now the Princes and the Saxon leaders in a pavilion adjoining were seated one and one, a Saxon and a Briton, in apparent good-fellowship; they toasted one another, and we heard their cries for more drink, and their laughter."

"So your proud Princes were sitting at table with these swine?"

"That was in the agreement. The treaty was made, and the lands allotted."

"Lands of Aurelian, I gather?"

"Lands of the Pendragon as we claimed," she said quietly. "But listen to what followed. Our Princes, as men do when they go to a feast, had gone unarmed, but each of these savages had a dagger hidden in his shoe. At a signal from their base and treacherous Duke, each one of these wretches then drew his knife and stabbed his neighbour, and thus, in one minute, fell and died the flower of our land of Cambria. Of all the Britons present at the feast, but one was allowed to live: the unhappy Guitolin was led away, covered with chains, to some foul prison, mayhap in company with beasts, for these dirty brutes live in stables."

I was horrified at this narration. I had, it is true, no sympathy with the traitor Guitolin who had tried to sell his countrymen, but I felt sick and disgusted at the baseness of the Saxon, who would slay at his own table a guest and ally.

"But what of Guitolin?" I asked.

"He is to be held, as I was told afterwards, until he has agreed to cede to these invaders the lands which they require, free from all condition and all overlord-ship, and of much greater extent than he was disposed to grant."

"He may cede, but he cannot grant. The land is Aurelian's. What lands do they now demand?"

"All the lands about the mouth of the river Thames, of one hundred miles in width, and one hundred in depth, with the towns of Verulam, Lundinium and Anderida."

A cunning scheme indeed, I mused. Thus they would hold our chief ports of Rudcester and of London; and, with their holdings at the Forth, close, to all effect, our commerce with the world. We should indeed be shut in. Still, a treaty unlawfully made is useless in law or against force of arms, in fact all treaties are useless against force of arms. The matter was of import, as indi-cating a further strong campaign by the barbarians, otherwise it left things very much as they were; though that Guitolin would concede any Saxon claim as the price of his liberty I had little doubt.

In truth the tale was no worse than I expected of Saxons, but having heard it, I looked with a gentler eye upon this maid.

"It seems that you have indeed passed through ter-ror and suffering, Princess of Cambria. But how did you escape, yourself, from the clutches of these outcasts?"

"When the murder was done our woman's pavilion was surrounded by armed men, who entered and seized those of us who were British. These Saxons had brought but few women with them, and their army was clamouring for wives. We were, therefore, shown to the heathen, who bid for us, those of them who had money, and they were few, for they are poverty-stricken wretches, a company of vagrants and footpads. However, the twenty ladies were sold, as I was myself."

"Did Guitolin raise no protest?"

"I saw him, chained behind a wagon, but he did not raise his eyes. He crouched low upon the ground, and moaned; but he never stirred."

"A hero prince indeed, and right worthy of the House of Cornwall."

She looked at me, and I saw a flicker cross her face, but she remained silent, and then began to weep.

"Come, come," I said, "this is useless."

"That it means much to me, you may guess," she replied with slow dignity, "that I should have met with these misfortunes, and now must live to hear ill-bred taunts against my house. Know, soldier, or slave of Rome, that my house ruled in this land, ere ever Rome was; that our great founder, whose duchy stretched from the Tin Islands to the Severn, was ruling men when your Romans were but the beaten serfs of the Gauls."

"As it seems to me now," I replied, "the Romans are not in much better case than they were then, at least in the mother city, while the head of the House of Corineus is in an evil position himself. We have other work before us than to plume ourselves upon ancient glories. But tell me how you freed yourself from the barbarians' clutches?"

"The brute who had taken me at the sale dragged me away to the wagon in which he lived. It was a large wain, with a tent upon it; it seemed that he was some leader among them. At the market that they held of these poor captured ladies there was much drinking and noisy laughter, and this man was drunk when he purchased me. In his tent, he cast me down in a corner, and then, seating himself upon a stool, gloated on the sight,

drinking at the same time deeply from a horn. In a little, for the liquor was strong, he became unconscious,
and fell from his stool in a stupor. His knife, that one
with the curved blade, with which, he boasted to me, he
had slain the Prince of Ysgarn, him whom they call the
'golden-haired,' a poor boy but a gallant, whose years are
less than mine; this knife I say, he let drop. I seized it,
and was in two minds whether to slay him or myself. I
was trembling with fear and hatred, and could scarcely
think. Then I saw my duty clear. I must escape, and
warn the land. I stabbed this Saxon beast where he lay.
He moaned in his torpor as the blood flowed, for I had
struck deep, and in a minute or two he was dead. It was,
by now, dark, but fires had been lighted about the
camp, and I could see the forms of the savages, like
shadows in the reflexion of the flames. They were, some
heavy, some wild, with drink, and were howling confused and horrid songs. I stood in the shadow of the
wagon, and as I watched, a girl whom I well knew, and
with whom I had laughed only that morning, leaped
from a wagon and died at my feet. She had stabbed herself with just such a knife as that which I had taken.
The seaxe, they call it, from which these people also
take their name."

"It is your knife, lady," I said, taking it from my
armour, and holding it to her, handle first.

"I thank you, soldier, for your courtesy," was her
reply. She touched the handle with her fingers and bade
me carry it for her. I liked this well.

"It is perhaps the better, lady," I said; "if perchance
you have again occasion for its services against a Saxon,
you will permit me, perhaps, to strike the blow on your
behalf."

"That would be well done," was her answer.

"But continue your story."

"You must remember we were upon an island, one of
a mournful tale, yet a tale cleaner than this I tell you. I
was fearful, but unfollowed. The trees were decked in
hideous fashion with the mutilated bodies of our poor
kerns nailed upon them, or strewn in pieces beneath

the branches, torn or hacked asunder, in some fit of
drunken bestial rage, by their slayers. Some of these
kerns were from my own village, men whom I had
known all my life. At the river's edge, I slipped gently
into the water, and swam to the main shore. From there
I travelled as slowly as a sorrowing woman must, weak
and often hungry, for I had brought but little food away
with me. I eked that out with wild berries and mush-
rooms. Once I came to a cottage burnt by these savages,
and found some scraps of food in an outhouse where I
slept. And so, for five days, I travelled through these
woods until I came to meet you by the pool."

"A wicked story," I told her. "Yet I cannot help thinking that you are more worthy of your House of Cornwall
than your cousin Guitolin."

"It is the motto of our house, that where one fails
some other must assume the burden."

"Are you observing this treaty with the Saxons then,
maid?"

"The treaty was violated, I am in no way bound by it
further, nor will I regard it, if it is within my right to
say."

"Your right to say matters little, but your sentiments
seem to me to be good law, and good sense. As to your
motto, maid: where one fails the other carries on. That
is for me now."

"How can you, a Roman Briton, carry on the work of
the Pendragon?" she asked, with astonishment.

"Where the master is ill, the servant must do his
work," I quoted. "I profess no dignity but that of a servant of Britain. Was Guitolin as much as this?"

"I do not think that aspect of it had crossed his
mind," she said slowly, "but there is truth in what you
say."

It seemed, in view of this remark, that she was better than the others of her clan, and had notions about
other things than her family pride and personal ambition. A girl who, after her experiences, could still see
that the State had claims beyond its leaders' strivings
for place and power, had parts about her worthy of

praise. True, her lesson had taught her that a mistake had been made. Guitolin, the cunning and unscrupulous, had led his trusting followers into death and slavery. A man less cunning, even such a one as myself, would never have been so foolish. Had I but heard that the Saxons were to hold a feast at which Guitolin was to be a guest, I should have contributed to the board, and right handsomely, by a secret present of poisoned wine. It was strange that the idea had never previously occurred to me. I hate gluttony and drunkenness, and after all it is but right, in war, to take full advantage of an opponent's weaknesses; for the opportunity lost I was in no way to blame, and mayhap some chance of the kind would come to me later, at least I hoped so.

CHAPTER III
THE GREY FATHERS

WHILE BIGOTS FIGHT AND SAGES DOUBT,
LET SIMPLE FAITHS BE TOLD;
FOR WHEN ALL THINGS ARE REASONED OUT,
THE NEW GODS ARE THE OLD.

It may be thought that Aurelian and I took the present disturbance very quietly; but in fact, for the past hundred and forty years armed invasion had been an almost yearly occurrence. The trouble began when the two Imperial brothers, Valens at Constantinople, and Valentinian at Rome, divided the Empire, and at the same time the inroads of Goths, Vandals, and other savages kept Rome so fully occupied with her own troubles, that she had no energy to spare for the distant province of Britain. Every uncivilized tribe in the universe appeared to have acquired a sudden longing to possess itself of other people's property. Our first taste of these disturbances in Britain came from an infamous wretch who, in consequence of some fabled adventures of his, gloried in the name of Niall of the Nine Hostages, and who attacked our province of Gwynnedd, or Britannia Secunda as it was called in those days. This pirate and villain ravaged the province, bore away countless numbers of the inhabitants into bitter slavery in Ireland, and, as some say, held large numbers of young children in captivity in pens like animals, where they were fattened and subsequently killed and eaten. When the news of these frightful deeds came to the great Cunedda, by name the Roman Proconsul in Valentia, but in actual fact reigning King of Strathclyde, he vowed the bestial atrocities of these Irish should cease.

"It was intolerable," said Cunedda, "that human

beings should be enslaved by dragons and wolves,"
and, after defeating some bands of mixed Scots and
Irish, a bastard race who had been driven out of their
own country, and were called Dal Righ, he marched into
Gwynnedd to liberate his fellow-countrymen. This
Cunedda was ever a man with a high sense of public
duty. Though Rome was, even in his day, a weakened
force, he still owed her his allegiance, and maintained
that his duty lay throughout Britain, and not merely in
his own province.

Niall of the Nine Hostages had established himself in
a sort of permanent residence on the coast of Gwynnedd,
and many thousands of his fellow-barbarians had settled there with him, stealing the produce of the mines,
enslaving the people, hocking the cattle, and outraging
the women. They remained there, however, but a short
space after the arrival of Cunedda. The Irish king, as he
called himself, was killed in a cow-house where he had
hidden himself in terror, and all his abominable followers were disbanded. Many thousands were slain and
thousands of others sent to work in the lead and copper
mines, of which in Gwynnedd there are a great number.
The work is hard and unhealthy, both copper and lead
being poisonous metals as well as being worked underground; so that even the overseers only worked on alter-
nate days. The Irish, being naturally lazy, had to work
under the lash, which was, I believe, very liberally
applied, so that they quickly died. In consequence of
this, Cunedda and his successors had to make frequent
expeditions to Ireland to obtain more slaves. The poisonous effects of the work in the mines were very curious.
The faces of the miners, and their bodies too, broke out
into evil-smelling sores, and in addition their teeth fell
out in great purulence. The people of Gwynnedd, therefore, would not work in the mines themselves. As the
metal was valuable, slaves were necessary and Ireland
was naturally the obvious source of supply; it was near
at hand, and the work and hardships were, when all
was said, but justice for the past evil deeds of the Irish
themselves. Cunedda and those who came after him

found the mines, under these conditions, well worth the trouble and very profitable, because the Irish slaves, being poisoned by the metals, did not cost very much in food.

After the Irish came the Picts. These people are of better quality than either Irish or Scots, being the degenerate descendants of the British race who have fallen back into savagery through the misgovernment of their own rulers.

After enormous dismay had been caused by their ravages, the great Consul Stilicho sent some legions to Britain who corrected their misdeeds, and drove them back to their native fastnesses. Then came a bastard lot of outlaws from Germania, mostly landless men who had no support in their own country, though in view of their natural loathsomeness it was commonly believed in Britain that they were originally criminals and refugees from justice. These were also defeated, and driven away, though some few remained in settlements at the mouth of the river Forth, in Kent and in Vectis.

Meanwhile, the Goths under Alaric destroyed the Western Empire, and thereafter our only overlord was in Constantinople. He was too far away to concern himself much with us, so that we became, in place of a province of the Empire, a group of kingdoms following more or less the Roman divisions of the island. Of old, before the Romans came, Britain was divided into three parts. Albania, the most northerly, from the Cheviot hills to the extreme north, was called after Albanact, its first king. Then came Cambria, called after Camber, his brother who governed all the region lying west of the river Severn. All the rest of the island, and much the best part of it, was called Loegria, or Locris, after Locrin, the third brother. It was the daughter of this Locrin, Sabrina, who drowned herself in the river, which is called after her to this day.

But when we split away from Rome, setting on one side the barbarous region of Caledonia, north of the Wall of Antoninus, the land was divided into six or seven kingdoms. First Reged, on the east coast, including the eastern portion of the old Roman province of Valentia, from the Wall of Antoninus to the river Tyne. On the west was Strathclyde, extending from the river Clyde to the Ribble, Ribchester being its most southern city. To the east again lay Elmet with its great capital city of York, for long the Roman headquarters in Britain, where the divine Constantine, the grandfather of Valens and Valentinian, was born. In the extreme south-west was Damnonia, reaching from the river Axe to the Scilly Isles. West of the Severn lay to the north Gwynnedd, a mountainous land surrounding the great hill of Snowdon, and to the south Demetia, or as we call it in the British tongue, Dynevawr, with its various divisions. All the rest of the land was Locris.

The rulers of these kingdoms were as follows. A very old man, so ancient that he was called "The Old," was King of Reged. He was named Coel, and was a wise and just King. In Strathclyde was Coroticus, Roman by descent and a good soldier. In Elmet was Justin, of whom all that can be said is that his province was worthy of a more adventurous and virile King. His people indeed, of the race of the Brigantes, were in no way inferior to other Britons, but their government was timid and unwarlike. In Damnonia reigned Constantine, a descendant of Constans, the father of the great and divine Constantine. In Gwynnedd ruled Maelgwyn, the grandson of that Cunedda of whom I have told. As to Dynevawr, it was split up into numerous small principalities, more or less loosely united under that rascally Guitolin, the third of the three curses of Britain. He claimed to be the descendant of Corineus and also of Sabrina, the daughter of Locrin, and consequently overlord of all Britain, from the Orkneys to the Scillies. Over Locris was the great King Aurelian, my friend, and the third of the great blessings of Britain.

Aurelian claimed overlordship by right of descent from the chief man of the island under Rome; not, as he said to me, through ambition, for he wished nothing better than to be left undisturbed in his own prosperous and fair dominions. But as he possessed the only really disciplined military force against invaders, and still maintained the same number of legions as had fought under Rome in the island in the palmy days of her great conquests, he was entitled to be regarded as head of the State. The other kings and princes, while in no way objecting to being protected against the Picts, Irish and Saxons, seemed to have an inexplicable prejudice against paying for this advantage.

Even in my time a change had come over Britain. At one time the language of Rome had been almost universal throughout the island, but now whole kingdoms had abandoned it, and relapsed into the original British. In Gwynnedd, Powys and Dynevawr they spoke British only; even in Locris, though many of us could write and speak the tongue of Rome, we for ordinary conversation used the British dialect, while in Strathclyde, Elmet and Reged they had a strange tongue which we of the south could indeed understand, but to which we had to listen carefully, or it became unintelligible. In Damnonia, near as they were to the great centres of culture and learning, such as Bath and Cirencester, they spoke a language of their own, British in origin but obscure, from certain local peculiarities, very like the tongue of the Armorican Britons.

We had ceased to speak of Roman names of places, and the old names had survived. They were older than the Roman dominion and persisted after Rome was dead.

It was true therefore, that we were growing into a nation. All that was needed was a measure of sense and agreement among the native populations; and, with Aurelian at the head of the State, difficult as was his part, I myself did not despair of triumphing in the end over our foes and our difficulties, and creating an Empire of Britain which should ride supreme above the tempestuous waves raised by the fall and engulfment of the city of the Cæsars. I like the old name for Britain used by our ancestors, and remembered still in the old tales: "The Island of the Mighty," as they called it, ere ever the Romans crossed the channel, ere ever Cæsar was born. That it might be in truth the Island of the

Mighty, as in the days of Bendigeid Vran who conquered Rome itself, and overawed the pestilent Irish, seven hundred years before the birth of Constantine at York, was indeed my earnest hope. National boundaries change, and there is nothing certain or secure in the fringes of States and empires. But the boundary of Britain is the sea, and if the land contained by these stormy waters were indeed the Island of the Mighty, no evil was to be feared that we could not hope with confidence to prevent.

On the day after I met the maid of the woods, we rode as best we might through the forest. I took a short cut and avoided the long detour of the military road to Uriconium round by Lichfield. For many miles we followed the winding of the river, until, some distance from the main road, we came across the old British trackway, over the Clee hills, that feeds it. Here we travelled in more comfort than before, until, half-way down a steep hill in a corner of the track, where it wound about a shoulder of grassland, we came in sight of two men. Even from that distance I could see that they were old, for their beards were long and grey, and they were clad in flowing robes and unarmed. I had therefore no fear in approaching them, but continued along the track unmoved by their presence there.

One was seated placidly upon a stone by the wayside, the other stood in front of him, and with waving arms and violent speech, addressed him in pouring eloquence. The first, clothed in a soiled white garment which reached to his feet, and with a long staff in his hand, remained seated even as we approached. He listened with calmness, and his quietude appeared to be rousing the other to the more fury. This other was indeed a strange-looking figure, thin and wild-eyed, an abbot by his mitre and his crook, but with his white robes tucked up to his thighs by a cord, exposing his hairy skinny limbs to the gaze of all. As we approached I heard his words, for he spoke in a loud shriek, with fierce gestures.

"For Britain has kings but they are all tyrants, she

has judges but they are unrighteous; they prey upon the innocent, and if they avenge or protect, it is the robbers and felons they favour. Bloody-minded and adulterers, fornicators, and false swearers, treating the altar of God as they would a heap of dirty stones."

"Whom do you especially bear in mind?" asked the seated one, calmly.

"This horrid abomination Constantine, the tyrannical whelp of the unclean lioness of Damnonia, who in the habit of a holy abbot, in his cloak red with the coagulated blood of countless victims, did many shames with vulgar and domestic impieties, and did add new wickedness to his former frightfulnesses by refusing to the Church her dues of malt, meal, and wine, honey and money."

"When was this?" asked the seated one. "And for how much did you ask him?"

"Vile scoffer, who with thy outrageous lord hast shamed and abused the priests and monks, the abbots and the priors, the canons and lay brethren."

"It is years since I was in Damnonia, yet when I was last with you, you told me nothing of this. You never even mentioned it."

"I speak not of thy misdeeds in Damnonia, for they are not to my knowledge. Yet black as thou art with sorceries and wickedness, I can well believe that there were many purple sins to thy discredit which thou didst in that lion's den. If thou wert there, there was wickedness in that land. Hast aught to confess of what thou didst in those parts? Forgiveness may come even yet unto thee, though I doubt it sorely; infinite as is the mercy of God."

"What is it particularly that you want to know?" said the other.

"Nay, my desire is as nothing. Thy horrid abominations are as discord in mine ears, thy sins fill me with a grief too bitter to be borne. I pray to be delivered from the recital of thy iniquities. Yet in my duty, and foreign to my own wish, I would wean thee from thy abominable pursuits, and guide thee to a better life, if it be possible, which I doubt."

"These things," said the seated one mildly, "are better expressed in simple language and with no unnecessary heat. I have not yet grasped what it is that you immediately desire to know, nor in what manner I have offended you. It appears that you wish me to go somewhere. Where?"

"To heaven, sinner."

"I prefer not. I am bound for Deganwy. Heaven later, perhaps, but not yet, if I have any say in the matter."

"To Deganwy; O woe, woe! To that city of the plain where the infamies of its earthly and earthbound Lord have raised a cry to heaven from the stench of its iniquities."

"Then it would clearly be the better for my presence, because on account of my age I have a dislike for these furious nights, to which you draw attention."

The two old men were so intent upon their quarrel that the step of my horse upon the grass had passed unnoticed; but as I came close to them, they at last perceived the presence of newcomers, and looked round with some surprise. The seated one acknowledged my presence with a slight though courteous nod; the other gave a wild jump and then shouted, "Another son of Belial, in armour of proof, with a countenance hard as the flints of the Southland, evil beyond a doubt, and as a further proof of his evil-doing, travelling alone with a woman. Art married to thy leman, man of blood?"

The question was a sudden one, being cast at me like a stone from a sling. The girl seated behind me on the pillion, her arms clasping me, looked out from over my shoulder, and said angrily:

"No, he is not."

I halted my horse. The two old men were so strange, alone together in such a wild place, and so unafraid, that the encounter seemed the oddest in my long life of wandering.

The girl slid from my shoulder and stood upon the road, and thus relieved, I dismounted, for I was stiff with two hours' riding.

"Who are you?" I asked.

The man with the girt-up loins cast his hands sky-wards in a despairing gesture; the other addressed me politely. It was a relief to me that the more excited of the twain refrained from speech; as I should judge from lack of breath, and out of no desire on his part to spare the company any of his eloquence.

"Sir Knight," said the seated one, "you may well ask who we are, for I find myself in an embarrassing situa-tion, and I am in no mood to be judged by the company in which I may happen to be found. This old gentleman, who is so angry with me, is the holy Abbot Gildas."

"A prophet of God, scoffer," burst in the other.

"Who claims to be a prophet of God. I have no infor-mation which would entitle me to dispute his assertion."

"And you yourself, old gentleman? I appeal to you, for you seem to have the more sense of the twain."

"I thank you, Sir, for your good opinion. I am no holy abbot but merely a humble bard of the Island of Mona. Indeed, though I am chief of them, I must necessarily be humble, for all bards are humble until they get what they want."

"And what do you want?"

"Chiefly, at this moment, to be relieved of this old gentleman's conversation."

"Scoffer and unregenerate. Vile spawn of the devil," said the other passionately. "If the devils believe, where is your belief?"

"He but repeats what has been commonly said about me," said the seated one apologetically. "It is indeed reputed that I am the son of the devil, with what truth I know not. It is not within my recollection what hap-pened either when I was born or when I was begotten."

"Son of the devil, who is the source of all evil," ejacu-lated his friend.

"It is regrettable to me," said the seated greybeard, "that the holy Abbot should be so inconsistent. He is commanded in his sacred books to enjoin upon all that they should honour their fathers, yet here we find him saying nothing good to the memory of mine."

"O woe, woe!" shrieked his opponent. "The devils

themselves no longer believe, and the spawn of the evil one walketh abroad throughout the land, mocking and blaspheming."

"Things are got to a bad pass indeed, my Lord Abbot. Let me beseech you to abandon me as hopeless, I am but as my father taught me. You cannot expect thistles to bring forth figs."

The Abbot lay down on the road, and began pouring handfuls of dust upon his head, having previously, I observed, carefully removed his mitre.

"He will be quiet now for a space," said the seated man. "That is a penance he is doing, either to assist in my conversion or to relieve his own mind, I do not know which. These mysteries, I confess, are beyond me. But you asked who I was, and I had not the opportunity for reply."

"I have no great curiosity," I said, being anxious to proceed.

"Nay, nay, Sir Knight, never refuse information. I may have knowledge which might be of service to you. For the future, if you desire to remain unknown, carry your shield so that it will not display that Imperial badge. Fourteen cities, and no less. Greeting, my Lord Duke."

"Who then are you, old man?"

"Sir, my name is Merddin, and I am chief of the bards of Mona. I am also Chancellor to the King of those parts, his name being Maelgwyn, of Gwynnedd."

"You are known to me by name, Merddin, as is your Lord."

"His Lord, his Lord indeed. Oh, unrighteous age," groaned the man lying in the road. He suddenly ceased to pour dust over his head and sat up.

"Maelgwyn, Maelgwyn, O dragon of the island, the first in mischief, exceeding many in power, yet foolishly rolling in the black pool of thy offences, and heaping upon thy kingly shoulders such a load of sins. Why dost thou show thyself unto the King of Kings, who hath made thee in stature, as in kingdom, higher than most of the Kings in Britain, no better likewise in virtue than the rest?"

"No, no," interrupted Merddin, "tell him to strive to aspire higher. I liked that bit best."

"Are we going to stop here all day?" asked the girl sharply.

"A word in your ear, Artorius," said Merddin, "for such I know you to be; if, as I guess, the errand on which you are bound is secret?"

"It is as well to keep any business in the knowledge of as few men as need be. I have heard that is your own opinion, Merddin."

"Then let us step a little to one side."

As we went together for a short space up the path, I leading my horse, the learned Abbot, who continued to grovel in the road, raised his head.

"The secret counselling of fools, and the temptations of the weak, the sins of the unregenerate, and the misdeeds of the unrighteous, behold them," he called out in a loud voice. "Sorceries and blaspheming without end and curses upon the children of men. Beware, beware, O man of blood and war, lest thy companion found by the roadside in this chance hour be not a devil from hell in human form to lead thee into perdition. Beware." Here he mumbled in a lower tone, and as we were fortunately beyond earshot, his eloquence ceased to trouble us.

"You go north, Artorius?" asked Merddin.

"That is as may be."

"Keep your own counsel. But assuming as I take it to be the fact, that you go north upon this business of the raids by the Picts upon Reged and Strathclyde, I have matters for you to hear. Many messengers have been sent by Coel of Reged and by Coroticus of Strathclyde, to Aurelian. Yet for many months he has ignored them."

"In such a business, Aurelian would ignore no messenger. You know, Merddin, that he holds it requisite, at all costs, to keep the kingdom clear of the Picts. They are but thieves, and yet he dreads alliance between them and the Saxons. Rightly so too."

"It is as I said then," he returned unmoved. "The

messengers were slain upon the way. The north, Artorius, as you do not seem to realize, is in an uproar. The walled towns still maintain their safety, for the Pict, or the Saxon either, is not fond of an assault, and has no engines for the attack; but the country farms and the villages in all the north are in terror, and the people have been slain in thousands."

"Then the sooner I am there the better. But how do you know this?"

"Despairing of aid from Aurelian, the Kings have sent to Maelgwyn for help, unwillingly I grant, for Maelgwyn has a great idea of price for such accommodation. Still, he would help them if he could, under the conditions. He has no desire to see the Pict and the Saxon under the walls of Deva."

"It is bad news indeed, then, if your story is true."

"It is bad, but it might be worse. So far they are but raiding parties. But my story is true."

"But on what business are you here, with that old fool, Merddin?"

"It is a part of the tale. He is a true man, and a Briton, though he comes from Armorica. It seems he had a notion that the Saxon could be kept from Britain by curses, and being, as you may have seen, skilled at that business, he established himself in a hermitage in the Lothians upon the seashore. There he daily stood, with girded loins, as he would say, shouting aloud to the east wind, which blows eternally there, his opinion of the northern swine. If he did as well as he did to-day it must have been good hearing."

"But what news was it he brought?"

"It was as I said. Ignoring the holy Abbot's curses, the heathen came in their long ships, and burnt his hermitage. I know only partially what happened next, but as likely as not he told them what would happen to them in eternity as a consequence. I say myself they were either so terrified, or so bewildered, or so amused at his language, that they allowed him to go away. It might be that they thought he was mad, and that it would be impious to kill him, for they have a belief that it is unlucky to kill a lunatic. However, he came, and brought us the news. A good man, but a nuisance."

"But what are you doing in these districts, Merddin? You belong as I know, to the court of Maelgwyn. Why so far from Deganwy?"

"We are on the march to Reged, Maelgwyn and I, with a full force. There are threatenings from the east, and we must face that trouble too. So we came into Powys here."

"But your road north is by Deva and Ribchester."

"It was our suggestion that Cadell of Powys should guard our flank upon the east, for we have heard of Saxons there, while we were away in Reged. To this Cadell has consented, and Maelgwyn is now at Uriconium with him, laying down the plans and conditions. This is supposed to be a State visit for the exercise of the armies, and it must be kept secret from the farms. The country people are easily frightened, and if they heard of Picts or Saxons they would come crowding into the towns. Our harvests were short last year as it is."

"That I can understand. I will come with you to Maelgwyn. But what are we to do with this old gentleman in the road."

"He is the devil in the form of a saint. He is in my keeping. In order to keep him quiet, Maelgwyn has instructed him to convert me to his beliefs, of which I know a great deal more than he does. Still he is an old man, and will be tired by sundown. He knows much that he has not yet thought it worth while to tell us, but it comes in driblets, in his own way. The holy Abbot is useful. Had he not been, I would have had him conveyed to the Saxons on a mission, in the hope that that would be the last of him."

I turned and looked at the Abbot. He had risen to his feet, and having resumed his mitre, was in conference with the girl. Presently she turned and came towards us.

"Merddin," she said, "for that is your name?"

Merddin turned to her. "I am Merddin. But, lady,

may I ask if by chance you have a black stone in the shape of a raven upon a string, concealed upon you?"

"I have indeed," said she.

"I could guess it. I should know that yellow hair and that arrogant face anywhere. You are of Dynevawr, then, lady, you who wear the chough?"

"I am of Dynevawr, indeed, which others call Demetia. And if you are a true bard, as you claim, you will know my descent."

"I know your descent, lady. As you say, it is my business as a bard to know it. You are then Gwendaello, the reigning Princess of the Creuddyn. Yes, at your age, which I take to be about twenty, you can be none else but she. Yet I have never met your Royal Highness before. Do I know my business as a bard?"

"I am Gwendaello."

"But what does your proud Highness so far from your cantrev, or from the court of Guitolin, your cousin and overlord? Nay, do not trouble to say, for I know the story."

"It is a sad story," she said. "Sad enough to make a black day in the history of Britain for a thousand years to come."

"Sad enough, yet it seems that the Princes of the Corinii might have foretold it, when even a poor bard from Mona could have warned them."

There was a mocking leer upon his face as he said this, which made me fear the man. It was the first change of expression that I had seen upon his ivory face.

She gave him a strange look.

"Are then," he said, "the Princes of the Corinii better concerned with looking back upon their thousand years of history than in looking forward upon the future?"

I realized now, for the first time, that she was a clever woman. Fair of face as all knew, but that was nothing. Pretty women are common enough in Britain. Brave and constant she had shown herself to be. Few maids would have shown so bold a front after such a matter as she had passed through; but now I saw that she was shrewd as well. She looked at this man Merddin as I had felt inclined to look; the thought that had crossed my mind had crossed hers. There had been some mystery of moment behind that cunning face of his.

"Old man, or Merddin as you call yourself, how came you to know what befell when Guitolin met with the Saxon?"

"Why, only that murder will out. The news spread fast, maiden; or Princess Gwen, as you are called."

"And you knew before that the murder would be done?"

"I guessed it, young lady, I guessed it. But attend, for I speak with meaning. Those things that I guess do happen, for I charge myself with them. Need I go further?"

She looked at him horror-stricken and afraid, with loathing in her eyes. He suddenly stood upright, and in a loud voice exclaimed: "Hear me prophesy. For I am Merddin, and I sing of what has been, is now, and shall happen in the years to come." He began to sing in a monotonous chant:

"Gone is Guitolin;
He and those who believed in him
Have been cut off in their strength.

Guitolin the King
And the youths of his house
Have been cut off, and their women are slaves.

With the knife that is like the half-moon,
Guitolin has been cut off
And the Princes of Dynevawr are few.

His own land he betrayed to the invaders,
He, the lord of the old house;
He was weaker than the bindweed when it is
    young.

I, the bard, knew what fate was coming upon
    him,
Death, and it was from the Saxon;
And I, the bard, whispered it unto the Saxon.

And in the future I foretell
That all those of the blood of Guitolin shall
    die,
That Britain may live unharmed.

And I will call forth the men
With knives that are like the sun, and keener
    than half-moons,
Who shall cut off the House of Cornwall.

Behold, the men with the sunlike knives are
    at hand,
They wait at the gates of Dynevawr,
And their sunlike blades shall be dulled with
    the blood of its princes.

Few are they who are left after their treachery;
Like weasels in the rocks do they hide,
But the avenging knife shall find them.

Behold the sun of Powys and of Gwynnedd
    and of Loegria has begun to shine;
As the sun travels in the heavens so shall
    their knives travel to the south,
And the moon shall be the midnight of
    Dynevawr."

The maiden looked not at him again. And he, having finished his song, turned his gaze elsewhere. He seemed for a space to be sunk into a trance. Then he spoke to me, but in an ordinary voice.

"Therefore, Artorius, we shall meet again at the camp of Maelgwyn; you will find it beyond Uriconium on the slopes of the high hill. Till then farewell."

He turned upon the road and went down the hill, and as he went, I heard him calling to the Abbot Gildas: "What curse wouldst utter against a Prince who has betrayed his people?" And the Abbot answered back, "Nay, why should I curse princes in these evil times, when each man, be he gentle or simple, is equally a betrayer?"

As for the maiden, though I saw her many times after this, she never again referred to the matter, and I, having other business on my hands, thought it better to let it rest.

CHAPTER IV

PLAS CADIFOR

EMPIRES MAY RISE OR KINGDOMS FALL,
GOOD MAY RESULT OR HARM;
YET IN THE END THE FATE OF ALL
IS FOUND UPON A FARM.

As Merddin and his companion disappeared behind the spur of the hill, the sun showed in its setting. We were still in a wild country, but much better than that which we had just crossed, well within the borders of Powys, and under an ordered government. It was no longer necessary for us to shelter in the woods during the night, for here there were dwellings of men within a few miles, and we should receive hospitality in some farmhouse. I stood for a while to scan the landscape, thinking that in the distance I might see the smoke from some chimney, where I should find a welcome. The maid stood silently beside me, and, far down the hill, I heard the voices of the two old men, the one repeating aloud some office from his book at the top of his voice, and the other grumbling at the interruption of the very peace of the evening by such discords. It was very still, and the noise was heard with clearness up these slopes for a long time, until finally, distance claimed her victory over sound, and the silence was complete except for the cry, rare and distant, of some evening bird.

This was the valley of Clun, a fair place, which in earlier days had been the wealthiest in all the land of Powys, and was a neighbourhood rich indeed in memories for the people of Britain. The hill on which we stood was known by a famous title, and still bore upon its scarred sides the upright and sharp stones which the tribesmen of Caradoc planted for their defence in their

last stand against the legions of Ostorius Scapula, more
than four hundred years before. Up this very hillside,
down which I now gazed, had the Roman soldiers,
under their carapaces and testudines, charged again
and again, only to be repulsed by the greatest Briton of
them all, with showers of stones and arrows. Then at
last Rome triumphed, and the invincible legions made
all Cambria subject to the Empire. Eastward lay
Leintwardine, a lovely village now, but once a Roman
station. It had perished in the Pictish inroads in the
time of the Consul Aetius, yet this place must ever be the
haunt of men, for it is at the junction of two rivers, the
Clun and the Teme, and as the old saying goes, "Where
waters meet, there men will greet."

A bend in the Clun encloses, with the Teme, a region
almost square, surrounded on three sides by these
sparkling waters. It is almost the shape of a Roman city,
so perfect and regular is it in its boundaries, though
many miles across. The soil is of the richest in Britain,
with deep pastures, breeding great and heavy cattle,
and fat cornlands. Yet if I were to compare these two
rivers, I should confess my allegiance to the Clun. I love
those pleasant low green hills that border it, the foot-
stools as it were to the greater hills beyond.

Upon the Clun was a strong fortress of former times,
facing that very Caer Caradoc on which I stood, but
many miles away. This fortress was built upon a
mound, piled, so the story went, as the foundations of a
house for Manocan, the King of all Britain; either
Manocan the father of Vran who conquered Ireland, and
was there killed, or the later Manocan, father of
Caswallon. Which of the two I do not know, nor do the
local people, for they mix the two in a most confusing
way. I myself think it must have been the first, for it is
said that he employed giants for his building, and it
seems natural that he should have brought these giants
from Ireland, because my ancestor Corineus would, by
his day, have killed all the giants that there once were in
Locris. It is indeed on record, that the last of these giants
were in Cornwall, namely Belin Baladr, Gocmacoc and

Caracorain, being all that were left of the primeval savages before the British came to Britain. If all these giants had been killed then, it follows that Manocan must have got his giants from somewhere else to build this mound. Now the only place from which he could have got them was Ireland. I never heard that the second Manocan went to Ireland at all, so it is clear that he had no giants in his service. In any case, in the time of Caswallon, there are no stories of giants at all, because it was just after his reign that the Romans conquered Britain. It must therefore have been the first Manocan who built the mound of Clun. Any one who has seen this mound will agree that it must have taken giants to build it.

This is all I have to say about Clun, except that there is a menhir near to the town, where Manocan is buried. It is a matter of regret to me that the people of his day could neither read nor write. If there were an inscription on the menhir we should know which of the two it was, either the first or the second Manocan. The bards say it was the second, probably because he fits in best with their poems, for they take in these too much licence with history. If it was the first, then it was here that he had the great feast at which his daughter Branwen was affianced to Matholwc, the King of Ireland. It was a great descent for a lady of such high ancestry to marry a mere Irishman, and resulted in great troubles as low marriages always do. This marriage was called the first of the three curses of Britain, and if it brought an Irishman here, I can believe the name was well bestowed.

Still, at this moment, being wearied with the journey, and even more wearied with the curses of that old man Gildas, my mind ran chiefly on the great feast which was given by Manocan at Clun. I could wish that he was again in the flesh with his feast; which recalled me to the necessity of finding some farmhouse near by where we could find shelter for the night, for there were some miles of the forest still to cross before we reached any of the small towns.

Far off, against the red glow of the setting sun, I saw

at last the smear of smoke which I sought, and mounting my horse, and bidding the girl get up behind me again, set off in the direction of that welcome cloudlet. It was dark when we reached the house, which stood on the side of one of those wooded hills sloping down to the Comot of Clun. It was of good size, plainly the residence of a prosperous farmer. The noise of animals moving in some enclosure, invisible in the dark, gave signs of a well-stocked holding, which the dark shadow of outbuildings outlined against the sky confirmed. The door stood wide open; it was a long house, and from within came the cheerful and welcome glow of a fire.

Holding my horse by the bridle, I knocked at the doorpost, and at once the master and mistress of the place came to meet me. The maid passed in at once with the lady of the house, but for me, before I entered, a duty remained, that of surrendering my sword, shield, and two javelins to the host.

"It is unnecessary," he said, declining the proffered weapons.

"It is the law," I replied, pressing them upon him.

"If you insist, then yes," was his reply. "It is wearisome to carry these things throughout the day. I am glad to ease you of the burden," then, calling to the inside of the house, "Nest, Angarwd, Myfanwy, where in the name of all that is evil have those sluts got to?"

Two girls came hurrying to the door.

"It is a vile thing indeed," said he, reproving them, "that this guest of my house should be kept waiting in the doorway. Had I not been here to welcome him he might have gone away, and I should have been shamed."

"My excuses to the gentleman," said the taller of the two girls, at the same time smiling into my face. "Give me his weapons. Ugly things at best."

"Having displayed your anger, you may now take the gentleman's horse to the stable," said the other girl, rubbing the farmer's head over in a familiar way with her hand, and taking the shield. "What a pretty picture!" She was gazing at the insignia on the inside of the shield. "Let me see, one, two," and continued to count, "fourteen great cities and towers, and a scroll and a book. Why, what does this mean?"

"My Lord," said the farmer to me, "I knew not this."

"I am of good repute, merely," I replied.

"Take the shield indoors, curiosity," said the farmer to the girl who held it, and who was listening to the talk; "clean it well, and place it too in a secret place."

"It is unnecessary," I said, repeating his own words, "I am among friends."

"True," he replied. "But strangers may enter in, though I can rely on my own household. You are then on business of the State, Lord?"

"Yes, on some small matter."

"Small indeed, which calls for so great a leader to venture alone these many miles. Yet small as it is, you go far beyond our valley of Clun, and I should guess, if what I hear is true, far beyond the borders of the kingdom of Powys. But it is all one, be your business great or small, you are more than welcome. Will you come with me to stable your horse?"

When we re-entered the house there was placed ready a basin of water in which to wash my feet. It is a sign among these people that when a stranger arrives he is offered water for his feet. If he declines, it means that he will leave after the meal, which is freely offered; if the water is accepted, it means that he desires to stay the night. Yet the host would in all cases prefer the latter, for the sake of hospitality and entertainment. In these lonely valleys they have no diversion but that afforded by chance travellers, yet they are cheerful and hospitable, giving of their best even to a guest who is poorly clad.

The room which we entered occupied the whole space of the house, for these farms of Powys, or of Dynevawr or Gwynnedd either, have but one room. It was large, perhaps a hundred feet long, and a fire, kept to a high blaze by the young men who replenished it from time to time with wood, burnt in the middle, the smoke escaping through a hole in the rafters above. It was necessary to preserve the blaze, for on this the household depended

for light. Around it were seated a mixed company of
people, men, women, and children, youths and maid-
ens; they kept some distance away from the hearth, for
it was warm, some sitting upon low wooden and leather
stools, the others squatting upon the rushes which covered the floor. The beds of the household were against
two walls of the room, and were merely piles of dried
heather arranged into the semblance of a bench, and
covered with homespun fabric of wool. Any one feeling
weary retired to this accommodation and slept when he
was inclined. When I first entered, the smaller children
were sitting at the fire, hearing some wild and strange
tales, but this amusement finished, they crept away,
and lying together at one end of the bed-place, crooned
themselves to sleep.

It was late, and the family had dined, but they
brought us food, a stew of mixed bear and goat with
onions and thyme, with bread of rye, and mead to drink;
and I, at least, ate and drank well, for I was hungry. I
had been dwelling so long in cities such as Bath or
Lundinium or even Rome, that I had to cudgel my mind
to recollect the manners suitable to these country
people. The maid for her part, though royal and of a
reigning house, behaved as one brought up thereto. She
knew well the life of her people, and I thought none the
less of her for that.

When our meal was ended we talked with the family.
From time to time some belated arrival entered, but
these were known as members of the household. Some
had been driving sheep to the fair at Wem, or had been
upon some other similar business, and had been long
delayed upon the road: they ate, and lay down and slept
after greeting us, joining no further in the talk of the
company. Those who had been about the business of
the farm, the older men and the women, were in favour
of a merry evening. They were pleased and proud to
have guests, whether great people or otherwise. Yet I
noticed the wife of the farmer, one Essyeult by name,
whispering to the girl whom I had brought with me: and
she, pulling from her breast the carved black stone,

showed it silently and rapidly. I saw thereafter, though all present conversed as if no distinction lay between any of the guests, that a sheepskin with the wool upon it, combed to a soft and silky texture, and dyed scarlet, had been placed beneath the feet of the girl as she sat upon the stool.

The claims of blood are strong among these country people. They still bear in mind the ancient tales, and from this Guitolin, the curse of Britain, had drawn the strength which he so shamefully misused.

"The scarlet wool, indeed," I thought to myself. "It is enough, I know their rules. They know from their secret channels of learning that Guitolin is dead or forfeit, and mayhap cast out from royalty by some strange secret meeting of bards and princes; that there is a change in their allegiance, and the scarlet is for his successor." I saw therefore that this maid was of the blood royal, and next in succession. Her pride was from no trifle, for she, in her own person, now claimed to be Pendragon. But what either Maelgwyn, or I, or Aurelian, would say to her claim was another matter. It was to Essyeult alone that the girl had whispered, but she by a queer sign, holding the finger and thumb of the right hand together in a ring, passed a signal among the company. I have been told that this is the sign of that ancient place Cornwall, and the Corinii, when they were driven forth from among the old tribes of the west, and found fresh thrones in Cambria and Strathclyde, brought the sign with them. However this may be, it is still sacred among them, and is now recognized among the country people who have kinship with their house. The Aurelii have never paid any attention to such childish memories, and herein I have always held them to be mistaken. It is not everything to be merely just and courageous. From a ruler, simple people demand also that their prejudices and superstitions shall be held in honour. This sign is very old, as old as the rock with the hole bored through it at which the Cornubii go to be married.

We were not the only strangers in this house, for other travellers had arrived earlier in the evening, and

the talk around the fire was brisk. From time to time
one would say a word of comment or news, or again
another would tell a tale, and the others would rest in
silence listening. It seemed to me that the tales told
were old and of a former age, but so confused in detail
that no one could name the time of which they professed to speak, yet with some hidden meaning in them
that conveyed news among the company. Finally one
began to sing, announcing, "I will sing a song of
Guitolin."

When he said this, I stole a glance around, pretending to look at the fire, and then away as if the smoke
were in my eyes, and saw that a look passed between
my charge, the girl, and Essyeult as if to say "by your
leave"; yet the girl gave no sign, and it was as if permission had been thereby granted. So the man who had
offered to sing, who was a bard, began his chant. And
indeed, though as he said he was not high in the order,
he was nevertheless of good repute and well worth the
hearing. Now although he had said that he would sing
of Guitolin, he never once mentioned that rogue, yet
these country people, quite unlearned as one might
suppose, understood as I did; for they nodded their
heads as if to say, "Yes, we have had the news. This is
for our guidance."

So this minor bard sang:

"Lo, the King of the sovereign land
Who supports heaven, the Lord of Cambria,
He has made drink a blessing to all;
He made every good thing and prospers it,
And will keep us secure from our enemies,
That the sheep may multiply
And our corn be not despoiled.
May Maelgwyn be lord of Mona and of all else;
His is the mead-horn and the joy of his people.
The bees store honey, but they do not enjoy it;
So others may plan as the bees planned,
But Maelgwyn shall take all their honey
And will share it with those who befriend him."

The song was a long one, but I had learned quite enough from this portion to understand the whole. I thought that the hand of Merddin was in this, and that he and his Lord, Maelgwyn, had laid their heads together to some purpose. Evidently the bards were abroad spreading the news of Guitolin's treachery, and Maelgwyn and Merddin between them had composed the plot. What fate they intended for the girl I did not know: probably they had believed her slain in the massacre at Shalott. Yet she had escaped, though Merddin had planned her death, and now he knew that she still lived. This meant another murder maybe. For my part, I cared little who schemed or who reigned in Cambria or in Powys, or indeed who was murdered, provided that Aurelian still reigned in Locris. "Let us," I thought, "rather guard against the foreigner than conspire amongst ourselves." However, Merddin's scheme had so far done this much good that it had rid us of the greater rascal, a benefit for which we must not fail to give him credit. Clearly my best plan was to secure his help against the barbarians, and Maelgwyn's too. I might prove the best schemer of the three in the end. It was plain that this Pendragon Princess, the rightful sovereign, as she and all these people believed, was still a factor in the business. Then, also, it had gone round, or must very soon, that she was still living and had escaped from the massacre. Merddin had not dared to slay her himself, he had had to contrive to get the murder done by Saxons, even to remove that wretched Guitolin. He could not now, clearly, get rid of the girl in the same manner, but must invent some other method of putting her out of the way of his plans. That she was still alive and adored, and recognized everywhere, had undone all the work which he had planned and worked out in support of Maelgwyn's ambitions. For me the incident of the scarlet-dyed sheepskin had settled all doubts on that point.

What was to be the next move? Maelgwyn's plan, if I was right, had miscarried to the extent of the life of the girl. As to Guitolin, in my heart I could find no blame for

Merddin at all. The rogue had always been a public danger, and in contriving his death the bard had wrought most usefully. But this girl was made of better stuff than that plotting fool, her uncle. She had agreed that it was better to be a servant of Britain than even to be acknowledged as Pendragon. I might, by some cunning, make her useful to the State even yet. Maelgwyn was astute, and his work against Guitolin had been well planned; but neither he nor Merddin could be concerned in this new alliance between Pict and Saxon in the north. I defy any man, gifted with ordinary sanity, to attempt to enter into an alliance with the Picts, unless he happens to be a barbarian Saxon with nothing to lose. Maelgwyn's principal anxiety was to keep his throne, and not to endanger it; though he doubtless wanted other thrones as well. He was alarmed about the Picts, for he was sending help to Reged and Strathclyde. It was due to him to admit that he had done good work here in Powys, as well, by his alliance with Cadell. In this welter of conflicting policies I could not well determine my own plan until I had seen him, and heard his views. I must also confer with Merddin; that aged bard took long views, and was cleverer than I in many ways, though scarce clever enough to make a fool of me. This stretch of thinking made me weary, and I retired to the couch, hoping to be lulled to slumber by the sound of an interminable tale told by one of the company relating to one Yspaddeden Penkawr, who was king of both Hell and Britain about thirty-five thousand years ago.

Here, in this simple Powysland farmhouse, I found myself in the midst of an underground whirlpool of intrigue, of plot and counterplot which annoyed me intensely. Small wonder if the enemies of Britain were making headway. The plain and immediate duty before us was to drive out the Saxon, and to punish the Pict, and yet all that these good people could do, apparently, was to discuss who should be honoured as head and Pendragon of a beaten nation. Men like this farmer, in whose house I now was, deserved better than this from their rulers. I made up my mind there and then to defeat the whole lot of them, and to trust to the ultimate success of myself and Aurelian. I believed I could do it, for neither Maelgwyn nor Merddin were altogether fools, and could see sound sense if it were pointed out and well explained to them. It was really only necessary to show them the risks, and to indicate the absolute necessity of making safe our own frontiers and defending our farms. Once that was done we could settle among ourselves who was to be Pendragon, if anybody wanted that legendary eminence for whatever it was worth.

Between Maelgwyn and Merddin, Gildas and Gwen, I was tired of the whole bunch of them. As for Essyeult, with her absurd scarlet sheepskin, why could not the silly fool of a woman mind her own business, instead of going out of her way to pay royal honours to a runaway trollop who was galloping about the country on a horse, with a strange soldier whose existence had been unknown to her a week ago? But I pulled my mind together again. This girl had power, and once I let her go she might do anything. I could see, here in this very house-place, her influence over her own people. Fool that she was, even if she was plotting, as she might be, her pride would not allow her to remain unrecognized. Clearly she had discovered in this Essyeult a kins-woman, or the wife of a kinsman; and as certainly, all the people gathered by this fireside were agreed in some common purpose, for I had noted well the sign of the looped finger.

Pretending to be asleep, I looked from the dark cor-ner where I lay, to the fire. It was burning low, and many of the company had gone to their beds, but a small cir-cle, the farmer (Cadifor was his name), the bard, Essyeult and the girl, or princess as she called herself, Gwen, were sitting together in deep converse. I could not catch a word that they said, because a chance guest, a goatherd from Wigmore, was asleep beside me. This hard-working and worthy man had been miles upon the road that day, and had, after driving his pestilent flock, become sorely wearied and hungry. As a consequence, he had eaten largely and drunk many horns of strong mead, and was now, worn out by the toils of the day, making a noise with his own snores which varied between the bleatings of his own goats, or several legions of them, and the grunts of a herd of swine in the woods.

Still this small group sat and talked by the fire. There was some deep game afoot, and the girl was in it up to the neck. It was some accursed business of the Pendragon doubtless, for bards as well as peasantry were concerned in that affair, with their chants about the ancient glories of their race, and the division of the world between Locrin and Albanact and Camber, ere ever Rome was born.

I could see that wretched bard beating time with his hand to a lilt, while the others nodded their heads. I knew quite well what they sang under their breath; the song had been common for many years. When I was a boy we treated it like the old tales of the fairies, but these fools were fitting a meaning to it.

Locrin is dead, and he and his sons are sold to
    the Romans;
The domains have passed into the hands of the
    aliens.
Albanact is a traitor, he has robbed his brothers'
    children;
He is accursed and his house shall be burnt,
His body shall feed the ravens.
But the sons of Camber shall triumph,
Camber the pure and the brave;
He shall defeat his enemies
And shall reign in the house of his father.

This miserable bard had either been seduced or terrified by the female, Pendragon as she called herself, with her superstitious black stone chough. Cadifor and his wife were in the matter too. There was to be no sleep for me that night. If that wretched girl got away to Demetia again she would raise another hornets' nest, at the very time when Aurelian was busied with a fresh invasion from the east. Any fool could have perceived that the Saxons were stirring again and threatening fresh troubles. Like all from Demetia, this girl and her fellow-tribesmen had no objection to our fighting the Saxons on their behalf, for that they thought was only our plain duty to them as our fellow-countrymen; but they would start their raiding upon our frontiers again, just when we were most occupied.

Then came a bitter thought. Here was I, who knew quite well what the talisman was, that would end, once and for all, this confusion. I was a fool after all, thinking as I had when younger, that the world was governed by reason, when all men of sense know that it is ruled by emotion. The cure for this situation I had in my possession at Bath; I had left there an amulet which would have dissolved this confusion at a stroke. This comes of too much sense, and too little romance, due no doubt to a Roman upbringing; never again will I despise popular superstitions. The great Agricola ever utilized them in his cynical and efficient way when he pacified Britain.

If the girl escaped, once on the other side of Clun, she would be in the Presteigne country and among friends, hidden among her hills, and escorted with music doubtless, back to the Creuddyn. The only course was to place her in the hands of Maelgwyn, and whatever quarrels they two might have between them was no concern of mine. Let these children of Camber settle their brotherly disputes among themselves. Maelgwyn at all events was a man and not a woman, and with him I should know where I stood. After all, the kinsman of this young woman had sought to sell us all to the Saxons, and she had known and abetted the entire disgraceful scheme. Maelgwyn was more to be trusted, since his henchman, Merddin, had defeated it. No, plainly Maelgwyn must deal with this problem; I had too much on my hands already. I decided therefore to watch the girl until I had her safely in the powerful hands of the King of Gwynnedd, so I must lie awake, and with the dawn, take what precautions were necessary.

I was very sleepy and tired out, and in that warm air, after many nights in the open, it was hard to refrain from slumber. The people round the fire had ceased their whispered conference, and it seemed from their silence, sitting there in the red glow of the embers, that they awaited something, but I could not guess what. Fortunately the very excitement of the problem served to keep me awake.

The fire was replenished, by whom I could not see, and a billet or two of wood thrown upon it; this started some small bright flames which shone upon the four, seated in close expectancy. Then suddenly, in the light shining full upon the door, I saw a figure appear in the opening, a form so grim and so exhausted that I wondered.

He was a short and slightly built man, obviously young, and strange indeed in looks. He was blackened all over with charcoal, and with the sweat dripping from him, it seemed that dark drops as of blood fell upon the threshold. He stood in the doorway, holding by the posts, heaving in chest and almost swooning for weariness. He was naked, save for a loin-cloth, and bare-footed; he carried nothing but a knife strapped around his waist by a light belt. So he stood, wild-eyed and haggard, and then, in response to a signal given, advanced swaying and panting into the room.

His speech came quick and in jerks, and though he said little, I heard every word, low as he tried to speak, for my bed-fellow had fortunately ceased to snore.

"The message, Lady of the Creuddyn. I have word from them whom you commanded that the escort is upon the way. The signal has gone forth and the tribes assemble. From Cardigan and from Gower come full assurances, and they whose lords have been slain are marshalling in order to obey your word. To-morrow, at the Bridge of Pengwern, will your servants await you."

Having said this, and without more ado, he dropped to the floor in collapse. He must have run the full sixty or seventy miles from Creuddyn to Clun within the limits of a few hours. It is what these kern runners can do, but my own progress with horse and arms has ever been slower. What puzzled me was how he had got the news, why he was here at this particular time, and on what information those who had sent him had formed their sudden and alarming plans. The Picts and the heathen of the north were in full cry like a pack of otter-hounds, the Dal Righ were out again and raiding into Strathclyde, Reged was in extremity, the Saxons were marshalling in the east and ere long were due to attack Aurelian upon the basis of their claims under the treaty with Guitolin, and now, to cap all, the whole of Dynevawr was in a tumult and out to avenge the death of their Princes, which they knew, as well as I did, was due to the machinations of Maelgwyn or of those who did his dirty work for him. It only needed an Irish attack on the coasts of Gwynnedd, which I quite expected in view of their present opportunities and their bitterness against Maelgwyn's slave raids, and the refusal of Constantine of Damnonia to pay his just tribute, as indeed he might refuse at any time, to complete the most perplexing problem that had ever as yet confronted the Aurelian house. This time we were to be attacked by all our enemies together, united for the first time. I lay for a while, planning and thinking. I could do nothing else until I had seen Maelgwyn, but, owing to the capture of Guitolin, and the secrecy of my present information, I had now a chance of ending the contumacy of the Silures and curbing the malevolence of that terror of the Creuddyn who called herself the Pendragon. She, at all events, should never live to carry out her plans. Her death was assured on the morrow, for I, who had saved her once, would myself slay her at dawn.

The runner still lay as if dead, flat upon his back. He would recover presently, for these men rarely die as a result of their journeys, being trained to the effort from birth. The others of the party, however, though they paid him some small attentions from time to time, continued, or rather resumed, their whispered conference.

At length the bard arose from his seat, and came towards me with stealthy footsteps. I had no fear of any sudden blow. By custom I was safe of my life so long as I lay within that house. I had surrendered my arms, and had eaten of the bread, meat, and salt of the head of the house, and Cadifor would have defended me as his guest to the death.

The bard stood over me. He was weaponless, and whispered gently in my ear.

"Do you sleep, Artorius my Lord? If so, wake, for you are needed by one who should receive obedience from all."

I roused myself. "I am awake," I said.

"We who sit by the fire have much to say to you, and pray your attendance."

"I will come."

I rose, and followed him back to the hearth, seating myself in the small circle there gathered.

It was the Princess Gwen who spoke first.

"Artorius, I have full news of the dangers that threaten Britain; and I, who am the most sacred head of the State, by the rights of my ancestors and the belief of the people, now do rule and command that all men must come henceforth to the rescue of the land, that our children may rule in the future in the Island of the Mighty, as they have ruled since first our ancestors came from Troy."

"It is what I myself have said all along," I replied.

"You have said it to me, I know well, and I acknowledged your rightness, though the manner of your saying it was worded, perhaps, in a manner that some crowned heads might have questioned. It was unusual, was it not? But that is by the way."

"For my part," I said, thinking little of this assumption of royalty, yet giving her credit for her good intentions, and indeed welcoming her dignity, for the maid was so young that she could not have played at being a queen and deceived me in the same breath— "for my part, I am heartily glad you have come to your senses. I am sick of these plots and counterplots when the enemy is in the gate."

"You say well," she replied. "But I had already

decided, and I did, accordingly, send word to my chieftains in Dynevawr to muster their armies and to prepare for war. I return to them on the morrow to complete the work, for my people will expect my leadership."

I was frankly curious. The girl had been alone in my company for a week past, and she had certainly spoken to no one in my hearing. By what means had she communicated with her people? Either she was lying now, a quite possible interpretation, in order to escape my company and return to play the mischief among her tiresome tribesmen, or she had resources at her command which I had not suspected. There had been no time since we arrived at Plas Cadifor to send a message to the Creuddyn and receive a reply, and yet that runner was undoubtedly from the Creuddyn, and had come as straight to her as an arrow to its mark.

"How did you get your message to the Creuddyn?" I asked somewhat sternly. "On the manner of your answer depends my reply."

She smiled. "You doubt my word? Well, I should expect no less of a warrior who is both cautious and occasionally discourteous. Know then, that from the time we entered the woods together my people have been searching for me. By signs that I know well, which they could not miss, I left messages. For days they followed us secretly, and at Severn-side—"

"Every man must sleep sometimes," I said sulkily, "and it was agreed that you were to watch upon that night."

"Yes, but that was my opportunity, so when you were asleep I spoke to a runner who had followed me: such a man as this kern here." She indicated the exhausted man still lying on his back, and now showing some signs of recovery. "That was the day that you said you would flog me, was it not, Artorius?"

Essyeult at this made a startled and horrified exclamation.

"Had you made that threat an hour later, when my people at last found me, you would have died. Their arrows do not miss."

"Then I am glad I did not flog you. But what has this to do with the high policies that we have now in mind?"

"I shall meet a party of my people to-morrow at the Bridge of Pengwern. They will escort me back to my lands. Once there, I will rouse my tribes to the defence of Britain, for the time has come, Artorius, as both you and I see clearly, when all men must defend the island; and all women too, I might add."

This was good hearing, but I could scarcely believe it. I never have believed any word spoken by these people from Dynevawr, unless it was a promise to accept payment of something valuable and to give nothing in return.

"Is this true?" I asked doubtfully.

"It is true," said Cadifor. "I swear it as a word spoken to my guest, who has eaten of my meat and sat at my fire."

"It is true," said Essyeult. "I swear it by my children and their children to come, by the purity of my daughters, and the lives of my sons."

"It is true," said the bard. "I swear it by the genealogies of the Princes of Britain, by the sea, by the land, by the trees in the forest, the flowers in the fields, the birds in the air, the grass upon the hillside, the fishes in the waters and by all living and creeping things. It is true."

"It is true," said the girl.

"Well," I said, "I will believe you," though I was still a little doubtful.

Cadifor looked at me humorously, as one man to another. "It is not always well to believe what a woman says," he remarked, with a dry smile. "But, as man to man, this is true enough. Besides, you ought to know that though I am not of this lady's vassalage, for I am of Powys, I am yet of her kindred. My interests, however, lie rather in keeping the invader from Powys under the guardianship of Cadell and his large friend Maelgwyn, than in playing the traitor and allowing the Saxon to burn my homestead."

"You are a sensible man," I said. "It is well. You may

go back to Dynevawr to-morrow, young lady. And now I want to sleep."

"Sleep well," said Cadifor.

"Yes, sleep well," said the girl. "We shall save Britain, Artorius, you and I together, for you are an honest and a clever man."

With this bouquet I returned to my couch and slept well until the morning.

CHAPTER V

THE BRIDGE OF PENGWERN

THE MUSIC OF THE WATER PARTS
THE LOVERS FROM THEIR DREAM;
YET HOPE REMAINS WITHIN THEIR HEARTS—
THE BRIDGE ACROSS THE STREAM.

The people of the household were astir with the first glimmerings of dawn, and as most of the company had retired to rest before me, I had small liking for the sounds that proceeded from these early risers. The young men, out of respect for the older people still asleep, did certainly creep silently out of the house for their baths in the river below, but, being enlivened by the water, came back in such merriment, with stories and laughter, that their earlier consideration was immaterial. Moreover, as both boys and girls (and there must have been twenty of them of one age or another, though I could not fathom all their relationships) went to the river in different parties at different times, and all came back roistering, rubbing their teeth with green hazel bark, and in hilarious mood, I soon gave up any attempt to rest longer, and after I had followed the earlier visitors to the river, returned refreshed to the house.

There was food spread upon benches, to which all helped themselves as they wanted, beer and milk in jugs, cold joints of meat, bread, butter and honey. It was strange to me to see a morning meal thus prepared without a decoction of the choava, to which I have become accustomed, but the berry costs heavily, and the transit from Alexandria or Constantinople is now so irregular that it would be vain to expect this luxury in a mere country farmhouse. There was, however, hospitality and plenty. The young women kept going and coming to and from some larder or pantry in an outer place, and bringing in such things as were necessary; and certainly, having far to go, and having been upon very short commons for many days, I made a breakfast which I expected would have to last me until I found the camp of Maelgwyn.

But I must first accompany the girl to the Bridge of Pengwern, where she was to meet her escort. It is best to keep such knowledge in as few hands as possible: and therefore Cadifor, with his wife Essyeult and the bard, drew the girl and myself apart, in fact over against the pigsty at the back of the farmyard, where, standing by a hurdle that kept the beasts from wandering, we conferred.

The runner who brought the message was by this time recovered. He had, like all the rest of us, bathed in a pool of the river, and had also spent some considerable time sitting in a barrel filled with hot water. He was now lying about on the grass in the sun, rubbing himself with grease. The black with which he had been smeared, to make him less visible by night, was now washed off, and he seemed to be a likely enough young fellow, like all his nation clean-shaven except upon the upper lip, and wearing his hair, as do all the women as well as the men of these western tribes, cut round at the eyes and ears. While the women, however, wear their tresses behind, flowing loose, and most frequently of great length, for they are proud of their hair, the men cut theirs short to save them from impediment in passing through the thick forests and woods with which the larger portion of their country is covered. This runner, it was arranged, should presently set forth again to meet the party expected as an escort for their Princess. He would then return to the place from which he had come as an advance messenger.

It is indeed curious how these foresters, half savage as they are, have yet a complete system of communications most accurately devised. It is from this service of chatter, as we say in the cities of Aurelian, that what is whispered in the west of Cambria is thenceforward shouted in the east, and what is whistled in the north is sung in the south.

At the pigsty the five of us bade farewell. I was to continue my journey with the girl in the ordinary course, and the bard, who came from the district of Ismenydd, would accompany us.

This settled, we thanked Cadifor and Essyeult for their entertainment, and set forth, the girl behind me upon the pillion, and the bard walking or running alongside. Indeed, though he was not a young man, he had no difficulty in maintaining the pace at which we travelled. So, together, we crossed ridge after ridge of these lonely hills, their lower slopes deep clad in pine and beech, with here and there a patch of small oaks, and their summits bleak and exposed, and covered with the dark green bushes of the whimberry which here grows in the most extraordinary abundance. It is an agreeable wild fruit, but staining to the lips, and for this reason, in Bath, it is not considered good manners to eat it.

The summits of these hills were welcome because of the breeze, for the sun was now high, and in the thick woods the enclosed heat was stifling. We spoke little, for we had far to go, but plodded on our way and came by early afternoon to the Bridge of Pengwern. This is but a narrow affair made of two pine trees with skins of oxen stretched thereon, but it affords, in spite of its seeming frailty, a ready and safe means by which men and their animals can be taken across the torrent, which here roars in great violence through a deep chasm.

At the nearer end of the bridge we seated ourselves to wait for the escort. The runner, who had passed us on the road, would shortly meet with the party and warn them of our arrival. He had from time to time and from place to place left messages, such as a leaf pinned upon a tree with a thorn, or some other such sign, giving notice that he had passed along the road.

"So you," said the bard of Ismenydd, "are the Lord Artorius? I have heard much of you." He said this calmly, but civilly enough.

"As you are so free with my name, perhaps you will return me yours," was my reply to this.

"Is it then unknown to you?"

"Well, as I never saw you before last night, and nobody took the trouble to mention it, I must be excused for my ignorance. But doubtless when I have heard your name I shall know it."

He seemed to be appeased. "It is true," he agreed, "that it was asking a good deal of you to expect recognition from my appearance, which is in no way remarkable. Yet I was surprised that so famous a man as yourself had never heard of Aneurin."

I was now no wiser than I had been before, and the man's self-confidence rather nettled me. But these bards are vain as peacocks. I therefore sought to placate him.

"My days," I said, "have been passed either in battlefields or camps, or in cities where the arts of music and song of high quality are sadly neglected. Yet, rude soldier as I am, even I have heard of Aneurin. I gaze upon him then?"

"You do," he said, smirking. "I am of the college of Holy Island in Mona, and was esteemed there even as a youth. Merddin, whom you know, is our chief. Yet, though he is a great man, and high in the councils of the State, I myself think very little of his verses. He is a poor enough hand at pennillion."

"As I understand, good Aneurin, his endeavours are rather in the direction of statecraft than of poetry."

"True enough," returned the bard good-naturedly. "It would be too much to expect of any man that he should shine in all departments. But you are right. I should be guided by Merddin in matters of policy, while reserving to myself the right to criticize his verses, though indeed, if I might express a preference, I would rather be spared the reading of them."

"Artorius," said the girl, who had been sitting silent during this discussion. "Artorius, are you now convinced of my rightness in this affair?"

"You would never have come by this road had I not been."

"I know, you were prepared to slay me, rather than have another wolf to tear at the throat of Britain?"

"Truly."

"You leave no stone unturned. It is your work then, the saving of the country?"

"I have no other aim, Princess."

"It is as I thought, and so, in spite of the fact that you would first flog and then slay me, I give you my confidence and praises."

This seemed to me rather like what the most sacred and divine Emperor Flavius Anastasius had said on another occasion, but I had noticed that his gratitude had stopped short at the words. The maid went on:

"Yes, you will save Britain. The *awen* is upon me. I can foretell events to come. Artorius shall save Britain, and the kings and princes of the island shall be the tools of his hand, and he shall save them. And in the future the bards shall sing his praises and the choirs shall chant their verses in his honour."

"Doubtless I shall be mentioned with distinction in the Notitia of the Empress of the Creuddyn," I thought to myself, but I said nothing, and for a time there was no word from any of the three of us. The bard Aneurin seemed to be deep in thought; his brow was abstracted and his lips moved silently. I thought, then and since, that he was composing an ode in honour of this or some other occasion, but no word of it has ever reached my ear, by which I was at the time secretly very much relieved. In moments of decision, both prophecy and poetry seem to me out of place as calculated to darken counsel. Aneurin, with that insight which these bards possess, may have esteemed me unworthy to hear his effusion, and kindly refrained from bestowing upon me an unmerited distinction.

So we waited long in silence until, towards dusk, a rustle in the bushes caught my ear. The girl, or princess, noted it too, and sat up listening. The bard alone took no note, for he was deep in his meditations. As I afterwards discovered, he was now in the act of composing the earlier verses of a series of odes to the months of the year, with many moral reflexions. These indeed I have since read, for he had the kindness to honour me by dedicating them to me with many benevolent expressions, and a hope that I would read them with pleasure and profit; which in truth I did, though it occupied me for some weeks, so valuable being the material that I thought it disrespectful to hurry over it.

Presently the Princess gave a soft whistle, hardly more than a hiss, at which the rustler emerged and approached with some show of dignity. He was, as his fellow had been at Plas Cadifor, naked except for his loin-cloth and knife-sling, blackened all over and barefoot; yet he was in better case than the other, his duty being merely to accompany the cavalcade and scout before them. One of these men can outrun and out-tire three or four horses in succession.

"It is well," was all the Princess said. "Bid them attend."

The runner vanished, and a few minutes later a party of men with horses broke through the bushes from some side track and approached the bridge. This they crossed in single file, for there was barely space for one at a time.

There were about a dozen of them, each riding a horse, and one leading a spare horse by the bridle. These Cambrian horses are hardy but of small size, though prettily made, and with their dark roan hides and flaxen manes and tails have a certain attraction of colouring. They are but ponies, or mannuli, as we would say, doubtless suited for their work, as these tribesmen are but light-armed at best, and prefer leather to mail. I much prefer the horses of Powys, which are heavier and bigger, being the best war-horses now to be found in Britain.

The men were of good appearance, and richly clad for their nation, with silver studs upon their dress, and their woollen tunics dyed in bright colourings. They all wore long scarlet cloaks, and each had his sword and long spear. When they reached our side of the chasm, they saluted their Princess in their own fashion, not speaking, but placing their hands upon their breasts and bending the head.

I was confirmed in my impression of this lady's dignity among her tribes. It would have been disrespectful and disloyal for these subjects of hers to speak before her until permitted. I remember well, in my father's day, how these old rules were observed by the country people. This was but a young girl vagrant, and of no great experience, but her vassals, men skilled in war, and proud by nature, with their haughty looks and wealthy dress, without debate acknowledged themselves her servants. Here she was, after a disaster, powerless and a mere beggar in a foreign country, for so Powys is regarded by those of Dynevawr, and yet they gave her obeisance as though she were in her own stronghold of the Creuddyn, that marshy duchy by the bay shores.

I stood up, for I had been seated upon a stone by the edge of the chasm.

"Greeting, men of Dynevawr," I said. "Here is one whom you have come to seek."

"Greeting, soldier of Rome," said the one who seemed to be the leader of the party.

"Your Lady has been safely conducted to this place by me," I said. "See to it that she meets with no undue risks upon her renewed journey in your care."

"She is as safe as the lives of us all can ensure," was his reply. "We thank you for the safe-conduct you have given her."

"It grows late," I added, "and you have far to go. Permit me to wish you a prosperous journey."

This fellow was very stiff, and I could read his mind like a book. He was doubtless one of those who had been concerned in Guitolin's conspiracy. Some of those Silures were as bitter against us Roman British as against the Saxons, or more, for they hardly knew the Saxons, since we of Locris lie as an impassable barrier between. Let me rather say that they hated us as much as they hated the Irish, and that is not a little. I believe the Demeti and the Silures say their prayers to the

memory of Caradoc when they say any at all, which is
as frequently as I do, for I have not even the memory of
Caradoc to pray to. I suppose my only god is the divine
Emperor, and I shall certainly say no prayers to Flavius
Anastasius in spite of the rescript of the divine Cæsar
Octavian. Flavius still owes me a considerable amount
of back pay, for did he not promise me the revenues of
three provinces of Gaul and a commission on the wheat
exports from Africa, and I never received a denarius of
either? I can hardly blame him for that, as the Goths
took the one and the Vandals the other, but in such circumstances it has always been the custom to make the
injured officer an Associate Emperor. Flavius broke with
the custom because, for two or three hundred years,
every time a Briton was made an Associate Emperor he
ended either by becoming Emperor, as did the great and
godlike Constantine, or very nearly doing so, like Maxen
Wledig or Maximian as the Romans call him, who was
slain in the attempt. But I, since I was twenty years of
age, never desired the supreme power. The Emperors in
the city of Rome are usually stabbed, while those in
Constantinople are poisoned.

The princelet of the Demeti, when I placed his
Princess in his keeping, showed no geniality of manner
whatever. I almost wished to be an Associate Emperor
after all. He would have been more respectful then. To
my civil remark that it grew late and that the lady had
a long journey before her, all he said was:

"I agree that there is nothing now that need detain
us." Even a Visigoth would have shown more politeness.

"Good-bye, then," I said, and went back to sit again
on my stone.

The lady turned to the bard:

"Aneurin, are you coming with us?"

"No," was his answer. "I have a poem to write, and I
find the scene by this chasm congenial to my soul. Hark
at the splash of the water. It is as a thousand pieces of
music played upon a million harps."

She turned her horse away, and then, upon an after-
thought, came back to me.

"Artorius, I leave you. I thank you for your safe-conduct and for your trust in me."

"That is nothing, Princess. See you well to the safety of Britain."

"As of my own child, did I have one."

"Come. Lady, it grows dark," called the leader from the thickness of the wood. He had crossed the bridge, leaving the lady with me at a sign from her.

"We shall meet again, Artorius."

"That is my hope."

"It shall be victory for you, and for me, or death for all faithful men. Great dangers are upon us; to you, and to all the faithful to their duty, is given the future. You have taught me somewhat, Artorius."

"You were teachable, lady."

"Then do not threaten to flog me again, school-master," said she, and crossed the bridge, throwing a smile behind her.

Within a second or two all sound of them was lost, and the bard and I remained by the bridge, looking at each other.

That I was sorry this lady was gone was the truth. It was as if I had been deprived of something that I valued; but I had other business on hand. If the conspiracies of those rebels from Dynevawr were checked for a space, it was something to the good. It would relieve Aurelian, and I must at once make shift to get the news to him. The bard Aneurin might contrive this message. This he promised to do; he would easily find a runner, and send him at once, as indeed he did. The lady had certainly promised to send an embassy to Bath, assuring the King of at least her neutrality, yet it was better to con-firm the news.

Yes, I was very sorry indeed that the lady was gone. Solitude, like everything else unpleasant, has to be borne until it mends. Yet I felt this present solitude more than a little, so I turned my thoughts to the busi-ness before me. My road lay now to the camp of Maelgwyn. The bard still sat by the chasm meditating. I wished that I were rid of him.

"Well, poet," I said, "do I leave you here to listen to the water?"

"I think not," was his reply. "It is a most commendable performance, this sound of splashing. I have, however, I think, by this time gathered the tune. Sometimes it is all the same and then it alters a little. I am unable to understand why. The water is in the same volume, and the rocks are still the same shape. Why should therefore the tune be altered every now and then?"

"It is always so with torrents," I told him. "The sound varies."

"I know that," he answered. "I have, in fact, just told you of it. I have just discovered it here by this waterfall. It will serve as material for my Poem of the Months. Now let us go. I have learned all that this little river has to tell me. I will come with you. It would be useless to sit all night by the waterfall."

"That is as you choose. You are welcome to come with me."

"I will do so. Soldiers are better at finding board and lodging than are poets. Yes," went on Aneurin after a pause. "We will find a farmhouse somewhere. Then there will be people to listen to my songs and praise them. The waterfall is too conceited. It talks all the time itself instead of listening to me. I am sorry to be critical, Artorius, of a man who otherwise has many good qualities, but I have a suspicion that your judgment in matters of poetry is defective. I do not want to be hard either on you or the waterfall, and this of mine is quite possibly a harsh judgment; I may be wrong, but I cannot help the feeling. You are impermeable."

"Yet I like your songs, Aneurin."

"It is clear, Artorius, that your natural taste is good, though its cultivation has been sadly neglected," said he, more hopefully. "With a little tuition you will be a worthy companion. I think I shall come with you to the wars in the north. I have a fancy to begin a battle piece. This waterfall put it into my mind, the eternal warring of the rocks and the waters. How the white waters rushed down from above as the Picts came from their mountains, and are broken upon the rock-like spears of the British heroes."

"A good poem indeed," I said approvingly. "I could see the sense of a poem like that."

"You like the idea?" he said in a patronizing tone. "It is as good as done. Now hear the beginning:

> *Gredyf gwr oed gwas*
> *Gwhyr un das*
> *Meirch mwth myngvas*
> *Y dan mordhuyt mygr was*
> *Ysguyt ysgafn llydan.*

So it goes on."

"I like it very much," I assured him. "As you say, it sounds just like that waterfall."

"Yes, but more varied," he said grudgingly, "and more skilful. The waterfall was very beautiful as far as it went, but it would be too monotonous in a book."

CHAPTER VI

Caer Maelgwyn

HONOURED IN ALL OUR BLOODY LORE
OF BATTLE AND OF STRIFE,
THE STEADFAST COURAGE OF THE POOR
WHO GAVE THEIR ALL, THEIR LIFE.

On the second day after leaving the Bridge of Pengwern we reached the hilly country to the north of Uriconium, where I hoped to find my formidable ally. Our journey had passed mainly through the pleasant land of Powys, scattered with prosperous farms, and the country residences of the lords of the kingdom. There was no trouble in foraging here: it was easy, at any of the farmsteads, several of which we saw in almost every mile, to obtain such rest and refreshment as we might need. The pastures, stocked with strong large cattle, white-faced and red of body, the glowing cornlands already yellow in the sun, and the orchards with their load of ripening fruit, all pleased me to see. It was a good land to defend: and that the men here needed no persuasion to come forward in defence of their heritage was proven at the farmhouse where we first lodged. We saw no men anywhere but those who were old and feeble, for the youths had vanished, and an aged man, carrying a bucket of pigwash, told us what was afoot.

"The women are in the house-place. I am too old for this bloody business of war, but the sons and the fathers of Powys have taken their spears, and are following Cadell."

"Are you then staying behind, old man?"

"The time comes," he said, "when old arms can no longer strike good blows. I should but be slain, and my sons would be lost too, in avenging me. Yet the duty will be upon me to avenge them should they die, and if the Pict and the Saxon defeat our armies, I shall defend, as well as I can, my ancient house. For nine generations have my fathers and I dwelt in this place, and if fire and slaughter should be upon us, then will be the time to die. I have my spear and my sword, and the women have their knives." He quavered to himself, and went upon his way with his pig-bucket. "To the house," he called back over his shoulder, "you are welcome; bid the women bring you water for your feet."

He was an old man, feeble in body and low-spirited, but his heart was sturdy, and his manner courteous and hospitable.

At this house I began to think better of the bard Aneurin. They still preserve, even in wealthy Powys, the customs of the ancient tribes. We were welcomed by the mistress of the farm, a young woman, whose brothers and husband were out with Cadell, yet she entertained us with ceremony, placing her guests and her household at their meal in parties of three, and remained standing to attend us while we ate.

"You are welcome," she kept repeating; but like the old man, who sat with the bard and me, she was in low spirits and very near to tears. So, too, were the young women of the house, showing none of the gaiety of their kind. The war had come when least expected, as is the way of war, and they all feared, because throughout Britain was the memory of the raids of former days. Yet I am glad to say that we left them more cheerful, and it was the poet Aneurin whom I must thank for that. I had hitherto felt but little respect for him and his kind, esteeming them as firebrands and shirkers, yet I found his use.

The supper over, he demanded a harp.

"I have left my own at the house of Cadifor of Clun," he announced. "I had a journey to tire me, and the harp was much to carry. Yet if you have a harp I will sing."

"It is no time for singing," said the woman of the house.

"I say that he shall sing," said the old man. "It is my

house, and from me, until I die, the orders come. If a
guest of mine desires to sing, sing he shall. I will be
shamed by no lack of hospitality. Besides, I want to hear
him sing. Can you sing?"

"Aye, aye, I can sing. I am Aneurin of Ismenydd.
Hear Aneurin sing."

All around the circle the murmur ran, as they all
settled themselves to listen. "It is Aneurin, think of that.
It is himself. He is famous everywhere. He sings the best
of all the bards of Britain. He has the *awen*. Sing,
Aneurin, it is an honour to us all."

So he tuned the borrowed harp, and sang:

"It is into Powys that I came;
And I found that the young were gone to the war,
And the old and the women were in distress,
But their distress was needless.
For all their family shall come back,
With honour shall they return,
And mead shall flow instead of tears,
And we will greet victory instead of dread."

So he began. I thought that there was cleverness in his
way of telling the story as it had happened, and he made
up a tune to it as he went along, of such merit, that I
found myself beating the time with my hand. Before he
was got as far as this, the entire family was becoming
more cheerful, and when he left off singing for a spell,
the woman began to tell me how good a shot was her
younger brother with the bow.

The old man announced that, for his part, he considered it cowardly in those who stayed at home not to
trust their relations in the field, while one of the girls
expressed her opinion that as soon as the enemy heard
that all Powys was going to attack them, they would run
away without striking a blow.

"It is absurd," quoth she, "as if it were any use for
them to fight against our men from Powys here."

"Yes, and from Gwynnedd as well," said another girl.

"Oh, yes, they from Gwynnedd are well enough, but

they are rude in their ways," said the old man. "For real military ability you must come to Powys here. I remember in the old days, when Rhiwallon was King of Powys, it was commonly reported that no less a man than Maxen Wledig said that of all Britain there were no soldiers to equal those of Powys. I myself," went on the old man, maundering as those of his age do, "was in the last Pictish raid. It was when I was a young man, and a good sixty years ago. I slew three Picts in one morning with my own hand. I waited outside a barn wherein they were drinking, and slew them as they emerged. They were terror-stricken at my fierce looks, and staggered with alarm. Yet I am in no way remarkable, for one of Powys."

"Oh, no, but, Grandfather, you were very strong and skilful."

"So, so," said the old man. "I should not be a man of Powys were I otherwise." Though he denied it, yet I noted that he regarded himself with pride, and began to test the muscle of his arm. "So, so," he said again. "Yet I misdoubt me. Perhaps it would have been better had I joined Cadell. I must think this over. With my experience now, what do you think, Lord?" said he to me.

"Some must remain at home to guard the women, Sir, and your wisdom in war will be needed to make up for the scarcity in number of them that are left behind."

"You are very right," said this ancient man. "My duty, as you say, is at home. Ah well, thus do I sacrifice my inclination. I lose honour, but yet I do right. Hear this, you womenfolk. You will be safe. I will remain here."

Seeing that they were more cheerful, I was grateful to Aneurin for his song, and to add my score to the entertainment I got out my shield and showed them the insignia, and told them what each thing painted thereon represented. It was a pleasure thus to cheer these simple people.

"Now here," I said, "here in this upper right-hand corner is York, also here we have Lundinium, and this below is Camulodunum, and here is Luguvalium."

"Yet, Lord, why do you carry this thing?"

"It is my right, for in all these places I have duties. I

must see to their defence, for so it was ordained before my time, when the God Constantine reigned at York and all men and all nations feared Britain."

The bard began to sing again, and as he sang, these strange and foolish people kneeled down before me. It made me sorry I had shown them the thing. Yet I suppose they were in trouble and, between boastfulness and grief, were agitated in their minds. The bard sang of many things that I should do, and named me the great one who should save all their land and kill all their enemies. I do not propose to repeat his song, for as I said it made me uncomfortable, yet the farm people were mightily cheered, and went to bed talking all together with boasting and laughter. As I was seeking the bed-place the old man came to me with a question. "Commander of all the legions, the legions of Rome, which were all-conquering once, I am old, and have fears. Say that all will be well."

"It will be well," I said. "Leave it all to me. Nothing shall harm you here."

The old fellow looked relieved and confident as he went off to bed; but before he went, looking around as if it were a secret, he produced an earthen bottle well-sealed, and we had out of this bottle a cupful each. It was the spirit, and very potent, that these people make from apples and pears, and so we each went smiling to bed. But before I went to sleep, in sober thought I wished that I was as certain as my own words, for the further I examined into the matter before me the less confident I felt.

I left the bard behind me in the morning when I departed. He said that he thought it necessary to visit the farms in the district. "Besides," he added, "the quarters here are uncommonly good, and the people appreciate me. As for the war in the north, Artorius, you can rely upon my being there; but tell me, would it be well for me to come after, or before the victory?"

"I should prefer to leave that to you, Aneurin. Whatever poem you write will be of merit."

"That of course is indisputable. But for writing a

poem properly I must have first-hand knowledge. You will have noted how closely I studied even that waterfall."

"Indeed I noted your conscience in that matter."

"Yes, and then there might be no victory. It would be useless for me to immortalize a victory which never took place."

"That is always possible."

"Then if I were not there I should be unable to sing of the defeat, for there would be nobody left alive to tell me anything about it."

"You might be better away in that event, Aneurin."

"I do not think so. No, I must be there before the battle is fought, and afterwards, if it is a victory, I can sing how I the bard was at the battle, and was uplifted, and all that rhetoric, and how I beheld the heroes overcome their foes, and so on; if it is a defeat, I can tell how Artorius fell in the midst of the battle, buried among the heaps of the slain. Or again, it might be that after seeing the young men of the Britons cut down like corn before the sickle, you sorrowed in your heart and fell upon your own sword. Either would be a good finish. Which do you like best, Artorius?"

"I do not like either of them very much, poet."

"Still," he added hopefully, "though it would be sad of course, it would be very touching. Sometimes I think that an ending of that sort rounds off a poem very nicely. There is certainly nothing more to be said after a finish like that."

"Farewell then, Aneurin, till we meet again. But there will be a sad poem for these good people here if their farms are burnt and their women carried away."

"All that I have considered. It works upon my mind till I can scarcely bear to think of it. Victory would be the best for everybody. If it were a defeat I might be killed myself before I had completed my song."

"I pray you may never sing that song, Aneurin."

"So do I. I should really be sorry for you to be killed, Artorius. But before you go, one word."

"What is it?"

"We of the college of the Holy Isle are skilled in men.

It is our trade, for how could a bard sing, unless he knew his fellows? And I know you, Artorius."

"I am glad that we are friends, at all events, Aneurin."

"I am depressed somewhat because we are going to part for a time, and I have not the *awen* upon me at this moment. I am rather thinking this, and thinking that, as we bards do, and setting the one against the other. This is not a prophecy, rightly considered, but still a foretelling, Artorius, from things that I know, as it were a reasoned judgment."

"And what is this foretelling?"

"Well, I am in no real alarm about these battles, Artorius. I feel a very great confidence that you will do all that any one could do. So, success."

With this we parted. He was a vain man, but a clever, and he played his part in the affairs of the State with much shrewdness and good sense. He waved a good-bye to me from the edge of the duckpond, on the brink of which we had held this conversation, and I went upon my way again, alone for the first time during many days.

The high summit of the hill for which I was bound lay now straight before me, the hill which they call the Wrekin in these parts, and within a space of three or four hours I was climbing up its first gentle slopes. I had a great anxiety to meet Maelgwyn once more, as soon as I could, and had wasted no time upon my journey, though that necessary detour to the Bridge of Pengwern had lost me a day or two. Still, it was a great good fortune to have the tribes of Dynevawr secured upon the right side. I had, indeed, by the cast of the Goddess Luck, accomplished a matter of high policy for which I took little credit to myself. It had happened well, and that was all there was to say.

About one quarter of the way up the hill of the Wrekin I met with a man whose face and figure I knew well. Of more than ordinary height, he stood within an inch or two of seven feet, stout and burly. His hair was black as jet, his face weatherbeaten, and at the first glance forbidding. His dress was of the usual fashion of the people of Gwynnedd, a single jerkin of leather, though in his case clasped at the neck with a buckle of gold, and upon his feet were sandals secured by garterings which crossed and recrossed nearly to the knee. He carried a large hunting-knife slung around his waist, but was otherwise unarmed. This was Maelgwyn, King of Gwynnedd, physically the strongest, and intellectually, probably, one of the most formidable rulers in Britain.

I hailed him.

He replied in singular fashion; seizing me by the elbow with a "Hist" implying instant silence, he drew me behind a clump of hollies. I had been leading my horse up the hill, and these bushes concealed the three of us most effectually. Maelgwyn, when we were safely concealed, again enjoined silence, and for the space of a minute or two we remained hidden. Mystified though I was by this secrecy, I am yet an old enough soldier to keep silence when that quality is desired. Presently I heard voices, as from two persons descending the road down the hill. "Ah," came from Maelgwyn under his breath, "silence on your life."

So dense was the screen of hollies that I could not see the pair until, as they came closer, I obtained, by peering through the foliage, a good view. They stood for a while near by and at length seated themselves upon a log close in front of us.

"By the ten scarlet dragons of the island, they are going to spend the day here," muttered Maelgwyn.

They resumed their converse.

"Nay, my son, I enjoin thee to abandon thy sorceries and thy iniquities, for if thou forsakest not thy evil life and refrainest from due repentance thou shalt burn for all eternity in everlasting torment."

"Gildas, why cursest thou me?"

"Nay, my son, this is no curse; it is but fatherly and kindly admonition."

"And the hundred thousand dragons of all other colours that seem to be arriving," muttered Maelgwyn. "That cursed Abbot or priest, or whatever he calls himself, is the bane of my life."

"But when I found that the present was an evil and a stiff-necked generation, and when I heard of the consummate iniquities of the bloodthirsty and deceitful Maelgwyn, which were crying aloud for punishment if not even for actual damnation, and when I realized that this proud and high potentate, who is nevertheless a hideous and mischievous ape of the mountains, was held in honour by his countrymen, then despairing of all, I retired to my hermitage by the sea at Leith in Midlothian and composed my soul by the writing of many books."

Thus went on the dreary voice of Gildas, though I myself was not without pleasure at hearing my companion described in these uncourteous terms without the possibility of replying thereto. If Maelgwyn had replied, knowing the violence and obscenity of his tongue, I should have listened with interest, yet wagering upon the ultimate supremacy of the Abbot; for his tongue wagged with great slowness and with consideration, whereas Maelgwyn's method was ever hasty and of the hit or miss type, as the archers say at the village butts.

"How many books didst thou write?" asked the voice of Merddin, for he was the learned Abbot's companion.

"Twelve books I wrote."

"Were they of such character and language as your admonitions to me?"

"They contained my message, such as I give to thee, my son; although, being composed in my studium with no haste, and with due consideration, they were perhaps more forcibly worded and better thought out, and in mayhap more bitter language. Four years was I engaged in the writing of these books, and never once did I relax from my toil between the rising and the setting of the sun. And in these books I set down all that I considered appropriate, in relation to the people of Britain, even to such evil-doers as Maelgwyn and Merddin, though perhaps I ought to put thee, Merddin, first, as the more intellectual of the two, and to the she-wolf of the Creuddyn, and to the imposter and usurper Aurelian, the bloodthirsty Artorius, and all other such vile and impious persons. And much mental pain and sorrow it cost me not only to describe such persons, but even to name them at all. Alas, alas, alas."

"These books must have been profitable reading."

"And then, seeing that the Saxons, and the Jutes, and the Angles, and the Frisians, and the Irish, and the Picts were coming either down from their mountains or across the sea in their long ships as the curse of God, being the vile spawn of Beelzebub, Belial, Shaitan, Lucifer, and Apollyon, and liking not the thought that those treasures, the books that I had written with such infinite toil and vexation of spirit, should fall into their impious hands, I waded into the sea at Leith and there cast my books into the deep waters."

"Did you do this because of the Saxons?"

"I did."

"It's the best day's work that they ever did."

"But I am writing another book which in volume shall be to the twelve as the mighty rock to the pebbles on the seashore where I drowned my children."

"And you a monk?"

"I spoke of the children of my mind and brain, scoffer."

"Do you say anything about the Saxons in this new book of yours?"

"It is not meet that the ears of those of Britain should be corrupted by tales of the misdeeds of those sons of the devil, with all pardon to thine own ancestry, Merddin. Nay, evil as are the children of this land, they are yet but as children, and must not be befouled by such accounts."

"I wish you would tell me something about the Saxons."

"Sorcerer, thy father's evil mind still persisteth in thee. Seeking to gratify thy craving for lust and cruelty, thy ears are open to the stories of wickedness. Were I to tell thee but the half of what I have seen, thy heart would be the more evil for the knowledge."

"Then you have been among the Saxons?"

"Truly, regarding them but as souls to be saved, I

journeyed among them to teach the Gospel, and to baptize. And in their camps I saw their wickedness, and heard of their evil conspiracies."

"I think that we are now getting at it," whispered Maelgwyn to me. "This old fool of an abbot is always thinking of our souls, and never once of our military necessities. I would give all the coin in my treasury to know what the forces of these blasted heathen are, and what is their chance of reinforcement. Their souls could remain damned for ever for all I cared."

"Does he know much, then?"

"The old fool knows everything. I have been for over a fortnight trying to get out of him what he knows, and he won't tell us anything. He says the knowledge would corrupt us. He refuses, he says, to tell us of any more sins than we know already, lest we should seek new experience in evil-doing. Old fool, as if any one knew more about sinning than I do; he couldn't teach me anything there, I promise you."

"Well, then put him to the torture, Maelgwyn. These are stories that we must know."

"Really, Artorius, you talk as if I never thought at all. I'd have put him on the rack long ago if it had been of the slightest use. Merddin, however, says that if we burnt the pious old lunatic alive at the stake he would only close his lips and die in a sacred rapture."

"I don't know about that. You remember that Pict whom we caught at Alcluyd?"

"Yes, that was well done. You had him scraped to death with oyster shells if I remember right. Of course that fellow did tell us all he knew before he died, in between his squeals. But that method, believe me, would be useless with old Gildas. He has only one weakness, and that is that infernal mitre of his. Sleeps in it, I believe. I might take it as a hostage till he told us all, but he wouldn't give way even for that. He would merely curse us and send to Gaul, where they gave it him, for another."

"Hush, Merddin is searching him again with questions."

"Gildas," said Merddin, "it is our business to save the land from the Saxons. I do not care two straws what their wickednesses are. You cannot tell me anything about their evil-doing that I do not know already. After all, you said yourself that my father was the devil, and he was ever an instructor of youth, and better qualified in knowledge of evil than thou art. But what I do want to know is where these Saxons come from, whether they are united among themselves, how far they are working together with the Picts, and, most of all, whether there are likely to be any more of them."

"I will tell thee nothing until thou art baptized."

"If that's all you want, I'll be baptized as soon as you like."

"Then, when thou art baptized I will instruct thee. For the space of seven years thou shalt receive my teaching, and then I will make thee a deacon, and when thou art a deacon, then I will tell thee all."

"By the Gods of all the oakgroves, there will not be any Britain left by that time."

"That, my son, is in the highest hands, but even then, if the worst cometh to pass, thy eternal soul at least will be saved, and then thou canst go among the heathen preaching the Word."

With this final intimation of his decision, Gildas rose from the log, and in a stately manner proceeded down the hill. Merddin followed him.

"It's always the same," said Maelgwyn bitterly. "There I've set Merddin on to him to find out everything, and although we have got out a bit here and there, it is nothing like all that he knows. He calls himself a missionary and goes among the heathen as he terms them, and is not of the slightest possible use to men like myself and Merddin who want to make profit of what he knows. No, after Gildas I have done with all Christians, Artorius. They have no sense. Then listen to this. After he had been mixing with these Saxons for years, lived with them, if you believe it, he came back here and I had him up at Deganwy. Curses, I ask you! It's only a couple of months since he came, but it seems more like twenty years. I had him up at the high table in the hall. He spoiled my dinner every night, and he's followed me about ever since, trying to convert me. He is a positive nuisance. I hide whenever I see him."

"Have you had any news from Coel the Old?"

"Yes, he has had his spies out, of course, though most of them have been caught and killed. He and all his people have taken refuge in the towns and abandoned the open country. There are either Picts or Angles all over the place. It is very difficult to get word to him."

"Will they not envelop the towns and come south?"

"Doubtless, but how far down will they raid? That is why I want to know their force. Look at this, Artorius. If they are but few their force will be exhausted before they reach Ribchester. In the hillier places the Brigantes are still as their fathers were before the Roman came. The enemy will find their small parties cut off here and there by our tribesmen, and their force will become exhausted."

"For the Picts, what you say is true, Maelgwyn, but the Saxon or Angle, or whatever he calls himself, is also in the north. What is his force?"

"That is the reason why I am troubling myself with that old fool Gildas. I believe the old devil knows all about it. Why, he lived among them for two years preaching. How they stood it is a miracle."

"Maelgwyn, we must go at once. You know the word of Aurelian that the asp must be slain before it strikes. What force have you?"

"The whole force of my kingdom that I dare spare on this venture is four hundred knights and two score thousand kerns. Then, I am in alliance with Cadell who can raise perhaps a score of thousand spearmen from Powys, and three hundred cavalry. What force was given you by Aurelian?"

"None. He is deeply involved on the east and fears an attack from the southern shore. This is confirmed by what I have heard upon my road."

Maelgwyn rubbed his chin, a practice common with him when he considered deeply.

"And that is all we can do. Sixty thousand light-armed kerns, against a good half-million Picts, Scots, Saxons, Angles and other spawn of the devil. A mixed company of unsanctified rascals all in alliance, with the odds ten to one against us."

"That is the truth of it, Maelgwyn."

"Well, if the worst comes to the worst, they can do little against me in Gwynnedd. You others must retire to the towns and let them wear themselves out. They are sure to quarrel among themselves over the division of the plunder."

"It is the plunder that I wish to prevent, Maelgwyn."

Indeed, I had in mind that old man at the farm in Powys where I had stayed only a night or two ago. I thought how he had taken down his old spear from the wall, and sworn to defend the farmstead that he and his had held, as he said, for nine generations. Before Hadrian ruled at Rome, the ancestors of that old man were ploughing their small fields, the bards were singing in his chimney corner, the fair and kindly women were going about the affairs of the house. At all cost, that old man, with tears in his heart, would die upon his threshold with the spear in his hand, and when he died his grandchildren would be dashed against the blazing walls of his homestead, and his daughters would be outraged by foul and bestial savages.

Of all living things I hated the Saxon most. He is a man with none of the wisdom of civilization, yet he has the cunning and the corruption of those who have lived in cities. He seeks loot, women, and drink, and thinks of all his victims as we think of the wild animals that we snare. The land must be saved, and its only bulwark lay in open war. The word that I gave in lightness and kindness to that old man, that he might sleep happily that one night at least, must be kept. Our word must be, to each other, that neither Saxon nor Angle, Pict nor Scot, should pass the line of the Wall.

Maelgwyn watched me closely. He read what was passing in my mind.

"There is something to be said for that point of view,

Artorius. For example, there is the rich plain that stretches from my city of Deva to the Mersey. I have no wish to see wild men raiding in those territories. They have been mine since the Strathclyders followed my grandfather Cunedda from the north. Still, they are a people used to war."

"Have you called them to your ensign?"

"No. Those I have mentioned are from Gwynnedd alone. These Cestrians are to be left to guard my kingdom. They will allow none to pass, for they have a dislike to being robbed. My point of view is that if there is war in my own borders the revenues will suffer greatly."

"Enough of all this. We must go north at once, Maelgwyn."

"When you say 'we' I differ from you. I am not going. My terms with Cadell are that half my force is to guard the frontier of Powys. Together we can hold the country safe by the line of the Trent and the Mersey. You are certainly right, Artorius, when you say that there must be war in the north, but you cannot complain if I leave you to attend to it yourself."

"They are already in defeat, from what you say, and in disorganization too, in Reged and Strathclyde. Coel is in a panic. What troops can you send with me?"

"I will spare you a score thousand spearmen, good fighting men, not old and fangless dogs. Cadell will add another half score, and that is our last word."

It was better than I expected when I saw how his mind was running. He watched me closely, and saw that I was satisfied.

"Do you think that you will require so many, Artorius? Surely, as you say, these Picts and Saxons are but savages, and with a well disciplined and well led army they will be easily defeated."

"Maelgwyn," I said to this, "do you not bear in mind the saying of the fisherman of Isca who said that his coracle needed no resin? Yet that man was drowned in the tide."

"I was but trying it, Artorius. It is a bargain between you and me, and it is my way to best you if I can. There is Cadell to reckon with too. If I reduce my levy to you, so will he, and the end would be that you would have none at all. It is agreed then, between you and me? I will answer for Cadell. Come now and eat. This talk has been long enough. It would have been shorter but for that perdition-deserving Abbot. Perhaps Merddin may have slain him before dinner. It is to be hoped so."

And so I dined with him in his tent far up the hill, and from the table at which we sat I could see as the daylight faded into dusk, and the twilight into the deeper blue of night, the fires of his dark, fierce men encamped among the trees, those wild tribesmen from his rocky hills, whom I was to lead to the battles beyond the Wall.

CHAPTER VII

THE WHITE CITY

WHERESOEVER I MAY ROAM,
IN WHAT CITY IS MY HOME?
IN THAT CITY, FAR OR NEAR,
WHERE I THOUGHT OF YOU, MY DEAR.

It was now my business to see the King of Powys, who had remained in his capital of Uriconium, marshalling his forces and collecting his military stores for a campaign. That he was a ruler of ability was clear. The readiness with which he had grasped the political position and thrown in his lot with Aurelian and Maelgwyn, in spite of the many private jealousies which he bore against both, showed that, in his own interests, he could rise superior to prejudice. Of many men deemed wise, much less than this can be said.

At the same time, Cadell was plainly by no means content to have the half-savage levies of Gwynnedd drafted into his civilized and wealthy province of Powys. He had an impression, not far removed from the truth, that these mountaineers regarded the fat lands of the plains as their lawful prey. As he was wont to say, it is simpler to steal another man's cattle than to catch and slay a wild goat or a bear, while hens in the roost are easier game than rabbits in the fields. He was chiefly anxious that Maelgwyn should retire home, or should send his armies out to fight, so that in either event Powys and her King should be relieved from the burden of their maintenance. That his fears of outrage and robbery from the men of his ally were groundless, I felt assured. Maelgwyn was a remarkable man in many ways, not inferior to his father Caswallon or his grandfather Cunedda. The policy of the family was always

wise, and had enabled them to rule for a long period
without reverses, and indeed with yearly increasing
strength and prosperity.

Powys and Gwynnedd formed a strong contrast to
their southern neighbour Dynevawr, where the tribal
organizations had continued uninterruptedly since
ancient times. As a result, there were fierce jealousies
and wars between Demeti and Silures, and even between
different septs of these tribes. In Gwynnedd, the house
of Cunedda had suppressed all tribal privileges with a
strong hand, and the country was governed as a united
nation. The boast of Maelgwyn was that from Cader
Idris to the Ribble, and from Holy Island to the Dee,
there was but one nation and one king, and, he would
say, "that one is myself."

I had been a week now in the camp of Maelgwyn
upon the Wrekin, and had made myself acquainted with
all the subordinate commanders of the force which I
was to lead, and also with the soldiers themselves.
Many a general has had less satisfactory armies under
his command. They wanted little in the way of food, they
were content with water as a drink if they could get
nothing else, being young men and fonder of sports
than of luxury. When I was fully acquainted with them
I regretted my legions in Bath but little. The legions
under Aurelian were heavy-armed Roman infantry with
swords and throwing javelins of steel, and with the
square curved shield, or scutum, and good body
armour, but the fault of these armies of heavy infantry
is the baggage trains that they necessitate. Here was an
arm to my hand that might perchance serve me better,
in the wild territories beyond the Wall, than the proven
troops that I knew so well.

These tribesmen were expert, in the first place, in
foraging, and though in camp here, in the friendly
country of Powys, they were under pledge of good
behaviour, and were daily well and plentifully fed by
Cadell; yet, beyond friendly territory, they would take
what toll they could of bird and beast, nut and berry,
and anything that the Picts had left behind (which was

likely to be little enough). Indeed, as their lord boasted
to me, while the Saxons were pirates and the Picts robbers, his own people were naturally skilled thieves. He
seemed to take some pride in the label. Again, the Picts
drink hugely of a liquor made by the distillation of oats
and barley, which produces much revelry culminating
in madness, and they have, too, a spirit made of heather
flowers which is wicked in its effects. The people of
Gwynnedd are, on the other hand, very abstemious, for
which, having sampled their liquors, I do not blame
them.

These kerns have another advantage in that they
make their own weapons, as it seems, out of nothing.
They have a saying that all the needs of man can be ful-
filled by a knife and three trees, the holly, the hazel and
the willow. With age-old skill and learning they make
out of these their favourite weapons, except the spear,
which is made from the ash trunks split into long staves
according to the grain of the wood, and then shaped and
polished with great labour and attention into truncheons
tapering almost to a point, longer than twice the height
of a man, and as thick as the wrist at the butt. The
truncheon is then topped with a blade of great keen-
ness, made of iron, which they used to get from Kent,
even long before the days of the great Cæsar. But since
the Saxons seized Kent we now get our iron elsewhere,
from Torbay over near Totnes, from a place on the Usk,
where the ore they say is very good, and also from Elmet
and from Furness. But none of this is so good as the
Kentish, as it requires more trouble in the manufacture
and is not so easy to temper.

With these spears they are very skilful, being able to
reach and kill a foe at almost the length of the spear,
with a sudden quick movement very hard to detect; as
they say, in teaching the young, the stroke of a spear
should be like the sting of a serpent.

More than once I have seen one of these spearmen
run away from his enemy and suddenly reverse his
spear, or, with the point behind him, transfix his pursuer
without turning himself about. They judge accurately by

the sound of their enemies' feet and breathing. It is a clever contrivance, though when I saw it first I thought it less like the sting of a serpent than that of a hornet, which always has her back to you when she delivers her venom.

These spear-rods are hardened and seasoned in the chimneys of the houses, and afterwards polished with oil and wax until they are black and shining. A good spear like this, if the blade be renewed from time to time, will last for many years.

Their bows they make of the hazel, taking the young branches, second year growths, with the brown bark and not the green. These they strip and plait very neatly and closely into a bow, the thickness of a man's forearm at the middle and tapering to a fine end each way. This is then wrapped smoothly and skilfully with a binding made from the guts of animals and strung with a piece of rawhide.

The holly they use not in itself, but for what it contains, and by boiling the bark of the younger branches they abstract a thick gum, used in its raw state for the snaring of birds; but by mixing it with pine resin they make a hard cement with which they affix the points to their arrows. They make their arrows of almost any straight wood, but prefer the hazel because of its magical powers, which are disastrous to an enemy. They top them with a very small sharp stone. I have seen a man struck in the neck with one of these arrows, and so strong was the bow and so keen the stone, that the arrow stood out a handbreadth behind his head. As for the willow, they use it for various purposes, but esteem it mainly for the inner bark which they make into cords.

All these weapons they keep greased to preserve their suppleness, but a man thinks but lightly of his bow, "for," says he, "if there be nut-bushes I can make another in a night."

It seemed to me that an army thus equipped was both formidable and of little expense to the State, for as Maelgwyn told me, his army cost him nothing, while one of our legions, what with armour, and weapons, and supplies, costs each year the entire revenue of a city. I asked him where his people learned these things. He replied, laughing, that they had always known them since there were giants in Britain. But Merddin, interrupting, said that when the British first came to Britain they brought the learning with them, but had since improved it, because nowhere do such hazel bushes grow as in Britain. Therefore they say the hazel is magic, and tend the bushes with care and respect where they grow near their homes, as they usually do.

About my fourth day at Caer Maelgwyn, there came a servant who said that a certain stranger desired to speak with me. Accordingly, I went to the secret place appointed, and there found a runner from the south concealed in the bushes. When he saw me approach he came out, and handed to me a piece of elder wood, from which the pith had been taken, saying that he desired to wait for such message as I might give him in return. Rolled up in the hollow was a parchment, written as follows:

ARTORIUS. This is to greet you on your departure to the dominion of Coel the Old, who is my kinsman, and whom I charge you to salute with affection in my name. But for yourself I say that I am in your debt for your courtesy for a week and more, and for your safe-conduct to me when in distress. Also I say that such things as you said to me as were threats of violence I will overlook, for the burden of the people of this land is heavy upon you. Therefore in your dealings be stern and relentless as you were to me, for you are now opposed to those who are unworthy of faith. Also I say that I shall be satisfied to hear of your safe return from your perils, and that I shall keep faith and do such things as are required of me for the end that is desired by us both. And I who say this am by birth and inheritance the Queen and ruler as of right of the Island of the Mighty and of her three adjacent islands. So for yourself great victory and a safe return.

"This," I asked, "has been sent to me from the Lady of the Creuddyn?"

"It is for you," he replied, "and it is from that lady." So I wrote in reply that I thanked her, and that the end was assured. I doubted this confidence myself, but it is ill to suggest to a woman that defeat may be contemplated. I also thought, though I did not put it in my letter, that it would be pleasing to me to see this lady again. In truth, though I have had many letters from ladies, this is the one of them all that I liked the best. The others were mainly complaints that I had been absent from some place where it had been appointed by themselves that I should meet them.

But I must tell how I came to Uriconium, which is but some ten miles from the camp of Maelgwyn; a fine city, though inferior to Bath in extent and in the size of its buildings, yet it is a noble town and much loved by those who dwell in it. They call it, in their affection for it, "The White City," because of the purity of the air, and also because of the whiteness of its buildings, for these, though built of stone and brick as is usual in Britain, marble being little used, are coated with a cement made of lime which reflects the sun in a most pleasurable manner. And though having seen Bath, as well as Rome itself, and other great cities such as Constantinople and Aquileia, I do not agree that Uriconium is the greatest and most beautiful city in the world, as its inhabitants with one accord assert, yet it is, nevertheless, a city worthy of a great king, as Cadell fully believes himself to be. It may indeed now be finer even than Rome, for even so long ago as when I was last in that place, much of the city had been burnt and destroyed by the barbarians.

There are in Uriconium several large places with gilded roofs, for they have gold in plenty from the rivers in Cambria, and particularly from the rocks in the islands near Penvro. There are also many other splendid buildings, and numerous temples and baths and two theatres. The houses have heated chambers, for in Powys the winters are cold; there are aqueducts, reservoirs and cellars in which to store food, and numerous very deep pits, such as we have at Bath, to store ice for when it is most wanted in the summer time. Round about the city are fine strong walls, about two miles in circuit.

The house of Cadell the King was a pleasant place. The courtyard was covered in grass, cut short like a carpet, and decorated in a curious way that I had seen nowhere else, by a number of yew trees cut into strange shapes, so that they resembled goats, peacocks, winebottles, and other images, a marvellous and ingenious scheme of adornment.

Cadell met me at the portal of his house, for he had been advised of my coming. He was a small, thin man with reddish hair and narrow grey eyes, and looked at me in a cunning way as if to see that I obtained no advantage over him by shrewdness. To this I felt no sort of objection. I knew him for a good king who, though his land had in former raids been desolated, perhaps as evilly as any part of Britain, had yet by sound government succeeded in making his country prosperous again.

It was indeed a smiling land through which I had lately passed. Cadell was himself no warrior, yet he thought deeply and, by schemes and subterfuges, had obtained more benefit for his people than had most of the Kings of Britain by wars and violence. That he was hated in Dynevawr I well knew. The princes of that large country had broken up their strength into many kingdoms, and fought in their tribal quarrels more savagely than in the defence of the island as a whole. Cadell it was who had profited most by their folly, for by treaties he would support first one and then another, and also by promises so vague that he had never occasion to redeem one of them, since nobody could understand their meaning. He had thus extended his domain to the south and west, and even to the boundaries of Brecknock. His country consisted of three great provinces, bearing the old names of Fadog, Wenwynwyn, and east of the Severn, or Salopia; but Cadell would hear nothing of any difference between these three, and would allow no man in any legal document to say from which he came. He held it unwise to foster these provincial feelings. So far as a man came from Powys, he would say, he is entitled to justice, but he knew of no privileges which they of Fadog could claim over Wenwynwyn, nor they of Salopia over either. Here I think he showed wisdom, for although he had stolen large parts of the lands of his neighbours to the south, it was observed that his new subjects became prosperous like the old, and if any did not like his government they received ample inducements to depart from it, and their places were then filled from other districts.

With Cadell himself I had no dispute, and after he had explained to me his situation, I understood why his wealthy land supplied only so small a force for my expedition. He had concealed his real strength even from Maelgwyn, though I doubt greatly whether the latter was actually deceived. Maelgwyn for his part, who never entered upon a war without hope of plunder, once he was entered upon the business liked to supply the main portion of the forces employed. Thus, when all was over, and the victory achieved, he would have the greater claim at the division of the spoils, of which he took no small portion for his own private purposes.

These two Kings interested me as being of such different characters. While Cadell thought but little of plunder, having a wide and a rich realm with a peaceful and industrious people looking rather for enrichment to the development of their lands and manufactures than to reiving and raiding, Maelgwyn inhabited a desolate and mountainous land which produced little except from the mines, and he therefore sought for war rather than for peace, and had ever a hope of plunder before him. In this spirit he was wont to say that his enemies were his best friends. Indeed he rather deplored the good terms on which he lived with his neighbours, and frequently complained that there was no one near except the Irish whom a gentleman could condescend to rob. That he was on good terms with Powys was, however, clear.

He had extended his realm northward to the marshes of the Mersey, and over the desolate moss lands which lay beyond that river up to Ribchester he claimed lordship. As to Dynevawr, his neighbour to the south, Maelgwyn agreed that there was nothing there worth the taking, for the people were as poor as his own, and the mountains as lofty and as rugged. "It would be useless," he stated, "to attack these Silures and Demeti. Who would look for the contents of a barn in the midst of a forest, or for a king's treasury upon a mountain top? They having nothing in Dynevawr except fierce men and wild goats, of which I have plenty in my own territories."

The manner of his family's coming into Gwynnedd was as follows:

The Romans, though they had at one time contemplated establishing a province in Ierne, had not in the end made the attempt; but while the divine Emperors ruled over Britain, they ever kept a fleet in the narrow seas to stop the depredations of these dishonest folk. The Irish said that they themselves were of two tribes, one descended from a god or giant called Heber, and the other from an even worse being, if that were possible, called Heremon. As far as we British could judge they were both equally objectionable. When the divine Emperor, however, being troubled by the Goths, Vandals, and other scoundrels who dared to attack him so impiously, could no longer maintain his warships in the Irish Sea, the Irish, whether of Heber or of Heremon, and probably of both, being enamoured of the wealth of civilized Britain, which they could not imitate in their own wretched, barbarous and cannibal island, began to raid the British cities on the coast of Cambria, particularly of that part which the Emperor called Venedotia, but which we call Gwynnedd.

By these raids the whole fabric of the State was destroyed, and even Deganwy, the capital, was razed and burnt. Now there was at this time a man called Cunedda in Strathclyde, a high commander under the divine Emperor, being in control of the legions that still remained in the north. He was also, luckily enough, descended from the great British House of the Corinii, which we call the House of Cornwall, through Dunwal Moelmud straight through to Corineus. Cunedda was consequently of royal birth, or so he claimed; though about this he told two stories, the truth of which he was calculated to know better than anybody else.

Maelgwyn himself said that Cunedda was the son of Gwawl, who was undoubtedly in the right line from Beli Mawr and Ludd, but, when discussing the matter before dinner, he would say that Cunedda was the right and eldest son of Gwawl and Edeyrn his wife. Then, after dinner, he used to say that Gwawl was the family disgrace, and make jokes about it, because, said he, this Gwawl was an old hound, and in fact he had twelve wives and called them all Edeyrn to prevent confusion, and to the last eleven of them he was not married at all, for they were minor or subsidiary attractions with whom he had entered into no pledges though undoubtedly he had children by them; that Cunedda was the son of the youngest of these and had murdered all the rest of the family. How true was this outrageous tale I do not know. From what I have heard from the bards, when I was younger and used to inquire into these things, Gwawl certainly had a wife called Edeyrn, and that is as near to the mystery as I can get. However, Maelgwyn himself was none the worse for these unhappy events, nor, as far as I can see was Cunedda either. As for Gwawl, he had been dead these two hundred years, together with Edeyrn and her namesakes, if any there were.

Because of his success as a general, and the repute of his high descent, in their troubles from the Irish the people of Venedotia asked Cunedda to come and aid them, which he did, with a large and well-equipped force. So fierce was he with the Irish pirates that within a generation they had ceased to trouble Gwynnedd at all. On one occasion, having captured sixteen ships of the Irish in the straits between Mona and Gwynnedd, he took all the men that he found in the ships and hanged them, after first cutting off their ears and noses. There were, it is said, over twelve hundred of these wretches.

Cunedda then, having armed one of the Irish vessels, filled it with men of his own in the armour and clothes of the Irish and sent it back to Ireland with a cartel professing to be from the chief Caicer Fionn, who had been the Irish captain and now was hanged. He said in the letter that there was so much plunder that more ships were required to take it away. Therefore, a number of Irish again came over with still more vessels, but Cunedda, having decoyed them into a trap, for he was expecting them and they were careless, being secure in their minds, took them all prisoners.

He then caused them to be conveyed to Deganwy, where they were shown the bodies of their countrymen, and were informed that in Britain these bodies were esteemed but as carrion, but that as the Irish were accustomed to eat men, these corpses would serve them as a meal in their poverty. He then put out the eyes of nine out of every ten of the Irishmen, but of each tenth man he only put out one eye, and having shipped them to a desolate part of the Irish coast, told the one-eyed to guide their comrades home. I believe that many of these Irish died because of the poisoning of their wounds, because Cunedda had had them all well flogged as well as blinded, and cut off their right hands. By this means he discouraged the Irish pirates who became, from that time, very unwilling to visit Gwynnedd.

Of Maelgwyn I may add that he had many fast and well-armed boats, in which he and his lieutenants from time to time visited Ireland, and brought away such things as they considered might be of service to them, such as cattle, slaves and horses.

As I sat at supper with him, Cadell referred to these tales and many others, so that from his manner I learned the notion that was in his mind, and, in order to make all clear, I said:

"Cadell, from what Maelgwyn has told me it seems that you have but one score thousand spearmen in all Powys?"

"Indeed," he replied. "That is what I did tell Maelgwyn, and he seemed to believe it."

"That is as well, but for myself I should say, having seen your great and rich country, that at least four times that number could be raised."

"There are, it is true," replied Cadell, "some few men too old for the force being now levied, whom I am retaining in case of further difficulties."

"Such," I said, "as those whom I have seen collected by night in the farmsteads and taken to the east secretly."

"Listen, Artorius, I am deceptive. I seldom tell all that I know, but, being wise in counsel, I fulfil all promises, though I never promise more than I choose to give. That, I expect, Maelgwyn himself understands, for between friends such as we are, it is unnecessary to say more than enough."

"Yes," I replied, "but it is I who am to lead these men into the war. If it were Maelgwyn, it would be for him to say, but for myself I require a larger force."

"Artorius," said he, "it is true that the armies under your command are but small. In my view, however, they are sufficient. You must do the best you can. I must guard my frontier to the east. All those lands which lie by the Trent are open to attack; they are but poorly defended by Aurelian. There are landings of Saxons now in large force, and a full invasion is, I fear, again in progress. We have watched now for a year. On this side they come very largely by the Trent, in boats, and are a threat of no small danger."

This ended my confidence with Cadell, yet I was satisfied that he was in the right, for he was always well informed, and, as I have said, of great cunning. Yet before I went I asked him if he had himself any news from Dynevawr, for his territories verged on that land to the south.

"Truly," said Cadell, "I hear much from Dynevawr, though most of it is but gossip."

"Still," I said, "even gossip may be sifted and turned to some military advantage."

"Well," said he, "the news that I have from Dynevawr is that the tribes are assembling for war, and being anxious about this, I inquired discreetly from high sources what was in the air. It is but five days since I was in Talgarth upon the borders of Brecknock, and there I had a conference with a red-haired bitch, one of the she-dogs inhabiting those woodlands, who assured me that I could go home with an easy mind, inasmuch as she deemed it beneath her to attack so wretched a land as Powys; but that she and her friend would see to it that so small a king as I and my pusillanimous peasantry were protected from harm. It seemed that she had raised some thousands of her tribesmen already, but they were but poorly armed, though busy improving their equipment with great speed."

To this speech of Cadell I said that the lady of whom he spoke was indeed in alliance with me.

"You are so concerned with your present errand, Artorius," said Cadell, "that the softer joys of dalliance do not touch you deeply." At this he looked more cunning than ever, and laughed at me. To me, however, his suggestion was not unwelcome, though I professed to be ignorant of his meaning.

I slept in a good bed at the house of Cadell, and left in the morning; yet early as it was, the streets of the city were full of people intent upon their affairs, for the market which they hold once a week was in progress. There were many sheep being driven by girls and dogs, and the white-faced cattle of the country were very numerous everywhere. This is a good breed which people say is the best in Britain.

Now one of these cattle, of dwarfish size compared to the larger beasts, with his reddish hair, white face and twinkling eyes, was so like Cadell that I smiled to see him. Some of the beasts were in a pen with a heap of fodder in front of each, yet this particular one, looking to the left and to the right, would snatch from time to time a mouthful from each of his neighbours, leaving his own untouched; yet if they came near to his pile, he was waiting, all alert, and would push them away. So I named him in my heart, Cadell.

Seeing the heaps of fruit for sale upon the stalls, and

the bunches of flowers, and merry-hearted girls looking at the bright fabrics displayed by the pedlars, and the busy scenes of traffic and commerce, I thought it no unworthy work for a soldier to defend such a city. For I should like to think that the market of the White City would continue to be held, and that these gay folk and their contented beasts would be immortal long after my work was done, and the name of Artorius forgotten. And then came into my head a queer thought: it was that I should like to take this lady from Dynevawr, whom Cadell had so rudely termed a red-haired bitch, by the hand, when peace was restored, and bring her to this market and there buy for her a blue cloak that I saw displayed on a stall, thinking to myself that it would go well with her appearance.

So, like a fool, thinking that I might not come that way again and should not see again another like it, I went to the stall and bought the cloak, which was a simple thing but handsome and of fine wool. I carried it away with me on my horse, and indeed carried it about for many weeks. The woman who sold it to me said that my wife, even though the lady of so great a lord as myself, would like it well. Yet she did not know that I had no wife.

In this way I left Uriconium, but when I came to it again does not matter now, nor whether I ever came again to it at all. Yet it was a pleasant place, and because I had heard from Cadell that the lady of Dynevawr was keeping her word to me, and because, strangely enough, with that foolish feeling I had bought the blue cloak, I loved it almost better than any place I had seen in all my wanderings. For all, they say, who have seen this city are fond of it, and they sing a song about it as follows:

The White City of the Plain,
Where the Severn flows by like a piece of silver;
A great city and yet very homely,
With flowers and fruit and other beautiful things;
A city with beautiful towers and palaces,

With residences of noble princes,
With great and ancient temples,
And where the people are kind to strangers.

That is their song, and, as a soldier who must drive men
to war when it is necessary for them to defend their
homes, I find that they fight all the better if their homes
are worth the loving. So I thought that these men from
Powys would be none the worse for their city. So, too, I
have often thought that Rome fell because the city was
too great for men to love, and that at the end they fought
ill for her because they knew that the city had ceased to
be their own even before the barbarians took it from
them.

CHAPTER VIII

THE HUNDRED-MILE WALL

A HUNDRED MILES BY FELL AND DALE,
  STRAIGHT AS AN ARROW SPED
THE WALL: EACH STONE HAS SOME FIERCE TALE,
  THIS RAMPART OF THE DEAD.

We had been upon the march some ten days, for most of the distance through hilly country, and were now come among great mountains, in as fair a region of woods and lake as I have yet seen. After passing the beaches of Morecambe, where I greatly feared to lose many of my force, so treacherous were the tides and shifting sands, we entered this mountainous region, and passing a great lake, and then a series of smaller ones, came out from a mountain pass upon a broad fair vale surrounded by high hills. There were two lakes in this valley, connected by a narrow torrent, the southerly of these two pieces of water dotted with small islands and wonderfully beautiful to see.

We were now well within the Kingdom of Strathclyde, and had received some small additions to our force; but the men of this part of the country had already been called up by their King Coroticus, and were, with the remnants of the armies of Coel the Old, manning the Wall in an endeavour to save their lands south of that bastion from the barbarians. Indeed, things were going badly for them. There had been defeat after defeat, the Pict and the Saxon were in full alliance, and the northern province, which the Romans called Valentia, was pillaged and desolate.

I had with my lieutenants some difficulty in collecting supplies, but what these Cumbrians could do they did, though they themselves were half-starved, having sent what provisions they could assemble to the Wall; and this was little enough to feed the troops there and the hordes of refugees from Valentia. Still, my force was hardy, and used to living upon little, and we made shift as well as we could. There were fish to be had from the lakes in some quantity, and our men foraged far and wide. We had by now exhausted what small stores we had brought with us, and delay was occasioned by the necessity of collecting more. I had half my force with me; the rest followed us, occasionally sending on complaints of being delayed because we had eaten in front of them all the food upon the road. Maelgwyn had despatched supplies by sea, which were to be brought up by our rearguard. We halted, therefore, to await them, within two or three days' march of the Wall.

In a few days we should be in the midst of the fighting, and it was certain that many of us would be dead. It is well enough to leave home with the girls strewing flowers, and the young men singing upon the march, but at the edge of the battlefield things assume a different complexion; and though I trust none of our party were faint-hearted, and would all of them, when put to the test, acquit themselves well, there were grave thoughts among all, which were best shown in the solemnity with which, from the highest to the lowest, they consumed their scanty rations. If men are to fight with a good heart, they should be well fed; yet here there were not even sheep enough for us to steal, as they had been sacrificed by the Picts who came roving into the regions south of Hadrian's Wall before Coroticus and Coel managed to man that line and drive them out. Moreover the richer portions of these two kingdoms lay to the north, among the fine valleys and wide rivers of Valentia, and from these they had drawn most of their troops and their wealth. South of the Wall it is mainly but lake, forest and moorland.

About the hour of sunset, as it was useless to move until our rearguard came up with us, I was sitting, as patiently as I could, upon a little hill which commanded a fine view of the road from the south. It was but a small hill which the people of those parts call the Cub, for they picture it as the young of the great hill lying to the north of it, a fine mountain of gentle slopes like a wolf asleep, which they call in their tongue, Skiddaw. So on the top of this Cub I sat down upon the grass and watched the southern road, while the sky faded, and the stars came out. Woods lay about the base of this little hill, and halfway up the sides; but the summit was green pure grass without shade or stone, as smooth as the cheeks of a young maiden, and while I sat there the reason of this smoothness became clear, for the rabbits came out from their burrows in the dusk, to play and browse. They seemed to me, sitting as one might say upon the edge of a death chasm, a proof of the futility of this business upon which I was engaged. Ere the Briton came to Britain, ere Rome won an empire, ere the Pict or the Attacottus began to ravage, to steal and slay, these pretty furred creatures had their empire here. And long after Briton, Pict, Roman and Scot, Saxon and Frisian, had finished their wars and were buried deep in the forgetfulness of time, the conies would still play upon the slopes of Skiddaw, revelling in the tender grass, and active in their innocence. To them, I said to myself, of a truth belongs this Island of the Mighty, as my Lady of Dynevawr called it, following the ancient phrases of her people. So I sat and mused upon this, and upon that, and strangely enough, would have been glad had this lady been with me to watch the play of the conies, for she had ever been of a pretty and playful humour, in spite of her pride and her dangers and my harshness; and in the forest, ere we came to Clun, had one day pointed out to me the ants, busy in their endless toils, making their processions and foragings. About these same ants she had made a tale, and of one, who was last of the gathering, carrying in his mouth a piece of seed, she had said he was a kern who was late, and would receive upbraidings from his wife for his delay. Yet silly as were her fancies, they were prettily put, and human. So I wished that she were here. For when there is war, or struggle, or risk before them, men think of their women in great kindliness, but their thoughts are very secret; yet as I am telling a true tale I may now say what I was thinking upon this little hill.

But it became too dark to sit longer thus alone. I must return to where the army lay in my care. So I left the hill, though I greatly desired to stay there for a while, and make up a tale that I might, did she desire it, tell to that lady if ever we were alone in the woods together again.

Across the valley but a short space away, there was a great mound, less high by far than that upon which I had been seated, and at the base of it, on the edge of a little river that flowed into the fairest of the lakes, were the troops encamped. I passed through their lines, and they were silent enough, for these men of the hills talk but little, and then I came out upon the top.

Now here is a circle of stones, famous throughout all Britain, being indeed one of those temples which the British put together before ever the Romans came to this Island of the Mighty, wherein it is said the early Britons worshipped the sun and moon and other gods, such as we find everywhere, like the spirits of rivers and hills and trees. This was before they had heard of the gods of the Romans, much less of the beliefs of the Christians. This stone circle, though much inferior to that which we call Stonehenge, is, nevertheless, a very noble and fine place; and I think it is better than Stonehenge, because here there is a circle of the biggest stones in the world beyond it, and those are the mountains which, if we define them aright, are but big stones. So here we have the greatest and finest temple in the world. Now here I thought I could be alone, for such was my mood, yet within call if my word were needed.

And here, seated with his back towards me, I came upon the bard Aneurin, and as I approached him, he, without turning, spoke aloud.

"But perhaps I was wrong in thinking that the maiden had hair as black as the winter ferns beneath the waterfall. I think now her hair was as the red wheat when it is ripe in the fields by the shore of Somerset, and that her eyes were blue like the sea of the Severn on a sunny morning in spring, looking towards the shores of Dynevawr."

But as I came nearer, he looked up and said, "Welcome, Lord."

So I told him how I was glad to see him again, to which he replied:

"Perhaps again I was wrong in the poem that I planned when you and I were in Powys, for I think now that victory is better for all men than is death."

To which I agreed.

Then said Aneurin as follows: "To all men there is home, and to all men there is a woman, and the two are the same."

"But," I said to this, "I have no home, and yet since I was a child I have been in many places."

So Aneurin reminded me of the saying of the King, who complained that half his life was past, and that he had been in Kaer Se, and Asse, in Sach, and in Salach, in Lotor, in Fotor, in India the Greater, India the Lesser, in the battle of Ynyr with twelve hostages, and in Europe, in the islands of Corsica, in Brythaec, and Brythwyc, Verthaec, and had slain the family of Clis, and Mildu the son of Ducum, and did conquer Greece in the East, and that he had come to his own place at the end, and his wife asked him where he had been all day.

"But Aneurin," I asked him, "where then is your home?"

But he would not say at first, merely smiling, yet in the end he said that he sought one in the hearts of such as these to whom he told his tales.

"For," he added, "when humble folk sit at dusk in the shelter of the hazels, when the May-moon shines through the trees, or when in the house-place a company are gathered round the fire, and one says 'tell us one of your tales, Aneurin,' then I know that I am in my own place."

On the morrow came messages from the Kingdom of Reged that the pressure upon the Wall was almost more than could be borne. They begged us to hasten forward,

which I was unwilling to do until the whole of my force
had arrived; for, as happens with armies on the march,
there were gaps in my ranks through sickness, and
some hundreds of our men had been lost in the crossing of Morecambe sands. For some time we had been in
touch with the armies of Coel the Old, and runners had
been interchanged, not once, but many times a day; and
now came the news that the front was nearly broken,
and that Coel was slain, but that they held the Wall still,
though pressed most sorely.

Early in the morning I climbed again to the summit
of the little hill to watch for my rearguard, and to my joy
beheld them coming. Now these tribesmen march not as
do our Roman legions in ordered ranks and a compact
body, but are spread over a wide front; yet so lightly
armed are they, and so mobile, and so deft in conceal-
ing their presence in wooded country, that a large force
may be quite near by and yet not apparent to the view.
They work together in small parties of four or five, yet
seem to maintain communication quite easily. The
troops that I saw were the knights, armed in the Roman
style, with shining weapons and insignia, riding their
horses and acting as guard to what small baggage they
had, some few score wagons and pack animals. These
knights were men of great dignity and honour, being
landowners of ancient lineage of Powys and Gwynnedd,
and very proud of their place in the councils of both
these kingdoms.

As my force was now complete we departed, and in
due course arrived at the Wall. It was many years since
I had been in this part of the great rampart; I had then
fought in common with Maelgwyn, near Carlisle, and
against the Niduarian Picts upon the Solway, a desolate
land, of sand, and grassy fields and mud-holes, overflowed at the spring tides, and much ado we had with
the horses and heavily armed men on such treacherous
ground; but now we were on the other side of Britain, on
the high moorlands to the east, for the Wall runs
straight as an arrow across both hill and plain.

These moorlands were waste and lonely as deserts,

wide undulating fields extending miles without either house or farm, covered by the waving yellow grass known as bent, swept in streaks of light and dark by the winds, which blow there unceasingly, and tenanted only by the curlews, which shriek and call to the passerby from the clouds. As for the Wall, one need have seen it but once to know it again, the greatest work in Britain, full thirty feet high, and the top of it wide enough for two horses to ride abreast, built of large grey stones, cemented and made as if to last forever. It is to be hoped that it may, to keep our country safe from these robbers beyond. The Wall was even now an ancient work, having stood four hundred years, the lives of twelve men, reckoning from father to son.

The commanders of Reged were glad enough to see me; yet they were in great distress. In the field, before they had retired to the Wall, many thousands had been slain, and their people were in affright. Standing on the broad rampart, I could see the smoke still rising from here and there a burning farm or sacked village. A young man named Urien stood with me, a grandson of Coel, and alone, for his father and brothers had been slain. Silent as the country lay to the north, there was tumult enough behind; the remains of Coel's forces were binding their wounds, or still manning their posts, though few of them were left, and great fires had been built in which they were burning the bodies of their slain, while women were wailing at the pyres, and children crying because of their fear and hunger. It was two days since the Picts and Saxons together had made a great attack upon the Wall, which had been repelled, and along the foot of the bastion I could see the bodies of many of these cursed beasts still lying, pierced by arrows, or crushed by stones hurled upon them from above. Urien told me that there had been a great landing of Frisians some way to the south; in Eboracum they feared a siege, and the people of Elmet were flocking into the city to seek the shelter of the walls.

"Indeed," said Urien, "we seem to be near the end. For many thousands of years have our people ruled in this Britain, which some in times past named the Island of the Mighty, but that it has ceased to be. Yet I would not readily accept the yoke of the stranger, so let us fight till we are finished, as becomes us, who once were lords of this island."

For my part, seeing to what a pass things had come, I thought he was in the right, yet I said that I had fresh and good men with me, and we might make an end of these attacks and robberies.

But Urien was in a sad mood, and said that it was perhaps useless, though he thanked me for coming so speedily. The Picts and Saxons, he said, as was their wont, had made their attack and been beaten back, and were now retired to their camps many miles away, mustering their strength to attack once more. "Yet, I fear," he said, "that they from the south will attack also. It is but a matter of days before Elmet is overwhelmed, and we of Reged shall be fighting on both sides of the Wall. It is the end, Artorius. I thank you for your presence, for it is meet that a General once so high in the councils of Rome should be here, where the Empire of Rome ends in this her farthest province. As Rome has fallen so will Eboracum, and the letter of death shall be written over the titles and honours of Reged and of Elmet."

Now to me, as one old in the wars, the thought always comes that when things are at their worst, it is time for a change for the better, and that a bold plan is justifiable when, with better prospects, it might be deemed foolish. It is time for a venture when there is no hope without, and the man with nothing in his pouch has often been known to win at the gaming table. So in council with Urien I made a plan.

That the attack had been beaten back was good, for it meant that there were many slain and wounded, and the barbarians were thus disorganized. I said that we must in our turn attack and seek these wild beasts out in their lair, and having tamed them, could then turn to the south, and clear the pests from Elmet. "And when we have done that," I said, "it will be an occasion for you to consider what the end of Britain shall be; but if we

have any say, who have but now come to the Wall, that
end is not yet." So Urien agreeing, we began to organize
our attack.

When he left me, I remained standing on that high
place, looking around to see the slopes and outlines of
the country; and turning this way and that, I saw in the
yellow grassland along the track by which I had come,
one toiling slowly and alone. An old man it was, with
bent shoulders and a grey beard, and thinking that I
knew him, I went forth to meet him and we walked
together. Now Gildas had come upon a strange errand,
upon which no other man, unless as mad as himself,
would have ventured.

His tale was that one had appeared to him in a
vision, saying that it was a fit time for him to go once
more among the wicked, and convert them, and upon
this errand he was now bound. "For," said Gildas to me,
"if I go among these unbaptized ones, and preach, they
will be converted to righteousness and believe. They will
then abandon their evil courses, cease from slaying and
stealing, and will return to their own places in repentance and sorrow."

I endeavoured to dissuade him, for of a truth I saw
little good in the project, and was sorry to see an old
man for whom, very strangely, I had a liking, for he was
indeed a good old man, thus about to throw away his
few remaining years among these violent and savage
invaders. I told him too, that when a robber had his
torch at the foundations of the house, and his hands
upon the plunder, it was no time for preaching. Yet
Gildas held to the contrary. "For," said he, "that is the
time when he must be called to the way of repentance."
Then he added with some acuteness, "When a man is in
his most evil moments, then it is most easy to uplift
him, for his mind is in a tumult. And I shall preach to
him with no uncertain words."

I never met a man with such faith in his own preach-
ing, considering the failure of his former attempts with
Maelgwyn and the bard Merddin, who, in spite of what
Gildas considered their obtuseness, were at all events

more promising pupils than a gang of idol-worshipping
Picts and Saxons. I reminded him of these failures. But
he replied that Merddin and Maelgwyn were unregenerate and obstinate in their sins, and used the art and
learning of culture to propagate their iniquities. "It is
said that the devils believe, but some devils, having
heard the good tidings, refused even to listen again.
Maelgwyn and Merddin," quoth he, "are confirmed and
malignant in their refusal. Knowing the good, they hate
it, and take their place among those who, having heard
of salvation, refuse to be saved, and are damned. But
the Saxons and Picts are ignorant, though evil, and as
the ore may be smelted and forged into iron, so shall I
make saints of these unbelievers."

"You will do nothing of the kind," I told him. "I forbid you to go."

This he treated with disdain. There was no authority
in me to say do this, or do that, to a Lord of the Church.
Who was I indeed, who but the watch-dog of his flock,
to give my commands to the shepherd himself. "For in
the Church lies the authority under God of all things
human," and that which had been commanded unto
him in a vision, that he would do, and neither the iron
nor the steel, the brass nor the copper, nor the gold nor
the silver, should prevent him, as a prophet of God,
from setting his hand to the plough in the field which
had been allotted to him or the saving of the souls of
these unfortunate children of men. "Besides," he added,
"they think I am mad and I therefore move freely among
them. I might indeed find out something which would be
of service, Artorius." There was something of a leer in
his face as he said this, that attracted me, though I
should hesitate to attribute double dealing to so holy a
saint. I nevertheless endeavoured to dissuade him, but
found it useless, and having other things to do, gave up
the attempt to keep him from his folly.

On the following day, therefore, he set forth. I stood
upon the Wall, and watched him cross the wild and savage plain that lay in front, to venture, a feeble old man,
among men even more wild and savage than the wolves

of the forest. Yet there seemed to be no fear in him. Even our scouts, fierce and cunning men from the fastnesses of Gwynnedd as they were, ventured with caution into this conquered land. Yet Gildas set forth sturdily and in good heart. I watched him, in his long white robe and sandals, with a small scrip slung about his shoulders, wearing his mitre with an air, and in his hand a long shepherd's crook, marching across the space before me, until he got to the dip in the ground. Here he turned, and waving his hand in farewell, vanished from my sight. I never expected to hear of him or see him again, and foretold to myself that he was gone to his death, with the tortures and mutilations which these Picts and Saxons practise upon their victims.

Yet he waved his hand gaily, if I may use that word of so venerable a man, and I thought to remember him as a very great fool, but yet a man of most noble and indomitable courage.

So Gildas went upon his way.

Now this Wall stretches right across the island, for, as some say, the distance of one hundred miles, though I should say rather less. The work consists of three parts: first the Wall by itself; then north of it, a broad and deep ditch, which by barriers, whenever there is an alteration in the level of the ground, is kept full of water. It was indeed not the most agreeable of our surroundings, being stagnant, bubbling and most uncommonly sour, and not improved by the bodies of men and horses that lay rotting in it, or floating about covered by great swarms of flies. There was some sickness among the people, caused, I suppose, by the smell, and by the flies, so that we kept great fires burning to protect us from these pests. But there was still a great stench, so that the soldiers standing on the Wall and watching the bodies as though they were swimming, would argue as to whether a Pict or Saxon smelt worse when he was dead, or when he was alive; on which there was never any agreement, for the British always say that neither of these people are cleanly, as they are themselves, but are covered with lice. So our trackers say that when a

Saxon has passed, even some hours before them, through the woods, they can detect his passage as one can that of a fox. This is one reason why our women, too, have such a hatred and fear of a Saxon raid, since they are revolted by the touch of these people. To sum up, the Saxons, and Picts too, in my view are not desirable neighbours whether quick or still.

The third part of the work is a high rampart of earth which was made before the Wall itself; some say, before the Romans came into the country, by the British of those ancient days who, according to the stories, even then hated the people to the north, because of the quarrel between Albanact and Locrin. This wall of earth is as high as the stone wall, and distant from it a hundred yards or more; so, having heard of the inroads into Elmet, and the advance of the barbarians to the siege of Eboracum, we moved into this space all our stores, animals and people, and very noisy and crowded it became. But in spite of the discomforts I admired greatly this wall, and have never seen it without wonder, for it is garnished well with great gates, stations, castles, and watchtowers, and is, provided it is defended with sufficient forces, a barrier impossible for these savages to pass.

Now as I said to Urien, it is ever the darkest hour before the dawn. Upon this day when Gildas went into the Saxon camp, a runner came to us from the west with the news that Coroticus had fought a battle with the Niduarian Picts, and had defeated them with great slaughter. This Coroticus was a great general, of a most noble Roman house in origin; but as his family had always, since the time of Claudius, lived in Britain, he had been deemed to be a Briton. There is an ancient rule that when a line has lived in Britain for nine generations, and always married with people of the country, and not with outsiders or foreigners, they are to be esteemed as British, and entitled to hold land; although when the Romans came the law fell into disuse, for the Romans took to themselves large estates irrespective of tribal rights. Yet when the divine Emperor ceased to collect the taxes, those who were of Roman origin and remained in Britain, agreed to abide by the old law, which we call the law of Malmutius. This King was the great law-giver of our people in ancient days and was the first of the British to be crowned as king. Coroticus, therefore, having won this great victory, by which he drove the Niduarian Picts into the sea, or such of them as were not slain in battle, sent us news of it, and this we deemed to be our chance of ourselves advancing, and attacking our enemies in their own strongholds. We had but few men for so great an attack, but if we waited, we should have fewer still. So we equipped ourselves.

The levies of Urien, or such as he had left, remained behind. They had been overpowered so often, and had suffered so from seeing their homes burnt, and their womenfolk and children slain and mutilated, that they were dispirited and useless; so I left them to hold the Wall as best they might, taking with me only those troops which I had brought from the south. What with losses by the way, and the sickness that had attacked us through the smell and crowding at the Wall, my whole force was thirty thousand men of Gwynnedd, with three hundred knights, and about fifteen thousand men of Powys, with two hundred knights. Each man carried his food for a fortnight, and a store of arrows; they were well armed according to their fashion, and so, in the dark of the moon, we left the shelter of the Wall and advanced to meet the wolves who threatened us, with as good a heart as we could summon.

CHAPTER IX

THE CALEDONIAN WOOD

WHEN ARTHUR FOUGHT BETWEEN TWO FIRES,
AND CAST DEFEAT UPON
BOTH PICT AND SAXON, NOW TRANSPIRES,
THE TALE OF CELIDON.

The King of the Picts was a man called Drust, the son of Erp, very old, for they said that he had been their King for one hundred years, and as these people never allow a king to rule over them until he be of warlike age, this Drust must have been at least one hundred and twenty years old; but old as he was, he was a man of great cunning, who had been the real author of the alliance between the Saxon and Picts.

Who Erp his father was, I never knew, for the Picts are an uncivilized people, who have no writing, but pass down the records of what history they have by repeating long ballads. Most of their ballads are but lies; as, for instance, they repeat in their genealogies the names of three thousand kings, in a straight line from father to son, some of whom reigned on the throne of the Picts for five hundred years, and none of them for less than one hundred and fifty. Of such as these they will say, "He was cut off in the flower of his youth, a great and noble king, amid the lamentations of the entire people." To me it seems a good thing he lived no longer, for these Picts should be cut down as we cut off stinging nettles in the spinney. Compared with the genealogies of the British, these Pictish ballads are childish and foolish; for though in Britain, before the Romans came, we had no writing, except the Ogams which are very hard to read, we still had colleges of bards whose duty it was to remember and study the histories of the kings, whereas in Pict-land it was an affair left to any doddering old grandmother. Besides, the records of the Picts agree with no other records, not even with those of the Irish, who are as big liars and thieves as themselves.

But of the British stories all people agree that they are as told by the bards. For instance, they have a tale that their great King Brennus, or Bendigeid Vran as some call him, captured the city of Rome nearly a thousand years ago. Now when I was in Rome, they showed me the place where this Brennus entered the city. He was eighth in succession from Greenshield, who also went to Gaul and fought ten battles there, as the records of the Gauls attest. The Picts view the records of their kings with some doubt among themselves, though they boast strongly and loudly to strangers, as, for instance, the Pictish poem about their kings beginning:

> Unmarked is your path in the air, you cloudy
>   children of the night.
> Often like but a reflected beam are ye seen in the
>   desert wild,
> But yet retire in your hosts, before our steps
>   approach;
> Knowledge with you there is none, but only light-
>   winged thought that flies across the soul.
> Years roll on, seasons unroll, and ye are still
>   unknown.

The bard Aneurin, having made a study of these things, recounted this to me, and observed very truly that it was not only descriptive of the Pictish kings, but also of their whole nation, who are all of them thieves and fly-by-nights.

Now when Coel the Old died at the Wall, he was buried quickly, for the pressure of the Picts and Saxons would not admit of any ceremony; but when Drust died the Picts determined to have a great feast, and after the feast to elect a new king.

So they went to a high hill many miles to the north with great speed, taking the body of Drust with them.

There were two claimants to the succession, Talore and his younger brother, Nectan Morbet, though Talore had the stronger party among the nation.

Now a quarrel was brewing between the Picts and the Saxons. The King of the Saxons, a man called Decdric, had assumed the command of these pirates and robbers in place of his father Ida, the Saxon who first came to that portion of Britain which lies north of the Wall. Gildas had known this Ida well, and had been in his camp for two years preaching his faith; it was because of his coming that he had thrown his twelve books into the sea.

Now Decdric was a young man, and hot-tempered, who was drawn to Britain mainly by hearing of the beauty of our women. Here he differed in no way from Talore, because Talore was more enamoured of the British women than of his own; for the Pictish women are hard-featured, with pale eyes, and their cheek-bones are placed just beneath their eyes, in a manner quite different from the disposition of cheek-bones in the features of the great statues which I have seen in Rome, and in Britain also. For neither British nor Romans would ever think of buying a statue of a Pictish woman, even if they were made; though no man, who was clever enough to make a statue at all, would ever consider it worth while to make a statue of a Pict or a Saxon either.

Now comes the cause of the quarrel. It was arranged between Drust and Ida that they should ravage the province of Valentia and anywhere else they could with any advantage to themselves, and then divide the spoil equally. There was not much chance of a dispute, because both Ida and Drust were old men, therefore the account was not likely to be confused by any difference in their estimation of the women they took captive. These women would be sold, and who bought them was immaterial, provided there was competition between the buyers, and a high price paid.

But when Ida was dead, and Decdric king of the Saxons, the position was changed, for if a particularly

fair maid was taken in the ravages, Decdric would frequently say she was part of his appropriation, and must
not therefore be sold. Now Ida died before Drust, and
when Decdric did this Drust only laughed, because, as
he said, there were women enough for all, and if Decdric
was so infatuated with the female part of the spoils, he
would be the less alert to an exact account of the gold
and silver, which Drust, being old, and a Pict, esteemed
of the greater importance. So the matter stood.

The quarrel between Decdric and Talore had begun
some years before, when a town called Giudi, which
stands on an island, was captured by the Picts, with the
help of several Saxon ships. Included in the spoil which
was carried away to the Picts' camp, was a British lady
called Tegid, daughter to the prince of that place. She
was an especially beautiful girl, and as soon as Talore
saw her he took her away and rendered no account to
any one, for he admired her greatly.

Then some of the Saxons went to Decdric and told
what Talore had done; so Decdric considered, with some
reason, that he had been defrauded. Decdric and Talore
quarrelled so much about the affair that it was referred
to their two fathers. As Ida was at this moment very
eager to be of service to Drust, the dispute was decided
in favour of Talore. The quarrel was bitter, and hard
things were said on both sides, although, as it turned
out, uselessly, because Tegid, when she was taken away
by the Picts to wait until Talore and Decdric should
have agreed who was to possess her, having found a
knife, stabbed herself with it, as did many of the other
women who had been taken captive at Giudi.

In spite of this, Decdric and Talore continued to hate
each other. Thus it was of importance who should be
king of the Picts; for though there was no great friendship between Decdric and Nectan, between Decdric and
Talore there was open enmity, and they never met without saying many hard and infamous things to each
other.

The camp to which the Picts had gone on the death
of Drust was on a high hill, many miles north of the

Wall. It stood almost alone in a plain, and was covered
with forest up to the summit. Around it the woodlands
were very thick, extending at least twenty miles in each
direction. The Picts, being a forest people, always
endeavour to make their camps in such places.

When I heard this tale, and understood the nature of
the country where my battle must be fought, I repented
of my thoughts about the troops under my command. At
the Wall, seeing the open country in front, I had yearned
for Aurelian's legions, for there they would have been
masters of the war; but in the dense woodlands the
legionaries were of little use, as the Emperor Severus
found when he penetrated into these fastnesses. But the
men I had with me now were as used to the woods as the
Picts themselves; so, sending on scouting parties, we
advanced with what speed we could, through as tangled
a forest as I have yet seen.

The hill where the Picts were encamped was called
in those parts Celidon, and was about five or six miles
from the seashore. On the shore the Saxons had been
established, as I was told, for nearly thirty years, during
the whole reign of Ida. Their camp had somewhat the
appearance of a town, with many wooden buildings, and
a stockade around it.

For the stockade they had a very good reason,
because although the Picts were their allies, the old
quarrel between Decdric and Talore left both parties in
mutual fear of an attack. But in any case the Saxons
knew that if Talore had broken faith once, he would do
so again, as would any other Pict over such things as
booty and women; and the Picts, being by far the more
numerous party, were the more to be distrusted.

In no part of the woodland through which we
advanced did we find traces of any guard being kept, or
of any outlook, by either Pict or Saxon. The Picts were
too busy with their funeral feasts and drinking, and the
Saxons too much occupied in watching the Picts, to be
in any way alarmed about us. They had both retired
from the Wall, considering, with good reason, that the
armies of Reged were beaten, and that they could return

at their leisure to take the Wall afterwards, and destroy
the remnants. They anticipated no possible attack upon
them, and retired as though they were within their own
borders, without watching to see if they were followed or
not. Besides, our march had been secret, and I believed,
as it turned out with truth, entirely outside their
knowledge.

Within some ten miles of this Pictish camp, I left my
heavy armed cavalry in an entrenchment with all the
baggage. The knights were little used to the labour of
making camp, being all, or considering themselves,
great lords and princes; but they worked well with mattock and spade, and made themselves a safe entrenchment, square in the Roman style, promising to defend it,
if need be, to the death.

We others advanced to the hill of Celidon. Up that
side which overlooked the sea was a broad beaten track.
For so great a host, about six score thousand men, with
many captured women, there had to be daily journeyings
from the camp to the plain, for food and water, so that
the path was well trodden. Though it wound but little,
from the beginning of the actual ascent it was a good two
miles to the summit, where, on a wide tableland more
than three miles in circuit, the Picts were encamped.
Here they were holding their celebrations, gathered
round great fires, of which we could see the glow, and
clearly feeling secure in their stronghold. There was a
great sound of howlings of grief over the dead Drust, and
many other sounds more of drunkenness than grief, and
much screaming and cries from the women.

Moreover there was no watch kept. Having by means
of scouts located the position of the Picts, we inquired
into the whereabouts of the Saxons. These, miles away
behind their stockade, were, I should judge, asleep, for
they are an early people. Besides, they had been told
they would not be welcome, having as foreigners no
voice in the election by acclamation of the new
monarch; and in some sulkiness at not being invited to
the feast, they had retired within their barrier and shut
the gates.

Our course was plainly to attack the Picts first, and, having defeated them, turn upon the Saxons, few men though we had compared with these savages, or either part of them.

My principal lieutenant of the Gwynnedd men was a noble called Cador, a young man, but shrewd, who was high in Maelgwyn's favour. The people from Powys were led by Gwlydr, a famous commander in that country, but well advanced in years; we therefore divided our army into three. One party, under Cador, was to attack on the south-west through the woods, while a second under Gwlydr attempted the eastern ascent. On both sides there were thick trees and undergrowth, but it was possible for woodmen to advance through these, though the climb was steep. With full half of the force, the rest of us were to make our attack up the footway I have described. Now Cador and Gwlydr, having reached, each on his own side, a place near the top of the hill, silently spread out their two armies, and began to shoot arrows into the camp of the Picts with great rapidity.

The Picts, seen by the light of the fires, were an easy mark; and being excited, and drunk, and not expecting an attack, ran hither and thither, nor did their general, who also was very drunk, know what to do. So a cry arising that they were attacked by the Saxons, they began to arm themselves, and without leadership, and in a great rage, after swearing with many oaths what they would do, began to rush down the pathway to the Saxons' camp.

Here we met them, for the ground was more open, and we could use the spear, though we had a rear rank, as in Roman armies, who shot with arrows over our heads. We in front held back the rush, while many Picts were killed by these arrows; but so great was their onset, and so ignorant were those behind of the spears in front, and so confused were they from the arrows falling among them from all sides, that they continued to shout against the treachery of the Saxons, and of how they disputed about the division of the spoil. We, being comparatively few, could not stop them, so they made

their way through us and madly poured towards the
Saxon camp. Yet from among the trees we continued to
kill many of them, and hardly a blow was struck in
return.

Cador and Gwlydr, finding the assault easy, continued on their way to the top of the hill, and came upon
all the loot of Valentia, or such part of it as had not been
wasted and spoiled by the Picts, in addition to many
women who were in great terror of being taken by the
Saxons. I should explain that, while the British women
are disgusted and revolted by the Picts, their feelings
are much stronger against the Saxons. For the Picts,
though foreigners, are at least something like us, as
using our own speech; they are dirty, but much cleaner
in their ways than the Saxon or Frisian hogs. These
women then, being assured that they were not now
taken by the Saxons, but freed by the British, their
countrymen, raised a great noise of thanksgiving.

Now what happened next is hard to describe, as I did
not see it all; but it appears that many thousands of
Picts reached the Saxon camp with arms, and began to
attack it. The Saxons, aroused from their sleep, were
angered and alarmed by the noise and the fires by
which the Picts tried to burn down the stockade; therefore they in their turn took up their weapons, and the
fighting continued with great fury, until daylight
dawned.

Before this Cador and Gwlydr, having left a strong
guard on the hill, joined with me, and we, being thus
reinforced, attacked the Saxon camp in our turn.

By this time both our enemies were entirely broken,
for the Saxons or such portion of them as were left, got
into their ships, for the tide was in and the ships floating, and made off in terror, although many of them were
left behind; of these we killed many, and made the rest
into slaves, to assist in the removal of all our plunder.
By this means was the power of the Picts and Saxons
broken utterly in this part of the country.

I sent runners to Coroticus who, being greatly
cheered by the news, and uplifted by his own victory in

the west, thereupon advanced into Fortrenn, and drove out the Picts still lingering there.

We now, in great spirits, made preparations to return to Urien, who was awaiting our arrival.

What became of Talore and Decdric I never knew, but I never again had dealings with them. It may be that their bodies as kings were carried away by their followers, for they were neither among the killed, nor among those found lying wounded after the battle was over. It seems that Nectan Morbet, on Talore's being elected King of the Picts, was angry, and left their camp, going to the western isles, and afterwards being slain in a sea-fight with the Norse at the Orcades. It may be therefore that Talore is still the Pictish King.

I was anxious that neither Saxon nor Pict should escape, thinking that the more of these people that were killed the better; and my followers, being angry at the robberies and particularly at the unhappy state of the women we had found, who had been ravished and beaten by these outcasts, needed no persuasion. All the wounded therefore whom we found we speared, to the number of about two thousand, but crucified about three hundred on convenient trees, as a more permanent warning.

Before I left this hill of Celidon, I had climbed to the top, to see the place where Cador and Gwlydr had launched their final attack. To handle some thousands of men in the dark, in the cover of trees, and on difficult and rocky ground, as they did, in absolute silence, was indeed a military feat of no small skill. I asked them, therefore, what methods they had followed in organizing the movement, and it seemed the only instructions that either of them gave his followers were, to go up the hill as fast as they could, to stop when they got to the top, to make no noise, and to shoot everybody they saw; and everybody agreeing that this was the best plan, did as he was told, and so the victory was won.

As I was meditating on this matter, I came upon the old man Gildas, whom I was indeed glad to see again, and with him the bard Aneurin. Gildas was proposing that we should hold a thanksgiving service, and all repent of our sins, while Aneurin maintained that the better method was to hold a great feast, with unlimited horns of ale and mead, and listen to odes, songs, pennillions, and chants sung in honour of the victorious arms of the British. "For," said Aneurin, "to show you the altogether superior nature of the entertainment that I desire, I will now repeat to you an englyn that I had already made up for the occasion. This is my englyn.

> Gildas will ask the Lord to have mercy on us,
> But, when Gildas preacheth, Gildas has no mercy
>   upon us."

For my part, thinking this was but discourteous to an old man, and determining to side with Gildas in this debate, at all events so far as would enable him to maintain his face with Aneurin, I asked the latter whether the song that he had made up, in which I was to have died beneath the bodies of a heap of the slain, was what he proposed to sing.

Aneurin replied that he had poems for all occasions, and that the poem he had now composed was even better than that one.

Gildas said that either poem would be equally untrue for this reason, that the bard had only come to see what had happened in the battle after it was all over; and that he himself, though he despised all such pagan forms of literature, could also compose englyns, and the one he had made up about Aneurin was this:

> The battle was fought in the dark, and no man
> there could see anything, but Aneurin, the bard,
> wrote a poem about it as an eyewitness, although
> he was not there himself.

Gildas's own story was that he had gone straight to the camp of the Saxons, who marvelled much to see him, and took him straightway to the King to be examined. Decdric the King, who dwelt in a large wooden

house on the seashore in the Saxon town, asked Gildas
what he knew about the Picts, for his mind ran on the
fraud that had been put upon him by Talore; and, moreover, being some way in drink, he had an ill humour
when he thought of Talore and the girl, and all his other
real or imaginary grievances.

To this question Gildas, who was a man without fear,
and thought, so he told me, to win this man Decdric
from evil companionship, said that Talore was accursed.
Now this pleased Decdric mightily, and he bade Gildas
continue. "For," he said, "you are the first man that has
said anything really sensible this day."

But Gildas went on to say, thinking that this poor,
ignorant heathen was at last seeing the light, that
Talore was a man whose dealings and companionship
were a corruption to the soul, and that any man who
dealt with him in the way of friendship was in deadly
peril.

Now Decdric was again pleased, and using a proverb
quoted among his own people, added that this was certainly true, "That if you lie down with dogs, you get up
with fleas."

Then said he to Gildas, "Being, as you are, a wise
man, and a prophet, and having the gift, curse for me
this man, Talore."

So Gildas, being in no way averse at any time to
cursing, particularly the Picts, whom he liked least of
any people he had ever met, cursed Talore. In his book
that I have read, Gildas wrote thus of the Picts:

> Like worms which in the heat of day come
> forth, or like the wolfish offspring of ravening
> beasts of prey, a nation of evil whelps, and every
> man a bastard.

Remembering this, I asked Gildas what curse he uttered
when, at the request of Decdric, he cursed the Picts.

"Indeed," he told me, "it was a good curse. I said that
I would deal with the commonalty of the Pictish nation
later, but that I would begin with Talore.

"Then said Decdric, that was what he desired.

"I then said this about Talore. That he would die in torment, and that the miserable fragment of sinfulness he called his soul would be transported to endless perdition. That the never-dying worm Fafnir, that lies at the foot of Yggdrasil, should lie about his feet and spit venom at his legs, that the wolf Fenris should gnaw his belly, that the frost giants should pile ice within his heart, and that Hel, the dread goddess of the regions of everlasting misery, whose body is half white and half black, should bestow her kisses upon his lips, whereby all his teeth should decay and drop out; that the beating of his heart, through fear and torture, should resemble the hammer of Thor thundering upon the granite rocks of Jotunheim; and that all this should continue without cessation for ever and ever, amen.

"It was a good curse, and having finished it, I told Decdric that I would now proceed to curse the other Picts. Decdric, however, said that he would prefer me to say that curse about Talore again, and he asked some of his chieftains and followers to approach nearer and listen to it.

"Now when they had listened, they said too that it was a good curse, and I think it was; so, having offered me a horn of ale, Decdric asked me to say it again, as he wished to memorize it so that whenever he thought about Talore, he could say it to himself with freedom. This I did many times, and having learned it so that he could repeat it without error, he again commended me."

"But, Gildas," I said, "how came it that you, who are one of the believers that are called Christians, and a holy Abbot as well, gave such a curse? This curse calls upon the gods and demons of the Saxons and not upon your own God."

"As to that," replied Gildas, "you have but a feeble understanding of the situation. The curse I used was in every way sincere, and who am I to say that the foul demons in whom the Saxons believe have no existence? Indeed I should say that they are extremely probable. In any event, you must admit yourself that these Saxons deserve no better gods, for God lieth in the hearts of men, and the hearts of the Saxons are beyond those of all men, except perhaps the Picts, deceitful, corrupt, and desperately wicked.

"Yet even they are not beyond the mercy of God, and it is our duty to bring them to a sense of their iniquity. This I, as Abbot, say can best be done by speaking unto them in the language they know, and the remarks that I have made about their deities were but figurative details calculated to bring great truths within their extremely imperfect understanding. Even as we all are, so the Saxons are but erring children, though they certainly err in a more comprehensive manner than some of us do."

"Well now," I said, "tell me what happened next?"

"Nay, there is nothing particular to recount beyond my thoughts. I considered the matter; for ever, when I was but a catechumen, the teachers in the monastery instructed me to consider all things. So I decided that Decdric had no liking for Talore, and that this dislike might, perchance, be turned to the advantage of honester men: taking my scrip and staff, therefore, I set forth, but on leaving the camp was stopped by one of the Saxon guards who took me again before Decdric. And Decdric asking me in a very civil manner whither I was bound, I replied that I was bound for the woods, as I wished to work an enchantment. I said it was a good enchantment from my point of vision, but an evil one from Talore's. Upon this Decdric gave me leave to depart.

"Now I was grieved in my heart at the uncharitableness shown by Decdric, yet as he seemed to have a grievance, that to be so poignant must be to some extent well founded, I next went to Talore, for the part of the peacemaker is indeed a blessed one.

"It was in my mind that if I were to show unto Talore the hard feelings that his injustice had caused in Decdric, he would repent him of his harshness. With these most worthy motives I went straightway to the camp of the Picts. Some of the officers on the watch seized me and took me before the King, who looked on me in no friendly light. So I said to him in fatherly admonition, 'Talore, why vexest thou thy friend Decdric?'

"And Talore answered that he had a grudge against Decdric, who was a Saxon swine.

"So I told Talore that Decdric had cursed him, and was seeking revenge, and that he had sworn enmity in spite of the advice of the Holy Books which bid us forgive our enemies; and I further said that Talore should visit Decdric, and extend to him his hand.

"To this Talore, being seemingly amenable to my admonitions, said that he would most certainly do so, though I was not quite certain what he meant by this, or whether the hand would be extended in friendship, or in some other manner, because of the curses and the fear Talore had of Decdric; still I hoped for the best, for as the Books again say, 'Think no evil.'

"Then I said to Talore, 'But Decdric being angry will shut his gates against thee. Therefore, when visiting him, enter by the weak place in the stockade.' So Talore asked me where this weak place was, and I told him, for I had observed it.

"'Behold, it is on the western side of the main entrance, where the tide hath washed under the piles of the stockade.'

"So Talore said he had not observed it but would remember it, 'For,' he said, 'I will visit this Saxon when he least expecteth it, lest peradventure if he had warning of my coming, he would harden his heart against me and close the gate.'

"At this Talore gave me leave to depart, so I gave him my blessing, and departed into the woods. It was on my second entry into the camp of the Saxons that I observed what the tide had done, and I therefore told Talore of it that he might acquaint his friend of this misfortune.

"Now in the woods I met some of those who have accompanied you, Artorius, and being happy that I had thus acted as peacemaker, and brought to those heathens, Talore and Decdric, the good tidings of forgiveness, I was vainly puffed up and could conceal my thoughts from no man. Thus I told these men in the woods what I had done, and they said this and that, and said they would spread the news among all men. Yet I have a misgiving that in thus telling them I was disobeying the strict rule of the Church."

"But tell me, Gildas, if you knew these things, why did you not tell them to Maelgwyn and Merddin, for they sought to know?"

"Nay, how could I tell them anything? I knew it not myself."

"You might at least have said so."

"It is not fitting," said Gildas, adjusting his mitre to a more proper angle, and assuming an air that had something of reproof in it. "It is not fitting for a teacher of the Church, and an Abbot, to say that he is ignorant; the Church is infallible, and extends her blessings to men by means of their faith. Why then should I destroy faith? Where would be my authority? Nay, nay, Artorius. Still, the Church hath to render duties that are equal to her power, and thus, not knowing, and reasoning that the question had some import, I came again to discover for ye, my ignorant babes, that which ye sought to know."

With this he turned away, for I had nothing to reply. Yet I thought, as he departed from me, that there was a movement of his eyelid, as if he had for a short space closed one eye, and that there was about him a look somewhat too knowing for so holy a man.

We then joined our knights at the camp that they had made, and having packed all our booty together, to transport back to Urien for his people, on the agreement that we should retain sufficient for reward for our kerns, when they should return to their homes, we departed for the Wall.

The booty was large and heavy, and the slaves, both Saxon and Pict, to carry it, were but few in number for so great a weight, so we travelled at no great speed. But while our march from the Wall had been silent enough, we made a great noise on our return, which to me, who am used to the orderly marching of legionaries, was vexing. Yet there was nothing to be said, for what with the dolorous cries and groans of the slaves and prisoners, who were carriers, under the beatings, for they moved slowly under their burdens, unless kept at a good speed with the lash, and the cursing of the knights who were using the whips, and with the singing of our kerns, who made up for themselves songs about the battle, there was a din such as I never want to hear again. The song that they sang was something like this:

> So we defeated all our foes,
> We, the men of valour who are unconquerable;
> And on the day of the battle
> The ash was exalted most,
> But the hazel was esteemed
> Because of the numbers in its quiver.
> And on the day after the battle it rained,
> Because it always does rain after a battle;
> But we did not mind being wetted,
> Because the rain will make the ash and the hazel
>   grow again,
> So that if need be we can kill more foes.
> But it will take many days of rain
> To wash away the blood of our foes,
> Which flowed in a stream
> Greater than the Severn in a flood.

On reaching the Wall we divided our baggage and plunder, and, having flogged and slain all the prisoners, prepared to depart for the south.

CHAPTER X

DEGANWY

GUARDING STILL THE SMILING BAY,
LIKE A LION'S CROUCHING FORM,
JUST AS IT DID YESTERDAY,
ROME'S ETERNAL, SO IS ORME.

At the Wall we met with great rejoicings, but those
whom I led were but tribesmen, soldiers of a sort
which it does not serve to keep long in the field. They do
not like a long war, but pine for their homes, and desert
if kept too long, so that the forces melt away; I therefore
judged it best to lead them back to Powys and Gwynnedd
at once.

What we had to do in the north was done, and well
done. The great alliance of our deadly foes in Valentia
was broken and destroyed. So also it had happened in
Elmet, where, hearing of the great destruction that had
come upon their brethren at our hands, the invaders
had fled away, and abandoned their plans for loot and
carnage. The siege of Eboracum was raised, and the
merchants and artificers, the princes and common populace, were rejoicing at the ease from anxiety they now
felt.

Be it said we had met with wondrous small loss,
either from sickness or in battle, at which I felt glad, for
I had ever in my mind that farmstead in Powys, where
the old men and women were weeping for their young
men who had gone to the war.

What became of the sage Gildas I know not. He vanished away, doubtless on some errand of his own that
he deemed vital; but Aneurin accompanied me. Soon
after our return to the Wall, when we were looking forward to seeing once more the pleasant land of Powys, I

fell into talk with him. It was a pleasure of mine thus to converse with one whom I felt to be wise, and yet his views differed from mine though we both, I consider, desired the same ends. At length after some idle gossip he said:

"And so, Artorius, this victory is achieved and many men have died as it was fated that they should. Sooner or later they would have died. Yet in how short a time will their deaths, and the victory too, matter little and be but as shadows upon the walls of the house of time."

"It was their work or at least their doom to die," I reminded him, "as it was ours who survived to complete the work which they began."

"Truly, Artorius, but listen, this is my expounding of the matter. Here is our Isle of Britain. What matters it whether Pict or Saxon, Frisian or Roman, Briton or Silure, shall rule and live here?"

"It matters greatly, Aneurin."

"It does, and it does not. In the life of a man, yes. Strive therefore, Artorius, for your country, for if a man in his own life striveth not, it would be better then if he had never been born. And each in his own generation should strive also, and so the world goes on. If I in my memory recall the old days, I seem to remember a time when the Britons strove against Rome, and when Caradoc fought at Clun, and the end of the world seemed to be come when he was made a captive. Yet five hundred years or less have passed, and you and I care little for Caradoc. Yet we strive, each in his own way, for the men of our own time. In three hundred years, or in six hundred, or in nine hundred, the people will be different according to the age, and yet each one will strive for that which he knows, and will think less of the three hundred, or the six or the nine, which have passed. Their ways will be different and their speech will not be the same. Now my teaching is this, that to each of us that only matters which he knows, and if the people of this time are happy in victory, it is well, and if they are miserable in defeat it will pass. Conqueror and conquered shall be the same in the end."

"Then all this effort of ours is in vain, Aneurin?"

"Not so; if there were shame there would be no men. If effort were abandoned there would be great shame. Do that which ye have to do, and all will be well, for if you are victorious, happiness results to those living."

"But what lives, Aneurin?"

"In all of our generations of men there have been people in the island. In each of these generations the people of the island gloried in it. There was that which lived, which was more than their bodies or their race, for the souls of the dead pass into the lives of the living, and the souls of the heroes of Caradoc became the souls of those who fought in the wood of Celidon, and those who died in Celidon shall fight again in a thousand battles yet. Men's bodies are nothing, Artorius, yet that which they strive for is much. Who cares whether a kern died on the slopes of Clun? Who cares whether Briton or Saxon shall die on some other hill nine hundred years hence?"

"I should care greatly, Aneurin."

"Truly, but would you in nine hundred years be the Pict or the Saxon, the Briton or the Roman? Yet the island would be inhabited, and each of those living would defend it. Their hope and endeavour would be the same. Attend, Artorius. I tell you now, for you are a wise man, something for you to consider. Bodies beget bodies, souls beget souls. The genealogies of the bards tell the story of our bodily descent, the knowledge of the wise teaches that there is a relationship of father to son in minds also. Yet whether this relationship is the same as the other I prefer not to say."

"But what of yourself, Aneurin?"

"As to that," said he, smiling, "if some one, nine hundred years hence, shall say that he has wept over, or smiled at, the odes of Aneurin, why then I will claim him as a son, and perhaps he may be. Three times must we all die before we come to our final repose. Or perchance more than three times. I, Aneurin, have been the blade of a sword, I have been a drop in the air, I have been a star, I have been light in a lantern, I have been a book,

I have been a bridge over threescore rivers, an eagle, a boat, a piece of foam upon the sea, a shield, the string of a harp, a man, a child, an animal, a thought; there is nothing which I have not been, and yet I am Aneurin."

"I am a little disappointed, Aneurin. I had hoped to hear something in your talk about the maiden whom you mentioned when you sat that summer night in the circle of stones."

"And what maiden was that, Artorius?"

"It was a maiden of whom you spoke before, whose hair was as the red wheat when it was ripe in the fields by the shore of Somerset, and whose eyes were blue like the sea of the Severn, on a sunny morning in spring, looking towards the shores of Dynevawr."

"Did I indeed mention such a maiden? I forget my tales, Artorius."

"Indeed, Aneurin, you mentioned such a one, but in a tone to yourself as if you meditated. I wondered, when you said it, had you met such a one."

"And did you meet one like that, great Lord, and General of all the armies of Britain?"

"It seems not once, but a thousand times."

"It is so," he said gravely. "If it were only once, yet it seems to have been many more when you remember that you have met a maiden such as that. I should forget it, if I were you, Artorius."

"I would willingly do so, but I cannot."

"Then advance, great General, to your first defeat."

"Nay, but, Aneurin, I wish to hear the tale, for it seems to me that your story is unfinished."

"I fear that you are not of the true breed of the poets, Artorius. It is not of the real spirit of my art, to place signs under all my characters. The tale is better told when it is left to the imagination what the end is."

"I think not, Aneurin. To my mind a battle is not over till all the enemy have run away, all the wounded been killed, and all the prisoners flogged and slain."

"I perceive, General, that you like a definite ending."

"Give one to your tale then, Aneurin."

"Well then, the ending is this. It is such an ending as

we give to an old story by the farmhouse fire, on a winter's night when pleasing the maids and the children, aye, the children of all ages."

"If the ending of the story is so simple, then tell it."

"Nay, it scarcely needs the telling. It is as you have heard it many times. It is merely that you get married and live happily ever after, Artorius," he said, laughing.

"A good ending," I said.

"A very good ending," he agreed. "There is none better."

When Aneurin had said this we sat awhile without speaking, and at last he said:

"Artorius, when do you depart from this place?"

So I told him that there was much to be done. Some of our numbers were wounded, and others sick, and we must arrange for their conveyance, for these men of Gwynnedd could not be left here in the north or they would die, as birds pine when taken from the nest. Also we must provision for the march, so that with one thing and another, I should be at the Wall for a month.

To this Aneurin said that he would go at once. "For," said he, "it has come across my mind that there will be work for us on a great river, in the land of Powys, and whether it is because I feel sick for a sight of that land again, or because I have been through many emotions, and have been in discomfort and distress, I know not, but the *awen* is upon me."

"Then tell me what the *awen* says, Aneurin."

To this Aneurin answered that he saw death. "And whether it be mine or yours, Artorius, I do not know. Perchance it is but the death of friends of whom we are fond."

"All friends must die, Aneurin."

"It is so," he replied. "But the *awen* bids haste, so I go at once, for I see a wide river reddened with blood, and I must be there, for the voice says at once, at once."

"It is a sad dream, Aneurin."

"Be it sad or not, it says to me and to you, come quickly; therefore follow me as soon as you may, Artorius."

Having said this with a serious look he left me, and I determined that whether there was ground or not for his foreboding, I would hearken to it; yet in spite of all my haste, it was three weeks before we were in a fit state to march.

On our way home we heard that the Saxons had made a secret and sudden attack upon the midlands, and had been met by Cadell with all his army. For two days that battle had been waged, in the open land by the river Trent in Cannock, a wooded country, with pleasant low hills and good wheat lands. Many thousands of the Saxons came up the river in their flat-bottomed boats, as is their way, and there was great slaughter; but in the end Cadell, being in this battle both brave and cunning, triumphed, and slew the foes of the island, and they broke and ran in fear from the charge of his Powys spearmen. On the evening of the second day the victory was won, at sunset, for all through two days and a night had these men from Fadog, Wenwynwyn and Salopia fought in the light and in the dark, singly, and in companies, and when their arrows were all shot away, and with no opportunity to get more, they fought with broken spears, and even, as I have heard, with pieces of stone and stakes of wood, to keep their hated enemies from their farms and women; so they died, to the number of seventeen thousand, and saved their land. I hope that the sons of the old man with whom I had foregathered were not killed, but I never heard, for they were but simple men, and their names would not be recorded. Yet I fear that they died with their countrymen, for my friend Aneurin would be with them, as he loved them, and was in the battle. Now of Aneurin I know the fate, for he died at the evening of the second day with a wood-chopper's axe in his hand. He had never during those days sung one song, but fought handily in the line with his friends. Now of this man I have to say, he had told me that he sought his home in the hearts of those to whom he told his stories and sang his lays, and he has found his place in my heart, for his example was the finest song he sang; and in all the farms and woodmen's huts the people wept, and hung wreaths of flowers upon the hazel bushes.

Deganwy, where the Princes of Gwynnedd had for more than a hundred and fifty years fixed their capital, lies on the flat lands where the coast-line looks across a narrow sea towards the Island of Mona.

To those who, like myself, are used to think of the capital of a State as a great and beautiful city, the place was a surprise. Here at Deganwy are no stone walls or temples with statues or arcades, nor the markets and forums which lend dignity and convenience to the life of a community. And yet the place suited the people, and was amply fitted to the purpose for which it had been built, the defence of the land of Gwynnedd against the beastly Irish.

In the middle of the sea-front was a great earth-work, on the summit of which was placed the palace of Maelgwyn. This mound was called Dinas Emrys, after a great man of those parts who reigned in Gwynnedd before the Romans came, and as the people there say, before even Prydain, for Emrys was a descendant of Hu Padarn, who was king before the Giant Alboin desolated the other parts of the island. Indeed, the bards told me that the giants never came into this part of the Island of the Mighty at all, because one of them, standing at a distance, saw the hill of Wyddfa and asked what it was, and a poor man, answering him, said it was the King of Cambria; upon which the giant went away with great speed, not liking to offend so mighty a king, who stood so high that he kept knocking the clouds with his head. For this reason I do not think there was ever a giant called Idris; it is much more likely that they told the same tale about that mountain to a giant who came into Cambria by the southern route and went away for a similar reason. Now this never happened at Plinlimmon.

The palace of Maelgwyn consisted of but a single story, with a great hall, and numerous other chambers for retirement and slumber. It was built of wood, and boasted little of the elegances of life as we knew them in Bath, and the other cities of Loegria. Indeed, for these things Maelgwyn confessed a certain contempt. He did not, he said, need statues, so long as there were beautiful women, nor pictures, provided that the sun was shining and he could look out from his hall door upon the bay of Deganwy, and from his bedroom window upon the hills of Gwynnedd. As for winter nights, when these were not visible, "Well," said he, "there is no picture so becoming as one of my friends asleep beneath the hall table." Yet, though he spoke in this way, Maelgwyn was an abstemious man himself for one of his inches.

The building was very large and surrounded by a stockade placed some little way below the crest of the mound; the space thus formed was entirely occupied by gardens, in which grew onions, leeks, and cabbages, as well as numerous fruit trees, which were tended by slaves with great diligence as being immediately beneath the master's eye. "For," as Maelgwyn observed to me while escorting me about this pleasaunce, "the Irish make good gardeners if they are well looked after." As to this method of securing attention, I could but commend his promptitude, for observing one of these slaves somewhat lacking in diligence, he took a kick at him as the man stooped, which measured him full length among the onions. "Let him smell that," said he.

The town itself was but small, for there is little trade among these people. What things they require they make for themselves, or steal from their neighbours, for their wants are simple. Those who lived in the town were fishermen, or sailors attached to the fleet. Compared to Bath, Deganwy is but a village. The harbour is a good one; there is not only the great river which is tidal, and navigable for many miles into the country, taking the ships right up to the base of the mountains, but the roadstead outside the harbour is protected from the winds by the great headland they call the Orme. There were many ships at their moorings when I first saw this harbour, because in consequence of the war in the north, Maelgwyn had refrained from raids upon Ireland for some weeks; moreover, as I have already told, he had used his ships for sending what supplies he could to our armies in the north by sea. However, he now announced that as his country produced little, and as his men, now home from their campaign, and somewhat disappointed at their small amount of loot, would as war-worn warriors expect some small luxuries, while their wives required presents and fairings, he supposed he would, very shortly, have to pay the Irish a visit. "But before that, Artorius, I have something to discuss with you. Also, I should like to know how Aurelian stands in this affair. With Cadell I have already come to an agreement." But what it was, he would not say.

The hall in Maelgwyn's palace was of large size, with a floor of great stones, set close together and strewn with rushes. The tables and benches were of plain oak and roughly worked, while the walls were hung, wherever there was a cranny of space, with the skins of wolves, bears and other wild beasts, cured and made into curtains. Many weapons, such as spears for use both in war and the chase, partisans, quivers of arrows, and axes, were hung in great display and were polished most lustrously. A fire burned in the middle of the room, the smoke escaping through a hole in the roof, and the place was lighted with torches of resinous wood which made a great smoke. Some perches at the far end held a dozen or more falcons, which now and again snarled at each other; when they made too much noise the birds had their heads enveloped in hoods to silence them, at which they grumbled in a comical manner. There were many dogs lying about the floor, very idle and lazy. They made room for none, not even for their master, but slumbered in the main passages about the chamber, and particularly near the fire. Maelgwyn, on passing by these beasts, and mayhap tripped up by one, would curse it for a lazy hound, and kick it, yet not so hard as he had kicked the gardener; then he would address it rather in remonstrance than in anger, as: "And to whom does this place belong, to me or to you, you bitch?" or again, "and who is the lord of this country, you or me, you mongrel?"

"They think they own the place," he would growl.

Yet for all its discomforts I liked the hall, and have had worse quarters.

Here I saw the reason why the learned Abbot Gildas had cursed both Maelgwyn and his city of Deganwy, for there were many traces of ladies about the hall, as a piece of sewing or embroidery, or a gay hood, left lying on a bench. At my perceiving this Maelgwyn cursed again, and said that of all living creatures, women were the most unseemly, and the most idle and untidy, leaving as they did their garments all over his palace. He said that he had too many of these hussies, but did not know how to get rid of them; it was indeed more trouble than to keep them, for did he so much as hint that there were too many of them, their tears and upbraidings destroyed his peace of mind. Then he laughed, and said it was for this that the sage Gildas had reproved him, and producing a letter that he had lately received from that holy man, read me a passage to which, he said, he always referred with pleasure. It was, indeed, a pretty letter to send to a king, and ran thus.

Yet neither is thy sensual mind, which is overcome by the excess of thy follies, at all checked in its course by committing so many sins, but hot and prone like a young colt that coveteth every pleasant pasture, running headlong forward with irrecoverable fury, through the intended fields of crime, continually increases the number of its transgressions.

He seemed to have had some ten or a dozen wives, but told me that he was not by any means certain of the exact number, but they were worse than the hounds and were for ever under his feet. Having seen some few of these ladies, I was in no mind to agree with Maelgwyn's harsh judgment of them, and said so. To which he replied that it was not their appearance to which he objected, but their ways and manners, and that had their appearance been in any way objectionable, they would never have been in his keeping at all.

"But indeed," said Maelgwyn, "I am reminded by the reproaches of this Gildas, of what a guest at a house said, when complaining of the butter with which he was provided. 'I think,' said he, 'there is too little butter with this salt.' So mayhap I should pay more attention to these adjurations of Gildas, if there were more butter with them."

I was anxious about the matter that he desired to discuss with me, particularly as he had hinted at some concern of Aurelian in the affair. That activity of some sort was in progress I was aware, for at times, with the coming of bards and other messengers, Maelgwyn would excuse himself from attendance on me, as having business to transact. On one of these occasions I took the opportunity of mounting to the summit of the great headland called the Orme, and there looking at the vista of the coast, which, with dotted islands and wood-clad shores, was indeed well worth seeing. My companion was a young girl called Regan, who knew the paths to the summit, and had been recommended to me by Maelgwyn for that purpose. "For," said he, "she is a pretty maid and not without mischief of her own, and will make the ascent of this rock the less toilsome by her chatter."

I will say in favour of Maelgwyn that he knew in a friendly way all the people about his palace, and would laugh and joke with all if he were in a good humour. To this I attribute his power in his own country, and the readiness with which his people not only supplied him with information but also served him in war. Even the Irishman whom he had kicked told me that there were men far worse than Maelgwyn, and that he bore no resentment for his blows. "For," said this Irishman, "he desires me to be at work, but the replanting of onions is less toilsome than digging of new ground. Therefore I, when told by the bailiff of the palace gardens to toil with mattock and spade to clear the large stones from a rocky part of the farm, was able to show that certain onions were spoiled and broken by my fall among them, so that I was bidden to replace these, and another of the gardeners was detailed to the clearing of the rocks. I was not indeed much the loser by the kick which you beheld, for," added this man, with a grin, "I fell down before it had quite reached me, knowing well the ways of the Lord Maelgwyn in his gardens."

This Regan, who went with me to the Orme, was, as Maelgwyn had said, a pleasant and fair companion. She was different from the ladies of Bath, being clad as one of the country girls of Gwynnedd, wearing but a short garment of white wool, and sandals, and upon her head a scarlet or purple hood. She had the most saucy pair of black eyes, and her hair hung down in a cloud of dark shadows, wonderfully becoming. She was lively in her speech, and amused me with stories and pleasantries not all free from humour at the expense of the lord to whom she was in allegiance.

When we had reached the summit and she had shown and described to me the various scenes and objects of which I ought to take note, we began to gossip and chat on matters that amused us. And presently she said:

"I have news for you of that lady whom you met in the woods by Clun, and a pleasant though haughty and troublesome lady she was, I make no doubt."

"Indeed," I said, "I liked that lady well."

"That we all know, for it is gossip throughout both Gwynnedd and Powys. When a great lord and general meets a pretty lady in the forest, and escorts her with great gallantry for many miles for a week or more, it is subject for report. Moreover she was a high and mighty princess. Therefore the story was repeated with pleasure by every charcoal burner's wife and daughter."

At this I was rather vexed, and said to the girl:

"Yet she was a princess, and one who holds high station, and carries a heavy burden in the State. And more than that, she gave me pledges that she would set the island even before her own sovereignty."

"Yet, Artorius, listen, for I am Regan of Pennal, and my father is of an ancient race. Under the Emperors he was Regulus of that district, and his father's father went with Maxen Wledig to Armorica. I am here at Deganwy as security for his peace, for Pennal is in Gwynnedd; yet we are of the kindred of the Creuddyn. I know that lady well, for she and all of us on the banks of the Devi are of the same blood."

"These," I said, "are strange matters to hear from a young girl such as you. Have you then complaints against Maelgwyn because of your lot as a hostage?"

"None," she said. "Maelgwyn would let me come to no harm. For the daughter of one of his chiefs in his palace, there is no fear from him. But of the Lady of the Creuddyn, you call her the sovereign Lady of Dynevawr. It is of just that sovereignty that I am in doubt."

"What wind blows now, Regan?"

"What I say, Maelgwyn has told me; to tell you himself without fair warning might raise a quarrel between himself and his guest, for he is pleased to have you as his friend. Tell me, Artorius, when three strands are entangled, which do you draw out first?"

"That which comes first to the hand, Regan."

"But it is always the woman that first comes to the hand, Artorius."

"Then if there is confusion, and a woman in it, I might leave her to the end. I thought you spoke of some mixture of cords and bow-strings."

"I spoke in a parable. To every man in authority there comes a time when he must unravel a tangle of three strands."

"And what are they, O wise young maid?"

"They are, war, women, and statecraft."

"As yet, Regan, my problems have not concerned women. I agree that the State and its politics, or the secrecies of its politicians, are not always of assistance to the aims of the soldier."

"Yet most men, Artorius, find that women confuse the issue between these two."

"I have heard of such things."

"I also. Now, Artorius, Maelgwyn's question was this: In such a confusion, which thread do you follow? The State, or the army, or the woman?"

"The State first, Regan. The State is that which shall live after the army has died."

"You are very simple, Artorius. How many armies, and how many States, have you known lost for the sake of a woman?"

"Many."

"Then are you superior to all other men, Artorius?"

"Remember this, Regan; if I and mine had suffered defeat at the wood of Celidon, not one woman only would have suffered, but all the wives of those kerns who earned their reward in victory. The State loves not the loves of one man in power, but the loves of all those who are in his keeping."

"I myself, Artorius, own a divided duty. I am under pledge here for my father the chieftain of Pennal, and to the King of Gwynnedd who is my rightful Lord. I am kin also to Gwendaello of the Creuddyn, and she is the woman in this affair."

"What follows, Regan?"

"This: you hold that the weakness of the Britons is in their divisions. When war comes, the Saxons who invade us fight as one nation, the Picts reconcile the differences among their tribes; even the beast-like Irish, whether of Heber or of Heremon, unite in face of a common foe."

"True enough," I said, thinking to myself that if we had not, by the good offices of the old Abbot Gildas, introduced divisions into the ranks of the enemy and set Saxon against Pict, we should never have left the hill of Celidon victorious.

"You say that to Aurelian, and you have said it to Maelgwyn. Now where does the danger lie? Not in Reged, or in Strathclyde. They are good and sound allies. Not in Gwynnedd; here in this mountain land, as in Powys also, they are friends of Aurelian. Not in Damnonia, which is but a tributary state; not in Loegria, the chief of the Island of the Mighty. Where then, Artorius?"

"There is but Dynevawr left, maiden."

"It is so: and after Vortigern, Guitolin it was who brought the wretches from Germania to strike at our unarmed backs. It is Dynevawr, by its tribal divisions, its pride, and its savagery, that threatens your State of Britain. Maelgwyn would end this."

"What can he do?"

"He will do this. In alliance with Aurelian, the supremacy of Demetia is to be ended by the combined forces of Maelgwyn and Cadell. The Silures, the breed of the traitress Cartismunda who betrayed Caradoc, shall no more own their own lands, but hold them of Maelgwyn. He can watch them, use their armies, and hold them fast to the common cause."

"There is reason in the scheme, yet I doubt it."

"Then, Artorius, here is one who ever puts the State before the woman. Yet never having cared about a woman before, what he said and did then counted for little. No man can say until he is tried."

"It is on other accounts than the woman that I doubt the wisdom of the scheme."

"So they all say, when blamed for the miscarriage of their politics. 'I acted for the best, but I was mistaken.' They never say, 'I did it for a woman.'"

It was a fair taunt. I wondered if there were truth in it. That red-haired gallant girl, whose hair was as the wheat ripening in the sun on the shores of Somerset, whose eyes were as blue as the Severn Sea looking towards Dynevawr—I must forget this, and view the matter without the woman. Yet I had trusted her, and she me.

"I know what you think, Artorius. If it were some other woman whose throne was to be taken and her pride humbled, what would you say then? What if it were I, now a hostage of Maelgwyn, whose royalty was to be taken away; what then, General?"

I said nothing and she went on:

"It was in truth an adventure worth while, to roam those woods with that lovely Princess; a memory to which a man might cling all his days, with that fond farewell upon the Bridge of Pengwern."

That was true. I thought of it sometimes.

"Think of our day here upon the Orme. Look upon the blue of the Mona Sea, look to the hills beyond the woods, see the vista of the valley of the Clwyd. See, there is Wyddfa, the monarch of all mountains. Think sometimes of this blue sky, and the white drifting clouds, and the warm air. Will you think of this with such sadness as when you look back on Severn-side, and the woods of Clun?"

"No, it has been pleasant, Regan, but I should not."

"No, you would sacrifice me to the interests of the State. But when you think of your other little friend of a day's romance your judgment wanders."

I saw that those were right who called Maelgwyn cunning. He had certainly chosen a good intermediary. I could see the whole game as it was played, yet there was truth in what this Regan urged. Britain was too much divided. Our only guarantee for the loyalty of the Southern Cambrians was the word pledged by a girl of twenty, in the absence of her treacherous uncle. There was no certainty that her people would abide by her law. If I trusted the girl, it did not follow that others would. Maelgwyn could be depended upon, if only for the reason that his interest lay with Aurelian's; the girl's pledge was one of honour and patriotism only, and for my part, in matters of State, I think that self-interest is a better support for patriotism, in the long run, than is honour.

We conversed little on our way back to the town. That night I raised the question with Maelgwyn.

"It is plainly," he said, "not fitting that these southern tribes should be any longer tolerated as disturbers of the peace. There was once a Pax Romana. Now we must aim for a Pax Britannica. All the States of Britain, with their agreed boundaries, must live in amity to resist the foreigner."

This coming from a man who had admittedly extended his boundaries at the expense of his weaker neighbours, was expected; but in this case it was clear that Maelgwyn and the boundaries of his land stood to gain. If an ambitious ruler acquires power and dominion by a well sounding argument, rather than by war, he but proves his capacity. I have noted that whenever a nation seeks to suppress one of its weaker neighbours, it is always easy to find quite satisfactory reasons for the aggression.

"But," I said, "there is now no risk of trouble from that source. It was a pledge that they should assist us in the recent invasion."

"True enough. But mark what led up to it. There was a sale by Guitolin of which I fear we have not even yet heard the last."

"But Guitolin is either a captive or dead."

"With the Southland there is no guarantee that his treason will not be repeated. There is no real unity among these people. They are not, like us in Gwynnedd, or you in Loegria, or Coroticus in Strathclyde, or Cadell in Powys, a strong and united State. They are split up into half a hundred tribal communities. Each village has its reigning prince, and the only link they have is the shadowy legend of Pendragon."

"But what do you intend, Maelgwyn?"

"I have sent messages to Aurelian, who agrees with me, and asks me to confer with you. Our plan is this: That the south shall be a lordship of Gwynnedd. They may, if they will, still maintain their local princes. Indeed it is better that they should. It is useless to make the servitude more of an humiliation than is required. But henceforth the military dominion is to be mine. Your Lady of the Creuddyn" (here he leered at me) "may keep her little marshy kingdom, but her teeth will be drawn. I can no more tolerate, nor can Aurelian, these disturbers of our security, whether Dynevawr, or Morgannwg, or Morfan, or the Creuddyn, or any other of these cantrevs that call themselves kingdoms. They must be ended."

"But there is no fear of more treason. The Lady of the Creuddyn is supreme there, and has given pledges."

"She behaved very well, but she was in dread; her plans and those of her house had miscarried. She is but one among many, and her shadowy authority may end to-morrow. There is no trusting the Silures. At any time they might throw off her command."

I knew in my heart he was right. Until a month ago

I should have agreed without debate. It had been the endeavour of years of my own life to bring about such an overlordship, either by him or by Aurelian, of this troublesome province. It was what I had never doubted was necessary, in the interests of Britain as a whole: to unite the land, and end these local divisions which had first enabled the Saxon to make prey of Kent, Vectis, and other fair portions of the island, never now, I knew, to be British again. No, Maelgwyn was right. And Regan had been right too. It was only because the lady had been honourable in her word, and fair to the eye, and my friend for a week and no more, that I stood out against the scheme. I would not, as Regan had said I would, sacrifice the State to the woman. I was a Roman citizen, or had been in fact, as I was still in law, and the code of the great days of Rome was ever that the private desire must be subordinated to the Respublica. The woman must go. Yet I felt sad at heart to think of it, and also that I was not a true and just man to my helpless friend, woman though she was.

"As you will, Maelgwyn. What do you and Aurelian require at my hands? Yet I wish, if this business means leading armies into Dynevawr, that you and he would place the business in other hands than mine."

CHAPTER XI

THE GWENT

A DARK AND ANCIENT BORDERLAND,
WITH WILD MEN FIERCE AND SHY,
PEERING FROM TREES WITH SPEAR IN HAND
AT EVERY PASSER-BY.

A plan such as Maelgwyn's, being for the advantage and concern of the country as a whole, had to be carried out with some regard for the forms of law and propriety. A council of the princes of the island must be held to decide all details affecting the future prosperity of the several dominions, and to give proper sanction to the settlement. After a long debate, and much interchange of cartels, it was at length agreed that a great council of the island should take place at Brecknock, in the region where, as we others knew, the sovereignty of these southern tribes was to be annulled and their independence ended. The South Cambrians, taking this as an acknowledgment of their rights under their Princess Gwendaello as overlord, under her style of Pendragon, made no demur; indeed that lady forthwith sent to each and every one of the Kings of Britain a most haughty summons commanding him to appear at her Council. Some of them, such as Constantine of Damnonia, professed to be most mightily offended at this, and because of her haughtiness and their resentment, it was many weeks before the conference was at last fixed with some degree of certitude. During all this time I was at Bath, whither I had returned after my stay with Maelgwyn, well content to be in my own home again with the comforts of a civilized and noble city ready to my hand.

The Council was to be held upon the sacred day of the British, called the Beltane, which is the first of the month of May. Now that the end was in sight, I felt a great sorrow that the Lady of the Creuddyn should within a few weeks more lose her authority and be shorn of her dignity. Aurelian, to whom I said this, showed no sympathy. "Was not this," he asked, "the woman who attacked you, and who was associated with Guitolin in the betrayal of Britain?" I had to assent. "It will be the last time that she is able to commit such treasons, Artorius," said he. "You were well out of that adventure." He was well satisfied that the preliminaries to the Council were completed, and I, knowing that the scheme was wise and right, said no more.

But Aurelian's satisfaction received some set-back on the morrow. We had agreed among ourselves that the representatives of the island should be: Aurelian for Loegria, then Constantine of Damnonia, Maelgwyn of Gwynnedd of course, Justin of Elmet, Urien of Reged, Coroticus of Strathclyde, Cadell of Powys, and this Princess of Dynevawr.

Urien and Coroticus sent messages that they could not attend in person, for, after the recent ravages of the Picts and others, they were re-establishing their king-doms, and could not risk leaving them at that time. Both, however, appointed me as their ambassador to Aurelian, and their deputy or representative at the Council. As not being a reigning prince of the island, I could not otherwise be present. It was, said Aurelian, a good solution, for I was at one with him on the question. As for Justin, it did not matter whether he came or not, for he was an idle man, and in no way wise in council. He would in any event do as Aurelian desired. Of Cadell and Constantine, Aurelian had no doubt. Of the six pre-sent, then, no less than five would support Maelgwyn's plan, and the Princess Paramount of Dynevawr would be helpless to oppose it. Thus the result seemed to be achieved. Yet now came a letter from the Creuddyn which promised to upset all our labours. It read as follows:

Of the princes who may be present at the Council of the Island of the Mighty, to be holden

at our city of Brecknock under the presidency of
me, the Pendragon, I desire to say that the fol-
lowing may by leave of me, and of the other
Princes Regnant, under my authority be present.
To wit, those of Loegria, Damnonia, Reged,
Strathclyde, Powys, Elmet and Gwynnedd; of the
others the following will attend, to wit, the Princes
of the Creuddyn, of Gower, of Morgannwg, of
Morfan, of Dyfed, Cydweli, Creulys, Gwent,
Neisgyn, Mabwynion, Syrwen, Isnafyr, Trahaiarn,
Selyf, Cethyniog, Isgenen, Rhwyngnedd, Talgarth,
Talacharn, Brycheiniog, Euas, Erging, Eucgdrud,
Pencaer, Mynyd, Penvro, Omawr, Carnwyllio,
Anlwnog, Swydd, Brwynllys, Perfellt, and Builth.
But as Pendragon I say that, at the Council, those
who appear for these princedoms of the island
shall have one voice for each of them.

To this Aurelian would not agree; "for," he said,
"under such conditions, it would be useless to hold the
Council at all, since each of these chieftains would give
his voice as the voice of the Lady Regnant of Dynevawr,
his overlord, and I, and Maelgwyn, Coroticus, Urien,
Cadell and Constantine, would be as if we had not spoken." With which I agreed; yet I admired the cleverness of
this lady who, as the saying goes, could see from the top
of Plinlimmon to the top of Wyddfa and tell whether a fly
resting upon the cairn of the latter had one eye or two.

After consultation with Aurelian, I wrote her a most
cunning letter. I said that as the subject of consultation
was the military defence of the island, only those could
have a voice in the proceedings who were Lords
Paramount. It was not a question of royalty of blood,
with which no part of the island could compare with
Dynevawr, or indeed with Dyfed or with Morgannwg,
but only of the levies which the greater military powers
could raise; and therefore equality of force, or something approaching it, was necessary in those who
should put their hands to such a treaty as was contemplated. We could not therefore concede to Southern

Cambria more than two, or at most three voices. That
Dynevawr, under her most noble and worshipful self,
was entitled to one, was of course beyond a doubt, but
it must be taken as representing its various small
though valiant subdivisions. Also we would allow one
voice to Morgannwg, and mayhap to Dyfed. If this were
not agreed, it would be better not to hold any council at
all, because, if the thirty and more voices from
Dynevawr were heard, the debates would be both pro-
tracted and purposeless, nor would there be any end to
the claims made by lesser princes than herself. For
example Cadell of Powys was already claiming that
Wenwynwyn, Fadog, and Salopia were each entitled to
an appointed deputy. As this could not be admitted, we
should be obliged if she would moderate her demands.
She replied that she would abide by the conditions
named and that it was right for no province to have
more than one voice.

This was more complaisance than I had expected of
her, but the readiness of her agreement gave me more
than a moment's misgiving. She would always, would
that young girl, try one way if another had failed, and I
pictured her as thinking deeply how to defeat the stratagem that was formed against her. For that she suspected some attempt to injure and constrain her I had
no doubt. Yet she was only, after all, a young girl, playing her own part against all the wisest and most powerful princes of the island. That our policy was necessary
and in the best interests of all, I had no doubt, yet my
mind misgave me that we could attain this reasonable
measure of security only by an injustice. Though now I
was determined that the scheme should go through,
and that I would spare no effort to that end, I confess,
that had she defeated us all, and kept her sovereignty in
spite of the great odds against her, my disappointment
at the collapse of our plan would have been tempered by
my willingness to see her triumph. Hers was but a tiny
and savage kingdom, she was but a fair and courageous
young girl, and when the weakest wins, all men that are
worth the name are pleased in spite of themselves.

Now it happened that Aurelian and I could not travel together. He had affairs at Gloucester, for since it had been almost completely sacked and burnt by the raid of Guitolin, who came as a Briton, and when admitted on terms of hospitality and friendship, took the opportunity to betray the city, Gloucester had been in great poverty and distress. However, in the worst times Gloucester has always had citizens with pride in their city and courage to advance her, and by now the city was in a fair way to recovery. Aurelian desired to inspect the defences that he had ordered, and also to distribute some reward to the legion there stationed, who had worked, with great honour to themselves, at the rebuilding of the walls. This was indeed a work of urgency, for unless the watchman watches the wall of the city, the protection of the gods is of small moment. Such at least, at the risk of being untrustful to the immortals, is my opinion, based on many years' military experience. I myself had business with Constantine, whom I did not trust. He was favoured by Aurelian, for he was occasionally prompt in the payment due from Damnonia, and gave in general but little trouble. He was smooth of tongue, as men are in his district, but I had some notion that, in close quarters, I should prefer to rely upon other men rather than Constantine. Before the princes met therefore, I desired to visit him in his city of Isca, and in conversation examine him unawares, ascertaining his intention from stray and random hints in his talk. My pretext was a deficiency in the tribute which, on account of the Pictish inroads and the devastation of Gloucester, we had been compelled to assess at a higher figure. The repair of Gloucester, as Aurelian maintained, the city being a national fortress, was rightly chargeable to the whole island, and was not the burden merely of Loegria. Constantine had demurred, and sent only the amount originally agreed. I heard what he had to say, and as the sum in dispute was small, told him that our knowledge of the facts had been incomplete, and that he was in the right. This pleased him mightily, and thereafter he treated me as a friend, expatiating upon what he called

the intended usurpation of Maelgwyn in Demetia. How
was he to know, he expressed his fear, that Aurelian
would not entertain the same projects against Damnonia,
as Maelgwyn had against Dynevawr?

"The truth is," said Constantine, "that when once
these amalgamations and apportionments begin, one
never knows who is to be the next victim."

"Aurelian," I replied, "does not desire greater territories. He finds his responsibilities heavy enough
already."

"Yes," replied Constantine; it was after dinner, and
he was in a mood more expansive, and therefore more
communicative, than was habitual in so secretive a
man. "That is what everybody says until he thinks it
over, and then he usually takes the profit which before
he said would be merely a burden. 'I would rather be
poor and virtuous,' said the farmer (when his wife
blamed him for the short allowance on which the family
lived), 'than a rich man with an evil conscience.' Yet how
self-sacrificing was this peasant. Out of a desire to
please his wife, the next time we hear of him he is not
only rich but dishonest. So do men mortify themselves
at the shrine of their duty."

I set down this Constantine as a doubtful adherent,
for when he said this, being drunk or part that way, he
was telling me the truth, in spite of his repeated profes-
sions that Aurelian was in the right, and that he would
support him through thick and thin.

So I left Constantine, and departed for Brecknock,
where Aurelian was already, as I judged, arrived; for it
was but four days before the Council. I am not one to
travel with a large train, though my position in the State
entitles me to full ceremony. I like to take the shortest
road upon my journeys, and an escort is of less use
than may appear. In the wilder portions of Britain, away
from the cities, the woods are thick and extensive;
indeed the island might be called a forest set in the sea.
Where men have built their houses, the woods have
been cleared, but elsewhere the trees are growing as
they did before men came to the land, thick and close,

with tangled undergrowth of raspberries and brambles, as well as other shrubs and briars with less fruit, and maybe with longer and more frequent spines. If there are robbers about, a lonely man can hide in the bushes. If he has an escort his party cannot hide, but the attackers can. With an escort, I could not expect to get through the woods of Gwent without some fighting, and against a number of brigands numbering as many as twenty, or fifty, or even a hundred as some bands do, all of them unscrupulous rascals, well armed and accustomed to forest fighting and concealment, the protection afforded by ten legionaries is not worth what it costs. On my return from Isca I remained only a few hours in Bath, and after passing through Gloucester, where I learned that Aurelian had been two days before me, entered the great forest of the Gwent, which I must cross on my way to Brecknock.

This forest is of great extent, and very wild and tangled. On the eastern side of it at least, it belongs certainly to no State; it is supposed to be a common sanctuary. The principality of Morgannwg claims it as within its borders, and in fact exercises a sort of jurisdiction over it, to the extent of slaying any officials who go there from Loegria to collect taxes or punish criminals. Only a year before this expedition of mine, a merchant setting out from Gloucester with two pack animals, to sell his goods among the scattered villages, was set upon and robbed of all he had by foresters. He was left for dead, but contriving to crawl for many miles, he at last got out of the forest and was conveyed by charitably minded herds back to Gloucester. There he made a most bitter complaint to the Ædile, and the Ædile saying that the offence did not lie within his jurisdiction, the merchant went to the Prætor of the city. This was a most costly matter for him, as no case can be taken to the Prætor unless a heavy fee is first paid. The merchants of Gloucester, however, angry at the ill-treatment of their colleague, paid this fee. They further made a subscription which enabled this unfortunate man to begin his business again in some small way. The Prætor made a short investigation, and then, having been paid the fee, said that he could do nothing further.

The merchants at this were very angry, and held an assembly in the forum of the city. Many townspeople attended, and Gloucester being a town which lives by its trade, many violent and indignant speeches were made, and the Prætor was called upon to punish the rogues who had robbed the merchant. He persisted however, that it was none of his business, and at the same time refused to refund the fee, which he said, quite correctly, had been his legal right. He insisted that he had made no overcharge, and had in fact charged less than usual out of his pity for the merchant. The merchants thereupon petitioned the Senate of the city, and held more assemblies in the forum, and also in the two markets: many of the townspeople too, though I think these were mainly young boys and people of the lower class, who had their own grievances against the Prætor and the Ædiles, wrote many disrespectful messages upon the walls of the city, and also made pictures on the walls in chalk, in some of which the Prætor was represented as a goose swallowing a large fish. The Senate then fearing that, at the next elections, other persons than themselves would be chosen for the city offices, commanded the Prætor to equip constables and seize and punish the men of Gwent who had robbed the merchant. It seemed an impossibility, but by good luck the constables did, as a fact, seize the three men who were said to have attacked him, and brought them into Gloucester, where they were imprisoned, and then hanged, after being well flogged.

But, knowing the way of constables, I rather believe that these, not caring to spend many days searching in these dense woods for a party of cut-throats, seized the first three men they saw there, in order to save trouble, and as they were, anyhow, men of the Gwent, there was not much harm done, had the matter ended there. But next came a demand from the Prince of Morgannwg for compensation for three subjects of his, who had been slain by the people of Gloucester; and the city saying that they would pay nothing, the Prince armed many of his men, and by stratagem, got them into the city at the annual fair. He then sacked and burned a great part of the town. The whole business was a great loss, and very foolish, and had some influence in determining me to suppress the independent rule of all the princes in Morgannwg and Dynevawr.

One has but to cross the river by Gloucester to reach the Gwent, which extends for many miles to Caerleon in the south-west, and almost to Brecknock in the north. There is between Brecknock and Gloucester only one town, but it is in ruins, and abandoned by the people, who in these parts are not fond of town life. This was called Ariconium in the days of Rome, and is now called Aberganway, and stands at the foot of the Pyramid mountain, a strange-looking hill. The woods have invaded all this region and it has gone back to its primeval wilderness, much to the satisfaction of its present inhabitants.

The Gwent consists of high, steep hills, clothed in forest trees to the summit, and narrow deep valleys filled by rivers, so that for a large part of the way the only road is by the bed of the stream. The old Roman road by Ariconium was, when I passed, overgrown, and in the marshy lands which are frequent in the Gwent, had sunk and disappeared into the swamp. Sometimes one could mark its former track by the brambles, which grew in dense patches just where the former road had been once the highway.

The reason for this is that when the Roman legions made the roads in these marshy lands, they built them upon a foundation of brushwood. Now the brushwood in these parts is largely blackberry, so that huge masses of brambles were planted in wattles for a thickness of many feet, to form a bed for the logs, stones and other hard material of the road. I have myself used a similar contrivance when ordering the making of a new road in the flat lands by Taunton. But when the roads ceased to be used, the brambles, which had been buried perhaps for a hundred years or more, began to sprout and quickly grew into a thicket. This is how we mark the roads now, but it is treacherous, for as the brambles grew, the hard parts of the roadway sank into the bog.

In this difficult country, therefore, I picked my way with the best care I might, wondering how Aurelian had thriven there, and rather envying Maelgwyn, whose road to Brecknock lay from Deganwy, along hard and dry ground, and mainly by a road the Romans had made for the transport of minerals to Caerleon from the mines in the north. This was another reason for placing these Silures and Demeti under Maelgwyn, for a military expedition through these fastnesses, from Bath and Gloucester, would be a long, risky and losing affair: whereas Maelgwyn could overawe them at once, by a force which could reach their heart in a day or two. No, much as I regretted the loss to the Princess of the Creuddyn, the decision was wise, and indeed inevitable.

By the end of the first day I had advanced well into the forest, half-way to Brecknock. At the junction of a small tributary stream with the main river of Usk, is a tump, built by the Romans as a watch-post when first they attacked the Silures in the time of Scaevola. It had been arranged that Aurelian who, on his long journey four days ago, was to make his camp there, should leave a shelter with food and a flask of wine in a cover for me, who was to follow him. From afar off I could see little of the tump, because of the trees, which I imagine must have grown considerably since the soldiers of Scaevola built this mound, otherwise it would have been of little service. However, within a hundred yards I was in full view of it. I tethered my horse and ascended the eminence. Aurelian's pavilion stood before me. I had hardly entered, when a noose was suddenly flung over my head and round my arms, prisoning them to my sides. I struggled to free them, but was seized by many hands from behind, and laid with no unnecessary violence, flat on my stomach on the ground outside.

CHAPTER XII

CASTELL DINAS

HERE MEN HAVE FOUGHT AND BLED AND DIED;
GREEN GROWS THE GRASS TO-DAY.
THIS LONELY MOUND HAS TIME DEFIED,
WHILE EMPIRES PASSED AWAY.

As I lay there helpless, a number of men surrounded me. The leader drew my sword from its sheath, and then allowed me to sit up. "I crave pardon, Lord, for this precaution," he said, "but knowing your reputation as a warrior, I imagine it will be held excusable even by yourself."

His gravity and courtesy in such circumstances amused me, and I replied:

"Certainly, Sir, it is a precaution I should undoubtedly observe myself were our positions reversed."

"Your courtesy, Lord, makes my task the more unwelcome."

The fellow was going to kill me, then. But it was ill done thus to play with a prisoner. When I take captives I waste no time on superfluous politenesses, but tell them plainly that they are either to be slaughtered at once or hanged in the morning, or at some moment when we have leisure for the work; this is the only gentlemanly procedure.

I said therefore, "Please waste no time on these unnecessary civilities, but get the affair over. I shall, I suppose, be dead by morning."

I took a look round me as I spoke. This then was the end of a career which I had endeavoured to make not altogether devoid of public service. When I was a boy I had thoughts that I might some day be the divine Emperor. It was a matter of election by the legions, and men from Britain, of lesser station and political favour than I, had achieved it. I do not know that I had built much upon the thought. Yet I was conscious of some ability, and should, I hope, have governed well. As my life proceeded, however, I found one thing to do after another. Men helped me and were good friends, and I served them in return; and so it came about that I abandoned the expectation of being Emperor, and was satisfied to do such work as came to my hand. So we all do. Our day-dreams melt away, and from one day to another we do, as well as we may, what we undertake between one night and the next. Well, all was ended now. I was a prisoner taken in attempting what I believed to be right, and yet knew to be cruel. All things must end in harm to some one. I have never liked the Gwent, or the people who live there, but I could well imagine that the dwellers in this fastness loved it. The early spring was upon the leaves, the sun shone between the boughs of the trees. The squirrels in these forests would be taking nuts years after I had been speared. I wished that these bushy-tailed, bright-eyed rogues might long enjoy their own forest after it had ceased to interest me.

The leader showed some surprise. "I contemplated nothing so violent," he said; "my orders are to conduct you to my mistress."

"Your mistress?"

"Our Lady the Pendragon, Lord. But we must not keep her Mightiness waiting. She is but a short distance away. Pray attend us."

I had no desire to be taken before their lady in any state, but least of all with a rope round my neck. I undertook therefore to accompany them without endeavouring to escape, if they would remove it. One of them led my horse, and in this order we proceeded to our destination. This, as I afterwards learned, bore the name of Castell Dinas. It was a round camping place, some hundred or more yards across, with a deep ditch and a flat-topped mound in the middle. It was therefore of British origin from the days before the Roman conquest, for the Roman camps were invariably square; though they would sometimes make use of a British work of this kind, as an economy of labour, if their party were on temporary business, and few in number. It was well known among the tribesmen, and was a gathering ground for such occasions as the present.

A wooden bridge had been erected across the ditch and some pavilions placed upon the mound. Seated outside the largest of these was the lady of the forest, whom a few weeks ago I had rescued and escorted to the Bridge of Pengwern. She greeted me courteously, yet with some haughtiness.

"You are welcome, my Lord Artorius, to my dominion."

I had little patience with this pretence of stateliness, particularly from a mere girl whom I had found wandering alone in a forest, in rags. I ignored her arrogance and said, "It would be more fitting to welcome me at Brecknock, whither I was bound, and where you yourself are under promise to appear."

"I preferred to meet you on the way, as showing you the more honour, Artorius."

She had not as yet invited me to a seat, which she might easily have done, as seats in that part of the world were cheap enough, and her own royal throne consisted merely of a bank of turves, with room upon it for two. I sat down beside her without more ado or invitation.

"I suppose," I said, "that the good Aurelian, the bulwark of Britain, has been served as I was in the excess of your enthusiastic welcome."

"Truly," said she, "he lies a prisoner in my castle of Brecknock. But with you, Artorius, I wish to treat on different terms. You are free to come and go as you please. The restriction my slaves placed upon you was but to secure to me the pleasure of this interview."

"Then I will go to Brecknock at once."

"And at the Council of the Princes of Britain, on which side will you give your voice?" she asked, with some glitter in her eyes.

I was amazed at her childishness. Did she think of me, or of Aurelian, or of that cunning old wolf-hound,

Maelgwyn, that we should abandon our plans for a girl's play-acting?

"At the Council of the Princes of Britain," I said, "young lady, I shall do what I have determined."

"Listen, Artorius. I know well for what this Council has been summoned. Nowhere in Cambria is anything said that we do not all know by the next dawn. I know well that a community of powerful robbers have determined to steal from me and from my people their land and privileges, under a pretext, and to rob our ancient people of our rights, which even the Romans did not dare to filch away."

"We act for the good of the island, girl."

"I am not here to argue. That is for the Council; for myself, I hold to my own view, which is worth as much as yours. Now, Artorius, a plain question. When the Council is held, on which side will you give your voice? To me and mine, or to Aurelian and Maelgwyn?"

I was silent.

"I will tell you, Artorius, that if you give your voice to me, or promise it, you shall go free away from here. If not, your death is assured."

I owed no obligation to this red-haired she-wolf, little more than a cub as she was. To her fellow-savages, Picts or Saxons, I should have said what was required and done what I thought fit afterwards. No prudent commander would scruple in such a case. The girl, who was watching me, read my mind.

"Artorius, if you give me your word I will accept it. Remember that this is my kingdom which I risk. I shall, however, believe you, whatever you say."

I saw now that what I said I should have to abide by. I did not choose to trick this girl. If I promised her anything I must keep my promise. She was not, after all, a Pict or Saxon, but one who had been in my care, and had now trusted me. No, the game was in her hands. If she chose to have me slain she might. But she needed a lesson. Some one must risk all for the State. She claimed to be Pendragon, to be head of us all. I would set her an example, but I would not deceive her.

I said, "It would be well, therefore, to get ready your executioner."

There was no other way out of the business. I was here through my own folly and lack of caution. Well, I would pay. After all, I could only die once. If she had Aurelian fast, Britain was in peril in any event. The work was over heavy for the young Ambrosius, his son. It was a wretched end after a life's work for the consolidation of Britain, but if I was to die, the troubles of the future lay with the future, as the bard Aneurin had said.

"I say truly, girl or Princess, as you call yourself, that I have come to this Council of Princes as accredited ambassador of two sister States of your own. From them I have instructions which you must know. I shall vote in accordance with my commission."

"But think, Artorius. If you will give me your pledge, for I know you would keep it, you shall go free. If not, it will give me great sorrow, I admit, to forfeit the life of one to whom I am under an obligation; but I will not sell my country, and having schemed until I can weigh the scales as I will, I should be a fool indeed to give up my advantage."

"There is no need of thought, girl, I have decided."

"Then you will give your voice against me."

"I shall."

"Yet I do not want you slain, Artorius, especially by a British spear, after all your service to us all."

"That you should have considered before."

"And can nothing change you?"

"Nothing."

"You are a most awkward and disagreeable person. Whichever way I look at the affair, I do not like it at all," said she. "Here I must in my ordinary duty order you to be slain, and yet you are a most worthy person, and old enough, or very nearly, to be my father. It is not suitable at all."

"I am not as old as that, I am merely forty."

"Well, perhaps you are not old enough to be my father, but you are a grave and experienced man, and I must respect you, even if I have to order you to be killed in my duty to my country. Yet I should regret that necessity greatly."

"Doubtless, and so should I until it had happened. Then it would not matter much to me."

"I think I should still regret it. I am sorry you will not support me at the Council. I should value your good opinion of my government."

"It is not your government yet, Princess of Dynevawr, or Pendragon if you prefer it. The fortunes of Roman Britain have claims superior to both yours and mine. Had I been a free agent, I would have given you any pledge that you might ask, and broken it, as is my way in war or diplomacy. You put to me a question that I should not have put to you, a woman's question. You can do as you like, but I have had enough of this talk. I have told you what I shall do."

"As you will. I think, on consideration, that I shall not require your voice at the Council. So go free, Artorius, I will not be the means of your death. I, too, have some notion of public service."

I hated this woman at this moment as much as one person can hate another, treacherous little auxiliary devil that she was. I could see no reason in her present attitude. If she wanted to have her own way, her right, as of force, was to get the killing over, but all this talk was futile. I looked at her and hated her all the more.

Yet she looked well, dressed for war, and not as the poor tattered wretch I had seen in the Severn woods. She wore a leathern vest with a chain of gold around her neck, her limbs clothed in breeches and gaiters, such as are worn by the northern legions on their marches, when passing through the heath and gorselands: and they fitted her and became her well, as I knew, for I had caught her glance admiring their fit. Had the occasion been less serious I should have laughed to see it, but indeed I was in no mood for laughter. But one thing I did notice in particular:

"Girl," I said, "where got you that coronet?"

She took no note of the question.

"Artorius, I have told you that you may go free. Now you may ask, if you desire, a favour of me. Will you travel in my train to Brecknock, or will you remount your horse and take your way by yourself?"

"I cannot accept the honour of travelling in your train," I said.

"Then come as my ally, or friend, if you like the term better."

"We travel in the same direction."

"Then let us go together. We have travelled in company before, without undue quarrelling, Artorius."

"But tell me," I said, "where got you that coronet?"

"You know it, Artorius?"

"I know it well."

"But it has been in secret keeping for these four hundred or more years."

"I am not without knowledge of the history of Britain, Princess."

"How old is it, Artorius?"

"More than a thousand years."

"Just that, and when Caradoc was taken by the Romans in the vale of Clun, a safe hand buried it. Artorius, where did he bury it?"

"At Dinas Dinnle, in Arvon, Gwendaello. It was buried with a chough."

"And to me, wearing it, you still say you owe no allegiance?"

"None."

"Not even to the crown of Dynwal Moelmud, the earliest and most stately symbol in the whole world, the crown of him who made the laws, who made a sanctuary at the plough, who made the roads, and gave to all men justice?"

"I prefer the work to the crown, Gwen."

"Yet it is a most stately symbol, Artorius."

"Wear it in a befitting manner then, girl."

"I think I will, yet it is but thin gold and light."

"It is nearly worn out."

"That I fear too, but let us keep that which it marks as long as we may."

"At the Council I shall give my voice for unity and against you. Would you give the symbol up?"

"I might; if it were claimed by one I honoured, I would, yet I doubt if he would claim it. Alas, poor old crown, poor mean work of an unskilful age, when men worked with unhandy tools, and knew neither wealth nor luxury. Will you guard it for me, Artorius? I should hate to have it taken by unseemly hands."

"Wear it then, Gwen, if you think thus. I will guard it while you wear it, as I did before, and when you cease to wear it, as you may, I will see to it that it passes into no unworthy hands. Now let us go to the Council. It is to-morrow. But I do not like the business, my poor girl."

"Yet I think your sorrow is misplaced, Artorius. Vote as you will. I shall suffer very little. I am in my own kingdom, and I wear still the Pendragon crown. I think that other people will regret the result more than either you or I."

Now of this crown there were many stories. After the quarrels of Fer and Por, in the ancient days, a king was elected over all Britain, a scion of that House of Cornwall to which this girl belonged. He it was who in order to inspire respect for his government, and end the quarrellings and civil wars of his people, had this ancient crown made from gold dredged from the river Conway, where in those days gold was in plenty. It was he who made the ancient laws of the Britons before we knew the code of Theodosius, and made the trackways that we had before the Roman roads. A great man, and a learned, in spite of the rough and evil days in which he lived. Now this crown had been treasured greatly. It was worn by Beli Mawr two generations before Cæsar came to Britain. It was the crown of Caswallon, of Ludd, of Cunobelin. I knew its story, for the old women had told it to me in secret, when I, a boy, played in Britain before ever I went to Rome to enter the service of the divine Emperor. There were marks upon it, by which all men who were in the secret might know it. Yes, it pleased me to see it at the last, just as it was to cease to be a symbol. It was a toy, and in the fierce work that lay before us, a small and poor Roman province, left almost helpless against innumerable and savage foes, it was a useless toy. Yet few men could have seen this ancient thing without a shade of feeling; and I am British by birth, and know the old stories of my ancestors.

CHAPTER XIII

THE CASTLE OF BRECKNOCK

ONE THING WE KNOW HAS EVER BEEN
WHERE WOMAN TAKES THE RULE;
IT DOES NOT ALWAYS NEED A QUEEN
TO MAKE A MAN A FOOL.
BUT SPITE OF ALL, THIS TRUTH IS RULED
AS PLAIN AND UNDERSCORED:
THE MAN'S CONTENT TO BE BEFOOLED,
THE WOMAN SEEKS A LORD.

It was barely twenty miles to Brecknock, and I urged upon her Mightiness, as she insisted upon being called in this, which at present was her own realm, the necessity of proceeding at once. The next day was the first of May, appointed for the Council, and in diplomatic conferences it is well to proceed to business promptly. Delay not seldom leads to division among the delegates. Some men are venal, others half-hearted, and ready for any excuse to escape from their obligations. Among these half-hearted, indeed, I might reckon myself; I was by no means enamoured of the violence which was in contemplation upon this ancient British State. If the conference met upon the day appointed, I would add my voice to the side to which I was pledged: otherwise, I was by no means sure that I might not, as one of the weaker-kneed brethren, seize upon the plea of delay to recant. How often is such an excuse heard, "Yes, had you approached me the week before last, how gladly would I have obliged you; but it is not now the week before last, and much water has flowed down the river Usk since then." Also, "Now I have made other arrangements, yet it would have pleased me to befriend you had I been able; but you will understand, I feel sure, how I am now placed."

Therefore, owing to the time, it was agreed that we should depart at once. By a track through the woods we could reach Brecknock in about three hours, that is by sundown or before. We had ridden perhaps two-thirds of the way, when we came to a small clearing, and there, seated by the pathside, was an aged man, eating some small pieces of bread which he took from a linen scrip at his side. As he ate, he seemed to think, chewing in a meditative way, and pausing some time before taking another bite.

It seemed to me that I had known this old man since I had been born, and in truth I was glad to see him again, though the lady who rode by my side did not apparently share my pleasure.

"There," she exclaimed, "is that ancient lunatic, who, on the road to Clun, detained us with his trivial converse and pestilent curses for a period that seems to me, looking back upon it, to have occupied a space of years in time."

"As for me," was my reply, "I like the old man well. He did me good service on one occasion."

"Then he is my friend also," said she, to my surprise.

We had now arrived beside the old man, who looked up in an astonished way and greeted us with a courteous nod, at the same time setting his mitre straight, which in his meditations he had pushed somewhat to the back of his head.

"Greeting, Gildas," I said.

"Greeting, Artorius," he replied. "I see you again with the young damsel. I should have thought at your age you would abandon these plays. But perhaps you are married to her. I should rejoice to hear of this ending to your misdeeds."

"That is another matter, Gildas, which at present does not concern us. This lady is, as you should know, the Lady Paramount of this part of Britain."

"Alas, then indeed are we in the company of the unrighteous. Yet herein is my good fortune; I can now address my reproaches to the mother of evil herself. I had not expected the approach to be so easy. Though," he added, with a cunning look, "I have rarely indeed failed in the end to secure an approach to the person whom I had in mind to admonish."

"What is in the wind now?" asked the girl.

"The flames of everlasting fire," answered the Abbot. "It hath come to my ears that a conference of the Princes of this land is to assemble. Britain has indeed kings, but they are tyrants; she has judges, but they are unrighteous ones who engage in plunder and oppress the innocent."

"Now that is a true word, old man," broke in the girl. "Proceed, old father, who are wiser than your earlier curses had led me to believe. 'Oppress the innocent' is true indeed. Truly are they tyrants, these Princes, all except myself, that is."

"A Daniel come to judgment, indeed," retorted the Abbot, "but thy words of seeming virtue are but a snare and a delusion. It hath come to my ears that on the first day of May, on the morrow, thy irreligious subjects, aided and abetted in their wickedness by thy encouragement and counsel, will celebrate by unholy fires the day of witchcraft and sorcery with Walpurgian orgies."

"He means the Beltane fires," said the girl; "we hold them indeed to-morrow night."

"Worshippers of false gods are thy people, and thyself as well," said Gildas. "I will attend, and will appeal to the multitude to repent and abandon their idolatries."

"Aye, do," said the girl, smiling. "Accompany us, Reverend Sir, and accept a shelter from me for the night. You are indeed welcome after your services in the north." I had told her on the way of the shrewdness of this old person in his dealings with the Saxons.

"Nay, nay, what I did was a trifle. The Picts and their unholy friends were but as children, and I have an old head upon my shoulders," said he, smirking. "It was perhaps not just to such poor innocents thus to delude them."

"There will be singing at the Beltane, and honours for those who sing well," said the lady. "I pray you to be present, and to sing for us."

"Aye, I will be present, and, as you press me, I will sing, but on one condition. And my condition is that you award not the prize, whatever it may be, to me. Give it to those who are younger. It is but just."

"You travel far about this land, Gildas," said I, not liking to see so old and clever a man made mock of.

"Yes, I like the country well, but it is not good for my soul. I become puffed up with pride, and the lesson of our order, of which I am Abbot, let me remind you," said he with some dignity, "Abbot and no less" (as he put his mitre straighter upon his head), "the lesson of my order is humility. And let me say this, that the powers of the mind being but corporeal and independent of those which are of the soul, just as reason is another matter than faith (for who can be cleverer than the devil?), I find that my vows here in Britain are in danger of being broken. I find the people of this land, as of most other lands, for I am a travelled man, such fools that I am really in peril of being conceited. I will come to your contest of singing, however, but as a teacher, mind, and not as a contestant."

At this Gildas dropped behind, saying that he would be with us at the castle. We resumed our progress and lost sight of him.

"Tell me," I asked, "if, as I suspect, Aurelian and the others are now in your power, how you have disposed of them?"

"Nay, you credit me with an impoliteness. They were but few, and found it useless as you did to resist my kindness. They are kept safe, and well lodged. You may meet them at supper if that be your wish."

"It is my wish."

"And mark this well too," she went on, with a meaning look, "I have not rifled their belongings, nor have my servants. It is not my practice, Artorius, as sovereign of this land, to rob other princes. Mark that well, I say."

I said nothing in reply. I should always have maintained, even with Maelgwyn, who said she was but a fool of a girl, that she had a ready wit, and some power of expression.

We were now within sight of the outlying farmsteads of the town of Brecknock, and our train, recognizing that their journey was nearly over, and full of the rejoicing common among these people at the first of May, began to sing songs. So loud was their singing that further converse, had I wished it, was useless. I liked those songs, which carried me back to old days before I went to Rome, for they were the old "arrival" songs of Britain. Thus, when as a child I had been with my father's shepherds upon the hills, and was tired after a long day of such pleasures, among the animals and the rocks and wild places, as are dear to such as me, and after many miles on the road, the old man who had the care of me sang just such songs when we came in sight of the lights of home. It was thirty or more years since I had heard these airs, and the memory made me feel a desire for silence, and also a sadness for this girl whose kingdom I was pledged to despoil.

So I listened to these songs, which first one and then another, and then all in chorus, would chant, with some pleasure, and melancholy also, not only for the days which were past, but also for the thought that they would never come again. It is at such times and with such memories that a power of judging the future comes to us all, and more to us who are of the ancient line. And with this vision upon me, I foresaw that evil would come to the land in the end, and that more joy lay in looking back than in looking forward. It might be that our day was indeed over.

In due course we entered the gateway of Brecknock Castle. It was a large place built in the Roman style, square in plan, with a wall and trench around it and four gates, with the main road running from gate to gate and a high stone wall; so it remained until after the first Pictish and Irish raids. In these troubles it was seized by Brychain, who called it after himself, though the Romans used to call the place Bannium. He was an ambitious man, and a great free-booter, a younger son of Edwal of Cardigan, and from him Guitolin was descended; though when Guitolin claimed to be of the

blood of Caradoc he lied, because there was only a very
distant relationship between Edwal and Caradoc. No
bard of Mona would admit the claim, but Guitolin had
paid other Druids, who were not of the College, to con-
struct his genealogy; and for this reason no bard of
Brecknock was ever allowed to sing anywhere in North
Cambria, being supposed to be unorthodox, and willing
to perjure the tables of descent for money. The precaution is necessary, for the genealogies are never written
down, but remembered by the bards, and passed on by
word of mouth. Brychain restored the castle and built
many towers and a hall to it, making it a very beautiful
and stately place; moreover it stands well where the two
rivers Hondu and Tarell flow into the Usk, in a broad
and fair vale, said by many to be the finest in all Britain.
But in my opinion it is not to be compared with the valleys of Somerset, and certainly not with certain valleys
such as Clun, with which I am acquainted in Powys.
However, it is a place deserving of admiration.

As we approached, I asked my companion again
whether Aurelian was really her prisoner, and what she
had done with the other Princes of Britain, Maelgwyn,
Constantine and Cadell. To this she replied that to her
mind it was discourteous in a guest to inquire what
other guests she might have in the house: that she had
a right to entertain or refuse whom she chose, and that
it might or might not be that the persons whom I had
named were still dependent upon her bounty. This
answer left me doubtful, because, knowing this lady's
proud and reckless nature, I thought her meaning
might be that they had fallen into her hands by an
ambush, as I had, and had since been slain by her
orders. I resolved to ask no more questions, but to
escape as soon as I could, and then, if it were true that
she had murdered Aurelian and the rest, to seek some
opportunity of ending for ever her power to do further ill.
As for her claim to be Pendragon, which was founded on
the legends of the Brecknock bards, I could have told her
that it was no better than Maelgwyn's, though, through
her mother, superior to Guitolin's. She had been made

to take the oath to him when very young, at a Beltane
fire some years before, with many incantations and sacrifices; and this oath she respected, though Guitolin was
no longer Pendragon, having been enslaved by the
Saxons, and therefore having gone beyond the threshold,
or as the Roman lawyers say, the postliminium. He was
civilly dead and no longer entitled to have oaths to him
observed.

As we entered the castle gates there were many
kerns with arms in their hands, and sewers and stew-
ards, as if a great feast were to be held. The enclosure
of the castle, once we had passed the gateway, was far
inferior to that of Cadell at Uriconium. The Roman
Britons hold that the grounds about the house should
be as carefully kept as the inside, as outside rooms to
the mansion; but Cambrians take little pleasure in gardens, saying that the gardens of the woods are more
beautiful than any they can make, and why therefore
should they waste toil and money and the labour of
slaves in making something that is better done elsewhere for nothing? With this I do not agree, and in my
villa at Bath, the gardens, as those of Aurelian, and
indeed those of Cadell at Uriconium, are cultivated, and
as well-swept and clean as the atrium: and even
Maelgwyn at Deganwy has most orderly onion-beds in
his curtilage. The yard of the castle of Brecknock was
crowded with great piles of wood for the fires, with
untidy grass in odd corners, and dandelions growing
between the stones of the paving, to say nothing of a pile
of horse-dung in the middle. There were men, also,
making great wicker-work images for the Beltane festivities. In the old days the Druids, at Stonehenge or
Amesbury or elsewhere, on the first of May would make
a great fire and burn slaves or enemies in these wicker
giants, but nowadays they are but childish toys. The
Romans said that these images were part of the
Phœnician worship of Moloch and forbade their use in a
rescript. Still, the people in Cambria among the hills,
and they in Valentia, and also the Picts, persisted in
their use with great obstinacy, and refused to obey the

edict. I myself doubt its wisdom, for when I was in Tyre and Sidon, the priests there assured me that no such images had ever been used in their worship.

When we reached the portals of the castle Gwendaello said to me:

"Artorius, I ask pardon for the jest I have played upon you. It was in a moment of anger that I ordered you to be taken, yet in a way it was to try you."

"Nay," I said, "it is as if it had not been done."

"No harm has been done your friends, nor is any intended, though I admit I have not much affection for them."

"You know," I reminded her, "but little of them. Of all that are here there is not one who has not played a worthy part in the defence of the State. They doubt you as too weak in yourself, and on too uncertain a throne, to join them in their struggle against the enemies of the island."

"I am not weak," said she angrily. "I thought I had given clear proof of my loyalty."

"Yet you should remember what cause for distrust Guitolin gave."

"It is true. I did indeed foolishly in joining in that treason."

"As for me," I continued, "I have constantly maintained that you were worthy of faith. I have also seen, in the trick that was played upon me in the Gwent, that your subjects obey you."

"Indeed, Artorius, that was one of the meanings in my mind when I commanded that ambush. I have influence over these tribes; greater indeed than my uncle's, for he was not loved. Many of our chieftains distrusted him, yet he has his friends even now."

"Yes," I said, "that was what we all feared."

"I do not," she said. "Every day I increase my influence. There are but a few, either bound by ancient habit, or disappointed of preferment, who now still work for Guitolin. You know that he is still alive, and is to be liberated in order to work disaffection here?"

At this I was startled indeed. I had regarded Guitolin

as dead, for no man used to the lot of a king in Britain could live for long as a slave in a Saxon camp. Even their captured women did not live long, but died soon under their ill usage and brutality. I may be thought fierce in my own treatment of captured Saxons, but I had so far repaid but a tithe of what we owed to them.

"But enough of that," said the girl. "I had hoped, Artorius, that you and I might sup together, away from others. What you have to say could be well said then. It is you and I who must support on our shoulders this island. Aurelian is well enough, but he is an old man and grows slow. The others, too, are good so far as they go, but they seek for themselves. In these times of peril, which I understand to the full, such self-seeking is not timely."

"With that I agree," I said, thinking yet that those who are thus single-hearted are most useful to others, and yet frequently come off but poorly themselves.

"Then you will sup with me alone? The others are well and suitably entertained; I told them that I should not be there, as I had other affairs on hand. There will be a riot of festivity to-morrow night, and a quiet evening with one friend is pleasant, Artorius."

"It is so."

"I think that the other gathering will be merry; a feast with Maelgwyn present would not be silent, and the mead will flow. Well, there is plenty for them."

I will not deny that I had great pleasure in being in this lady's company and delighted much in her courtesy to me, which was shown when she escorted me across the courtyard. She apologized most profusely for the untidiness of her court, of which perhaps, as a man unmarried, and old enough to love exact order, I took undue note.

"We are entertaining many important guests," she said, "and our resources are but slight, so we must make many unwonted preparations; yet it is ungrateful to a guest to show him thus—nay, not show him, for there is nothing in my poor castle to show; rather let me say unwillingly expose—the machinery of the feast. Forgive, if you please, the disorder of the approaches to this old house. Truly to a man who has refused the high office of Associate Emperor, this squalor is little less than an insult."

"Nay, Gwen, I never refused the office."

"I think the better of them for that. Truly to a man such as yourself, with the Empire in its present disorder, they refrained, in natural delicacy, from offering it."

I was not altogether convinced by her explanation of the shortcomings of Flavius Anastasius, yet it was an interpretation that had not previously occurred to me. There might be a grain of truth in what she suggested; truly she was a most far-seeing lady. I was glad to sup alone with her, for any one, even a young girl such as this, with such an accurate and right appreciation of high politics, must have much to say of value on the smaller affairs of the island.

She very prettily entrusted me to the care of her seneschal, a man named Kai, who was most respectful and gallant in his bearing towards me, and took me into a large chamber for my exclusive use, where every comfort was prepared; he then asked if there were anything else that I required, and was most gravely distressed that I made no demands upon him.

I had not been there many minutes when the old man Gildas came to me. He had been given suitable accommodation in the castle, and professed some liking for his hostess, who, so he said, although a pagan, yet had a most proper appreciation of what was due to the Heads of the Church. I said it seemed truer to me that the lady liked him for himself, and had no more exact knowledge of his clerical standing than I had. This he regretted greatly, saying that he had always endeavoured to bring his cloth into no disrepute, yet he would rather we acknowledged him as our spiritual head than as our intellectual superior. To this I had nothing to say, being in some doubt as to his meaning. To me the mind and spirit are identical terms. Gildas, seeing my lack of comprehension, shook his head at me. Then he spoke in graver terms.

"Artorius, on another occasion I brought you certain information of the doings of your enemies. Now again I have a message for your ear."

I bade him speak on, saying that I respected his knowledge greatly, and in view of my experience of him would do as he advised in most matters.

"Then," said he, "the matter is, that the lady of this castle is in very grave peril. It is reported that great changes are to be made in the constitution of Dynevawr, though what these are is not certain. Unquestionably, most of the princes of the tribes have full confidence in their lady, regarding her as the bulwark of their independence; but there are some, of Guitolin's party, who say that she, in common action with Maelgwyn and the others, desires to suppress their small sovereignties, and govern as supreme, absorbing to herself all their powers."

This had not occurred to me, but I could see that nothing was more likely. I told him that I would gladly hear all that he had to say.

"There is not time for a long story," said he, "but the truth is briefly this: there are men secretly in this castle, either tribal princes or, as is more likely, servants hired by them, who will take a chance this night of placing it beyond the lady's power to do them any injury."

"The secret knife?" I asked.

"Truly. To-morrow is the Council. If the deed is done to-night there will be no Council, for any ruler of Dynevawr that took her place would require an adjournment for consideration. Therefore these traitors think, reasonably enough, that if the Pendragon be slain to-night this injury to their interests will be avoided."

I besought him to tell me all he knew.

"Well," said he, "I know the men, but what I do not know is the hour when they intend to do the abominable deed. What you and Maelgwyn and the rest of you propose to do with this girl's inheritance to-morrow, I do not know or care very much, yet I like the girl, and wish her well. In any event, I will certainly go to some lengths to frustrate the accomplishment of her assassination."

"In an hour, Gildas, I sup alone with the girl. We are friends. The scheme of the Princes is not to her advantage, but is, as I think, or did think, for I have changed my views somewhat, to the advantage of the island as a whole. But I say that though I am bound to keep my pledge to those with whom I am acting, yet still, what I can do to soften the blow to this girl, I shall do at the Council. I shall indeed urge another course, giving reasons for the change; though if they hold me bound to my former pledges I shall have no choice."

"The attempt is most likely to be made in the dark of the moon, which sets about an hour before midnight."

"The attack will then be after I leave her, when she is retired."

"That is the usual time for such work, so far as my experience goes," said Gildas seriously. "Unless of course she is to be poisoned at supper. I think the knife is more probable. There are few opportunities for poisoning in this castle, where all eat out of the same dish as it were."

"How did you learn so much?"

"I have my methods," he replied serenely. "I tell you the attempt will be made in her own chamber. The criminals will meet secretly in the small court, into which your own chamber looks. Keep your lights hidden, and profess to be asleep at the dark of the moon. I will watch from another place. When you are sure that you have them, descend and strike a blow for her that you love."

"What do you know about that?" I asked him.

"Old eyes see a great deal, if they have at the back of them a brain with eighty odd years of worldly experience. Never mind, Artorius; if you are shy, I doubt whether any one else has noticed it, unless it be Maelgwyn, or that young she-cat Regan, both of whom know a great deal more of such subjects than they ought."

"I will be ready."

"Wear full armour, and bring your sword. You will have to do the fighting. I should, at my age, be useless, even did not my holy office forbid such bloodthirsty work. It is permitted to me as a churchman to say how, why, when and where people should be killed, but I must not do such carnal work with my own hands. Besides, I prefer scheming to fighting, like all abbots and bishops."

"But why risk the matter on a single arm like mine?"

"My good friend, I have mentioned it to several of the closest friends and most devoted admirers that the girl has. They refuse to believe it. These fools regard Guitolin as dead, and the conspiracy is secret, while there are many blood-ties among these folk of Dynevawr. No, there is no man to be trusted but yourself. Besides, time presses, and the lady has, expecting you to supper, given orders that she is not to be interrupted. Thus does love imperil our lives! Also, I had some notion that you would like the work yourself. I am sure the lady would prefer her liberation, or salvation, whichever it may be, to come from you. But all these, Artorius, are but childish reasons."

"To me, they do not indeed sound convincing."

"The real reason is the man who will do the murder: who is he?"

"Nobody. I will prevent it."

"Listen, Artorius: the plan is to defeat the Council of the Princes. If a certain person be present the Council is without authority. In the superstitious devotion of these Dynevawr people to ancient conventions and prohibitions, we dare not tell them the truth."

"You speak in riddles, Gildas. Let me speak plainly and briefly. If the life of this girl is threatened, I will defend her. If there is a fight in prospect I shall not shirk it. No matter how many are in the plot, I will kill them all. How many are there?"

"One that matters."

"Then I will kill him before morning."

"But we must bury him secretly, Artorius. If you will bring your sword, I will make shift with a spade."

After this we parted, agreeing that as soon as I left the girl, I should go straight to my own chamber and watch from the window, with the room darkened. I then went to supper. Gildas had some affair of his own in prospect, into which I did not inquire, for he would not have told me.

The chamber of Gwendaello to which I was taken was an upper hall of the castle, and lay beyond the court. It was tidier than I should have expected from the appearance of the yard, of which Gwendaello, judging from the look of her room, was no more enamoured than I was. The floor was of stone, but there were dyed sheepskins on it, and a cheerful blaze of logs upon the hearth; and ancient robes of embroidered stuff, brought hither by the Roman lords of the old time, and carefully preserved by these local princes, served as curtains, for this castle was most draughtily constructed.

I sat at supper alone with this girl, at a table well spread with glass vessels, of a pale blue tinged with green, such as I have in my house at Bath. I could see from the spreading of the table, and the attentions of the girl, that she desired to treat me with honour. Yet she would say nothing of the Council of the Princes or of the Beltane, and I asked no questions, thinking that this was a woman, and if I questioned her she would tell me lies, but if I left her to speak, then she would gossip freely and tell me all on which she thought deeply; yet in this I was disappointed. She talked all the time I was with her of trivial matters, and was very gay, saying she hoped that all my gear was correctly bestowed. "Indeed, Artorius, I with my servants went through all your property, but it seems that you soldiers carry some odd things about with you. What, for instance, did you do with that peasant woman's cloak of blue that was in your saddlebag?"

"Nay," I said, "I bought it at Uriconium, being attracted by the foolish thing, and brought it away with me, for I loved that city well, and it came into my mind that I should like to have the cloak."

"But," said she, "had you no maid in mind to whom you would give it?"

To this I would say nothing but that it was an idle fancy.

"But you are a great prince, Artorius, visiting a

sovereign who is not of your house. What gifts have you brought?"

Now here she was within her rights, for I had brought no gifts, so I was discountenanced, and said, "Indeed I am ashamed, but being troubled with many contrary things, it escaped me. Pray overlook my discourtesy."

"Artorius," said she, "as you must give me a present, and you have no worthy gift with you, I will accept the blue cloak."

"Why, it is but a peasant's garment of wool."

"No," said she, "but I think it would become me; blue goes well with my hair."

Now when she said this I asked for a servant to go to my chamber and bring the cloak, which I prayed her to accept, and she put it upon her and it looked marvellous well, as I had thought it would.

So presently, without knowing where my friends were, I sought to go back to my room.

"Artorius," said she, "I give you a pledge. Your friends shall come to no harm in my castle, and still less shall you. Yet for the Council of Princes I will give you a promise that neither will I come to any loss. So rest well to-night, easy in your mind upon both scores."

So I bade her good night, and when I left she was prinking about before a shield of silver, admiring herself in the blue cloak.

CHAPTER XIV

THE OUTER COURTS

NOW COMES A TALE OF PLOTS AND BLOWS,
WHILE WEAPONS GLEAM AND SPARK;
OF HUSHED ATTACKS ON SECRET FOES,
AND FIGHTING IN THE DARK.

When I parted from Gwendaello, I returned with speed to my own chamber. For some short space I maintained in full blaze the torches with which it was illuminated. I thought, as I most watchfully listened, that I could detect some slight sounds in the court below; yet, as I did not wish to seem suspicious, I could not venture to the window. I desired to create upon those below the impression that I was retiring to rest, and knew nothing, and cared less, about them, being entirely carefree and mayhap a little merry with liquor. I therefore moved freely about in full view of anybody that might be watching the apartment, singing, very badly, snatches of old songs; this seemed the best way of conveying to them a sense of my ignorance of their proceedings.

When I thought that I had played this deceptive game long enough, I dragged to the middle of the apartment the couch set for my use, and placing all my gear handy, extinguished the torches, making noises as of a man very sleepy and taking to his bed. I made these artificial yawns most resonant in order that the sound of them might travel to those below, and, before I put out the torches, I took care to stand, so that I could be seen from below, yawning with my hand in front of my face, and then sitting on the window-sill with my back to the outside, quavering a little in my song.

The torches out, I slipped into my corslet, and placing

my sword ready to my hand, crawled on all fours to the window. In few of the buildings of Dynevawr is there glass, and in the winter-time they try, very partially, to keep out the cold air by means of fine linen stretched upon frames and well greased. But in Brecknock now, as it was the last day of April, and the winter afar off, the windows were but embrasures, and had no glass or curtains. When crouching on the floor by the window and looking out, I held a dark cloth above my head and shielded my face all except the eyes.

It is strange how in all hiding-places a face stands out as a landmark. Something in the gleam of the flesh is, more than other things, noticeable in the dark. I suppose this is why these Cambrians smear themselves with charcoal. There is a story that the ancient people of these Islands, in going to war, dyed themselves with blue. This I should say was better in the British landscape than black, particularly at night, for all things at night are blue, or grey, like all cats. However, the woad was more in use to the east, in the country of the Iceni and the Trinobantes, and all the grounds in which it grew best are now in the hands of the Saxons, I fear permanently. I never heard that the soldiers of Caradoc used woad, and think that with them it was customary to use charcoal as we do now.

There in the window I crouched, with my eyes just above the sill, waiting for what might happen. I had faith in old Gildas. Never yet had that old man failed in wisdom or knowledge, though he had perhaps a somewhat strange manner of communicating his advice. For this his friends must make allowances if they desired to profit by his abilities. Yet for his manner there was some excuse. The man was old, and provided that I get from any man profitable wisdom I am prepared to forgive any difference in manner and outlook. So I watched at the window, in faith and expectation, though among the litter, and piled billets and brushwood in the court, I discerned no sign of the presence of my old friend, the Abbot.

I heard, however, another sound, a stealthy scrape

of heavy wood being cautiously dragged from a hiding-place, and the panting breath of men engaged in a laborious task. There was also a whispered word or two, in such low cadences that it was more like the sighing of the wind through fractures in the masonry than human speech. It was too indistinct for me to hear the words.

The opposite wall of the court contained, as I guessed, the window of Gwendaello. While I was conducted by the man Kai from my chamber to hers, I had counted and measured my footsteps, thus estimating the location of the rooms of the castle. Many years of soldiering have taught me the good general's habit of noting such things as angles of buildings and distances. I guessed, though I could not see in the dark, that a ladder was being raised; and not daring to wait over-long, I slipped through the window. The servants had brought all my horse furniture to my chamber when they had cleaned it, the same being gold-mounted and excessively valuable. With the straps I had made, after Gildas had left me, a rope long enough to reach from my window to the flooring of the court, a distance of some thirty or more feet. The two men opposite had their backs to me. It was some time before they could plant the ladder, for they had to move much wood and rubbish out of the way, and were absorbed in their occupation. I took advantage of their engrossment, and of the slight noises they made, and fixing my rope of harness to a staple, gently got through the embrasure and slipped down the rope nearly to the floor. The men, some forty feet from me, turned at the sound of my scraping against the wall, and saw me descending. I reached the ground speedily, letting the rope go, and dropping the last six feet or so; and then, drawing my sword, leaped at them. It was a poor half-light, the only gleam coming from the window of Gwendaello's chamber. What there was of it shone upon me, while my foes were dim shapes in the shadow, though I caught the flash of a seaxe in the hand of the taller. He must have seen the gleam of my corslet and the shine of my sword quite easily. Without a word he leaped back into the

darkness, and rushed for a narrow gateway closed by a
ramshackle gate or hurdle, for it was little else. I chased
him down the dark alley-way which led under the main
tower of the castle. The other, unluckily for himself, fell
over a log of wood. I struck at him as I passed, and felt
the yield of flesh and bone beneath my sword; he
remained still, lying where he had fallen, and emitting
moans as I followed his friend. This fleeing rascal, for
his part, ran lightly, too fast for me in my armour. He
wore, as far as I could observe, nothing beyond sandals
and a leathern shift; the attire of a slave. So we went, he
gaining, until we were clear of the castle, and were out
upon an exposed piece of ground that had been included
in the old British camp, and used by the Romans, but
had not been required by Brychain when he rebuilt his
castle. There were many remains of old walls, and a
tumble-down gateway at the end, a hundred yards
away, which I could just see in the starlight. I judged
that we were upon the old Prætorian Way.

Out here, away from the castle, we came into a short
stretch of waste ground, full of brambles and nettles,
the sort of place where, in the day-time, one can see
hens and poultry clucking about, and cottage children
playing, and cats asleep; but it was all silent now except
for the sound of our running and my own pantings, for
I was out of breath. The man was perhaps twenty feet in
front of me, and increasing his distance, as he made for
a copse of trees. If he once reached that I judged I
should lose him in the dark among so many hiding-
places. The brambles made the only path to the wood,
and along this he fled, with me after him.

To my delight, just as he reached the first trees, he
fell with a loud cry. I leaped upon him and came to the
earth with him. As I grasped him he struck at me with a
knife, and gashed my naked leg upon the thigh, just
where the loose plates of my corslet over-lap the kilt. I
dropped my sword in my hurry, for after striking the
other man down with it, I still held it in my hand as I ran.

We rolled together, and as we did so I felt for my
sword, to end the affair, and could not find it. It was a

tumbling scramble on the ground, and I had, moreover, to guard against his knife. As we struggled there amid the nettles, Gildas came out from behind the bushes and stood waiting. First I was on top and then my quarry, but I had felt the hilt of my sword with my outstretched left hand, while with the other I grasped my enemy's wrist. At this moment Gildas struck him on the head with the flat of his spade. The man's limbs relaxed, and I stood up, recovering my sword as I did so.

"Come, let us bind him before he comes to himself," said Gildas, taking from about his waist a hempen girdle. So we tied the man's hands.

"There is a cord around his neck. He seems to wear a heathen charm. Surely by that you may identify him?" suggested the Abbot.

The vagabond being securely bound in the Abbot's girdle, I pulled the charm from his breast where it lay beneath his shift. It was the Cornish chough.

"Know you the man, Artorius?" asked Gildas.

"I know him by this sign, Gildas."

"Then let us try him for his sins."

"There is no need for a trial. He dies within a minute."

"Who is he? He seems to be a Cornishman by the cutting of his hair." It was not cut away at the ears in the Cambrian fashion, but long and matted over the brow; nor was he shaved like a Cambrian, but heavily bearded, and his beard was tinged with grey.

"This is no true Cornishman, Gildas. He wears his hair thus for disguise. See the stitching of his sandals."

Gildas looked closely at the foot. "That is a Saxon shoe," said he.

"The other shoe, Abbot. That one has been repaired."

"You are right, Artorius. This man has been in a Saxon camp and in poverty. The sandals are old. This is a Brecknock sandal. I should know, for as a young man, in the monastery, I was in the shoemaker's workplace for a spell. I was in charge of it after, so great was my skill."

"Then we both know him now, Gildas."

"What did you do with the other one, Artorius?"

"I struck him down before we left the castle."

"We had better fetch the body. Kill this fellow first and then we can bury them both together." Thus decreed the Saint.

While we spoke thus, the man came to his sense. He heard us, and looked at us with fear, and opened his mouth to speak.

"Silence," said Gildas, lifting the spade again. Then he turned to me, and said, "Strike quickly, he has lived too long."

I saw that Gildas was right, and lifted my sword to strike. Gildas, however, commanded me to halt. "For," he said, "it would be wrong to slay the wretch thus, without giving his immortal soul a chance; God forgive me, that aspect of the matter had escaped me in this hurry."

"Do what you will, Gildas."

Said Gildas to the man: "My son, believest thou in Holy Church?"

Now the man spat at him for this most civil question most kindly put, and I, watching, saw that Gildas was grieved at this ingratitude, and at the man's indifference and hopeless lack of religion. I myself did not in the least understand the matter at issue, though, as Gildas seemed to think it of importance, I had yielded to him. I loved the old man and did not desire to cause him sorrow for my unbelief. However, when I saw that there was no community of thought between them, and that it was useless to prolong the scene, I lifted my sword again and smote the man upon the skull. It split his head open to the ears, for I struck hard.

"So he dies," said Gildas. "Now let us fetch the other."

This we did, and considered, as we examined him, that he was a man of the district, as I should judge, some henchman of Guitolin of former days. He was alive when we came to him, but lying on the ground and very feeble. His right arm was nearly severed where I had struck him, and he had almost bled to death, and was very faint. Yet he told us, what we knew, that this was Guitolin whom we had slain, and that he had come from the Saxons in treason again to Britain. Then, after telling us this, the man died.

The chough I took from Guitolin's neck. If it were found near the body by some person afterward digging in the ground, the news would have been abroad at once that it was a king who had been thus slain in his own territories, without postliminium, and therefore the table of descent would have been in confusion. Very probably also there would have been war between the tribes in consequence. I therefore threw the chough into the river beside the castle, where doubtless, though of black stone, it speedily became smooth and unrecognizable by the rolling of the gravel in the floods.

Gildas dug a deep enough grave, I helping him, for he was an old man, and we buried the two bodies.

"Now it is useless," he said, "to debate this matter further. We know that this man was Guitolin, and there was a plot between him and his Saxon captors. The man had forfeited his throne, and they, relying on their treaty with him, gave him liberty to achieve this murder. The Saxons, Artorius, fear you greatly, but, intent on conquest, they fear the unity of Britain more. Therefore, hearing of this council, they strove to disturb the significance of the meeting."

"No Saxon could conceive so deep a plot, Gildas."

"Yet, if it were explained to them by Guitolin, a very cunning man although a fool, the matter becomes understandable. He sought by murder to get both his throne and his liberty."

I told him that he seemed to have the rights of the matter, and that we, having done a night's work, had better return to the castle. To this he agreed.

"However," said he, "let me first return this spade to the shed from which I borrowed it." This he did, after cleaning it with a handful of grass, talking as he did so of the earliest lesson he had received in his monastery, where, as he said, they cultivated the gardens with very great diligence, and a man who put away a dirty spade was flogged. This was a sound lesson, for a dirty spade makes useless toil.

When we returned to the castle, Gildas said he would sleep in my room because of the lateness of the hour, and because to reach his own chamber he would need to pass through a guard-room where there were irreverent young fellows sitting up all night, drinking and being merry, who would call to him with ribald comments on his midnight adventures. This amusement he was in no way inclined to give them.

In my chamber, to which we ascended by the ladder left behind by the two conspirators, and then threw it down, I asked Gildas for a full account of his doings.

"Nay," he said, "I did nothing beyond guiding foreseen events, forecasting what was likely to happen, and making dispositions accordingly."

"Yes," I said, "but your plan nearly miscarried, for the man ran faster than I did, and had he not fallen I should have failed to overtake him."

"Now that," said Gildas in reply, "is where I do indeed take pride, if I as a humble son of the Church may do so. For forecasting in my mind that the chase would take the road it did, I had tied a cord between the trees, ankle-high above the ground, and I waited there with my spade to complete the event. See therefore, my son, a tale in which there is a lesson for thee. Let us, instead of trusting to fortune, fortify ourselves with good works. The rewards, both here and elsewhere, are to the careful and the industrious, and they who assist the decrees of heaven by bending their own shoulders in effort become truly blessed. The man fell because, in accordance with Holy Writ, I laid a snare for him which was not in the sight of the quarry."

"That," I said with warm praise, "was well done indeed." Yet, although I praised him thus, I thought that so old a man and so fierce, had a strange way of describing his acts, which were, in spite of his mildness and virtue, singularly efficient.

We sat there talking in my chamber for some little time, for my leg, where I had been cut with the knife, was sore and pained me, and was also bleeding. This Gildas noted, and seeing it, he knelt before me to dress it. While he was doing so, and with some skill, there came a knock at the door. On this I stood up, and going to the door threw it open.

"Surely I may enter," said Gwendaello. "And now tell me of these doings: guests in my house asking neither with your leave nor by your leave, abandoning their chambers by ladders in the middle of the night, and slaying men with swords in my curtilage, and old men leaving their most comfortable beds that they may take part in these random excesses."

So I asked how, as we had been so secret, she came to inquire.

She looked at me very straight, and said:

"It came this way. After you had parted from me I sat at my window, for I desired to look at your chamber, hoping that you as my guest were in comfort and sleeping well. Thus I saw what took place in the court. But before you tell me about these trifles I desire to see that wound of yours."

"Nay," I told her, "it is but a mere bramble-scratch or a gravel-rash."

"Truly a gravel-rash acquired by the small boy-child who plays in rough games without permission," said she, wondrously soft. "Yet it bleeds, and I, seeing you as you returned, perceived that you limped, and knew thus that you were injured. Therefore I brought with me the remedies taught me by the wisdom of my ancestors. Yet first we must soothe it. As yet it is a month short of mid-summer, yet the hypericum has virtue and so the red oil will soothe, and having thus calmed your pains," said she, bathing the cut with the oil of the hypericum, a wondrous liquid made from the common yellow flowers of the hedgerow, "we will stop the bleeding with the styptic."

"Alum, I say," was the rejoinder of that rival surgeon, Gildas. "I have it here."

"Nay," she said, holding up a small vase. "Here I have oil of nettles which is better than alum. "Saying this she bathed the wound with the liquor and the bleeding ceased. She bound it up most tenderly, and Gildas highly approved her skill.

"It is nothing," said she. "The people of my race have always been in battle, and we women, their sisters, have learnt by ancient wisdom to heal their wounds. Now, tell me, Artorius, does it feel more easy?"

I was most grateful to the lady for her gentleness; and after this we sat a while talking and telling tales that we knew. I had some stories of the older days of Rome, when I fought in the Cæsar's armies, and rose to be legatus. Gildas told most marvellous tales of saints and of early days in his monastery when he was but a young boy in a convent in the country by the rivers of Eastern Gaul. He told also of the evil workings of witch-craft and of devils, and of the good that comes from a pure heart, with the which, though I know but little of his religion, I heartily agree; and so the time passed. And then after this, we said that we had talked too much and had been awaiting a tale from her. Thus sitting round the fire of logs in my chamber, it would be a great pleasure to us; but she, saying that she knew no tales like ours, who had the one fought and the other preached, as you might say, half across the world, would tell us a fairy tale suited for the eve of May Day. So we sat to listen.

"Now, once upon a time, there was a man who lived in a little narrow valley, and his name was something that I have forgotten, so let us call him anything that we like; the name Uffa will do as well as anything else."

At this I interrupted, thinking of all old things, as I do when anybody tells a story of this kind, and trying to get thoughts of real people out of it. "Why," I told her, "Uffa was the name of my father's grandfather."

"Was it indeed?" said she. "Now I ask whether I am to tell a tale, or whether you, having already talked much to-night, desire to tell me of your father's grandfather?"

At this I begged her pardon, and she, looking most severe and yet wanting to laugh, resumed her tale.

"Well now, this Uffa, who was a much younger man

than your father's grandfather can possibly have been, felt a longing to get away from the little narrow valley, and every day, when he got up from his bed, he went to the door and saw the sun shining over the mountains and wondered what there was on the other side of them, and yet he knew quite well what was there, for he had crossed those hills many a time when he went to market; yet he liked to think that there were other hills beyond those yet again, and other valleys, and great plains and so on to the end of the world, and things that he had never seen, as indeed there were.

"Now one night, when it was hot, and he could not sleep because of the heat, and because he was unsatisfied in his mind, he arose and went to the door, and looked at the night, for it was quite dark; and in front of the house, where the river had every spring overflowed, was the marsh that spread to the hills opposite, and that they called the Morfa Helen."

"Yes," I said, "there was in front of our house a Morfa Helen as you say."

"Now before I proceed," said the lady, "I pray that I may have no more about your father's grandfather. The tale is not about either you or him. It is about a certain Uffa. You are as ill-mannered as a kern listening to a travelling bard.

"Well, as I said, Uffa stood awhile by the Morfa, and he saw a movement upon it, and as he watched, the thing that moved came nearer until it came right up to his feet; and he stretched out his hand to it, for it was a most beautiful maiden, and as it says in the poem that you doubtless remember quite well:

> Her eyes were like two mountain lakes
>   Beneath a sky of blue,
> When at the dusk the twilight takes
>   Its softest, darkest hue.
> Her cheek was like the meadowsweet,
>   Tinged with a dog-rose blush;
> Her lips like poppies in the wheat
>   Or scarlet campion's flush.

Her hair fell drooping gently,
As the yellow catkins look,
From the branches of the alder
On the margin of the brook.

But, as Uffa reached out his hand to the maiden, she moved a little away, and as he reached still farther, she did not seem to move at all, but he could not touch her. So he stood and admired.

"Then she said 'Uffa.'

"And as she said 'Uffa' it seemed that she was calling him to great deeds and to far countries beyond the mountains, and he saw empires rising and crowns and kingdoms falling and himself on a great and high throne, and all the peoples of the earth bowing at his feet.

"So she said again 'Uffa.'

"And then Uffa saw himself admired and worshipped by all the peoples of the world, and he had a great army which obeyed him and won all battles, and wherever Uffa went he won victories, and after the victories he made peace; and there was in the world nothing but peace, and all the farms had good crops, and there was no more poverty or cruelty, or bad men or bad women, but all the people of the world lived in amity and happiness because of the wise laws of Uffa.

"So Uffa stood a while, and for a moment he did not see the maiden, but seemed to see a misty land beyond the mountains, and then he closed his eyes, for his heart was very full, and then he looked at the maiden again, and again she said 'Uffa.'

"Now when Uffa heard this the third time he saw the world after he was dead, and there was a great temple with marble porticoes and columns, and groves of cypress leading to it, and it stood on the edge of the great sea, where flowers bloomed down to the water's edge; and all the ships of the world came to visit it, and there was a great winding road leading to the temple, and crowds passing up continually, going to the temple where they worshipped Uffa, after he was dead, as a god, though he had been dead for more than a thousand years. And when the crowds mentioned the name of Uffa, some called him a great warrior, and some a great legislator, and all said he was the greatest and best man that had ever lived.

"Then Uffa woke up again, and asked the maiden what was her name, and she said her name was Morgan, and she would guide him to the land beyond the mountains which she had shown him in a vision, so she turned about and departed, and Uffa followed her.

"But after they had crossed the Morfa, for the maiden was always in front, Uffa found himself upon the mountain-side, and the maiden had disappeared. But he was ashamed to go back, and climbed up the mountain and went through wild passes and travelled into far countries, and did many marvellous things, and yet was never satisfied and never got what he desired; but he was happy enough for a time, because all he had to do he did well. And sometimes, and indeed more often than not, other men claimed and got the credit for what he had done; and Uffa did not care greatly when this happened, for there was always something else for him to do, and he said that if the work was finished, it did not matter who did it, provided he was at liberty to proceed at once to the next achievement.

"But Uffa sometimes felt angry, when he had asked to be allowed to serve people, both great and little people, and they had said they would rely on the efforts of others, and the others failed, and all the time Uffa had really known what required to be done, and the people had not been guided by him.

"And once, when he was feeling like this, he was on the edge of a dull and watery plain, and again he saw Morgan, whom he had not seen for many years, and he cursed her in his heart. 'For,' he said, 'I am now past my youth, and am weary and often sad, and not valued at my true worth; and if it had not been for you, I should still have been in the little narrow valley, making horseshoes, and growing corn in a small field, and quite content, as my fathers were before me.'

"And again Morgan said 'Uffa.'"

"And when she said this her voice was the sweetest thing that he had ever heard. It seemed as if all the music of the universe was gathered into that one word. 'But,' he said, 'I have no time to listen to that talk of yours any longer. There are roads to be made and a war to be fought, and best of all,' said he, 'the marshes to be drained so that you will no longer be able to lead men away from their happiness.'

"But she said again 'Uffa,' and he turned and followed her again.

"And this time she led him through many troubles, and through wild mountains, where there were robbers and many dangers. And he was in peril of his life, and he saw friends of his suffer loss, and many kingdoms destroyed, and evils triumph, and all the time everything that he did was unsuccessful in a way; and people said that nobody else could have achieved so much, 'for he has been most earnest and painstaking indeed, but the day of great men is over, and Uffa is as good as we can expect to-day, but is not as good as we ought to have.' And Uffa was very bitter in his heart, because he knew that if what he had said before had been done, these troubles would not have happened.

"Now, one day Uffa was looking out of his tent, because for many years he had had no house, and he was journeying everywhere and being told nothing but lies, and was feeling very weary. He looked out of his tent, and the maiden appeared again, and though for all these years Uffa had hated her, and thought that she was outworn and ugly, yet when she came this time she looked as she had seemed that day when he first saw her. And again she said 'Uffa.'

"And when she said 'Uffa,' he thought of mountain lakes and meadowsweet, and dog-roses and campions in the hedge, and the catkins on the alders in the little narrow valley.

"And again she said 'Uffa.'

"And when she said this, he dreamed again, and he saw himself as a young man singing to the sound of the anvil as he made horseshoes, and sowing corn in the little field, and laughing as the birds quarrelled over the seed.

"Again she beckoned to him as she had done before, and said no word, but instead turned away, and Uffa followed her without a word either, and he found himself back in the narrow valley as a very old man, and he was talking to a child.

"And the tales that he told to the child were about many great lands overseas, and about the wars that he had been in, and the emperors and kings that he had spoken with, and the great cities and temples and palaces that he had visited. And when he told all these tales he got quite excited, for an old man, in the telling of them, and the child's eyes grew very large and round at the magnificence of the things of which he was told. And having told all these true tales Uffa began to feel hungry, so he said to the child:

"'Ask your mother if supper is ready yet.'"

CHAPTER XV

THE COUNCIL OF PRINCES

THE PRINCES ROUND THE COUNCIL BOARD,
WITH MUCH TO LOSE OR WIN,
HAVE NO MORE WISDOM THAN THE HORDE
WHO GATHER AT AN INN.

I had been curious to see whether the Council would be held according to the rites and customs which had always directed gatherings of this kind even during the Roman overlordship. The Romans, indeed, had governed largely by respecting and using the old ordinances and laws of the Britons, at all events where they found them useful. It was a saying of the wise Agricola that if you respect people's prejudices with sympathy they will allow you to rob them, and this was Roman rule in a nutshell. Even while the divine Emperor ruled in the island, he would from time to time convene meetings of princes to register his decrees, just as he submitted them to the Senate in Rome itself. In neither case have I ever heard that his wishes failed to receive the assent which he had a right to anticipate. I therefore expected the conference to be held on the ancient plan, for she who seemed to be directing the ceremonies had shown her attachment to ancient custom on every occasion, and in this I guessed rightly. To hold it on the feast of Beltane was another compliance with the ancient rule. The old procedure was as follows:

First a private meeting would be held, at which the princes, meeting as it were unofficially, made their decision. Each would be attended by his bards and secretaries, and the rights and wrongs at issue would be examined at great length. A disagreement might cause angry scenes, and weapons even might be drawn and some of the gathering killed, but in any case, a conclusion was reached. It was then correct for all to present themselves before the people, as if the agreement were acceptable to all; it was not good manners to show public heat or anger. In fact very few agreements were acceptable, and not seldom princes would assemble their followers and depart for their own territories, saying that the proceedings were not in accordance with their wish, or with what was right or fair, and that it was useless to remain. For this reason it had been agreed by all of us to hold this council at Brecknock.

After the private meeting, at which some of the bitterest feelings would be worked off, came the Council proper, at which everything, having been previously arranged, would be only very briefly discussed; though even with this precaution sometimes untoward events occurred, as when a speaker in the heat of his eloquence forgot what he had agreed to say, and then introduced fresh subjects of discord. Thus a council might take many weeks, and in the end accomplish nothing; so many speeches would be made, everybody saying what he had said already many times over, and contradicting his neighbours with acrimony. At the present Council there was no reason why this should happen. First, we had decided that the comot of Talgarth should be taken from Dynevawr and incorporated in Powys. It is a fine valley, on which Cadell had had his eyes for many years; it was his price as part of the bargain. Next, Maelgwyn was to be overlord of Dynevawr, to command its armies in the field when he needed their assistance, and to have the right of coining all the money in use in that province. Dynevawr was to pay to Locris full damages for the sack of Gloucester, and most of the smaller Princes of Dynevawr were to cease to be sovereigns and semi-independents, and become mere Arglwyddi, or lords. This was the part of the scheme that I liked best, apart from the repayment of our losses at Gloucester, which was only fair.

There were three votes which would be given against these proposals. First, the vote of the overlord of Dynevawr, which we could count as certain. Then Hwyl of Morgannwg would of a surety cast his lot with Dynevawr, for these States were old allies. The third was Rhys, the Prince of Dyfed, for at the last moment his claim to be present was allowed. His rights were indeed supported without question by all the bardic genealogies, as a sovereign Prince and a descendant of the great ruler Pwyll, son of the Queen of the Fairies, whose name was Rhiannon, and who could make a bird sing whenever she commanded it. It would have lowered the dignity of the whole assembly had not Rhys been there. Now Rhys was greatly enamoured of Gwendaello of the Creuddyn, but she would have nothing to say to him: at first, as she told me, because he had refused to join with Guitolin in the bargain with the Saxon, and afterwards for another quite good and sufficient reason; but what this was she would not say, nor could I guess, though I desired greatly to know what politics lay at the root of her objection.

Against these three there were six votes: Reged and Strathclyde, which I held as plenipotentiary; Aurelian of Locris; Constantine of Damnonia; Maelgwyn of Gywnnedd, and Cadell of Powys.

Consequently, however much everybody talked, the conclusion appeared certain. We assembled in the large hall of the castle at an early hour. I was unattended, but Aurelian had with him his Chancellor and two scribes, neither of them men of whom I thought very highly, as they, being officials, always did most unintelligently exactly what they were commanded, with the result of many mistakes which might have been avoided. Then there was Cadell, looking as much as ever like a skinny red and white heifer, who greeted me most cordially, and took me on one side to recount a supper-room jest at great length, relating to a lady residing at Corinth whose name I have forgotten; but if the story was true, it would have been right to tell her husband of her misdeeds. Justin of Elmet had not come. He was ever of an indolent disposition, and as he had not been expected he was not missed. Constantine of Damnonia was there, looking at me and at Aurelian rather shrewdly. I whispered to Aurelian that he would prove treacherous unless concessions were made about his tribute, but Aurelian said that he would not abate a denarius, as the man would go on making claims until he had paid nothing at all. This was indeed not unlikely, nor inaptly applied to any Damnonian. Then there was Maelgwyn, who, of course, had brought with him his Chancellor Merddin and his secretary, as he claimed, who turned out to be that young and deceptive she-cat Regan. At the very onset there was a passage of arms between the two young women, Gwendaello saying with a sniff that she would have thought it beneath the dignity of a Princess of Pennal, as Regan was, to travel about with a man of Maelgwyn's character, who, as everybody knew, respected the virtue of no woman.

"Why," said Gwendaello, "all will assume that you are his concubine, and will probably think correctly."

To this Regan was tart in her reply. "I have not as yet," she said, "journeyed alone in a forest with any man as you did, and it ill becomes the cat who has lost its tail to abuse one who has not."

Maelgwyn commanded her to step back and refrain from speech, which Regan did, putting out her tongue at Gwendaello as she did so, to which the other replied by shrugging her shoulders and turning away her head, as if to say that this was a vulgar slut indeed. Then a thought striking her, she called across the room:

"And if you, Regan, had had my chances you would have rejoiced, as you did at Deganwy."

But Regan shouted back, "I will give you an englyn.

"When Gwen has taken a bite out of an apple,
the apple is glad that she does not get the chance
of a second, but Regan would not bite an apple
that had been gnawed by Gwen."

This as an englyn made me laugh, although it was incorrect in literary form; and Gwendaello replied that all apples, to Regan, were cider apples and useless till they had turned bad. Maelgwyn, to change the subject, asked me where I had been the night before, as they had had an agreeable banquet. From this I gathered that no threats had been made to them, and indeed thought that the trick played upon me was an attempt to seduce me from my allegiance to our plan; for I remembered well the hint given me by Regan, at Deganwy, about men who sold their kingdoms for the sake of a woman. Now as I had made up my mind that nothing of that sort should be urged against me, I thought the Lady of the Creuddyn foolish and childish in expecting it. I noted this Gwendaello, and to my surprise saw that she was wearing the blue cloak that I had bought her, and indeed it became her well. To her came Regan saying:

"Let us not be bitter to each other; I came to see your cloak. In the poverty of Dynevawr it is indeed appropriate that its sovereign should wear the cloak of a peasant. Why, I have seen cloaks like it at the market stalls. The price is low at the best. But I pray that it had not the moth in it when you bought it, for I see that it has been put away, and is sadly creased."

"The cloak is well enough. Being the cloak which the women of my country wear, it is not too vile for me. Yet, Regan, with your black complexion, you could not wear a blue cloak. It requires some presence, and a figure, to become one well. The shape and tint are trying."

At this they parted, using affectionate terms one to the other, Gwendaello thanking Regan most sweetly for her truth-telling about the cloak; but as for myself, I felt sore that a cloak which I had given should thus be discussed, and thought little of Regan for what she had said. It is true I had a grudge against her for her cozening of me upon the Orme.

Now before we began our conference, there was a dispute who should hold the principal place in the chair at the end of the table. It was Regan who raised the question, for the supernumeraries had the right to speak, but not to vote. They were Regan, Merddin, although up to now he had not spoken, and one or two others, such as the officials of Aurelian, who, I may say, were better behaved than some others I could mention, although by nature inclined to stupidity. One of them, a man called Abbius, was already seated, industriously making notes of all that was said, which seemed to me most unwise, and I made him clean all the writing off his tablets. That is the worst of all the meetings of these Britons, of whom indeed I am one, but more prudent and less talkative than most, because of my Roman upbringing; they always say too much. As for the scribe, a pure Roman, he was as bad in another way, being too fond of recording trifles which could only make trouble in the future unless promptly forgotten; though the rude things those two women had said to each other would, I am quite sure, be remembered by them for a hundred years, if they lived so long.

This Regan, then, at once said, "It is indeed true that Maelgwyn, as the most powerful sovereign of Britain who is of pure blood (for that Aurelian is not, being but Cæsar), has the right to sit in the great chair. There can be no question raised over this."

So said Gwendaello in reply, "And who are you, I pray, to lay down the law in this castle of Brecknock? I am Lord here, and Lord also by right, of all Britain."

Now Cadell was in some degree jealous of Maelgwyn, and was a natural-born intriguer. He would take all, whether he wanted it or not, in the way of privilege, lest if he did not, an unwelcome precedent might be established. As he said to me, "If anything seems unimportant, and yet is claimed by another, you should dispute the claim lest you lose in the future. If you do not understand the value of a thing you are a fool to give it away." Now Cadell had no jealousy of Aurelian, so he said that in his view Aurelian should be the chief, and added several fine things about his services to the island. Aurelian rejoined that he did not desire any dispute, but that he would sit where he was most likely to be of service. At this there were many voices, and Gwendaello most shrilly said that she was Pendragon, and by ancient constitutional usage was the chief of all those present; and that if that were not acknowledged by all, then there would be no conference in her castle, for she would not brook any derogation of her rights. When the girl Regan began to dispute this, Gwendaello said that if her supremacy were denied by any lesser person than a contracting prince, whose person as ambassador she must respect, she would immediately send that person to the lower chambers to be whipped as guilty of treason.

At which Regan was most indignant and yet afraid as well. "Sit in the big chair for all I care. Yet you will look ugly there as you would anywhere else, you red-haired heifer, like a cow of Salop." Now upon this Maelgwyn asked me what in my view was the proper course. "For," he said, "you are a man of judgment and discretion." At this Gwendaello said to me in a most heated manner, "Don't you dare to say to this man what is against my wishes. If I cannot sit in the chair of my ancestors I will sit nowhere." So answered she, but Maelgwyn, not in any way disconcerted, said, "If I had the keeping of you, young woman, you would not desire to sit down at all." But nobody paid any attention to what he said, except that Regan whispered, in a tone loud enough for all to hear, that with this she agreed, and that it was so far the best thing that had been said in the debate.

It was some vexation to me that this great Council, called to decide matters of vital import to the State, should be thus led astray into side paths and matters of trifling moment; but it is always so when women get together, whether they are originally in agreement or not. If only the occasion is great enough they will be sure to fall out. I think they get worked up to excitement by its importance, and then their heat of mind takes the form of savagery one against the other. It is to me a strange weakness, and for that reason I have always been in favour of keeping women as far as possible out of public affairs. One woman might be tolerable, but two spell contention. Therefore when I was appealed to by Maelgwyn, I decided that in order to produce peace and stop all disputing, it was right that Gwendaello should preside. "For," I told them, "this is her castle, and inasmuch as no one here disputes her title to be Pendragon, and as this gathering is held under the ancient customary laws of Britain, upon a date formerly the most sacred in the whole year, that of Beltane, upon which the Pendragon must officiate as chief even if he were totally disregarded on all other occasions (as not seldom happened in the past), it seems beyond question that Gwendaello must sit in the big chair. I ask her to take the place she claims."

The others agreed, and Merddin, speaking for the first time, declared that what I had said was correct bardic law. Gwendaello with some amount of indifference, very well assumed, took her place and gave the remainder of us permission to seat ourselves; for which Regan did not in the least thank her, having made a jump for a chair in order to be seated before she was bidden. Girls are fond of these little independences. However, she was too late, for she received permission actually in point of time before she obtained a chair for herself.

I confess that Gwendaello opened the proceedings with dignity and sense. Having commanded our attention, she said as follows:

"We, fellow Princes of the Island of the Mighty, are met here to take such measures as we can best imagine for the protection of our land, for the maintenance of our supremacy over our foreign and barbarian foes, and for the establishment of such governance and military defences as may be best contrived to secure that object. Now it becomes me, as chief of you all, to command of you your speech, that is, from any of you that have anything of value to deliver yourselves of. I shall listen with due patience to you all in any case, but pray you to be brief."

At this, Constantine was the first to open his mouth. "Provided," he said, "that the measures to be taken do not involve other than a just equality in the bearing of the burden of the cost, that is a correct statement. Now in the matter of the tribute paid to Aurelian—"

"That," said the Pendragon, "is a matter of detail and could be best dealt with at a later hour in our Council."

"As for me," I said, "I do not appear here as a prince myself, but as the envoy of the two Lords of Reged and Strathclyde. There is little purpose in threshing brambles. Everybody here knows what is to be suggested and who is the proposer of it. Let Maelgwyn therefore say what he has in his mind."

With this Maelgwyn said what he had told me, that he desired to be overlord of Dynevawr and to have the right of coining their money, and calling up their troops for war, but otherwise they could govern themselves as they liked.

"Now," said Cadell, "I have little concern with the claims or desires of my friend Maelgwyn, though they seem to me, as an impartial person, not devoid of merit. All that I desire is a declaration that the comot of Talgarth shall be included in the boundaries of Powys. It was in ancient times reckoned as part of Wenwynwyn, which is a part of Powys. That which I ask is but justice, and as far as I am concerned, something less. I might have demanded the comot of Trahaiarn as well."

Aurelian had been sitting with his eyes half closed, taking little note of what was said, but now he spoke. He said that the needs of the island demanded unification, and that provided the independent Princes of Dynevawr paid for the losses inflicted on Gloucester, and ceased to exercise sovereign rights at all, that was, he thought, a moderate settlement of the matters about which he guessed there would be some debate.

The young woman Regan, as the issue was so clearly defined and all ready for the voting, said, putting her spoon into the stew without invitation: "Now I think that all that has been said is most excellent. It would rejoice me to hear that the Lord Artorius on behalf of his two kingdoms at the Wall also agrees."

Now this was ill judged, because a long debate ensued as to whether I was to speak as one man for two kingdoms, or was to have a vote for each. Constantine held that I was to have one vote only, because he claimed that no man could have two votes unless he spoke with the wisdom of two men, and so far I had given no indication of being able to do so. Maelgwyn somewhat angrily remarked that if I were considered by two kingdoms to be wise, then clearly I was as wise as two men such as Constantine, who only represented a mere feudatory province. Then said Constantine:

"Whether I am compelled by tyranny to pay a tribute to Aurelian or not, has no bearing on the rights of the question. What is more to the purpose is that Isca and Teyngrace are two of the thirty-three cities of Britain, and I have yet to discover that Deganwy is more than a collection of wooden shielings. Moreover it was at Totnes, in my duchy, that the foundation of this realm of Britain took place."

Aurelian was looking extremely wearied at this most unprofitable debate, and indeed I had some doubts in my mind, whether Maelgwyn was quite wise in thus belittling Constantine. Maelgwyn, of all the Princes, was most anxious for the decision we had agreed upon, and had the most to gain from it; and yet here he was taunting Constantine, who at best was but an untrustworthy supporter. I shook my head at him as if to suggest silence on his part, but Maelgwyn affected not to understand me. Aurelian, too, was tactless, being irritated by Constantine's reference to the tribute, for he said:

"It is no more true that Britain was founded at Totnes than it is true that Rome was founded at Alba Longa. Just so much and no more, for just as a gang of Trojan pirates under Æneas founded Alba, so a thieving gang of similar race seem to have established themselves in Totnes. We have done with all those old stories now. We have to face the Pict and the Saxon."

Now this put the crown on the discussion. Gwendaello, whose only religion, as far as I could estimate it, was a profound belief in the sanctity and ancient descent of the House of Cornwall, was infuriated at this reference by Aurelian. She despised him, at the best, as not a Briton at all but a mere Roman; and reddened in cheeks, and shrill in voice, she now intervened in the debate.

"It is ill doing," she said, "at a time when the loyalty and service of all men are called to the deliverance of the island from its foul enemies, to cast scorn on that which stimulates best our pride in our home. I rule therefore that Aurelian is at fault. As for the voice of Artorius, it is my duty as President of this assembly to rule on that matter also. My ruling is that Artorius shall have but one vote."

Now at this there was some disputing, but Gwendaello having recorded her decision, refused to abate it, and the voice of protest continuing, she turned herself around, and sat with her back to the rest of us till the clamour had subsided. I could not but admire her firmness in her office as well as her readiness to take advantage of all side-winds in her own favour, and was reminded secretly of the adage that red hair and respect for other people's wishes are never found under the same fillet.

Now there was nothing more to be done but vote. For a time we sat quietly conferring among ourselves, and, when there was complete silence, Gwendaello again turned to the table, and said as follows: "This Council has assembled under the pretext of organizing the defences of the Island of the Mighty. It seems, from what has been proposed at this board, that its real object was to deprive the region of Dynevawr of its ancient and unquestioned rights of independence. Therefore I call upon you, assembled here, to decide whether this wrong shall be done."

"I," said Maelgwyn, smiling as at the obtuseness of the question, "I vote in favour of my own proposition."

"I," said Aurelian, "vote as Maelgwyn votes, for the unification of the island."

"As for me," said Cadell, looking more like a red heifer than ever, "I support Maelgwyn, provided that I obtain the comot of Talgarth."

"And that is really all you care about," interjected Gwendaello scornfully. "And what do you say, Artorius?"

"As for me," I said, not liking the business much, but realizing that it was for the best in the end and was inevitable in any case; "I also, for Reged and Strathclyde, vote in aid of Maelgwyn."

"Now here," came the harsh voice of Constantine, "is where I differ from my eminent friends. When I consider how my duchy of Damnonia has for many years been mulcted of an unfair tribute, I will be no party to the oppression of the ancient State of Dynevawr. I oppose Maelgwyn."

"I knew it was coming," I whispered to Aurelian; "this was but to be expected," and he rejoined that he also had thought that Constantine would prove false.

"But it does not matter greatly. After all, he may protest against the tribute, but he will have to pay it, and for those nasty remarks, I shall have an excuse for insisting on the payment of the arrears."

"That is all very well," I said. "But you are going to get a surprise."

The old man Merddin was sitting opposite me. I saw him shrug his shoulders with an air of disgust. Then his face became a mask once more.

"I," said Rhys of Dyfed, "vote in defence of my kin of South Cambria. There shall be no rifling of the realm of the Pendragon with my leave."

"And so say I," came from Hwyl of Morgannwg.

"And as for me, as a Princess present at this gathering, and more concerned than any, I, for my part, naturally give my voice against the theft of my prerogatives," said Gwendaello.

"Ten thousand dragons," interjected Maelgwyn. "That is four and four. And I thought it was a sure thing. She's dished you, Artorius."

At this I was most indignant, though I kept my voice within compass. "It was no scheme of mine, Maelgwyn, and you can never say that I failed either in my pledge to you, or in my duty to the State, however unwelcome."

"True enough, old friend," said he good-naturedly. "But, blast the women every time. It's young Regan here who's to blame, just as much as you, you young puss-cat," he added, turning to Gwendaello.

"A thousand mercies for my further speech," said she. "But the vote being four and four, nothing is yet decided. As president of this gathering of the Princes, I have a deciding vote. This matter stands equal at present. I therefore give my final voice that the proposal of Maelgwyn has not our approval. I direct the scribes properly to record this decision. Hear you that, Merddin?"

"This is an unofficial meeting," said he sulkily. "The real meeting is at the Beltane table of turf."

"No, no, that will not do," said Maelgwyn with decision. "It would only be the same thing over again. We must draw up proper plans for our defences, as Artorius has for years been telling us. We must abandon the attempt at coercion of the free State of Dynevawr. I always feel a sort of glow in my breast when I oblige a lady in a business matter. It is no disgrace to be out-manœuvered by them."

With that, which met with general approval, we sat to a late hour discussing the interplay and mutual reinforcement of the provinces, and I think the work went smoothly. For my part I was indeed glad that my Lady of Dynevawr had come out safely from the plot against her with such credit. Yet she owed much to the treachery of Constantine, and I often wondered by what means she had bought him. For Constantine was a man who in any one's real need would require a heavy price. What he said about the tribute was a mere colourable pretext, for, as I have told, he had been by me excused the greater portion of it. I suppose I was not as generous in my remission as Gwendaello had been with her payments in hard coin of the Empire.

Now it may be thought that Maelgwyn surrendered to the defeat of the Council more readily than from a man of his character was to be expected. I had, however, before the debate privately told him and the others separately what had happened the night before, and how this girl was now sole and undisputed ruler, supreme in her office. I told Cadell that Powys was surging with devotion to this Lady of Dynevawr, while to Aurelian I suggested that there was little advantage in forcing an unfair bargain merely for the advancement of a subordinate of his own like Maelgwyn. In the end Maelgwyn, deciding that his raids on Ireland would be fostered better by a friendly use of the ports of Penvro, and that the people of Dynevawr being little accustomed to work would be useless as slaves, thought that the balance of advantage lay in the solution to which we had come. All alike were rejoiced that Guitolin was dead.

CHAPTER XVI

BELTANE

OLD MEMORIES OF A PURPLE SKY,
A TURF-CLAD SEAT OF EARTH;
OF FESTAL BONFIRES FLAMING HIGH,
AND GAY AND SIMPLE MIRTH.

In the afternoon of this day, as I sat in my chamber, waiting till I should be called by the Fetial to take my place in the procession that was to conduct the Princes of the island to the Gorsedd, there came a summons at my door, and the old man Merddin, on being given permission, entered. He closed the door, and dismissed the slave who had accompanied him. Then he approached me in a secret manner, till he was quite close, and spoke in a whisper, lest he should be overheard.

"Walls have ears, Artorius, and I speak of a matter too high for the vulgar."

"Speak on, Merddin. I shall respect your secrecy."

"Then speak low, Artorius. This is between you and me alone. None other knows it."

"Then there is the less reason to discuss it."

"Truly. Yet I would know what is in your mind, Artorius. I am chief of the bards of Britain, and though there are many things that we as wise men may say, and indeed I know, are but ancient superstitions, yet they are of import."

"All matters of ancient superstition are of import, Merddin, when many believe them."

"True. And vast issues hang upon them."

"That is also true," I answered. "If the bulk of men believe a thing it is so, Merddin. The belief produces the effect."

"Where learned you that wisdom, Artorius?"

"From my father, Merddin."

"Aye, from thy father Eutherius, the son of Brothen."

"Brothen was my grandfather as you say, Merddin."

"And in view of this you say that the girl Gwendaello is yet Pendragon?"

"Who is to prevent my saying so, Merddin?"

"None, Artorius. Will you yourself at any time dispute her claim?"

"Not I. Why should I? The world goes on. Those who have, let them keep. I am a Roman. I say that the order of the State is the first consideration."

"I know all, Artorius, as chief of the bards of Mona, with the secret tables of the royal house alone in my keeping, passed down to me and wearily learned until I was faultless in the repetition."

"This is vain, learned bard. I have the wisdom of my house, and mean to observe it. The sacred word of Dunwallo Moelmud was what?"

"That the Lord Pendragon held all in trust, for the most sacred people of Britain. What was the word, Artorius?"

"I will give you the half."

"Nay, Artorius, the third."

"If the third will suffice."

So we repeated it, I beginning this ancient ritual, a thousand and more years old. It is a secret word.

"You have answered the test, Artorius, and yet I knew, ere you confirmed my knowledge. And you make no claim, and the Lady of the Creuddyn reigns at the Gorsedd without a counter-word from you?"

"She does, Merddin."

"By the sign of the chough? Show it to me, Artorius. Nay, I see the cord. The pierced black stone. Let me see it. I am an old man and a high. Yet the Great Chough I have never seen. I thought it lost."

"A toy, Merddin, and a very old toy; what interest can you, an old and a wise man, have in toys?"

"It is not a toy, Artorius. Listen to this tale. An ancient king died, and upon his tomb was built a lordly pile centred round a menhir. And the pile of earth was washed away by the rains of a thousand years, and the bones were washed away with them. Yet the memory of the king survived, and still the menhir stood."

"Very likely it did. It was an ancient black stone, and founded deep."

"But while the stone stood the people had faith, and they said: 'Here is the menhir of the great king. He watches over us, and as long as the great stone stands the land will be safe, and what matter if we die in battle? for even if we die the ghost of the menhir will give us the victory.'"

"So they believed."

"Yes, they believed. And they said that if at any time the stone were removed, then would come disaster, and the end of their safety. Then came an evil and unbelieving king to their throne, and he said that the stone was but a stone, and that he required a stone such as that in another place. For, said he, it is an ancient stone and curious, and it will add an interest to my palace if I place it as a gatepost. And so, with slaves of foreign breed, he removed it, and it was the gatepost of his house."

"This is a good tale, Merddin."

"Nay, it is a bad tale. And when he removed it the people wept."

"Where did this deed take place, Merddin?"

"It was in Ierne, Artorius, and the name of the king that removed the stone was Dorcha."

"All this I know, Merddin."

"Let me proceed. This Dorcha was of the blood of Partholanus. Now an invasion came, and Dorcha assembled his people at the hill of Howth and armed them. And the name of the invader was Nemedius. Now these invaders came to Howth with spears and bows and a great equipment, yet they were fewer than the people of Dorcha. But the people of Dorcha said one to the other, 'Why should we fight? for the end is certain. The menhir has been removed and our ancient gods will not aid us. Dorcha the accursed has removed our strength': and so they died, and the sons of Nemedius reigned in their place."

"It is an old tale, Merddin."

"It is a tale that will always be true, Artorius. This Nemedius was one of the race of Gocmacoc, who reigned in Cornwall before the coming of Prydain. He was the son of the first of the curses of Britain: a curse so old and so great that he is not included among the Three."

"Well, Merddin, what is the application of this legend?"

"It is, that you leave the people their beliefs, Artorius. For as long as the common man, and more especially the common woman, believes a thing it is true; but if you destroy their faith the end comes quickly, an ending in tears and sorrow and loss. For with their faith the common men lose all else."

"This is true indeed, Merddin."

"Then what will you do, Artorius?"

"I shall do this. I shall leave the common people, the kerns who fought with me at Celidon, the farm folk of Powys, the archers of Dynevawr, the beaten and yet struggling soldiers of Reged who still fought in the ruin of their land—I shall leave them their beliefs. Why should they be destroyed? It would but dishearten them. They do that which they have to do, and the end marches on. In time they will have other beliefs, but let us make no break in the story of the people, Merddin. Let them go at their own pace, as I do my horse. They will get to the place to which they go all the sooner. They know the past, but no man knows the future."

"Then you leave this girl as Pendragon?"

"So long as there is a Pendragon, what matter who it be?"

"You are a strange man, Artorius. Yet knowing what you do, and what I know, I think you are not so strange as I say. Well, provided you make no break with the past and keep your own secret, I will keep mine."

"You know too many secrets, Merddin."

"What does it matter how many secrets I know, provided they die with me?"

At this Merddin departed, leaving me wondering at the knowledge of these bards, for I had thought that this was a secret which only I myself knew. Yet Merddin had said that only he beside myself was aware of it, and he was under an undertaking not to disclose what he knew. He, like myself, was tired of, and alarmed by the divisions of Britain. The chief need was to have this old quarrel settled for good. What matter who was Pendragon, provided the holder of that title wielded its power for the good of the island? And I believed in this girl Gwen. She was the cleverest of us all. The last few months had made an enormous difference in her character.

So in due time, headed by the bards playing on their harps, and with a music of trumpets made from long horns of Kyloe cattle, we made our way to the Gorsedd.

All the morning the young men of the neighbourhood, helped or mayhap hindered by the young girls, had been digging a circular trench for the meeting of the Council. The trench was a most perfect circle, perhaps two feet deep, with a step in it which was to form the seat for the company. The inner portion was a level piece of turf carefully shorn, and as smooth as art could make, and in the centre was a pile of wood for a fire. In this trench the seats were covered with sheepskins dyed scarlet, and there was room for sixty persons to seat themselves. The fire in the middle, when kindled, would serve for the lighting of this round banqueting table.

These things I knew well, for I had, when a boy, assisted in the making of more than one of these Beltane tables, and found it a most amusing experience; for, while the young men were digging, the girls were supposed to take the soil thus dug out, and carry it away in baskets to a distance, so as to leave all tidy. However, with mixed companies preparing for a feast, and all of them of youthful years, the work proceeded most unsystematically; for what with the girls laughing and spilling their baskets of sand and gravel on to the young men digging in the trench below, and the young men catching hold of the girls' ankles, there was a great tumult. However, the work was finished at last. A circle of stones was placed outside the trench, and decorated with oak boughs, then in their tender green clothing of spring, and all was ready. Such a circle we in Britain call a Gorsedd, and it sets forth the equality of all men, be they princes or kerns, before the law of Britain; for there is neither beginning nor end to the circle, neither first place nor last place. Outside this inner circle others like it were made, to the number of two or three or even more, each one bigger than the last, so that when all the work was done there was accommodation for several hundred people to seat themselves at the feast, to listen to the decisions of the Council, and to hearken to the songs and entertainment provided for the company.

Between the castle and the tables two mounds had been raised with the soil dug from the trenches, and upon these were placed piles of wood for the two Beltane fires. Between them was the place of disgrace. All those who had throughout the past year given cause of offence were assembled there, and there they had to remain until the punishments decreed by the Gorsedd were administered. These were not serious crimes, for criminals were as a rule killed on the spot if of British race, or were flogged and burnt alive if merely foreign slaves. The wrongdoers between the fires were those who had been guilty of what may be called social bad manners, as a young man who had jilted a girl, or, often enough, a girl convicted of a like discourtesy to a young man, and similar acts which cause unhappiness and yet are not punishable by law.

Another most important work was the kindling of the fire. This was done with an oak plank well dried, in which a small hole was cut, and a wimble of dried oak made to revolve in it. This produced great heat, and when, owing to the friction, the wood grew red, a powder made of the fungus growing on old birch trees was applied and the flames came. This fire was most carefully fostered, for it was the sun fire. But indeed all fire is sun fire, for the sun alone makes fuel. There would be nothing to burn if there were no sun.

Now before we set out, the old man Merddin came to me again, and he said, "You are set on your purpose, Artorius?"

"I am set on my purpose. Listen, Merddin, there have always been quarrels among us here in Britain. You know the old tales, countless numbers of them. There is the tale of Por and Fer, when brother fought against brother, or again the same story when Beli fought with Bran, and the tale of the daughters of Leir. These quarrels came because men set more value on a fancied honour than upon the peace of the State."

"Artorius," said Merddin, "it is, in my view, necessary to have peace and unity. Your father at Verulam was murdered by Vortigern, your father Eutherius, the son of Brothen. I knew that his successor Guitolin was an evil man, and a usurper, and I procured his death; also I tried to procure the death of this Gwendaello of the Creuddyn, so that the true Pendragon might hold the throne of Moelmud Dunwallo as the Holy King."

"And so your plan failed, Merddin; mine will succeed."

"There is now no other way than your plan, Artorius, if peace is what we need, and if we are to have peace."

"Merddin, I am a Briton, and love this land, but I am also a Roman, and place small value upon this title of Pendragon."

With this Merddin left me, but I wished he had not come.

However, we set out for the Gorsedd, and in the inner circle sat Gwendaello and the other Princes who had been at the Council, and the chief of the bards, together with young Regan, for even she was of royal blood, and other Princes of the tribes of Dynevawr to the number of sixty. Then all the outer circles were filled with the lesser people, and there was a great noise of laughing and talking and squealing from the girls; but what they were squealing at was only a joke here and there, and being pinched and such like, as always happens when young people are merry. Though why it should be pleasurable to make girls squeal and scream is a mystery, yet none the less a fact.

The first business was to announce, to the people assembled, the decisions of the Council; and as these amounted to nothing that could be put into words, one

after another of the representatives of the States arose
in his place and made most solemn and high-sounding
speeches which meant nothing at all, being mainly
adages that nobody could dispute, which therefore met
with great applause.

Now came the trial of the offenders. The first step
was for the Pendragon, as chief of us all there, to light
the three fires, for by now it was growing dusk; so with
a torch kindled at the oaken wimble, she did so, and
then the offenders were duly assembled between the two
fires. At some distance was placed a plough with a
wooden handle. The meaning of this was, that under the
law of Moelmud, a plough was sanctuary. By the
ancient laws of Britain no man engaged in ploughing
could be arrested or slain, for he was fulfilling a public
duty, and so long as his hand was on the plough, so
long was he safe from arrest, and so was any other person who ran to the plough for shelter.

Any person between the two fires therefore at a given
signal was to run to the plough, and on the way he was
pelted with eggs and lumps of wet moss and other matter. The girls who were offenders were not compelled to
run, but could, if they chose, pay forfeit in kisses
instead, which all of them did, as I thought, being heart-
less young jilts, very willingly.

This over, the great wicker images, made in the
shape of giants, were brought in, and five of us were
appointed to announce their names and the reason for
their punishment. These were: Maelgwyn, who indicted
Niall the King of Ireland; Cadell, who accused Elfric the
King of the Saxons; Aurelian, who prosecuted Igmar
Duke of the Jutes who had desolated the Island of
Vectis; and myself, who was to describe the misdeeds of
Drust, the son of Erp, King of the Picts. I never knew
who was to do a similar service for Decdric of the
Northern Saxons or Angles, as they call themselves,
because there was a dispute here, some saying that
Cador should be called upon, and others calling out
other names. But when the debate was waxing warm,
the old man Gildas arrived, and demanding a seat at the

inner circle as a saint and Abbot and the spiritual superior of any there, announced that he was at the disposal of the company for any high solemnities that were needed.

What he meant by a spiritual superior none knew, but as he seemed to think with sincerity that his claim was founded on law and justice, it was conceded.

Now while all were describing the battles, I thought a little upon my companions in them, and called to mind the deeds of old Gildas, and of my friend Aneurin; and being but a schemer in war, and having knowledge and experience of battle, I think but little of my deeds, but of Gildas and the poet who died upon Cannock I thought much, for these men were courageous beyond any valour I could have myself displayed. So, in my speech, I said this, meaning it beyond all I could say, for my words in speech-making are by no means what they should be. However, everything was done in the appointed way, and the wicker-work giants were duly burned amid great rejoicing.

At other Beltanes, in peaceful times when there were no existing villains to burn, it has been customary to make images of the old giants of Cornwall, mainly such old monstrosities as Caracorain, Belin Baladr, and Gocmacoc, but long ago people got so tired of these that they actually sent the image Gocmacoc to Lundinium, telling them there as a jest, that it was the effigy of the Duke of Cornwall. Now the language of Lundinium differs somewhat from that of Cornwall, for they in Lundinium and Verulam speak the dialect of the Trinobantes (saying, for example, Adrian, while we in the west say, Hadrian), for in the west they speak the pure British. Now, when the image arrived, the Trinobantes ignorantly thought that Gocmacoc was two words and not only one name, and therefore, thinking that one of the images had been destroyed or lost on the journey, they made themselves another and have ever since preserved it and its fellow in their council chamber.

We made our speeches of accusation, and the images were duly condemned. The last was the image of

Decdric, and in reference to this the Abbot Gildas rose to accuse this bad man. Now Gildas cleared his throat, and setting his mitre in place, looked at us with severity, and then spoke as follows:

"My beloved, this man whose evil deeds I recount to you was but as we are, one of the children of God, and a prodigal and evil-living son as accursed in his deeds as Belial. And why is it that he has come to this evil and painful end? It is because he has ever set his face against the light, and has in consequence come to taste the fire of damnation. His crimes as they appear in your minds, my beloved, but superstitious and misguided hearers, are those of lust, avarice, anger, pride, gluttony, envy, and sloth. These are the seven deadly sins, and of all these he is guilty. Yet that is not the reason why he is burnt to-night. He was guilty of an even worse crime than any of these. His offence was ignorance. It was because of this, that I, a God-fearing old man, learned indeed, for there are few know as much as I do, but nevertheless innocent almost beyond belief, so that even my friend Artorius has called me a lunatic—yet idiot though I was, I was enabled to outwit him."

At this there was a disturbance, some crying out that I had no right to call so learned a man a half-wit, and Maelgwyn, being half intoxicated, for the feasting had now been in progress for some time, rising in his seat, proposed that, as guilty of an offence, I should be placed between the two fires and pelted with eggs. But his suggestion was frowned upon as being brought forward too late, for the judging was by now over. So the disturbance ended.

Gildas, continuing, then warned his hearers against the sin of ignorance, whether they were high or low in station, and reminded even that high and mighty Lord Maelgwyn, that he had as yet much to learn both in decorum of behaviour and in respect for the Church. As for Cadell, for him he also had a warning: let him remember in storing his barns to store them with his own goods only. And so he went on, for there was not one who escape the castigation of his tongue; and yet there was truth in all he said, so that all present laughed, except those whom he admonished.

This done, the images were placed upon the fires and burnt, and while they were burning, the young men, having brought up some tethered pigs, twisted the tails of the beasts and jerked their legs so that there was a piteous wailing and squeaking, to which we listened with pleasure, symbolizing the torments of the heathen barbarians.

Then came songs and competitions of bards, and the telling of stories, so that it grew late before the passing of time was noticed.

In the midst of all this cheerfulness there came runners, messengers from the west as the rumour said, but they went to Gwendaello and whispered to her. Now there was no soul left in the castle, so these men had searched for the Princess, as the message was for her ear alone. So she, rising in her seat, said as follows:

"Friends, I have news for you. We have had a merry meeting, in friendship, and a settlement of all our differences, as is right upon the first of May; but now this festival must end, for there is work before us. To-day, in conference with the Princes of Britain, I drew up a scheme for the defence of this island. Now will that scheme be tested. It is but a few weeks since we repelled grave attacks upon us in Powys and in the north. The valour and skill of men, Princes, and chiefs who are here by me now, gave success to our arms, but the quarrel to-day is for us near at home and in our beloved Dynevawr. The Irish have landed in Penvro, and are burning and slaying. My friend Rhys, they are in Dyfed; we must assemble the tribes and give them such a lesson as will end these disturbances."

Now here I was interested to see in what a swift manner this remarkable girl had established her ascendancy in her troublesome and chaotic kingdom. She gave swift orders in a quiet manner to one or two of her squires, and the assembly of the Beltane began to melt away. An equerry called out a list of names, and spoke to those who gathered round him swiftly, giving them

their orders to go here and there throughout the realm
to call their tribes to war; some were for Morgannwg,
some for Gower, for Talgarth, and other appointed
spots. "Bid them meet at the ford of Cwmamman, every
last man, and all with weapons, spear, arrows, and two
bows, and a bag of meal."

Now immediately these young men stripped off their
clothes, and mixing the charcoal from the fires with
mead and beer from the tables, smeared themselves
therewith, and disappeared into the outer darkness
beyond the fires upon their errand.

Rapidly the Princes of Dynevawr mounted their
horses and galloped for their villages, to lead their
tribesmen. Rhys of Dyfed had already departed with his
followers for his town of Narberth, while Gwen, her manner calm, sat with us at the tables of turf where we had
dined. Throughout the disturbance Maelgwyn had slumbered peacefully, for he had fallen into unconsciousness
before Gildas had been preaching for three minutes. A
can of water standing handy, Regan seized and emptied
it upon him. "It is the best way," she explained.

"What's this?" growled Maelgwyn.

"The Irish," screamed Regan in his ear.

"The Irish, what do I care for the hounds?"

"They have landed in Penvro," screamed Regan.

"Landed, the Irish, nonsense, child. I am as wet as
Llyn Ogwen," grumbled Maelgwyn.

"Indeed it is true, runners have brought the news;
look around," said Regan rapidly.

Maelgwyn, much sobered, looked about him. "It
looks as if you were right. It does seem that I had a
dream about a turmoil. A thousand dragons. Well, well,
get me my horse. Waking me this way. Am I never to
have a quiet evening? You, Regan, get all ready, and if
you have another can of water handy, give me another
swill."

Regan, without more ado, reached out her hand for
a wooden pail that stood on the bank behind, and threw
it over him.

Maelgwyn gasped. "You young she-devil, you should

have warned me. Where's Merddin? Arawn and
Annwvyn, must I call out for my Chancellor when I want
him? He ought to be here. Now did I not say," he questioned indignantly, "that if I gave the Irish any peace
they would become presumptuous? I have shamed the
memory of Cunedda, my grandsire, by my mercy. It is
six months since I harried their coasts. Me for Deganwy.
I want some more slaves and cattle."

He stood up, shaking the water from him like a great
dog, and rolled off to the park where the horses were
tethered. "What's the news, you, Gwen?" he called over
his shoulder.

She told him.

"I gather," said he, now sober, and master of the
facts. "At them with your spears, young woman. I shall
be at Deganwy within a few hours, and I'll light a torch
there to stick under the dogs' tails. This trouble comes
of my not attending to my business. The Irish indeed,
the crimson-gutted swine."

Now as Aurelian and I mounted our horses, a gal-
loper from Bath, with his horse in a foam, met us. I recognized him as an equerry of mine, a youth named
Lortus, of pure Roman ancestry. His grandfather had
been a centurion in the legions under my father,
Eutherius. This boy brought us vile news. "Tell my Lord
Aurelian," said he, "that the Jutes are on the march.
We have news from Sarum that they have passed their
boundary, and are reinforced by many from Saxonia."

Aurelian, at this moment giving the equerry his
attention, heard this.

He nodded his head.

"There is purpose in all this, Artorius. We get no
news of these combined attacks, yet there is a plan in it.
How is it that Irish and Pict, Frisian, Saxon and Jute
link themselves up in this way to compass our destruction? Well, we must to Bath. Send word to the legions to
be under arms, Lortus."

At the castle I met Cadell, making ready for his
departure for Uriconium. He looked at me with a somewhat solemn face.

"I have heard the news from Bath, Artorius. I have just been speaking with Aurelian."

"Bad enough, Cadell."

"I would help more if I could, and I will do what I can. This attack comes from the crossing of the southern Avon, and I hear the Jutes are already masters of Sarum."

"Not so. They are about to invest it, Cadell. They will never take that hill unless they starve it out. My fear is for its water. Jupiter send that it rains. There are no wells in Sarum, and the water tanks are small."

"I will march from Powys in a day or two, but my armies! Seventeen thousand of my people slain at Cannock, and many maimed. Yet what I can raise, I will. They are all good men. We will take these Jutes on their flank, but you will have your full legions, Artorius, and be in your own country."

"Nay, I fear not for the result, Cadell. But my gratitude for your promised help."

"Listen to me, Artorius; you are a soldier, I a statesman. Your business is to be confident, mine to be fearful. You will need all the aid you can get. This is a large and great matter."

"War, Cadell, is a matter in which one may say that the guests bring their own meat. The bigger the army, the better the entertainment. The stronger the line, the sooner the end. So speed in your efforts."

Cadell departed, looking somewhat doleful. I felt, however, more confidence in him than when I had met him in his palace at Uriconium. He had his deeds at Cannock to his credit; a self-seeking man, but an honest, in spite of his cunning. I absolved him then and there from being a red heifer.

After leaving Cadell, I turned to seek Aurelian, for we were to proceed together across the Gwent with a Dynevawr guide (for on that I had insisted), when I came upon the sage Gildas. He was seated in the courtyard of the castle, watching with placid mien the departure of the armed men, and the bustle and hurry of the garrison placing the castle in war array.

"Greeting again, Artorius. You depart then, now upon an errand of blood. Spoil you the Egyptians."

"There are no Egyptians," I answered him, thinking that the old man wandered in his thoughts. "These that we go to war with are Saxons."

"I spoke in a metaphor, Artorius, which you do not understand. You are indeed a pagan and an irreligious dog."

"You are too learned for me, Abbot."

"Truly, my son, I am more learned than thou art. I depart, myself, for the assembly at the ford of Cwmamman. I have been in Ireland."

"Then I expect you will be useful at Cwmamman, Abbot," I said, remembering this ancient's quaint knowledge, which he gathered on his pilgrimages.

"Wherever I go I save souls," said he calmly. "But the souls of the Irish are best saved when at the point of death. I hope to save many."

Waiting there for Aurelian, I watched this man making his preparations. He folded his mitre in a careful manner, and placed it in a scrip at his side, then bound up his long robe about his middle till it left his legs bare to the knee. "This," he said, "is indeed girding up my loins."

He then tied about his head a woollen scarf. "The nights are cold," he explained, "and I must guard against the infirmities of age." He hoisted upon his shoulder a small bundle, and assuming his shepherd's crook, announced himself ready.

"Farewell then, Artorius. We shall meet again when the Amalekites are slain."

"There are no Amalekites, Abbot, they are a tribe of whom I have never heard."

He shook his head at me. "After the war is over I will instruct thee, my very ignorant and brainless son. As it is, I am upon urgent affairs and cannot tarry. I must be at the ford of Cwmamman before the men of blood." He strode forth, vigorous and yet bent in the shoulder, for he had said he was eighty years of age, and at the portal he waved his crook, saying:

"Artorius."

"Yes, Abbot."

"If thou achievest not a victory over these sons of Belial, the Saxons, I will lay this stick about thy shoulders. I, thy father in God, aver it. Farewell then, and slay the Amalekites and the Edomites, the Hivites and the Hittites, the Jebusites and the Ammonites, and also the dwellers about Cyrene."

"But, Abbot," I called after him, "I never heard of any of these tribes. Are they varieties of Saxon? Cyrene I know, for I was there with Flavius Anastasius."

"Farewell, Artorius. I pray that thy military knowledge be better than thy comprehension of Holy Writ."

To this day I have not the slightest comprehension of what he meant, but he was a sensible old man, and there must have been some meaning in it, for I observed that he was laughing as he departed. I do not in truth think that he was mad, or that the people of whom he spoke had no existence; but I have commanded armies in Britain for many years, and I will swear, by all the Gods, that none of these names ever landed or fought here. I at one time after this incident took some Saxons as prisoners, and inquired of them, under torture, whether they belonged to these peoples, for I was curious about the matter; but they averred with tears that they were not of that kindred, that they disliked them as much as I did, had no information concerning them, and had never even heard of them. One of these men I kept as a servant, wheeling manure in the farmstead and such light duties, for he was badly injured by the torture; and he, like me, had some curiosity about the matter, for he inquired frequently whether the Ammonites and the Hittites had landed in Britain, and being an intelligent man, had some idea that they were a branch of the Huns.

As Aurelian and I with our staff set forth, we met Gwendaello in the court, about to depart.

"It seems," she said, "that we are to have no peace, Artorius. So I bid you good-bye, and if you, or I, should not return or meet again, I hope that we shall think of each other kindly."

Her words reached me, for I remember them well, yet at the time they meant little to me. I was looking at the girl, and made no reply till she spoke again.

"You see," said she, "that I wear the blue cloak."

"It becomes you well," I answered. "I am glad I bought it for you."

"It will serve well for the rough work on which I am engaged," said she. "These peasant homespuns wear well, and if it rains it will keep me warm and dry."

We said nothing more, and set forth each on our respective journeys.

It was but two hours after that first news came that we started, and the early grey shades of the dawn were already showing as we crossed the first stretches of the forest of the Gwent; yet the runners, hasting to bid their lady's tribesmen to the war, had passed before us. As, riding hard, we passed by a lonely woodman's cot, we heard one of the messengers at the door.

"Out, out, woodman. You are bidden to war. By the word of the ruler. Bow, spear, arrows, and meal. To the ford of Cwmamman."

And a sleepy voice inside the hut: "Coming, coming. Wife, where are my breeks?"

And ever, on the way, we met these denizens of the forest passing us in twos and threes, and once a party of six, and many times lonely men laden with their war gear, and lurching forth, yawning and stumbling in the early dawn, to their tryst with death. Yet there seemed to be no hanging back; the summons had been enough. I watched them as they came by, for we saw some with every mile we passed, stalwart men of middle life, striding stolidly, young boys laughing and talking, silent old men, keen-eyed and white-haired; bow and spear, spear and bow, bare-footed and bare-headed, like wasps issuing from a nest that has been threatened.

CHAPTER XVII

THE BATTLE OF THE ISLANDS

SKOMER AND DYRDDOD, FROWNING ROCK,
AND WINE-LIKE ENDLESS BREEZE,
WHERE GANNETS NEST AND EAGLES FLOCK,
WILD SKIES AND ROARING SEAS.

We had been in the field now for three weeks, and with every day that passed it became clear that this was real war, and that the end for us might be disaster in the field. If we, the legions of Aurelian, were beaten it was an end to the Britain of the British. In moments of sadness I pictured to myself this great and civilized province overrun and ravaged by these hoggish barbarians, and the scenes of woe and torment, of ravished girls and smoking homes repeated on a scale ten times greater than in Valentia. However, to anticipate failure is useless for a soldier charged with the defence, and so I laid my plans and met the foe on occasion as well as I might, though in truth we were continually driven back, for the numbers of the enemy were as the sands of the seashore; a phrase that every defeated general has used since battles first began, which, knowing human beings as well as I do, I should say was a long time ago.

The only general, of whom I have ever heard, who never complained after the battle of the numbers of the enemy, was Leonidas at the battle of Thermopylæ, but then doubtless he too would have complained had he survived. I have thought occasionally with pleasure of what Leonidas would have said to the Magistrates at Sparta had he survived and won the battle; but I really think that the Ephors counted upon his being killed. Thus do the politicians play with the lives of us poor soldiers; we are but pawns in their game.

Since the German barbarians had established their hold upon the Channel, between ourselves and Gaul, their possession of Vectis, and particularly of Kent and the mouth of the Thames, had forced us to abandon Richborough, Lundinium, and Winchester, as main military stations. True, we maintained troops there, but these districts were so liable to be overrun that it was unsafe to treat them as other than a first line of defence. Our main stronghold was in the west, in what was called the Triangle, the three great cities of Bath, Cirencester, and Gloucester. This was the base from which we defended the entire island. If this Triangle once fell or was breached, we could write "departed" over British rule in Locris.

We had, at the outside, some thirty thousand legionaries, mostly centred in these three cities, the heart of the island, from which we deemed it our duty to defend the whole area just as the heart makes alive all the members of the body. In the present war we sallied forth from our base on these beautiful towns to drive the enemy back into their kennels. On arriving at Bath I found myself in command of twenty-three thousand troops. Over a third of these I had to post in outlying stations, and took the field at the last with three legions, and these rather depleted. These were the Grumblers, the Fur-caps and the Defensores: the latter were older men, but good veterans. The number in all was some fifteen thousand heavy armed infantry. Our cavalry was negligible in quantity, and the horses in the main poor, and small in size. Indeed, since the Saxons held the east, our best breeding-grounds for heavy war-horses had been lost to us, and those we had were mainly from Damnonia, with a few from Cambria, only mannuli in real truth, and too small for the work. They were useless in an attack upon such mobile assailants as the Jutes and Saxons. They would, of course, be useful in a pursuit, but unfortunately the pursuit of a defeated enemy was at present outside our experience. The greave, as is said, was upon the left shin.

We first met the enemy upon the banks of the Avon,

about twelve miles to the south of Sarum. These were mainly Jutes, and they essayed to cross the river. We contested hotly, but they were ten to our one. I spread out my line to defend the river until it was dangerously thin, for we were on the outer curve of the bend in the water, the Jutes having attacked, from their point of view, very wisely at that point. In places we were but one file deep; still, we held the river, though constantly in danger of being outflanked, for two days, which involved much movement of legions from one point to another, a very wearisome business. In the end we had to fall back in the respite that night brought us.

In this battle of the ford we lost a good sixth of our force, yet those men, who thus died in battle, if they have now any knowledge of it, may know that we slew twenty for every British legionary who fell. Our arms indeed in this sort of open country were better than theirs, and their spears and knives, with bucklers, proved but weak in comparison with our javelins and short swords, with the square curved shield. Twice under cover of a tortoise we crossed the river, and penetrated almost to the pavilion of the Jutish King, but we were, in the end, beaten slowly back again, and in these two crossings, and in the retreats, our losses were greatest. Yet twice we had this Jutish King well frightened, and his alarm enabled us to draw in our cohorts and combine upon a shorter frontage; for the Jute, in reply to our most spirited second attack, drew in his flanks and concentrated in a massed attack on our centre. This was a foolish move which we repelled so pleasurably that the river was red with their bodies. The centurion in command of the garrison at Sarum, just as the Jutes were pouring across the river, by a happy thought released the weir, with the result that many of the Jutes were overwhelmed in the flood water, and we took them in confusion. In our second attack across the river, I noticed that I had part of an arrow sticking in my left shoulder. This must have been done in our first crossing, though I had no memory of it, for the blood was dried. It shows how, when one is busy and occupied

in mind, some small hurt will pass unnoticed, but when
I had noted that the arrow was there my shoulder felt
wondrous stiff, and indeed bled for the best part of the
next day. Thus it is that, even amid the gravest affairs,
we take note of trifles; as when, in retreating the second
time, I noted that one of the Jutes had reddish hair but
a single white lock on his forehead. I had never seen this
man before and never want to see him again.

So then we fell back upon Sarum, where there was
much to do. I was unwilling to surrender such a fortress
to the barbarians, knowing well that they could never
take it by assault if it were properly defended. Its one
weakness I had named to Cadell. It is a big city at the
summit of a high hill, and it has no wells, depending for
its supplies of water upon rainwater tanks. There were
many people there, and if the city were beleaguered they
were all like to die of thirst. I therefore told the old men
and women and the children to depart, assuring them
that their property would be safe. With many doleful
cries they went, to the number of about ten thousand,
and found shelter in Cirencester and other places
beyond. Yet such was their terror that some went even
as far as the Gwent and made themselves huts in the
woods. The rest of us, having formed a garrison among
the young men and able-bodied, took up our camp on
the slopes of the hill, and waited for the enemy's next
move, for we had arms to repair and many wounded to
tend, in addition to burning the bodies of those dead
whom we had brought away with us, or who had died
since the fighting ceased. The Jutish and Saxon dead
we threw into the Avon, for as this flows afterwards
through Jutish territory, it did not matter what we did
with the water, and I hope that many of the Jutes were
poisoned thereby. It is a good thing to do when the
enemy are downstream.

I was by now taking a very serious view of the whole
situation. I had with me practically the whole force of
Aurelian's kingdom, for those detailed elsewhere
amounted to but little. It was certain that I must defeat
these Jutes, else the whole of Britain were ended. Yet

how to do it I could not discern. My people had fought as well as any general could expect, and better.

While I was thus, like a dog, licking my wounds, there came to me a most haughty and impudent message from Igmar, King of the Jutes. He had noted, he said, that the treaty made by Guitolin, King of the Britons, had not been kept; he consequently hesitated to enter into a treaty himself, with men so utterly without faith, and he preferred rather to take what he required of our territories by the strength of his arm. In his great generosity to the weak, however, he would contract with me that, if I would surrender to him, without further slaughter, the lands he had already seized, he would allow the remnants of my army to retire. He added that I should be well advised to profit by this offer, as his good friend the King Elfric, of the South Saxons, was intending shortly to march against me; but if I retired peaceably he would find opportunity to persuade his friend also to content himself with his present conquests.

At this I was in two minds. We were the weaker side, in great straits, with little hope of reinforcements. Cadell had lost sorely in the former fighting, when my friend Aneurin was killed; he could advance but slowly from the north, being hampered by raiding parties of Saxons, which, though not very strong, were yet sufficient to delay him. He dared not leave Powys, with its rich farms and homely simple people, open to be raided behind his back, and he had to cover a wide front to seek out and destroy these pests as he advanced.

As for Aurelian, that truly great man, my own and my father's friend, he was busy in the Triangle, arming and marshalling the people there; but at the best I feared that these would never make legionaries, nor were they used to war like the Cambrians. Still, they would be better than nothing. In Dynevawr I had little faith. I knew too well the divisions of its people, and that the Guitolin party were likely to contest the predominance attempted by the girl Gwendaello.

On the other hand, Igmar would clearly never have

sent me such a message had he felt strong enough to take what he desired without parley. We had hit him hard by the river, there was no doubt. I therefore replied, telling him to commit himself to the care of what evils spirits inhabited the Saxon or Jutish Hades, if there were any there worse than he was, or if that place were worse than any place that had been infested by his bestial compatriots for more than three days. At the same time I considered retiring on the Triangle, where we could regather our strength, and attack from the shelter of our fortresses. But meanwhile, I received a long letter from the Pendragon.

"To Artorius, greeting. It would appear that you have been in great danger, and are even yet in no satisfactory plight. I say, therefore, keep what courage you may, for assuredly your cause is righteous. If you desire news of our doings here, I send you such as there is.

"The Irish made a landing near Penvro between the islands, their leader being one Congall. They came in many ships, professing revenge for the ravages of Maelgwyn in the north of their land. At their landing-place they made a great stockade with large stones and earthworks, and leaving there a sufficient garrison, got the most of them into their ships again, and made off for the river Teifi, to ravage there. We heard from Maelgwyn in Deganwy that his ships were afloat in great numbers, and that he was sailing for Ierne, with a whip that would make these Irish dogs of Ynys Saman yelp.

"We thought that if Maelgwyn thus attacked them at home while we defeated and slew them here in Dyfed, we should give them such a lesson as would end these raids for many years to come. So we assaulted them in their great stockade, but had little success and great losses, for we were but light-armed with spears and arrows, and when the ships that had gone to the Teifi returned we should be in worse case still. Now this bay of Penvro is a fine and broad water, with high cliffs all around, but a good harbourage, and a most notable beach. The Irish had made bases for their ships at the islands.

"At the north end of the Bay is the great island of Hyrddod; at the southern, Gwales in Penvro, which some call Skomer, a most holy place, for thereon the seven men who came back out of Ireland buried the head of Bendigeid Vran; it is also said that fairies live there.

"This isle is separated from the mainland by a very rough water through which the tides make much turmoil four times a day. There is also the Mid Isle, on which it is most difficult to land, since the waves upset the coracles. The Irish had stores and men and ship-building materials on all these islands.

"Now we had no boats at all but coracles, for the fishermen in these parts use no other, and most brave and skilful they are in the use of them, as indeed the people of Dynevawr are brave and skilful in everything, and proud indeed I am to be queen of such a place, the best on the face of the earth under the eternal skies, and admire and love all my people most greatly, as they do me. The fishermen said an attack might be made and were eager to try, though it is risky indeed in these waters to take two men in a coracle. Therefore the fishermen from all over Penvro, and indeed from Caerfyrddin and elsewhere, came over the hills in the night-time, each man carrying his coracle over his head, so that having invested the stockade, we assembled about two thousand coracles, which was enough and to spare; we had two men to each coracle, which we considered a sufficient force to seize the islands.

"Hyrddod is but half a mile from the shore, and we took it by surprise upon the second night. It is a high isle with great and perilous cliffs and several farms upon it. The Irish had slain all these poor people, and fearing us mightily, made a great defence in the dark. I went with them in that attack, for being of the Creuddyn, where the waters are shallow with a ground swell, I can paddle a coracle well, as I was taught when I was young. So, taking with me an armed man with a spear, and having a sword, I went to see how the attack proceeded.

"We landed in a party of two hundred, having crossed silently, and in landing and fighting among the rocks on the shore, lost about half of these, with a dozen or more drowned in the crossing, for there was a rough sea in the narrow channel that overturned the coracles. The fight was fierce enough while it lasted, but at last the Irish broke, and ran to the top of the island; and there we took them all and threw those that were left alive into the sea. So this was well done. There were by this time about sixty of the force I took with me still alive, so these I left on the island and crossed back alone to my camp where the Princes of Dynevawr were arraying our main force. The Prince Rhys, whom you met with me at the Beltane, had with him many men of Dyfed, better armed perhaps than mine, for Dyfed is a rich land with mines of iron lying ready to the hand.

"On the next night, we attacked Gwales, for I had news that the Irish ships were coming back, though delayed by contrary winds. But the fishers were sure that the wind would change, so there was no time to lose. The water was too rough to reach Gwales, much less the Mid Isle, in coracles; so we got poles of young pine trees, and lashed twenty or more coracles together into rafts, each carrying about twenty men. By this means we got to Gwales, but lost many men in the crossing, for the high waves broke up some of our rafts.

"On Gwales it was the same tale as on Hyrddod, except that we took a prisoner who said that he was the King of Ireland; but this I thought a lie, for these people commonly say, when taken, that they are kings so as not to be slain. However, we afterwards heard that this young man was indeed a son of the King of some place in Ireland of which I did not quite catch the name; so I am sorry that I had him thrown into the sea with the others, for if I had known that he was the King of Ireland, I should have kept him for the torture.

"On Gwales we found all the Irish shipbuilding materials, much pitch and canvas, and fine masts for boats, most of which we burnt, for we could not take them away on our rafts. We slew there about four hundred Irish, and on Hyrddod perhaps as many. Their numbers were more than ours, but we took them by surprise, as it was dark, and our men blackened all over. Myself I used the charcoal like the others, but like many more I fell into the sea at the landings, for the water was rough, and many of us were thus washed white again, before the fighting began. I had tied up my hair in a cloth, but in the turmoil and the scrambling about among the rocks, and being knocked down as a number of men came at me, my hair got tangled up in the bramble bushes and much of it torn and knotted with briars. It took two hours and more the next day to get it combed straight.

"When we got back to our camp from Gwales, where we again placed a garrison, it was already day. The old Abbot Gildas came forth to meet us, and, seeing me, raised some outcry, for he said, 'My child, it is indeed wrong in you thus to go about among men without the decent habiliments of women'; and when I asked what was wrong in what I did, all he could say was that some magician of great authority among those of his belief said that a woman in making her appearance among men in public should have her head covered. Now there is much sense in that, in view of what happened among those thrice accursed blackberry bushes, and I replied as I think most aptly, did I not tie it up in a cloth? and, in losing this cloth I suffered great misfortune, as I have said. But Gildas seemed to think that the magician of whom he spoke, had it indeed occurred to him that any person would wear no clothes at all, except a cloth round her hair, would have commanded her to wear the cloth elsewhere than upon her head. In that there is no sense at all, for we of Dynevawr always fight without any clothes, to say nothing of swimming in the sea. Had I had clothes I should have been drowned many times over.

"So now having destroyed their base in the islands, we were ready to resist their landing when Congall's ships came back; for on our way back from Gwales we put in at the Mid Isle with one raft, for it is but a small place. There were but ten men on it, and having seen the blazing of the ship stores on Gwales they were in great terror, and made no fight at all, but, when we landed, were all on their knees; so we put spears through them and threw them into the sea. They will do no more stealing and slaying, or praying either. I could not but laugh, for it was as if we were tedding hay, to see the bodies tossed on the end of a long spear, two of our men to each spear, for these Irish are heavy.

"We surrounded the Irishmen's stockade so that as we could not get in, they should not get out; and wherever we were threatened, we put up a stockade ourselves, till it would have taken all the dragons of Britain a thousand years to come out without being slain. All these days more and more had been assembling from all over Dynevawr, so we feared nothing from any landing; but to tempt the Irish to land, we concealed our force in the rocks and woods behind, with only a few fires permitted, and these put well back so that we seemed but few, and eager to run away.

"After two days, a rumour came that the Irishmen had put back to Ireland, abandoning those whom they had left in their stockade. Many of my army were for another assault on it, so as to end the business and go back to their farms. But I said we would wait until the barnacles and cockles ate through the bottoms of the Irishmen's ships. There was much grumbling at the delay; but Rhys said that these people were hot-headed, and it was not good to lose so many men in a hopeless assault on the stockade, for indeed this Rhys agrees with all I say, as is but proper when I am his overlord.

"But early on the third morning we saw the Irish fleet to the west off the Strumble, making straight for our beach with a favourable wind as our fishermen had foretold. Over two hundred large vessels we counted, with a hundred or more men on each of them. As they came near, we set fire to a great pile of dry wood covered with wet bracken and such matters, between the stockade and the shore, so that those in the stockade could signal no messages to the ships; and a great smoke it was, so that we could hardly see ourselves, a stinking, smarting business. And this gave us an unforeseen advantage, for the smoke spread so as to hide our doings on shore. We stationed our bowmen in easy distance on open ground, with spears in plenty at hand. First sixteen ships came in, shouting one to another, 'Let us land quickly for the stockade is on fire,' eager to save their friends and stores. But as they were beached, we killed every one in them with the arrows, before a man left his ship. The flight of the hazel twigs was like gnats over a wet ground in summer, and with us never a man hurt, except one who slipped on a rock in the smoke and broke his leg.

"More and more ships came to shore, and we took them as they came in, and at last about fifty came at once, and many men landed, and the smoke having died away, they could see our numbers; so they formed up and our spears came into play, and there was much hard fighting. Yet we destroyed all that landed, about two thousand. So then no more came, and the ships that were left put out to sea again, abandoning their stockade, and their men and stores, and all the bodies of them that were killed; which we thought a most disgraceful thing, for the dead bodies of them that die in battle should be decently burned, as we do.

"Our people were now so full of battle that they said, 'put out to sea in the coracles and destroy all those Irish,' which was not to be thought of, and I forbade it. However, what was our delight when round the great rocks that lie out beyond the little island, we saw the ships of Maelgwyn, far more than the Irish had, with the red dragons of Britain on their wide sails, come up before the norther. Now the Irish were rowing with sweeps against the wind, and were soon overhauled.

"Then there was a great fight, for the ships of Maelgwyn, with great hooks made of twisted and bent oak branches, made fast to the other vessels, and the Gwynnedd warriors came into them with swords and axes and spears. I never saw a fight on the water before, and I wished to see it closer, but the sea was rough with the wind, and the coracle in which I set out was over-turned by the waves, and so I must swim back to shore.

"Now what with the yelling of the Irish, and the roaring of the wind, and the splashing of the sea, and the shouting of our people on the land, there was such a din of mixed music as it would be hard to surpass; and as the wind was a strong norther though the sky was blue, the ships of the Irishmen got out of control and were one after another dashed ashore, and, as they beached, we slew all that were in them. At which after-wards Maelgwyn was wroth, as he wanted them for slaves in the mines. It was a great mercy therefore for these wretches that we speared them. We could see well, for the smoke had all died down; but I laughed to think that the people in the stockade must have been well-nigh choked with the reek of it. Now as Maelgwyn's ships had driven the Irish ships on shore, except such as were rammed in the fight, we could see the sea all dotted with Irishmen's heads like bobbing corks such as the fishers place on their nets, and our archers wager-ing on shooting arrows at these moving and very diffi-cult marks, and getting many of them, which was a clear waste of arrows, for they would have been drowned anyway. Still, it was great amusement for them, and I did not prohibit it, because these good men had lived in great dullness for five or six days.

"Next day Maelgwyn, being disappointed of a great capture of prisoners, and anxious to obtain more slaves for the mines, sailed for Ireland. About seven Irish ships were uninjured, and as they were good vessels, he put crews in them and took them with him for the cargoes of cattle and slaves and horses for which he hoped. I have not as yet heard from him again, but wish him great success in his undertaking.

"And now, my dear friend, having done our task here as well as it might be done, I forget not the peril of you and your legions, so within a few days you may expect us in your aid with what force we can. We are making great store of arrows, as many as we can carry, and there has been another slaughter since that of the

Irishmen, such cutting down of hazel bushes that the region is denuded, and the crop of nuts for the next two years will be scanty. As the arrows are made they are assembled in sheaves, and many witches have made incantations on each bundle, that they may fly true to the mark and cause rankling wounds and death to our foes. Besides this we have great store of spears, and the chimneys have been ransacked throughout Dynevawr for seasoned ash staves, and many new handsome blades forged.

"We are moreover in great spirits, and day and night there is such a din of music played on cowhorns, and beating of anvils, and chopping down of trees, as deafens everybody. We shall shortly be equipped and shall march on our way, silently enough, to be not only welcomed by you, but also to give some greeting to those who so vainly and insolently oppose you. We are attempting other engines of war and have had some success. We shot into the stockade burning arrows, wrapped with tow and greased with pine resin. Also under cover of a shelter or tortoise made of wettened cowhides with seaweed on top, we advanced to the barrier and built many fires against it. The place being shortly in a great flame, the Irishmen inside tried to come out. There was great smoke and bother, but we made shift to kill, I think, the most of them, though some got away into the woods, and these we are looking for; for giving us all this trouble after they had plainly been left to our good offices by their own lord who had sailed away and deserted them, and indeed for coming here at all when they were neither desired nor invited, we have administered some correction to these undutiful stragglers by beating them before the hangings which they had earned.

"I send my dutiful greetings. I would there were some silence in this camp, for I find it most difficult to write well in all this uproar. The wind is blowing a great gale, and now the smoke is all abated, the smell of the air is most healthful and grateful to me. There are some white clouds in the sky speeding across the blue at a great pace, and the sun is shining most brightly, which I take as a good omen for your endeavours."

Enclosed in this packet was a message from Gildas, very short, which in itself was strange, for when Gildas set pen to paper he was, if I may say anything to the discredit of so learned and old a man, inclined to a certain prolixity. He wrote thus:

"Truly we have smitten the Assyrians. Smite you now the Amalekites."

This I found incomprehensible, but the letter of Gwendaello pleased me; yet I was not unduly elated by it, though I was glad that she had had her moment of great triumph. That she would march with her tribesmen, and even now was on her way, I had no doubt. Yet that she could be of great assistance I doubted. Of all the States of Britain Dynevawr is the poorest and most thinly populated. Her subjects would be like all these tribesmen, unless they are closely governed, volatile and easily tired of war, desiring always to fight for two days, and rest for three months as the saying goes. However, it is a soldier's business to work with the tools at hand, and hope for the best, building victory upon certain and sure foundations, and not relying upon promised help which may never come.

My letters from Aurelian were not of the most cheerful description. I had already decided to fight, and not retire upon the Triangle if that could be avoided. "Let us all," I said to the commanders of my legions, "die in our rearguard actions and not give up, rather than abandon all these fair territories to the Saxon and Jute, to be lost like Kent and Vectis." Aurelian said the same in his letters.

"The people driven out by this inroad," he said, "must have at all costs their chance of recovering their lands and towns. The barbarians have already laid the most beautiful city of Silchester in ruins. There is not land in the Triangle, or in the safer regions protected thereby, for so great a multitude of people; and in so small an area our future power of resistance would be less. Fight therefore, my good Artorius, as I know you will, or we must all die. And indeed it is the easier way. These people who are now dispossessed and in terror and misery, living in the woods or on sparse charity, must have their homes back again, and surely we should be wrong to desert them, for, even if we do, our sons will be no safer. Fight therefore. I, who am born of the tribes of the Romans, recall the heroism of the older Rome in defeat, when she strove with men of your race, and yet came through the bitterest hour of her defeat to the dominion of the world. I ask you to carry the dragons of Britain backward or forward in defeat or in victory, yet never in surrender. Ten thousand troops, I fear but half armed, and as yet but inexperienced, are now being arrayed for your assistance. Hold on therefore."

To this I agreed: I had to fight. To lock myself up in Sarum would be worse than the Triangle. Once contained there I should never be able to get out, not to mention the question of the water supply. Besieged troops deteriorate over-rapidly; it is better to keep in the open, even with a slender chance. Every fortress, in the failure of relief, must surrender in the end when opposed to almost illimitable force. I therefore put the garrison of Sarum on a sound footing, quite sufficient to hold such a strong place, and took up my camp on the high ground at Amesbury, resolved to contest every inch of the land. If we were beaten back, which would not be done if we could help it, we should at all events have done all that we could.

I am not going to tell a long tale about these deeds of ours at Amesbury, which is indeed holy ground to all of our race, but we fought here against the Saxons and the Jutes who attacked us again. For some days they had been intimidated by the haughty nature of my reply to their king; but watching, and seeing that we got no reinforcements, they attacked us again. At Amesbury we fought for several days, and in the end were pushed out of our ground again, and I, who had set forth from Bath with fifteen thousand legionaries, was now in retreat with but seven thousand. Yet we took toll of the barbarians, and though compelled to retire were yet undefeated. In this battle two of my legion commanders were killed, and I was again struck in the arm by an arrow, yet not badly; but shortly afterwards, in the press that took place by the outer circle of the great temple of the sun, I was struck in the same arm by an uncouth ruffian with a seaxe, while I was surveying the forward slope of the ground, seeking to make a counter-attack, and thus not watching the vagabond. The wound bled abominably, but was bound up, and I was not much the worse, though I could not use that arm, which by great good fortune was the left one.

By now the barbarians had overflowed all the country, and we were wide of Sarum, which was contained and wholly enveloped; yet the garrison, whenever they could get an opportunity, made diversions against the Saxons. I had placed the young Lortus in command there, and he was in truth a most capable youth. Now we had nothing more to do than to retreat again, which we did by night, breaking our ground as silently as we could, and taking our stand, after a long march, in a good defensible position, upon the high ridge of the downs, some miles to the south-east of Bath. Here we were reinforced by Aurelian's new levies, and resolved to give battle once more.

We had barely entrenched our position when, in the early hours of the morning, we were aware of advance swarms of the Jutes again placing themselves against us. It had before struck me as singular that it was always the Jutes who attacked first. My own view was that they were the weaker tribes, and because of this were always given the most dangerous work, and forced on in front by the Saxons. It is indeed curious that there should be any tribal or other difference between living creatures so low in the human scale as Jutes and Saxons. Yet the difference, whatever it was, though so inexplicable to me, appeared to be quite obvious to the barbarians themselves, in spite of the fact that they both offered sacrifices to the same demons, and were equally oblivious of all the decencies of life.

CHAPTER XVIII

MOUNT BADON

AT SUNSET IN THE DOWNLAND
THE HILLS ARE FAIR AND BRIGHT;
THE GRASS IS GILDED WITH THE GLOW
OF DAY'S DECLINING LIGHT.
WHEN BRITON FOUGHT WITH SAXON,
UPON MOUNT BADON HILL,
THE GOLD WAS BLOOD OF LEGIONS
AND THE GRASS IS GILDED STILL.

With the earliest dawn we were aware that the fourth attack would come. Three had we beaten back the previous day, the last at dusk, yet in this last, which, had I been directing the movements of my opponents, would have been delivered an hour earlier, we were only saved from final defeat by the coming of the blessed dark. The fighting had been both fierce and perilous. My men were weary to the point of death. I had sent messages among the legions saying that at all costs we must save the city which was our home, and also the other cities of our great and ancient land. All knew that there was little hope for us in the future, if we were defeated. There would be nothing, then, before us but a long retreat into the forests and hills, to be no longer citizens of a great and civilized empire, but mere outlaws of the woods. Defeat meant that we should be driven from our homes, that we should have to listen to the shrieks of ravished girls and wives whom we dare not stop to save, and that we should be quickened in our departure by the reek of the thatch of our own burning farmsteads. This the legions understood well enough, the new levies as well as my own veterans of many battles, and they stood to the long test as steady as the pillars of the temple which they were, answering all calls upon them without a quaver.

Indeed, as over and over again I saw them bend and then recover beneath some fierce stroke of a heavy mass of Saxon demons, howling and slashing like the wild beasts of their own stinking forests, I thought that if, as seemed probable, this was my last fight, it was not one of which my ghost, soon to be liberated from its earthly habiliments, could have any reason to be ashamed. Long before that first day of battle closed, I had thought that the end was come. Only the valorous resistance of those princely legions put off the final death. We were but as a stag at bay before the hounds, standing with our horns down, waiting to be pulled to the sodden earth in the last death grips.

Of a truth our losses were severe. We took our stand some fifteen thousand strong when the tempest opened, of whom nearly two-thirds had never fought in the line before, yet there was little to choose between old and young. The enemy could not take Bath as long as we stood before them, and therefore, in the night, we retreated yet another mile and occupied the summit of Mount Badon, a sweep of downland that rose in a gentle slope culminating in a sharp crest, and about thirty miles from Bath. The nature of the ground was such that we could deploy our line on a shorter length with less risk of being outflanked than on the lower ground. The third attack had been delivered at dusk, and though we had again lost heavily, still we beat it back, and so were able in the darkness to take up our new position. The shortened line was necessary, for we had lost a third of our number. These lay scattered as dead bodies up the long slope by which we had retired. They were all dead; no legionary would willingly fall alive into the hands of the Saxons, and as they lay dead or dying upon the ground they were mutilated by the hooked knives of their beastlike foes.

So the dawn came, hopelessly enough, and with it no need for speeches to the legions. We knew what we had to do: it lay before us plain. It might be that help would come, though I believed in it but little now. The armies against us were too numerous, our resistance had been eaten away, so that whatever help was now available must come from the States of the west and the north. This would surely be too feeble to be of much service. There might be, for there sometimes is in war, a miracle or an earthquake; the enemy might, as savage peoples sometimes do, give way to superstition and panic. Anything might happen, and probably would not happen; but while there was life there was hope, and for us there was nothing for it but to fight to the last, on the bare chance that when we were finished with there might still be hope for others.

On the second day I expected the Saxons to attack at dawn, but they did not. Hour after hour we stood to our arms, but the attack never came. I had, all the time, in my mind the fear of an enveloping movement, and I searched far and wide throughout the day for signs of its preparation. My scouts, however, brought me no news of any such movement.

It was very warm at an early hour, and as the day passed it became sultry. What the Saxons were doing I tried hard to imagine, but from their lines, although we heard occasional signs and sounds, there was no distinctive indication of their intentions. That there was a purpose in this I could not doubt. I had from this waiting a higher opinion of their leader's generalship than he had given me cause to hold before. The three previous attacks had been badly conceived and unduly delayed, and, though perilous and costly to us, had unduly sacrificed the lives of his own men. It now seemed to me that the Saxons were dispirited by the extent of their losses, and were, therefore, seeking to bring a similar discouragement on us. There is something very disheartening, even to the best of troops, in being kept as it were on the tenter-hooks too long; it works upon their spirits and takes away their courage. Still we waited.

However, about three hours after midday, the attack came. It was on a wide front; far too wide to please me.

The Saxons had brought up new tribes who had been kept behind in readiness for this attack. I tried to estimate their numbers, and should have reckoned them, at the least, at one hundred thousand. Our great circus in Bath, which we now hold three times a year, and held twice in those days when it was a recognized observance to hold a circus on the birthdays of the Emperors of the East and of the West, took place in a field, surrounded by the populace sitting on wooden stages, so that all could have a good view. The field held ten thousand people; it was, of course, always full. I estimated that the Saxons would have filled the field at ten to a dozen such circuses, irrespective of those whom they might have behind and out of my sight; though I should imagine that those would not be many, knowing that the Saxon method, like that of all savage peoples, is by mass attack with little thought for the morrow. With legionaries in ordered formation I should, of my military knowledge, be able to estimate their numbers by their formation and length of line, for that is a matter of science. With a dense mob of Saxon barbarians thrown together anyhow, according to my notions, though they doubtless have some ideas of how to use their own human material, no real military rules would apply, and more ready methods were required. I should say therefore that the Saxons were between one hundred and one hundred and fifty thousand men, those, that is, within vision. I knew that they had more reserves in the eastern fens, though to what number I cannot of course estimate. A loathsome thought crossed my mind, that many of these abominable savages might be the descendants of British mothers, poor girls who had been captured in former years in their swinish raids.

Still, in this attack at three o'clock there was some method about the formation. The front was wide, with a thick mass of pikemen in the centre, and on the flanks many archers as well as seaxe-bearers and pikes and spears and axes. I liked the look of this attack very little. The foe, of a verity, outnumbered us by ten to one, and I saw a stiffening go through the ranks of my legions, a slight movement that taught me that they, as well as I, guessed that the end had come. We were by now but nine thousand strong, mixed-up legions old and new, drafted together by cohorts to make a formation; for on the previous day entire cohorts had perished, leaving a ragged grouping which was not appropriate to the art of war.

I heard the Saxons' whistles and yells, uncouth noises in which they indulge when about to attempt an overwhelming assault (for these people must ever be grunting and squealing like the pigs that they are, and do not fight in silence like our legions, keeping their breath for the dealing of blows, but make much empty noise). At this moment a messenger brought me news from Cadell. He was as yet no nearer than Tetbury, more than fifty miles away, and could not reach us for, as I guessed, a day or more nearly two. By that time I reckoned that all would be over, unless the news of his coming alarmed our foes. Yet even then I doubted whether he could have with him sufficient force to make any difference. However, he was coming, and I therefore circulated a message among the legions that Cadell of Powys had beaten the Saxons at Alcester, as indeed he had, and also at Lechlade on the Thames, where he had forced a crossing and was victoriously coming at great speed to our help. "Let us all," I said, "remember what our brothers have done in these battles ere they died, and continue to uphold the name of Britain." At this a great cheer went up, and all prepared to hold the crest of Badon. So we, being in spirits, met the attack and beat it back once again.

Yet as we slew the first and last of those who reached our lines, throwing our javelins at the front rank, or what the Saxons call a rank, and then, when they were in confusion, advancing with the sword for a few steps, and if possible recovering the javelins, we failed where we had always succeeded hitherto. For in this attack there was no cessation because of the throwing of the javelins, but for some time it was sword-work with the lines interlocked, in which we lost fewer than was to be expected, so much superior is the Roman sword and the square shield, to the buckler and seaxe of the Saxons. The seaxe is, as I have always said, more a weapon for an assassin than for a soldier.

We were much assisted in this defence by the new arms sent to us in the last resort from Bath, including some good catapults with a great store of flint stones got from the chalk. Also Aurelian, remembering the Balearic slingers, had mustered some boys and others too old or too young to be in the line, and lame men and partially recovered wounded, who made some diversion with brook pebbles and clay balls. The clay balls we had made at Bridgewater, where the clay hardens well, and many thousands of these were thrown with a very good effect. The long and short of it was that we repelled this fierce attack with a good deal of sweat and pushing, and from what I have said regarding our weapons, it will be clear that we had used what resources our province could afford.

Still, there was a long time before we could expect Cadell, though the hope of our relief by him was an inducement to hold on. After this attack, the Saxons again retired, and played their former game of waiting. They had lost heavily, for before our lines were so many dead bodies that they formed a rampart. We employed the respite by clearing the front of our lines and cutting the throats of those among our assailants who still lived.

After this, preserving our lines, we sat down upon the turf of the downs and waited for what the Saxons would do next. We moved, as well, all our wounded to the rear of our lines, and the country women carried them in stages in litters; and afterwards many ladies in Bath came out and carried them into the city, and brought them into the shelter of the walls to be there tended and cured of their wounds. Yet many died in the litters, and for these the women built pyres by the road-side and burned their bodies, with many tears. A thing like this I have never heard of before. This work had to be done by the ladies, as all the men, even the old men and young boys, were assembling to join our legions; and in the supreme danger of the State it was well that even the women should be at work. So Aurelian judged, for he held that panic in danger, when the women and civilians were not at work, was as great a peril as the enemy in the field. For my part I was more concerned with how long we of the legions could continue to resist the Saxons. A good deal depended on the barbarians themselves. If they had repeated their attack more often they must have worn us down, for our line was all the while wearing thinner and thinner yet. I do not mention here all the minor attacks that were made, but only those assaults which I should call general, in which the whole of our force was engaged. Yet in spite of our losses we took such toll of them that their leaders had to urge the savages to the attack, calling upon the names of gods and demons hitherto unknown to us, to drive them onward and compel them to their deaths under Roman-British swords.

I had great reason for watchfulness. The three o'clock attack, with its ominously lengthened line, had given me cause to fear. The long delay on the former occasion had resulted in an enveloping movement by the barbarians, which we had repelled. I doubted very seriously whether we could defeat such another; and so the hours passed.

We were, as I said, on high ground, among vestiges of some ancient works. They were like mounds, grass-grown, of some ancient Beltane feast, but on a colossal scale; low mounds, but still quite a defensible position. Our lines spread right and left of them along the crown of the hill; then came a dip in the ground, and on the farther side of this was the Saxon centre. Curiously enough, this was also around rings made in the turf similar to ours, yet the difference in height between this low hollow, and the height occupied by either of us, was little more than a hundred feet.

We were in the month of high June, and daylight might be expected to last for some hours yet, for it was but five hours after noon when, watching the Saxon lines again, I saw that alarming stretching out and deploying, if such an orderly word can be used for this undisciplined marshalling, towards the right and left again. At this, in my own mind, I acquitted this Saxon General of lack of skill, and recognized him for a man that I hated indeed, but yet one whom as an opponent I could admire. Indeed he was doing the right thing in his own interests, and the delays that were a handicap to him were a result of the stupidity and ill-discipline of his men. The General himself was working with great and powerful, and yet ill-made tools, clumsy to his hand. Yet he was no fool, and it would need shrewd judgment to beat him.

At last the attack was launched. From all sides they came sweeping across the half-mile of turf between us, trodden now, and blood-soaked for large patches in a thousand places. In another half-hour or so we should be surrounded, and the end would come; an end like that of Leonidas at Thermopylæ, which I did not in the least desire to imitate. For Leonidas had all the rest of Greece behind him, and I had, to my regret, nothing at all, unless it might be Cadell, who was, for I knew his force, no better armed than the Saxons, and inferior to them in numbers. As for them of Dynevawr, I had given up hopes. From where they had fought the battle of the Islands, to where we were, was over a hundred and sixty miles, and a bad road. I doubted whether they could reach me until I had been dead for about a week.

But I would not wait to be enveloped. A desperate throw was needed in this last spasm of Roman Britain. We would at all events die fighting, and snatch what chance we had, a poor one at the best, of victory at last. Our trumpets therefore sounded the swell, the order for a general attack. The wearied legionaries, with javelins and swords and shields, advanced to the attack, and the catapults hurling the last flints we had at the Saxon centre, with the slingers running behind us, we charged in line across the dip in the ground, and reached the Saxon centre unbroken.

The barbarians rallied to meet us; we were fighting

up-hill, and yet such was the weight of our attack, that we broke their centre in the fierceness of our onslaught, and in a few minutes were in possession of the highest ground of their camp. Yet what can six thousand men, which was by now all our number, do against a hundred thousand? The desperate throw, I saw at once, had failed, and only postponed the event. We were enveloped on the enemy's ground instead of our own, and were surrounded by the howling mob of the barbarians. Our slingers and catapulters saw what had happened, and fled at once. They could not assist us, and went to save their lives. I blame them not in the slightest; they could have done no good by staying. As for us in the legions, we knew, every man of us, that we were now to fight to the death indeed.

For once the silence of the legionary was broken. We encouraged one another by shouting out the name of some ravished farmhouse, some sacked town, some violated girl. We called aloud the names of the great ones of our race for a thousand years back. We sought to lash ourselves into a rage, that we might feel no fear, and with blows we repaid blows, and men fell on either hand, with the blood soaking the turf.

It was a wild scene of shouting and groaning men, with working faces, and many clashes of blows. There were hoarse calls and snarls, and men falling to the ground, biting in their deaths the feet of those who rushed across their bodies. For a time we were in confusion, but at last, by the aid of discipline, my commanders got their cohorts and details together again, and we formed a ring with the shields close locked around us as a wall, and moved, by disciplined movement, now slowly to the right, and now again slowly to the left, to keep the battle alive until Cadell should come. He might come indeed, he and his men of Fadog, of Wenwynwyn, and of Salopia. Let him come then. We should either be alive and fighting still, or it should be beyond the power of the Saxon to triumph over us.

Now I can no more describe this combat in set terms, for there was a wailing of men, and people falling piecemeal to the earth, and many shouts of anger and bitter woe, and colour before everybody's eyes as it were black or red, and dazzling rainbows and stains of blood, and pain, and noise, and clash of arms. There were wrathful and fierce and high spirits, and as it were the shaking of the wings of great birds in the air, when there were no birds, but only the ghosts of dead men taking their flight from the horrors and terrors of battle. There was anger and damage and blindness, whereby men lost their eyes, their most treasured possession, so that they were doomed never to see the sweet colours of the flowers, or the sun, or the laughter in their children's eyes. This was taken from many. Then it seemed to me again that the ravens who shall come at the end of the world were all there, flapping their wings, and yet we were set in our minds that we would never yield up life, sword, or a yard of soil to the Saxons; and yet we had no land to yield, for he had already taken it from us.

In the thick of the fury I thought I heard a blowing as it were of a million cowhorns, and some low felon struck me upon the head. My ears were singing and my eyes all bloodshot, and the cohort commanders asking me this and that, and I smote a man dead, for I saw he was a Saxon, and the noise continued, and I was struck again, and fell forward upon one knee; and the cowhorns continued to blow louder and louder, and there was a noise of rivers in my head, and men shouting, and the waves of my enemies were broken and I fell forward again, and rose again.

As I rose the whole of everything that I could see was bright scarlet, and my face was wet, and I had a most dreadful pain in my side, and thought that this was caused by a man that was in front of me with his face looking most horrible and evil; so I struck at him for causing me that pain, and wiping my face I saw clearly for a short space, but everything became cloudy crimson again and I felt wondrous dizzy and like to faint. Yet a voice called me to slay and to slay, and to slay, and I slew, and it seemed that they avoided me. Now a blow came upon my breast, but did not penetrate, for I fell

backwards from the violence of it, and a man with a
spear struck at me from behind. Now, for a moment, I
was clear in my head, and I thought that this was a
most foul blow, to strike me thus behind when I was
with sore trouble engaged in killing another man in
front; so I turned round, very indignant, to kill the
craven, and slew him. I did not now know where the sun
was, because when we began the fight it was on my left
hand, and now it was upon the right; from this the fight
must have been many hours in length, yet I could
remember nothing of it.

Now I had a pain in my head that seemed to belong
not to me, but to a great cave in which I was walking,
and that arched over my head; and I wondered that the
cave, being so great and so many miles away, should
allow any pain so great as that to live, and I called to the
cave, which was the vault of the sky, "slay, slay, and I
will also slay." After this I fell again. Now there were
many men around me, and all pressing to slay me and
I eager to kill them too. But I could not stand up, so I
got to my knees, and it seemed to me that my enemies
were running away from me. So again I tried to stand
and follow them, and could not, but moved after them
upon my knees, and taunted them for cowards who ran
thus from only one man, thus in pain, and with only one
arm, for the other pained me so that I could not use it.
So I shouted to them to stay and let me kill them, yet
they continued to run, and because of the scarlet cloud
over my eyes I could not see, and dashed it away; but it
came back again and I was marvellously annoyed that
it should thus blind me, and dashed it away again.

Now I saw the Saxons running, and a great swarm
of men with blackened skins and no armour, and nothing but great spears, running at me and spearing all
that stood in their way; and the men in the blackened
skins were wet and sweating, and they ran with their
mouths shut, and all around were men screaming and
spearing and being speared and fleeing.

In the middle of the blackened men came a wondrous great charge of horses, and wooden chariots with

scythe-blades upon the axles that mowed men down like corn; and in front of all the others was a chariot driving with wild horses, with manes and tails blowing about, and in it a figure with red hair streaming in the wind, holding a spear and shrieking aloud in fury, and a man crouching at the front of her guiding this chariot with foaming horses, and all about were the men with the spears and the blackened skins, white in patches because of the sweat, and the noise that was dying away and the sky going round. Now after this I fell and there was silence except for the singing of many thousand birds.

My head ached most wondrously, and a soft arm was holding my neck as I lay upon the ground, so I called out "My legions, my legions," and I beheld them very small and far away, yet in good order as I had taught them to be; and away in the distance, both near and far, came screams and a great flashing of spears and a view of silent black men hunting.

So I said, not feeling well, yet realizing that as commander I must know all, "Then it is victory?"

And a voice said most gently in my ear, "It is victory."

"Then who are those that come? Those that looked so fierce?"

"Indeed it is victory, and you must rest, for your head is hurt."

"Yet there was no hope and we had determined to die."

"There was hope, for all of Dynevawr is here, from the grandsire to the just-weaned babe, and each with a spear."

"Then you have saved Britain, Pendragon."

"Truly," said she. "And also something that I value even more. For I have come, and mine with me, forty miles this day that I may keep it."

Then with a fine cloth she wiped the blood from my face and softly kissed me.

Historical Notes

p. 21. *Cirencester*: Corinium, or Caer Ceri.

p. 22. *Bath*: Aquae Sulis.

p. 23. *Arabian or Egyptian holly*: Fructus Euonymi Aegyptii or choava, i.e., coffee.

p. 23. *Demetia*: Dynevawr, or South Wales.

p. 23. *Teyngrace*: Caer Teim.

p. 23. *Damnonian*: Damnonia, i.e., Devonshire.

p. 24. *Demetia*: South Wales.

p. 24. *Guitolin*: Vitilinus.

p. 24. *Reged*: The counties of Durham, Northumberland, Berwick and Haddington.

p. 24. *Strathclyde*: The western coast, roughly stretching between Glasgow and Preston.

p. 25. *Cambria*: Wales, or Britannia Secunda.

p. 25. *Cornubia and Damnonia*: Cornwall and Devon.

p. 25. *Vectis*: Isle of Wright.

p. 26. *Gloucester*: Glevum, or Caer Gloui.

p. 26. *Isca*: Exeter.

p. 28. *Gwent*: The Forest of Dean, then many times its present extent.

p. 29. *Uriconium*: Viriconium, or Wroxeter.

p. 30. *Verulam*: St. Albans, or Caer Mencipit.

p. 33. *a small piece of black polished stone, carved into the shape of a raven*: The Cornish chough, "talons and beak all red with blood," is the raven. Cervantes in *Don Quixote* (Jarvis's translation) tells us that after death

King Arthur was changed into a raven, "and from that time to this no Englishman has ever killed a raven."

p. 38. *Carlisle*: Luguvallium, or Caer Luilidd.

p. 43. *Verulam, Lundinium, and Anderida*: St. Albans, London, and Pevensey (Caer Pensavelcoit).

p. 43. *Rudcester*: Vindobala.

p. 51. *Ribchester*: Coccio, near Preston.

p. 51. *Elmet*: Maxima Cæsariensis.

p. 51. *York*: Eboracum, or Caer Ebranc.

p. 51. *Snowdon*: Wyddfa.

p. 51. *Locris*: Loegria, or England, the two Roman provinces of Britannia Prima and Flavia Cæsariensis.

p. 53. *Lichfield*: Etoceto.

p. 59. *Deva*: Chester, or Caer Ligion.

p. 59. *Armorica*: Brittany, or "Little Britain."

p. 60. *Powys*: Mid-Wales, with Shropshire and Hereford.

p. 61. *Creuddyn*: The northern portion of Cardigan.

p. 70. *Wem*: Rotunio.

p. 71. *Cornubii*: The British tribe inhabiting Cornwall.

p. 76. *Locrin*: England.

p. 76. *Albanact*: Scotland.

p. 76. *Camber*: Wales.

p. 76. *house of his father*: The entire island, Great Britain.

p. 94. *Gredyf gwr oed gwas*
Gwhyr un das
Meirch mwth myngvas
Y dan mordhuyt mygr was
Ysguyt ysgafn llydan.

Manly the Youth in breed,
First in the stricken field;
Gallant and fleet his steed,
Shining his sword and shield.

p. 98. *Lundinium*: London.

p. 98. *Camulodunum*: Colchester.

p. 98. *Luguvalium*: Carlisle.

p. 119. *Ierne*: Ireland.

p. 120. *in the straits between Mona and Gwynnedd*: Menai Straits.

p. 140. *the Pictish poem about their kings beginning*: Ossian.

p. 147. *Fortrenn*: Stirlingshire.

p. 181. *Ariconium in the days of Rome, and is now called Aberganway*: Abergavenny and the "Sugar-Loaf" Mountain.

p. 249. *Sarum*: Salisbury.

p. 258. *Ynys Saman*: The Island of Dogs.

p. 259. *the great island of Hyrddod*: Ramsay Island.

p. 260. *Gwales*: Skomer.

p. 266. *city of Silchester*: Vindomi.

ABOUT THE AUTHOR

Wilfred Barnard Faraday was born in March, 1874, the son of F. J. Faraday, a commercial editor for the *Manchester Guardian*. He was educated at the College of Technology and University of Manchester—where he earned his LL.B. in 1897—and was called to the bar in 1900. During World War I, he served in the 5th Battalion, The Royal York and Lancaster Regiment, and was appointed, upon demobilization, secretary of the Royal Aeronautical Society, later serving as editor of the *Aeronautical Journal*. In 1925, he became Recorder of Barnstaple and of Bidford, a position he held until his death, at age seventy nine, in June, 1953. Faraday maintained an active interest in politics and economic policy throughout his life, and wrote about the topics in *Democracy and Capital* (1921) and *The Collapse of the Foreign Exchanges* (1922). His works of fiction include *Pendragon* (1930) and *The Milk in the Cocoanut* (1933).

More PENDRAGON™ Books from
GREEN KNIGHT PUBLISHING

IN BOOKSTORES JUNE 2002

Cian of the Chariots
by William H. Babcock

In the dark days after Rome's departure from Britain, the people of that beleaguered island find themselves torn between the hopeful promise of Christianity and the mystical traditions of the Druids, the desire to revive the Empire's lost splendor and the need to maintain their heathen ancestors' wild and warlike ways. No man feels this tension more strongly than Cian Gwenclan—Cian of the Chariots—a Celtic warrior who wears a badge of silver mistletoe upon his mail in reverence of the pagan mysteries, yet serves the young emperor Arthur, upon whose shield is painted an image of the Virgin Mary. But in his quest to forge an army united by faith rather than necessity, Arthur increasingly declares himself an enemy of Cian's beliefs, leaving the loyal soldier to face a terrible question: Is the emperor even more of a threat to his way of life than the Saxon marauders?

Originally published in 1898, *Cian of the Chariots* is the first American historical novel set in Arthurian Britain. It is also the most significant and compelling work of fiction by historian, poet, and novelist William Henry Babcock, author of *Two Lost Centuries of Britain* and the groundbreaking *Legendary Islands of the Atlantic: A Study in Medieval Geography*.

GK6214. ISBN 1-928999-30-1. 320 pages.
$19.95 US; $31.95 CAN; £13.99 UK